RICHES

— AT HOME WITH THE BOSS —

Rags to RICHES
COLLECTION

April 2017

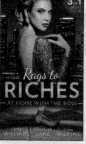

May 2017

June 2017

July 2017

August 2017

September 2017

Rags to RICHES

— AT HOME WITH THE BOSS —

Cathy
WILLIAMS

Elizabeth
LANE

Gina
WILKINS

MILLS & BOON

Published in Great Britain 2017
By Mills & Boon, an imprint of HarperCollins*Publishers*
1 London Bridge Street, London, SE1 9GF

RAGS TO RICHES: AT HOME WITH THE BOSS
© 2017 Harlequin Books S.A.

The Secret Sinclair © 2012 Cathy Williams
The Nanny's Secret © 2014 Elizabeth Lane
A Home for the M.D. © 2011 Gina Wilkins

ISBN: 978-0-263-93065-8

09-0517

THE SECRET
SINCLAIR

CATHY WILLIAMS

Cathy Williams can remember reading Mills & Boon Modern Romance books as a teenager, and now that she is writing them she remains an avid fan. For her, there is nothing like creating romantic stories and engaging plots, and each and every book is a new adventure. Cathy lives in London, and her three daughters – Charlotte, Olivia and Emma – have always been, and continue to be, the greatest inspirations in her life.

PROLOGUE

RAOUL shifted as quietly as he could on the bed, propped himself up on one elbow and stared down at the woman sleeping contentedly next to him. Through the open window the sultry African night air could barely work itself up into a breeze, and even with the fan lethargically whirring on the chest of drawers it was still and humid. The net draped haphazardly over them was very optimistic protection against the mosquitoes, and as one landed on his arm he slapped it away and sat up.

Sarah stirred, opened her eyes sleepily and smiled at him.

God, he was beautiful. She had never, ever imagined that any man could be as beautiful as Raoul Sinclair. From the very first moment she had laid eyes on him three months ago she had been rendered speechless—and the effect still hadn't worn off.

Amongst all the other people taking their gap years, he stood head and shoulders above the rest. He was literally taller than all of them, but it was much more than that. It was his exotic beauty that held her spellbound: the burnished gold of his skin, the vibrancy of his black, glossy hair—long now; almost to his shoulders—the latent power of his lean, muscular body. Although he was only a matter of a few years older than the rest of them, he was a man amongst boys.

She reached up and skimmed her hand along his back.

'Mosquitoes.' Raoul grinned, dark eyes sweeping over her smooth honey-gold shoulders down to her breasts. He felt himself stirring and hardening, even though they had made love less than a few hours ago. 'This net is useless. But, seeing that we're now both up and wide awake…'

With a little sigh of pleasure Sarah reached out and linked her hands around his neck, drawing him to her and wriggling restlessly as his mouth found hers.

A virgin when she had met him, she knew he had liberated her. Every touch had released new and wonderful sensations.

Her body was slick with heat and perspiration as he gently pulled down the thin sheet which was all they could endure out here.

She had the most wonderful breasts he had ever seen, and with a sudden pang of regret for things to come Raoul realised that he was going to miss her body. No—much more than that. He was going to miss *her*.

It was a situation he had not foreseen when he had decided to take three months off to work in Mozambique. At the time, it had seemed a fitting interlude between the conclusion of university—two hard-won degrees in Economics and Maths—and the start of what he intended to be the rest of his life. Before he threw himself into conquering the world and putting his own personal demons to rest he would immerse himself in the selflessness of helping other people—people as unfortunate as he himself had been, although in a completely different way.

Meeting a woman and falling into bed with her hadn't been on his radar. His libido, like everything else in his life, was just something else he had learnt to control ruthlessly. He had intended to spend three months controlling it.

Sarah Scott, with her tangled blonde hair and her fresh-faced innocence, was certainly not the sort of woman he fancied himself drawn to. He generally went for tougher, more experienced types—women with obvious attractions, who were as willing as he was to have a brief, passionate fling. Women who were ships passing in the night, never dropping anchor and more importantly, never expecting *him* to.

One look at Sarah and he had recognised a girl who would be into anchors being dropped, but it hadn't been enough to keep him away. For two weeks, as they'd been thrown together in circumstances so far removed from reality that it was almost like living in a bubble, he had watched her broodingly out of the corner of his eye, had been aware of her watching him. By the end of week three the inevitable had become reality.

They made love now—quietly and slowly. The house they shared with six other occupants had walls as thin as tracing paper, and wooden floors that seemed to transmit sound with ruthless efficiency.

'Okay,' Raoul whispered, 'how close do you think I can get before you have to stifle a groan?'

'Don't,' Sarah whispered back with a giggle. 'You know how hard it is...'

'Yes, and it's what I like about you. One touch and I can feel your body melt.' He touched her accordingly, a feathery touch between her generous breasts, trailing a continuous line to circle her prominent nipples until she was squirming and breathing quickly, face flushed, her hand curling into his over long hair.

As he delicately licked the stiffened, swollen tip of her nipple he automatically placed a gentle hand over her

mouth, and half smiled as she tried very hard not to groan
into the palm of his hand.

Only a handful of times had they taken the beaten up
Land Rover and escaped to one of the beaches, where
they had found privacy and made love without restraint.
Between work and down-time on the compound, however,
they were confined to a type of lovemaking that was as
refined and guarded as a specialised dance.

Sarah half opened her eyes, simply because she could
never resist watching Raoul—the dark bronze of his body
against the paler gold of hers, the play of sinew and muscle as he reared up over her, powerful and strong and un-
tamed.

Although it was after midnight, the moon was bright
and full. Its silvery light streamed through the window,
casting shadows on the walls and picking up the hard angles of his face as he licked a path along her stomach, down
to where her legs were parted for his eventual caress.

Quite honestly, at times like this Sarah thought that she
had died and gone to heaven, and it never failed to amaze
her that her feelings for this man could be so overwhelm-
ing after only a matter of three months...less! She felt
as though, without even realising it, she had been saving
herself for him to come along and take possession of her
heart.

As their lovemaking gathered urgency the uneasy tangle
of thoughts that had been playing in her head for the past
few days were lost as he thrust into her and then picked
up a long, steady rhythm that became faster and harder,
until she felt herself spiralling towards orgasm, holding on
so that their bodies became one and they climaxed. The
only sounds were their fast-drawn breaths, even though
she wanted to cry out loud from the pleasure of fulfilment.

As she tumbled back down to earth the moonlight illuminated his suitcases, packed and standing to attention by the single old-fashioned wardrobe.

And then back came the disquieting thoughts.

Raoul sank against her, spent, and for a few seconds neither of them spoke. He draped his arm over her body. The sheet had managed to work itself into a heap at the foot of the bed, and he idly wondered just how long it would take for the mosquitoes to figure out that there was a new and much bigger entrance available to get inside.

'Can…can we talk?'

Raoul stiffened. Past experience had taught him that anyone who wanted to *talk* invariably wanted to say things he didn't want to hear.

'Okay, I can tell from the way you're not jumping with joy that you don't want to talk, but I think we should. I mean…your cases are all packed, Raoul. You're leaving in two days' time. And I…I don't know what's going to happen to us.'

Raoul swung off her to lie back. He stared at the ceiling in silence for a few seconds. Of course he had known that this was where they would end up, but he had conveniently chosen to ignore that because she had bewitched him. Every time he had considered giving her one of his little speeches about expecting nothing from him he had looked into her bright green eyes and the speech had melted away.

He reluctantly turned to face her and stroked the vanilla blonde hair off her face, neatly tucking loose strands behind her ears.

'I know we need to talk,' he admitted heavily.

'But you still don't want to…'

'I'm not sure where it's going to get us.'

Hearing that was like having ice cold water thrown in her face, but Sarah ploughed on bravely—because she just couldn't see that what they had could possibly come to *nothing* the minute he departed. They had done a thousand things together. More than some people packed into a lifetime. She refused to concede that it could all melt away into nothingness.

'I never intended to come out here and start any kind of relationship,' he confessed, his eloquence for once gone, because he was just not accustomed to having emotional conversations with anyone. He never had. He just didn't think that he had it in him. But there she was, staring at him in the darkness with those big, questioning eyes... waiting.

'Nor did I. I mean, I just wanted to get some experience and live a little—do something a bit different before starting university. You know that. How many times did I tell you that—?' She'd very nearly said *falling in love*, but an innate sense of self-preservation held her back. Not once had he ever told her what he felt for her. She had only deduced from the way he looked at her and touched her, and laughed at the things she said, and when she teased him. 'That meeting someone wasn't part of my agenda either. The unexpected happens.'

Did it? Not to him. Never to him. He had endured a childhood that had been riddled with the unexpected—all of it bad. Top of his list of things to avoid was *The Unexpected*, but she was right. What had blossomed between them had taken him by surprise. He drew her against him and searched for the right words to explain just why the future staring them in the face would be one they each faced on their own.

'I shouldn't have given in, Sarah.'

'Shouldn't have given in to what?'

'You know what. To you.'

'Please don't say that,' she whispered with heartfelt dismay. 'Are you saying that what we did was all a big mistake? We've had so much fun! You don't have to be serious all the time.'

Raoul took her hand and kissed the tips of her fingers, one by one, until the radiant smile reappeared on her face. She smiled easily.

'It's been fun,' he agreed, with the heavy feeling of someone about to deliver a fatal blow to an unsuspecting victim. 'But this isn't reality, Sarah. This is time out. You pretty much said it yourself. Reality is what's in front of us. In your case three years at university. In my case...' *The world and nothing less.* 'A job. I really hoped that we wouldn't have to have this conversation. I hoped that you would see what's pretty clear to me. This has been great, but it's...a holiday affair.'

'A holiday affair?' Sarah repeated in a small voice.

Raoul sighed and ran his fingers through his too-long hair. He would get rid of it the second he made it back to civilisation.

'Don't make me out to be an ogre, Sarah. I'm not saying that it hasn't been...incredible. It has. In fact, it's been the most incredible three months of my life.' He hesitated. His past had never been something he chose to discuss with anyone, least of all a woman, but the urge to go further with her was overpowering. 'You've made me feel like no one else ever has...but then I suppose you know that...'

'How can I when you've never told me?' But it was something for her to hang onto.

'I...I'm not good with this kind of emotional drama. I've had a lot of emotional drama in my life...'

'What do you mean?' She knew only the barest of facts about his past, even though he pretty much knew everything about hers. She had waxed lyrical about her childhood—her very happy and very ordinary childhood—as an only child of two parents who had always thought that they would never have kids until her mother became pregnant at the merry age of forty-one.

He had skirted round the subject aside from telling her that he'd had no parents, preferring to concentrate on the future which, as time went on, suited her very well—even though any mention of *her* in that future hadn't actually been voiced. She liked the thought of him forging his way with her at his side. Somewhere.

'I grew up in a foster home, Sarah. I was one of those kids you read about in the newspapers who get taken in by Social Services because their parents can't take care of them.'

Sarah sat up, lost for words. Then her natural warmth took over and she felt the prickle of tears, which brought a reluctant smile to his lips.

'Neither of your parents could look after you?'

'Just the one parent on the scene. My mother.' It was not in his nature to confide, and he picked carefully at his words, choosing to denude them of all potency. It was a trick he had learnt a long time ago, so his voice, when he spoke, was flat and detached. 'Unfortunately she had a problem with substances, which ended up killing her when I was five. My father… Who knows? Could have been anyone.'

'You poor soul!'

'I prefer to think of my background as character-building, and as foster homes went mine wasn't too bad. Where I'm going with this…' For a second he had to remind himself where he *was* going with it. 'I'm not looking for a relationship. Not now—probably not ever. I never meant to string you along, Sarah, but…you got under my skin… And all *this* didn't exactly go the distance in bringing me back to my senses.'

'All what?'

'Here. The middle of nowhere. Thrown together in the heat...'

'So nothing would have happened between us if we hadn't been out here?' She could hear her voice rising and had to control it, because she didn't want to wake anyone—although there was only one other English speaking person on the compound.

'That's a purely hypothetical question.'

'You could try answering it!'

'I don't know.' He could feel the hurt seeping out of her, but what could he do about it? How could he make it better without issuing promises he knew he wouldn't keep?

Frustration and anger at himself rushed through him in a tidal wave. Hell, he should have known just by looking at her that Sarah wasn't one of those women who were out to have a good time, no strings attached! Where had his prized self-control been when he had needed it most? Absent without leave! He had seen her and all trace of common sense had deserted him.

And when he had discovered that she was a virgin? Had that stopped him in his tracks? The opposite. He had felt unaccountably thrilled to be her first, had wanted to shout it from the rooftops. Instead of backing away he had rushed headlong into the sort of crazy quasi-romantic situation that he had always scorned. There hadn't been chocolates and jewellery—not that he could have afforded either—but there had been long, lazy conversations, a great deal of laughter... Hell, he had even cooked her a meal on one occasion, when the rest of the crew had disappeared for the weekend to camp on the beach, leaving the two of them in charge.

'You don't know? Is that because I'm not really your type?'

He hesitated just long enough for her to bitterly assume the obvious.

'I'm not, am I?' She slung her legs over the bed, kicking away at the mosquito net and finally shoving it aside so that she could crawl under it.

'Where are you going!'

'I don't want to be having this conversation.' In the darkness she hunted around for her clothes, located them, and began putting them on. An old tee shirt, a pair of denim shorts, her flipflops. 'I'm going outside. I need to get some air.'

Raoul debated the wisdom of following her for a few seconds, then leapt out of the bed, struggling with his jeans, not bothering with a shirt at all, as he watched her flying out of the room like a bat out of hell.

The bedroom was small, equipped with the most basic of furniture, and cluttered with all the bits and pieces of two occupants. He came close to tripping over one of his shoes and cursed softly under his breath. He shouldn't be following her. He had said all there was to say on the subject of any continuing romance. To prolong the conversation would be to invite a debate that would be stillborn, so what was the point? But watching her disappear through the bedroom door had galvanised him into instant, inexplicable action.

The house was a square concrete block, its front door accessed by sufficient steps to ensure that it was protected against flooding during the cyclone season.

He caught up with her just as she had reached the bottom of the steps.

'So, what *are* your types!' Sarah swung round to glare at him, hands on her hips.

'Types? What are you talking about?'

'These women you go for?'

'That's irrelevant.'

'Not to me it isn't!' Sarah stared up at him. She was shaking like a leaf, and she didn't know why she was getting hung up on that one detail. He was right. It was irrelevant. What did it matter if he went for tall brunettes and she was a short blonde? What mattered was that he was dumping her. Throwing her out like used goods. Tossing her aside as though she was just something insignificant that no longer mattered. When he was *everything* to her.

She literally shied away from the thought of waking up in three days' time in an empty bed, knowing that she would never lay eyes on him again. How on earth was she going to survive?

'You need to calm down.' He shook his head and raked his fingers through his hair, sweeping it back from his face. God, it was like an oven out here. He could feel the sweat beginning to gather on his body.

'I'm perfectly calm!' Sarah informed him in a shrill voice. 'I just want to know if you've had fun *using* me for the past three months!'

She swung round, began heading towards the central clearing, where the circular reed huts with their distinctive pointed roofs were used as classrooms for the twenty local children who attended every day. Raoul didn't teach. He and two of the other guys did brutally manual labour—building work in one of the communities further along, planting and harvesting of crops. He gave loads of advice on crop rotation and weather patterns. He seemed to know absolutely everything.

'Were you just making the best of a bad job out here? Sleeping with me because there was no one else around to your taste?'

'Don't be stupid!' He reached out and stopped her in her tracks, pulling her back to him and forcing her to look up.

'I know I'm not the most glamorous person in the world. I know you're probably accustomed to landing really gorgeous girls.' She bit her lip and looked away, feeling miserable and thoroughly sorry for herself. 'I knew it was odd that you even looked at me in the first place, but I suppose I was the only other English person here so you made do.'

'Don't do this, Sarah,' Raoul said harshly. He could feel her trembling against him, and he had to fight the impulse to terminate the conversation by kissing that lush, full mouth. 'If you want to know what kind of women I've always gone for, I'll tell you. I've always gone for women who wanted nothing from me. I'm not saying that's a good thing, but it's the truth. Yes, they've been good looking, but not in the way that you are…'

'What way is that?' Sarah asked scornfully, but she was keen to grasp any positive comment in these suddenly turbulent waters. She realised with a sinking heart that she would be willing to beg for him. It went against every grain of pride in her, but, yes, she would plead for him at least to keep in touch.

'Young, innocent, full of laughter…' He loosened his fingers on her arm and gently stroked her. 'That's why I should have run a mile the minute you looked at me with those big green eyes,' he murmured with genuine regret. 'But I couldn't. You summed up everything I wasn't looking for, and I still couldn't resist you.'

'You don't have to!' Before he could knock her last-ditch plea down in flames she turned away brusquely and walked towards the clearing, adopting a position on one of the fallen tree trunks which had been left as a bench of sorts.

Her heart was beating like a jackhammer and she could barely catch her breath. She didn't look at him as he sat down on the upturned trunk next to her.

The night was alive with the sounds of insects and frogs, but it was cooler out here than it had been in the stifling heat of the bedroom.

Eventually she turned to him. 'I'm not asking you to settle down and marry me,' she said quietly—although, really, who was she kidding? That was exactly what she wanted. 'But you don't have to walk away and never look back. I mean, we can keep in touch.' She threw him a watery, desperate smile. 'That's what mobile phones and e-mails and all these social networking sites are all about, you know.'

'How many times have we argued about the merits of throwing your personal life into a public arena for the world to feed on?'

'You're such a dinosaur, Raoul.' But she smiled. They'd argued about so many things! Light-hearted arguments, with lots of laughter. When Raoul took a stand it was impossible to deflect him, and she had enjoyed teasing him about his implacability. She had never known anything like it.

'And you'd be happy to do that?' Raoul thought that if she were the kind of girl who could be happy with that kind of distant, intermittent contact then they wouldn't be sitting here right now, having this conversation, because then she would also be the kind of girl who would have indulged in a three-month fling and been happy to walk away, without agonising about a future that wasn't destined to be.

For a fleeting moment he wondered what it would be like to take her with him, but the thought was one he discarded even before it had had time to take root. He was a product of his background, and that was something he was honest enough to acknowledge.

Deprived of stability, he had learnt from a very young

age that he had to look out for himself. He couldn't even really remember when he had made his mind up that the world would never decide his fate. He would control it, and the way he would do that would be through his brains. Foster care had honed his single-minded ambition and provided him with one very important lesson in life: rely on no one.

Whilst the other kids had been larking around, or pining for parents that failed to show up at appointed times, he had buried his head in books and mastered all the tricks of studying in the midst of chaos. Blessed with phenomenal intelligence, he had sailed through every exam, and as soon as he'd been released from the restrictions of a foster home had worked furiously to put himself through college and then later university.

Starting with nothing, he had to do more than just *be clever*. A degree counted for nothing when you were competing with someone who had family connections. So he had got two degrees—two high-powered degrees—which he intended to use ruthlessly to get where he wanted to go.

Where, in his great scheme of things, would Sarah fit in? He was no carer and never would be. He just didn't have it in him. And Sarah was the sort of soft, gentle person who would always need someone to take care of her.

Heck, she couldn't even bring herself to answer his question! When she spoke of keeping in touch, what she really meant was having an ongoing relationship. How responsible would he be if he told her what she wanted to hear?

Abruptly Raoul stood up, putting some vital immediate distance between them—because sitting next to her was doing crazy things to his thoughts and to his body.

'Well?' he asked, more harshly than he had intended, and he sensed her flinch as she bowed her head. He had to use every scrap of will-power at his disposal not to go across and put his arms around her. He clenched his hands into fists, wanting to hit something very hard. 'You haven't answered my question. *Could* you keep in touch with me with the occasional e-mail? When you should be moving on? Putting me behind you and chalking the whole thing up to experience?'

'How can you be so callous?' Sarah whispered. She had practically begged and it hadn't been enough. He didn't love her and he never would. Why should she waste her time lamenting the situation? He was right. E-mails and text messages would just prolong the hurt. She needed to cut him out of her life and leave no remaining bits to fester and multiply.

'I'm not being callous, Sarah. I'm sparing you the pain of building false hopes. You're young, with stars in your eyes…'

'You're not exactly over the hill, Raoul!'

'In terms of experience I'm a thousand years older than you, and I'm not the man you're looking for. I would be no good for you…'

'That's usually the coward's way out of a sticky situation,' she muttered, having read it somewhere and thought that it made sense.

'In this case it's the truth. You need someone who's going to take care of you, and that person is never going to be me.' He watched her carefully and wondered if he would ever again be in the business of justifying himself to another human being. *Walk alone,* that was what he had taught himself, *and you don't end up entangled in situations such as this.* 'I don't want the things that you do,' he continued softly.

Sarah would have liked to deny that she wanted any of those things he accused her of wanting, but she did. She wanted the whole fairytale romance and he knew it. It felt as if he knew her better than anyone ever had.

Her shoulders slumped as she struggled to look for the silver lining in the cloud. There always was one.

'I'm not equipped for playing happy families, Sarah...'

She eventually raised her eyes to his and looked at him coldly. 'You're right. I want all that stuff, and it *is* better for you to let me down so that I can have a fighting chance of meeting someone who isn't scared of commitment.' Her legs felt like jelly when she stood up. 'It would be awful to think that I might waste my time loving you when you haven't *got it in you* for the fairytale stuff!'

Raoul gritted his teeth, but there was nothing to say in response to that.

'And by the way,' she flung over her shoulder, 'I'll leave your clothes outside the bedroom door, because I'll be sleeping on my own tonight! You want your precious freedom so badly? Well, congratulations—you've got it!'

She kept her head held high as she covered the ten thousand miles back to the house. At least it felt like ten thousand miles.

Memories of their intense relationship flashed through her head like a slow, painful slideshow. Thinking about him could still give her goosebumps, and she hugged herself as she jogged up the flight of stone steps to the front door.

In the bedroom, she gathered up some of his clothes and buried her face in them, breathing in his musky, aggressively male scent, then duly stuck them outside—along with his cases.

Then she locked the bedroom door, and in the empty quiet of the bedroom contemplated a life without Raoul in it and tried to stop the bottom of her world from dropping out.

CHAPTER ONE

CAUGHT in the middle of crouching on the ground, trying to get rid of a particularly stubborn stain on the immaculate cream carpet that ran the length, breadth and width of the directors' floor of the very exclusive family bank in which she had now been working for the past three weeks, Sarah froze at the sound of voices emerging from one of the offices. Low, unhurried voices—one belonging to a man, the other to a woman.

It was the first time she had been made aware of any sign of life here. She came at a little after nine at night, did her cleaning and left. She liked it that way. She had no wish to bump into anyone—not that there would have been the slightest possibility of her being addressed. She was a cleaner, and as such was rendered instantly invisible. Even the doorman who had been allowing her entry ever since she had started working at the bank barely glanced up when she appeared in front of him.

She could barely remember a time when she had been able to garner a few admiring glances. The combined weight of responsibility and lack of money had rubbed the youthful glow from her face. Now when she looked in the mirror all she saw was a woman in her mid-twenties with shadows under her eyes and the pinched appearance of someone with too many worries.

Sarah wondered what she should do. Was there some special etiquette involved if a cleaner come into contact with one of the directors of this place? She hunkered down. In her blue checked overalls and with her hair scraped back under a matching scarf, she figured she might easily have passed for a heap of old clothes dumped on the ground, were it not for the elaborate trolley of cleaning materials by her side.

As the hushed voices got closer—just round the corner—Sarah put her all into the wretched stain on the carpet. But with a sinking heart she was aware that the voices had fallen silent, and the footsteps seemed to have stopped just in front of her.

In fact, sliding her eyes across, she could make out some hand-made Italian shoes just below charcoal-grey trousers, sharply creased, a pair of very high cream stilettos, and stockings with a slight sheen, very sheer.

'I don't know if you've done the conference room as yet, but if you have then you've made a very poor job of it. There are ring marks on the table, and two champagne glasses are still there on the bookshelf!'

The woman's voice was icy cold and imperious. Reluctantly Sarah raised her eyes, travelling the length of a very tall, very thin, very blonde woman in her thirties. From behind her she could hear the man pressing for the lift.

'I haven't got to the conference room yet,' Sarah mumbled. She prayed that the woman wouldn't see fit to lodge a complaint. She needed this job. The hours suited her, and it was well paid for what it was. Included in the package was the cost of a taxi to and from her house to the bank. How many cleaning jobs would ever have included *that*?

'Well, I'm relieved to hear it!'

'For God's sake, Louisa, let the woman do her job. It's

nearly ten, and I can do without spending the rest of the evening here!'

Sarah heard that voice—the voice that had haunted her for the past five years—and her mind went a complete blank. Then it was immediately kick-started, papering over the similarities of tone. Because there was no way that Raoul Sinclair could be the man behind her. Raoul Sinclair was just a horrible, youthful mistake that was now in the past.

And yet...

Obeying some kind of primitive instinct to match a face to that remarkable voice, Sarah turned around—and in that instant she was skewered to the spot by the same bitter chocolate eyes that had taken up residence in her head five years ago and stubbornly refused to budge. She half stood, swayed.

The last thing she heard before she fainted was the woman saying, in a shrill, ringing voice, 'Oh, for God's sake, that's the *last thing we need*!'

She came to slowly. As her eyelids fluttered open she knew, in a fuddled way, that she really didn't want to wake up. She wanted to stay in her peaceful faint.

She had been carried into an office and was now on a long, low sofa which she recognised as the one in Mr Verrier's office. She tried to struggle upright and Raoul came into her line of vision, taller than she remembered, but just as breathtakingly beautiful. She had never seen him in anything dressier than a pair of jeans and an old tee shirt, and she was slowly trying to match up the Raoul she had known with this man kneeling over her, who looked every inch the billionaire he had once laughingly informed her he would be.

'Here—drink this.'

'I don't want to drink anything. What are you doing here? Am I seeing things? You can't be here.'

'Funny, but I was thinking the very same thing.' Raoul had only now recovered his equilibrium. The second his eyes had locked onto hers he had been plunged into instant flashback, and carrying her into the office had re-awakened a tide of feeling which he had assumed to have been completely exorcised. He remembered the smell of her and the feel of her as though it had been yesterday. How was that possible? When so much had happened in the intervening years?

Sarah was fighting to steady herself. She couldn't believe her eyes. It was just so weird that she had to bite back the desire to burst into hysterical, incredulous laughter.

'What are you doing here, Sarah? Hell...you've changed...'

'I know.' She was suddenly conscious of the sight she must make, scrawny and hollow-cheeked and wearing her overalls. 'I have, haven't I?' She nervously fingered the checked overall and knew that she was shaking. 'Things haven't worked out...quite as I'd planned.' She made a feeble attempt to stand up, and collapsed back down onto the sofa.

In truth, Raoul was horrified at what he saw. Where was the bright-eyed, laughing girl he had known?

'I have to go... I have to finish the cleaning, Raoul. I...'

'You're not finishing anything. Not just at the moment. When was the last time you ate anything? You look as though you could be blown away by a gust of wind. And *cleaning*? Now you're doing cleaning jobs to earn money?'

He vaulted to his feet and began pacing the floor. He could scarcely credit that she was lying on the sofa in this office. Accustomed to eliminating any unwelcome emotions and reactions as being surplus to his finely tuned and highly controlled way of life, he found that he couldn't control the bombardment of questions racing through his brain. Nor could he rein in the flood of unwanted memories that continued to besiege him from every angle.

Sarah was possibly the very last woman with whom he had had a perfectly natural relationship. She represented a vision of himself as a free man, with one foot on the ladder but no steps actually yet taken. Was that why the impact of seeing her again now was so powerful?

'I never meant to end up like this,' Sarah whispered, as the full impact of their unexpected meeting began to take shape.

'But you have. How? What happened to you? Did you decide that you preferred cleaning floors to teaching?'

'Of course I didn't!' Sarah burst out sharply. She dragged herself into an upright position on the sofa and was confronted with the unflattering sight of her sturdy work shoes and thick, black woollen tights.

'Did you ever make it to university?' Raoul demanded. As she had struggled to sit up his eyes had moved of their own volition to the swing of her breasts under the hideous checked overall.

'I…I left the compound two weeks after you left.'

Her strained green eyes made her look so young and vulnerable that sudden guilt penetrated the armour of his formidable self control.

In five years Raoul had fulfilled every promise he had made to himself as a boy. Equipped with his impressive qualifications, he had landed his first job on the trading floor at the Stock Exchange, where his genius for making money had very quickly catapulted him upwards. Where colleagues had conferred, he'd operated solely on his own, and in the jungle arena of the money-making markets it hadn't been long before he'd emerged as having a killer streak that could make grown men quake in their shoes.

Raoul barely noticed. Money, for him, equated with freedom. He would be reliant on no one. Within three years he had accumulated sufficient wealth to begin the process of acquisition, and every acquisition had been bigger and more impressive than the one before. Guilt had played no part in his meteoric upward climb, and he had had no use for it.

Now, however, he felt it sink its teeth in, and he shoved his fingers through his hair.

Sarah followed the gesture which was so typically him.· 'You've had your hair cut,' she said, flushing at the inanity of her observation, and Raoul offered her a crooked half-smile.

'I discovered that shoulder-length hair didn't go with the image. Now, of course, I could grow it down to my waist and no one would dare say a word, but my days of long hair are well and truly over.'

Just as she was, she thought. She belonged to those days that were well and truly over—except they weren't, were they? She knew that there were things that needed to be said, but it was a conversation she'd never expected to have, and now that it was staring her in the face she just wanted to delay its onset for as long as possible.

'You must be pleased.' Sarah stared down at her feet and sensed him walk towards her until his shadow joined her feet. When he sat down next to her, her whole body stiffened in alarm—because even through the nightmare of her situation, and the pain and misery of how their relationship had ended, her body was still stirring into life and reacting to his proximity. 'You were always so determined...' she continued.

'In this life it's the only way to go forward. You were telling me what happened to your university career...'

'Was I?' She glanced across at him and licked her lips nervously. For two years she had done nothing but think of him. Over time the memories had faded, and she had learnt the knack of pushing them away whenever they threatened to surface, but there had been moments when she had flirted with the notion of meeting him again, had created conversations in her head in which she was strong and confident and in control of the situation. Nothing like this.

'I...I never made it to university. Like I said, things didn't quite work out.'

'Because of me.' Raoul loathed this drag on his emotions. Nor could he sit so close to her. Frustrated at the way his self-control had slipped out of his grasp, he pulled a chair over and positioned it directly in front of the sofa. 'You weren't due to leave that compound for another three months. In fact, I remember you saying that you thought you would stay there for much longer.'

'Not all of us make plans that end up going our way,' she told him, with creeping resentment in her voice.

'And you blame me for the fact that you've ended up where you have? I was honest with you. I believe your parting shot was that you were grateful that you would have the opportunity to find Mr Right... If you're going to try and pin the blame for how your life turned out on me, then it won't work. We had a clean break, and that's always the best way. If the Mr Right you found turned out to be the sort of guy who sits around while his woman goes out cleaning to earn money, then that's a pity—but not my fault.'

'This is crazy. I...I'm not blaming you for anything. And there's no *Mr Right*. Gosh, Raoul...I can't believe this. It feels like some kind of…of…nightmare… I don't mean that. I just mean…you're so *different*…'

Raoul chose to ignore her choice of words. She was in a state of shock. So was he. 'Okay, so maybe you didn't find the man of your dreams…but there must have been someone…' he mused slowly. 'Why else would you have abandoned a career you were so passionate about? Hell, you used to say that you were born to teach.'

Sarah raised moss-green eyes to his and he felt himself tense at the raw memory of how she'd used to look up at him, teasing and adoring at the same time. He had revelled in it. Now he doubted that any woman would have the temerity to tease him. Wealth and power had elevated him to a different place—a place where women batted their eyelashes, and flattered…but *teased*? No. Nor would he welcome it. In five years he had not once felt the slightest temptation to dip his toes into the murky waters of commitment.

'Did you get involved with some kind of loser?' he grated. She had been soft and vulnerable and broken-hearted. Had someone come along and taken advantage of her state of mind?

'What are you talking about?'

'You must have been distraught to have returned from Africa ahead of schedule. I realise that you probably blame me for that, but if you had stuck it out you would forgotten me within a few weeks.'

'Is that how it worked for you, Raoul?'

Pinned to the spot by such a direct question, Raoul refused to answer. 'Did you get strung along by someone who promised you the earth and then did a runner when he got tired of you? Is that what happened? A degree would have been your passport, Sarah. How many times did we have conversations about this? What did he say to you to convince you that it was a good idea to dump your aspirations?'

He didn't know whether to stand or to sit. He felt peculiarly uncomfortable in his own skin, and those wide green eyes weren't helping matters.

'And why cleaning? Why not an office job somewhere?'

He looked down at his watch and realised that it was nearing midnight, but he was reluctant to end the conversation even though he queried where it was going. She was just another part of his history, a jigsaw puzzle piece that had already been slotted in place, so why prolong the catch-up game? Especially when those huge, veiled, accusing green eyes were reminding him of a past for which he had no use?

If he politely ushered her to the door he was certain that she would leave and not look back. Which was clearly a good thing.

'You can't trust people,' he advised her roughly. 'Now perhaps you'll see my point of view when I told you that the only person you can rely on is yourself.'

'I've probably lost my job here,' Sarah intoned distractedly.

She had seen him look at his watch and she knew what that meant. Her time was coming to an end. He had moved onwards and upwards to that place where time was money. Reminiscing, for Raoul, would have very limited interest value. He was all about the future, not the past. But she had to plough on and get where she needed to get, horrible though the prospect was.

'I couldn't countenance you working here anyway,' Raoul concurred smoothly.

'What does this place have to do with you?'

'As of six this evening—everything. I own it.'

Sarah's mouth dropped open. 'You own *this*?'

'All part of my portfolio.'

It seemed to Sarah now that there was no meeting point left between them. He had truly moved into a different stratosphere. He literally owned the company whose floors she had been scrubbing less than two hours ago. In his smart business suit, with the silk tie and the gleaming hand-made shoes, he was the absolute antithesis of her, with her company uniform and her well-worn flats.

Defiantly she pulled off the headscarf—if only to diminish the image of complete servility.

Hair the colour of vanilla, soft and fine and unruly, tumbled out. He had cut his hair. She had grown hers. It tumbled nearly to her waist, and for a few seconds Raoul was dazzled at the sight of it.

She was twisting the unsightly headscarf between her fingers, and that brought him back down to earth. She had been saying something about the job—this glorious cleaning job—which she would have to abandon. Unless, of course, she carried on cleaning way past her finishing time.

He'd opened his mouth to continue their conversation, even though he had been annoyingly thrown off course by that gesture of hers, when she said, in such a low voice that he had to strain forward to hear her, 'I tried to get in touch, you know...'

'I beg your pardon?'

Sarah cleared her throat. 'I tried to get in touch, but I...I couldn't...'

Raoul stiffened. Having money had been a tremendous learning curve. It had a magnetism all of its own. People he had once known and heartily wished to forget had made contact, having glimpsed some picture of him in the financial pages of a newspaper. It would have been amusing had it not been so pathetic.

He tried to decipher what Sarah was saying now. Had she been one of those people as well? Had she turned to the financial news and spotted him, thought that she might get in touch as she was down on her luck?

'What do you mean, *you couldn't*?' His voice was several shades cooler.

'I had no idea how to locate you.' Her heart was beating so hard that she felt positively sick. 'I mean, you disappeared without a trace. I tried checking with the girl who kept all the registration forms for when we were out there, and she gave me an address, but you'd left...'

'When did all this frantic checking take place?'

'When I got back to England. I know you dumped me, Raoul, but...but I had to talk to you...'

So despite all her bravado when they had parted company she had still tried to track him down. It was a measure of her lack of sophistication that she had done that, and an even greater measure of it that she would now openly confess to doing so.

'I came to London and rented a room in a house out east. You would never have found me.'

'I even went on the internet, but you weren't to be found. And of course I remembered you saying that you would never join any social networking sites...'

'Quite a search. What was that in aid of? A general chat?'

'Not exactly.'

Sarah was thinking now that if she had carried on searching just a little bit longer—another year or so—then she would have found him listed somewhere on the computer, because he would have made his fortune by then. But she had quickly given up. She had never imagined that he would have risen so far, so fast, and yet when she thought about it there had always been that stubborn, closed, ruthless streak to him. And he had been fearless. Fearless when it came to the physical stuff and fearless when it came to plans for his future.

'I wish I had managed to get through to you. You never kept in touch with your last foster home, did you? I tried to trace you through them, but you had already dropped off their radar.'

Raoul stilled, because he had forgotten just how much she knew about him—including his miserable childhood and adolescence.

'So you didn't get in touch,' he said, with a chill in his voice. 'We could carry on discussing all the various ways you tried and failed to find me, or we could just move on. *Why* did you want to get in touch?'

'You mean that I should have had more pride than to try?'

'A lot of women would have,' Raoul commented drily. She turned her head and the overhead light caught her hair, turning it into streaks of gold and pale toffee. 'But I suppose you were very young. Just nineteen.'

'And too stupid to do the sensible thing?'

'Just…very young.' He dragged his eyes away from the dancing highlights of her hair and frowned, sensing an edginess to her voice although her face was very calm and composed.

'You can't blame me if I couldn't find you…'

Raoul was confused. What was she talking about?

'It's getting late, Sarah. I've worked through the night, hammering out this deal with lawyers. I haven't got the time or the energy to try and decipher what you're saying. Why would I *blame* you for not being able to find me?'

'I'll get to the point. I didn't *want* to get in touch with you, Raoul. What kind of a complete loser do you imagine I am? Do you think that I would have come crawling to you for a second chance?'

'You might have if you'd been through the mill with some other guy!'

'There *was* no other guy! And why on earth would I come running to *you* when you had already told me that you wanted nothing more to do with me?'

'Then why *did* you try and get in touch?' He felt disproportionately pleased that there had been no other guy, but he immediately put that down to the fact that, whether they had parted on good terms or not, he wouldn't have wanted her to be used and tossed aside by someone she had met on the rebound.

'Because I found out that I was pregnant!'

The silence that greeted this pooled around her until Sarah began to feel dizzy.

Raoul was having trouble believing what he had just heard. In fact he was tempted to dismiss it as a trick of the imagination, or else some crazy joke—maybe an attention-seeking device to prolong their conversation.

But one look at her face told him that this was no joke.

'That's the most ridiculous thing I've ever heard, and you have to be nuts if you think I'm going to fall for it. When it comes to money, I've heard it all.' Like a caged beast, he shot up and began prowling through the room, hands shoved into his pockets. 'So we've met again by chance. You're down on your luck, for whatever reason, and you see that I've made my fortune. Just come right out and ask for a helping hand! Do you think I'd turn you away? If you need cash, I can write a cheque for you right now.'

'Stop it, Raoul. I'm not a gold-digger! Just listen to me! I tried to get in touch with you because I found out that I was having your baby. I knew you'd be shocked and, believe me, I did think it over for a while, but in the end I thought that it was only fair that you knew. How could you think that I'd make something like that up to try and get money out of you? Have you ever known me to be materialistic? How could you be so insulting?'

'I couldn't have got you pregnant. It's not possible! I was always careful.'

'Not always,' Sarah muttered.

'Okay, so maybe you got yourself pregnant by someone else…'

'There *was* no one else! When I left the compound I had no idea that I was pregnant. I left because…because I just couldn't stay there any longer. I got back to England and I still intended to start university. I *wanted* to put you behind me. I didn't find out until I was nearly five months along. My periods were erratic, and then they disappeared, but I was so… I barely noticed…'

She had been so miserable that World War III could have broken out and she probably wouldn't have noticed the mushroom cloud outside her bedroom window. Memories of him had filled every second of every minute of her every waking hour, until she had prayed for amnesia—anything that would help her forget. Her parents had been worried sick. At any rate, her mother had been the first to suspect something when she'd begun to look a little rounder, despite the fact that her eating habits had taken a nosedive.

'I'm not hearing this.'

'You don't *want* to hear this! My mum and dad were very supportive. They never once lectured, and they were there for me from the very minute that Oliver was born.'

Somehow the mention of a name made Raoul blanch. It was much harder to dismiss what she had said as the rantings of an ex-lover who wanted money from him and was prepared to try anything to get it. The mention of a name seemed to turn the fiction she was spinning into something approaching reality, and yet still his mind refused to concede that the story being told had anything to do with him.

He'd never been one to shy away from the truth, however brutal, but the nuts and bolts of his sharp brain now seemed to be malfunctioning.

Sarah wished he would say something. Did he really believe that she was making up the whole thing? How suspicious of other people had he become over the years? The young man she had fallen in love with had been fiercely independent—but to this extent? How valuable was his wealth if he now found himself unable to trust anyone around him?

'I…I lived in Devon with them after Oliver was born,' she continued into the deafening silence. 'It wasn't ideal, but I really needed the support. Then about a year ago I decided to move to London. Oliver was older—nearly at school age. I thought I could put him into a nursery part-time. There were no real jobs to be had in our village in Devon, and I didn't want to put Mum and Dad in a position of being permanent babysitters. Dad retired a couple of years ago, and they had always planned to travel. I thought that I would be able to get something here—maybe start thinking about getting back into education…'

'Getting back into education? Of course. It's never too late.' He preferred to dwell on this practical aspect to their conversation, but there was a growing dread inside him. There had been more than one occasion when he had not taken precautions. Somehow it had been a different world out there—a world that hadn't revolved around the usual rules and regulations.

'But it was all harder than I thought it was going to

be.' Sarah miserably babbled on to cover her unease. He thought she had lied to try and get money out of him. There was not even a scrap of affection left for her if he could think that. 'I found a house to rent. It's just a block away from a friend I used to go to school with. Emily. She babysits Oliver when I do jobs like these...'

'You mean you've done nothing but mop floors and clean toilets since you moved here?'

'I've earned a living!' Sarah flared back angrily. 'Office jobs are in demand, and it's tough when you haven't got qualifications or any sort of work experience. I've also done some waitressing and bar work, and in a month's time I'm due to start work as a teaching assistant at the local school. Aren't you going to ask me any questions about your son? I have a picture... In my bag downstairs...'

Raoul was slowly beginning to think the unimaginable, but he was determined to demonstrate that he was no push-over—even for her. Even for a woman who still had the ability to creep into his head when he was least expecting it.

'I grant that you may well have had a child,' he said heavily. 'It's been five years. Anything could have happened during that time. But if you insist on sticking to this story, then I have to tell you that I will want definite proof that the child is mine.'

Every time the word *child* crossed his lips, the fact of it being his seemed to take on a more definite shape. After his uncertain and unhappy past, he had always been grimly assured of one thing: no children. He had seen first-hand the lives that could be wrecked by careless parenting. He had been the victim of a woman who had had a child only to discover that it was a hindrance she could have well done without. Fatherhood was never going to be for him. Now, the possibility of it being dropped on him from a very great height was like being hit by a freight train at full speed.

'I think you'll agree that that's fair enough, given the circumstances,' he continued as he looked at her closed, shocked face.

'You just need to take one look at him… I can tell you his birth date…and you can do the maths…'

'Nothing less than a full DNA test will do.'

Sarah swallowed hard. She tried to see things from his point of view. An accidental meeting with a woman he'd thought left behind for good, and, hey presto, he discovered that he was a father! He would be reeling from shock. Of course he would want to ensure that the child was his before he committed himself to anything! He was now the leading man in his very own worst nightmare scenario. He would want proof!

But the hurt, pain and anger raged through her even as she endeavoured to be reasonable.

He might not want her around. In fact he might, right now, be sincerely hoping that he would wake up and discover that their encounter had been a bad dream. But didn't he know her at all? Didn't he *know* that she was not the type of girl who would ever *lie* to try and wrangle money out of him?

Unhappily, she was forced to concede that time had changed them both.

Whilst she had been left with her dreams in tatters around her, a single mother scraping to make ends meet and trying to work out how she could progress her career in the years to come, he had forgotten her and moved on. He had realised his burning ambitions and was now in a place from which he could look down at her like a Greek god, contemplating a mere mortal.

She shuddered to think what would have happened had she managed to locate him all those years ago.

'Of course,' she agreed, standing up.

She could feel a headache coming on. In the morning, Oliver would be at playgroup. She would try and catch up on some sleep while the house was empty. It hadn't escaped her notice that Raoul still hadn't shown any appetite for finding out what his son was like.

'I should go.'

In the corner of her eye, the cleaning trolley was a forlorn reminder of how her life had abruptly changed in the space of a few hours and suddenly become much more complicated. She doggedly reminded herself that whatever the situation *between them* it was good that he knew about Oliver. She sneaked a glance at him from under her lashes and found him staring down at her with an unreadable expression.

'I'm very sorry about this, Raoul.' She dithered, awkward and self-conscious in her uniform. 'I know the last thing you probably want is to have bumped into me and been told that you've fathered a child. Believe me, I don't expect you to do anything. You can walk away from the situation. It's only going to clutter up your life.'

Raoul gave a bark of derisive laughter.

'What planet are you living on, Sarah? If...if I am indeed a father, then do you really think I'm going to walk out on my responsibility? I will support you in every way that I can. What possible choice would I have?'

Tacked on at the end, that flat assertion said it all. He would rise to the occasion and do his duty. Having wanted nothing in life but to be free, he would now find himself chained to a situation from which he would never allow himself to retreat. She wondered if he had any idea how that made her feel, and felt painful tears push their way up her throat.

She found a clean white handkerchief pressed into her hand, and she stared down at the floor, blinking rapidly in an attempt to control her emotions. 'You never owned a hankie when I knew you,' she said in a wobbly voice, reaching for anything that might be a distraction from what she was feeling.

Raoul gave her a reluctant smile. 'I have no idea why I own one now. I never use it.'

'What about when you have a cold and need to blow your nose?'

'I don't get colds. I'm as healthy as a horse.'

It was only a few meaningless exchanged words, but Sarah felt a lot better as she stuck the handkerchief in the pocket of her overall, promising to return it when it had been washed.

'I'll need to be able to contact you,' he told her. 'What's your mobile number? I'll write mine down for you, and you can contact me at any time.'

As they exchanged numbers, she couldn't help but think back to when he had walked out on her with no forwarding address and no number at which he could be contacted. He had wanted to be rid of her completely—a clean cut, with no loose threads that could cause him any headaches later down the road.

'I'll be in touch within the week,' he told her, pocketing his mobile, and then he watched as she nodded silently and walked out of the room. He saw her yank off the overall and dump it in the trolley, along with the headscarf. She left it all just where it was in a small act of rebellion that brought a smile to his lips.

Alone in the office, and alone with his thoughts, Raoul contemplated the bomb that had detonated in his life.

He had a son.

Despite what he had said about wanting evidence, he knew in his gut that the child was his. Sarah had never cared about money, and she had always been the least manipulative woman he had ever known. He believed her when she said that she had tried to contact him, and he was shaken by the thought of her doing her utmost to bring up a child on her own when she had been just a child herself.

The fact was that he had messed up and he would have to pay the price. And it was going to be a very steep price.

CHAPTER TWO

SARAH was at the kitchen sink, finishing the last of the washing up, when the doorbell went.

The house she rented was not in a particularly terrific part of East London, but it was affordable, public transport was reasonably convenient, and the neighbours were nice. You couldn't have everything.

Before the doorbell could buzz again and risk waking Oliver, who had only just been settled after a marathon run of demands for more and more books to be read to him until finally he drifted off to sleep, Sarah wiped her hands on a dishcloth and half ran to the front door.

At not yet seven-thirty she was in some faded tracksuit bottoms and a baggy tee shirt. It was her usual garb on a weekend because she couldn't afford to go out. Twice a month she would try and have some friends over, cook them something, but continually counting pennies took a lot of the fun out of entertaining.

She had spent the past two days caught up in trying to find herself some replacement shift work. The cleaning company that had hired her had been appalled to find that she had walked out on a job without a backward glance, and she had been sacked on the spot.

Her heart hadn't been in the search, however. She'd been too busy thinking about Raoul and tirelessly replaying their unexpected encounter in her head. She'd spent hours trying to analyse what he had said and telling herself that it had all happened for the best. She'd looked at Oliver and all she'd seen was Raoul's dark hair and bitter chocolate eyes, and the smooth, healthy olive skin that would go a shade darker as he got older. He was a clone of his father.

If Raoul saw him there would be no doubt, but she still hadn't heard from him, and her disappointment had deepened with every passing hour.

On top of that, she couldn't make her mind up what she should tell her parents. Should they know that Raoul was Oliver's father and was back on the scene? Or would they worry? She had confessed that she had had her heart broken, and she wasn't convinced that they had ever really believed it to have been fully pieced together again. How would they react if they knew that the guy who'd broken her heart was back in her life? She was an only child, and they were super-protective. She imagined them racing up to London wielding rolling pins and threatening retribution.

She pulled open the door, her mind wandering feverishly over old ground, and stepped back in confusion at the sight of Raoul standing in front of her.

'May I come in, Sarah?'

'I...I wasn't expecting you. I thought you said that you were going to phone...'

She was without make-up, and no longer in a uniform designed to keep all hint of femininity at bay, and Raoul's dark eyes narrowed as he took in the creamy satin smoothness of her skin, the brightness of her green eyes in her heart-shaped face and the curves of her familiar body underneath her tee shirt and track pants.

He recognised the tee shirt, although it was heavily

faded now, its rock group logo almost obliterated. Just looking at it took him back in time to lying on the bed in the small room in Africa, with the mosquito net tethered as best they could manage under the mattress, watching and burning for her as she slowly stripped the tee shirt over her head to reveal her full, round breasts.

Raoul had planned on phoning. He had spent the past two days thinking, and had realised that the best way forward would be to view the situation in the same way he would view any problem that needed a solution—with a clear head. First establish firm proof that the child was his, because his gut instinct might well be wrong, and then have an adult conversation with her regarding the way forward.

Unfortunately he hadn't been able to play the waiting game. He hadn't been able to concentrate at work. He had tried to vent his frustration at the gym, but even two hours of gruelling exercise had done nothing to diminish his urgent need to *do something*.

Sarah read everything into his silence and ushered him into the house.

'I didn't know if I should be expecting a call from… somebody…about those tests you wanted…'

'On hold for the moment.'

'Really?' Her eyes shone and she smiled. 'So you *do* believe me.'

'For the moment I'm prepared to give you the benefit of the doubt.'

'You won't regret it, Raoul. Oliver's the image of you. I'm sorry he's asleep. I *would* wake him…'

Raoul had no experience of children. They weren't part of his everyday existence, and in the absence of any family he had never been obliged to cut his teeth on nephews or nieces. He was utterly bewildered at the notion of being in the presence of a son he had never laid eyes on. What did a four-year-old boy *do*, exactly? Were they capable of making conversation at that age?

Suddenly nervous as hell, he cleared his throat and waved aside her offer. 'Maybe it's best if we talk about this first...'

'Then would you like something to drink? Tea? Coffee? I think I might have some wine in the fridge. I don't keep a great deal of alcohol in the house. I can't afford it, anyway.'

Raoul was looking around him, taking in the surroundings which were a stark reminder of how far he had travelled. Now he lived in a massive two-storeyed penthouse apartment in the best postcode in London, furnished to the very highest standard. Frankly, it was the best that money could buy—although he barely glanced at his surroundings and was seldom in to take advantage of the top-of-the-range designer kitchen and all the other jaw dropping features the high-tech apartment sported.

This tiny terraced house couldn't have been more different. The carpet, the indeterminate colour of sludge, had obviously never been replaced, and the walls, although painted in a cheerful green colour, showed signs of cracks. Standing in the hall with her, he was aware there was practically no room to move, and as he followed her into the kitchen there was no change. A pine table was shoved against the wall to accommodate random pieces of freestanding furniture—a half-sized dresser, a chest of drawers, some shelves on which bottles with various cooking ingredients stood.

He had managed to climb up and away from these sorts of surroundings, but it still sent a chill through his body that but for a combination of brains, luck and sheer hard work beyond the call of duty he might very well have still been living in a place very much like this.

This was precisely why, he told himself, he had refused to be tied down. Only by being one hundred percent free to focus on his career had he been able to fulfil his ambitions. Women were certainly an enjoyable distraction, but he had never been tempted to jettison any of his plans for one of them.

The more wealth he accumulated, the more jaded he became. He could have the most beautiful women in the world, and in fact he had had a number of head-turning girlfriends on his arm over the years, but they had always been secondary to his career.

Dim memories of living in a dingy room with his mother while she drank herself into a stupor had been his driving force. This house was only a few steps up from dingy. He imagined the landlord to be someone of dubious integrity, happy to take money from desperate tenants, but less happy to make any improvements to the property.

The notion of *his son* had somehow managed to take root in his head, and Raoul was incensed at the deplorable living conditions.

'I know,' Sarah apologised, following the critical path of his eyes. 'It's not fantastic, but everything works. And it's so much better than some of the other places I looked at. I don't even know where *you* live…'

Raoul, who had been staring at a dramatic rip in the wallpaper above the dresser, met her eyes and held them.

He couldn't understand whether it was her familiarity that was making him feel so *aware of her*—inconveniently, frustratingly, *sexually* aware of her—or whether he had just managed to make himself forget the attraction she had always had for him.

'Chelsea,' he said grimly, sitting on one of the chairs

at the table, which felt fragile enough to break under his weight.

'And…and what's it like?' She could feel hot colour in her cheeks, because he just dominated the small space of the kitchen. His presence seemed to wrap itself around her, making her pulses race and her skin feel tight and uncomfortable.

Coffee made, she handed him a mug and sat on the other chair.

'It's an apartment.' He shrugged. 'I don't spend a great deal of time in it. It works for me. It's low maintenance.'

'What does that mean? Low maintenance?'

'Nothing surplus to requirements. I don't like clutter.'

'And…and is there a woman in that apartment?' She went bright red as she asked the question, but it was one that had only occurred to her after she had left him. Was there a woman in his life? He didn't give the impression of being a married man, but then would he ever?

'What's the relevance of that question?' He sipped some of the instant coffee and looked at her steadily over the rim of the mug.

'It's relevant to this situation,' she persisted stubbornly. 'Oliver's your son, and he's going to have to get used to the idea of having a father around. I'm the only parent figure he's ever known.'

'Which isn't exactly my fault.'

'I know it's not! I'm just making a point.' She glared at him. 'It's going to take time for him to get to know you, and I don't want him to have to deal with a woman on the scene as well. At least I'd rather not. I suppose if you're married…'

Having never had to answer to anyone but himself, Raoul refused to be railroaded into an explanation of his private life—although he could see the validity of her question.

'No. There's no little lady keeping the home fires burning. As for women… I'll naturally strive to ensure that a difficult situation isn't made even more difficult.'

'So there *is* someone.' She tried desperately to take it in her stride, because it really wasn't very surprising. He was sinfully gorgeous, and now wealthy beyond belief. He would be a magnet for any footloose and single woman— and probably for a good few who *weren't* footloose and single.

'I don't think we should get wrapped up in matters that don't really have much to do with this…situation. We just need to discuss what the next step should be.'

'Come upstairs and see him. I can't have this conversation with you when you don't even know the child you're talking about. This isn't a business deal that needs to be sorted out.' She stood up abruptly and Raoul, put on the spot, followed suit.

'He's sleeping. I wouldn't want you to wake him.' Raoul was more nervous than he could ever remember being— more nervous than when he had chased, and closed, his first major deal. More nervous than when he had been a kid and he had stared up at the forbidding grey walls of the foster home that would eventually become his residence.

'Okay. I won't. But you still have to see him, or else he's just going to be a *problem that needs solving* in your head.'

'Since when did you get so bossy?' Raoul muttered under his breath, and Sarah spun around to find him looming behind her.

Standing on the first stair, she could almost look him in the eye. 'Since I ended up being responsible for another human being,' she said. 'I know it's not your fault that you weren't aware of the situation...' *Although it was, because if he had only just given her a contact number she would have been able to get in touch with him.* 'But it was terrifying for me when I discovered that I was pregnant. I kept thinking how nice it would be if you had been around to support me, and then I remembered how you had dumped me because you had plans and they didn't include me, and that if you *had* been around my pregnancy would have been your worst nightmare.'

'My plans didn't include *anyone*, Sarah. I did you a favour.'

'Oh, don't be so arrogant! If you'd cared enough about me you would have kept in touch.' She was breathing heavily as all the remembered pain and bitterness and anger surged through her, but staring into the depths of his fabulous dark eyes was doing something else to her—making her whole body tingle as though someone had taken a powerful electrical charge to it.

Raoul clocked her reaction without even consciously registering it. He just knew that the atmosphere had become taut with an undercurrent that had nothing to do with what they had been talking about. It was a type of non-verbal communication that sent his body into crazy overdrive.

'I don't know why I'm bothering to tell you any of this.' She jerked her hand in clumsy dismissal, but he caught her wrist. The heat of physical contact made her draw in her breath sharply, although he wasn't hurting her—not at all. He was barely circling her wrist with his long fingers. Still...she was appalled to find that she wanted to sink against him.

That acknowledgment of weakness galvanised her into struggling to free herself and he released her abruptly, although when she could have turned around and stalked up the stairs she continued to stare at him wordlessly.

'I know it must have been a bad time for you…'

'Well, that's the understatement of the decade if ever there was one! I felt completely lost and alone.'

'You had your parents to help you.'

'That's not the same! Plus I'd left for my gap year thinking that I was at the start of living my own life. Do you know what it felt like to go back home? Yes, they helped me, and I couldn't have managed at all without them, but it still felt like a retrograde step. I never, ever considered having an abortion, and I was thrilled to bits when Oliver was born, but I was having to cope with seeing all my dreams fly through the window. No university, no degree, no teaching qualification. You must have been laughing your head off when you saw me cleaning floors in that bank.'

'Don't be ridiculous.'

'No? Then what *was* going through your head when you looked down at me? With a damp cloth in one hand and a cleaning bottle in the other, dressed in my overalls?'

'Okay. I was stunned. But then I started remembering how damned sexy you were, and thinking how damned sexy you still were—never mind the headscarf and the overalls…'

His words hovered in the air between them, a spark of conflagration just waiting to find tinder. To her horror, Sarah realised that she wanted him to repeat what he had just said so she could savour his words and roll them round and round in her head.

How could she have forgotten the way he had treated her? He might justify walking out on her as *doing her a favour*, but that was just another way of saying that he hadn't cared for her the way she had cared for him, and he hadn't been about to let a meaningless holiday romance spoil his big plans.

'I've come to realise that sex is very overrated,' Sarah said scornfully, and then flushed as a slow smile curved his beautiful mouth.

'Really?'

'I don't want to talk about this.' But she heard the tell-tale tremor in her voice and wanted to scream in frustration. 'It certainly has nothing to do with what's…what's happening now. If you follow me, I'll show you to Oliver's room.'

Raoul let the conversation drop. He was as astounded as she had been by his own genuine admission to her, and he was busily trying to work out how a woman he hadn't seen in years—a woman who, in the great scheme of things, had not really been in his life for very long—could still exercise such a powerful physical hold over him. It was as though the years between them had collapsed and disappeared.

But of course they hadn't, he reminded himself forcefully. Proof of that was currently asleep in a bedroom, just metres away from where they had been standing.

Upstairs, if anything, seemed more cramped than downstairs, with two small bedrooms huddled around a tiny bathroom which he glimpsed on his way to the box room on the landing.

She pushed open the door to the only room he had seen so far that bore the hallmark of recent decoration. A night-light revealed wallpaper with some sort of kiddy theme and basic furniture. A small bed, thin patterned curtains, a circular rug tucked half under the bed, a white chest of drawers, snap-together furniture, cheap but functional.

Raoul unfroze himself from where he was standing

like a sentinel by the doorway and took a couple of steps towards the bed.

Oliver had kicked off the duvet and was curled around a stuffed toy.

Raoul could make out black curly hair, soft chubby arms. Even in the dim light he could see that his colouring was a shade darker than his mother's—a pale olive tone that was all *his*.

In the grip of a powerful curiosity, he took a step closer to the bed and peered at the small sleeping figure. When it shifted, Raoul instantly took a step back.

'We should go—just in case we wake him,' Sarah whispered, tiptoeing out of the bedroom.

Raoul followed her. The palms of his hands felt clammy.

She had been right. He had a son. There had been no mistaking those small, familiar signs of a likeness that was purely inherited. He wondered how he could ever have sat in his office and concluded that he would deal with the problem with the cold detachment of a mathematician completing a tricky equation. He had a child. A living, breathing son.

The cramped condition of the house in which he was living now seemed grossly offensive. He would have to do something about that. He would have to do something about pretty much everything. Life as he knew it was about to change. One minute he had been riding the crest of a wave, stupidly imagining that he had the world in the palm of his hand, and the next minute the wave had crashed and the world he had thought netted was spinning out of control.

It was a ground-breaking notion for someone whose only driving goal throughout his life had been to remedy the lack of control he had had as a child by conquering the world. A tiny human being, barely three feet tall, had put paid to that.

'You're very quiet,' Sarah said nervously, as soon as they were out of earshot.

'I need a drink—and something stronger than a cup of coffee.'

The remnants of a bottle of wine were produced and poured into a glass. Sarah looked at him, trying to gauge his mood and trying to forget that moment of mad longing that had torn through her only a short while before on the staircase.

'You were right,' he said heavily, having drunk most of the glass in one go. 'I see the resemblance.'

'I knew you would. It'll be even more noticeable when you see him in the light. He's got your dark eyes as well. In fact, there's not much of me at all in him! That was the first thing Mum said when he was born… Would you like to see some of the drawings he's made? He goes to a playgroup two mornings a week…I get help with that…'

'Help? What kind of help?' Raoul dragged his attention away from the swirling wine in his glass and looked at her.

'From the government, of course,' Sarah said, surprised. How on earth could she afford childcare otherwise, when she worked as a cleaner? On the mornings when Oliver was at nursery, she helped out at the school at which she was due to start work, but that was unpaid.

Raoul controlled his temper with difficulty. 'From the government?' he repeated with deadly cool, and Sarah nodded uneasily. 'Do you know what my aim in life was? My *only* aim in life? To escape the clutches of government aid and own my future. Now you sit here and tell me that you're *reliant* on government aid to get you through life.'

'You make it sound like a crime, Raoul.'

'For *me*, it's obscene!'

The force of his personality hit her like a freight train travelling at full speed, but she squared her shoulders and glared at him defiantly. If she allowed him to take control just this once then she would be dancing to his tune as and when he wanted her to. Hadn't she done enough of that years ago? And look where it had got her!

'And I can understand that,' Sarah told him evenly. 'I really can. But your past has nothing to do with my present circumstances. I couldn't afford to put Oliver into a private nursery,' she informed him bluntly. 'You'd be shocked at how little I earn. Mum and Dad supplement me, but every day's a struggle. It's all very well for you to sit there and preach to me about pride and ambition, but pride and ambition aren't very high up in the pecking order when you barely have enough money to put food on the table. So if I can get help with the nursery, then I'll take it.' She wished that she had had some wine as well, because she was in dire need of fortification. 'You were never such a crashing snob before, Raoul,' she continued bitterly. 'I can see that you've changed in more ways than one.'

'Snob? I think you'll find that that's the last thing I am!' He was outraged that she could hurl that accusation at him in view of his past.

'You've moved away from your struggling days of when we first met! I'll bet you can't even remember what it was like, darning those shorts of yours when they got ripped because you couldn't afford to chuck them out!'

'*You* darned them.' He looked at her darkly. He could remember her doing it as if it had been yesterday, swatting mosquitoes and moths away while outside a dull rumble of thunder had heralded heavy rain. She had looked like a girl in a painting, with her hair tumbling around her face as she frowned in concentration.

Sarah bit back the temptation to tell him what an idiot she had been, doing stuff like that, worshipping the ground he walked on, eager to do whatever he wanted.

'And I *haven't* forgotten my past,' he said grimly. 'It's always there at the back of my mind, like a stuck record.'

Her heart softened, but she held her ground with grim determination.

'I may not have planned for this, but I want you to know that things are going to change now. This place is barely fit for habitation!' He caught the warning look in her eyes and offered her a crooked smile. 'Okay. Bit of an exaggeration. But you get where I'm going. Whether you think I've become a monstrous snob or not, I can afford to take you away from here—and that's got to be my number one priority.'

'Your number one priority is getting to know Oliver.'

'I would prefer to get to know him in surroundings that won't challenge me every time I walk through the front door.'

Sarah sighed. It would certainly make life easier not having to worry so much about money. 'Okay. I take back some of the things I said. You haven't completely changed. You still think that you can get your own way all the time.'

'I know. It more than compensates for *your* indecision. Now, you could put up a brief struggle to hold on to your independence, maybe give me a little lecture on things being just perfect here, with your quaint, outdated kitchen furniture and the walls in need of plasterwork, but we both know that you can see my point of view. I can afford to take you out of this, and I consider it my duty to do so.'

The word *duty* lodged in her head like a burr, and she looked down at her anxiously clasped fingers. There was nothing like honesty to really hurt.

'What do you suggest?' she asked. 'Do I have any input

here? Or are you going to just walk all over me because you have lots of money and I have none?'

'I'm going to walk all over you because I have lots of money and you have none.'

'Not funny,' Sarah muttered, remembering his talent for defusing a situation with his sense of humour. Given the conditions years ago, when they had been cooped up on the compound, tempers had occasionally run high and this talent of his had been invaluable. Was he using it now just to get his own way? And did that matter anyway? The prospect of no longer having a daily struggle on her hands was like being offered manna from heaven.

'I intend to take my responsibilities very seriously, Sarah. I think you should know that. It would be very time-consuming to travel out here every time I wanted to see Oliver. Somewhere closer to where I live would be a solution.'

Now that they were discussing things in a more businesslike manner Sarah could actually focus on what was being said—as opposed to fighting to maintain her equilibrium, which showed threatening signs of wanting to fall apart.

'I feel as though I'm suddenly on a rollercoaster ride,' she confessed.

'Spare a thought for me. Whatever rollercoaster ride you're on, mine is bigger, faster, and I'm a hell of a lot less prepared for it than you are.'

And yet he was rising to the occasion. It didn't matter that the only reason they were now even having this conversation was because she had become a responsibility he couldn't shirk. He had taken it all in his stride in his usual authoritative way. That there was no emotion involved was something she would have to deal with. It wasn't his problem, and she wasn't going to let that get in the way of the relationship he had to build with his son.

'So we move to another place… There are still all sorts of other things that need sorting out. I'll have to try and explain to Oliver that he has a…a father. He's only young, though. I should warn you that it might not be that easy.'

'He's four,' Raoul pointed out with impeccable logic. 'He hasn't had time to build up any kind of picture for or against me.'

'Yes, but—'

'Let's not anticipate problems, Sarah.'

Now that he had surmounted the sudden bout of intense nervousness that had gripped him in the bedroom, Raoul was confident he would be able to get Oliver onside. Having had a life of grinding poverty, replete with secondhand clothes and secondhand books and secondhand toys, and frankly secondhand affection, he was beginning to look forward to giving his son everything that he himself had lacked in his childhood.

'We take things one at a time. First the house. Secondly, I suggest you try and explain my role to Oliver. Has he… has he ever asked about his father?'

'In passing,' Sarah admitted. 'When he's been to a birthday party and seen the other kids with their dads. Once when I was reading him a story.'

Raoul's lips thinned but he didn't say anything. 'You will obviously have to tell your parents that you are moving, and why. Will you tell them I'm on the scene? What my position is?'

'Maybe we shouldn't go there just yet,' Sarah said vaguely.

'I won't hide in the shadows.'

'I'm not sure they're going to be overjoyed that you're on the scene, actually.' She flushed guiltily as she remembered their distress when she had told them how she had fallen hard for a guy who had then chucked her. The hormones rushing through her body had made her all the more vulnerable and emotional, and she had spared nothing in her mournful, self-pitying account.

Honestly, she didn't think that Raoul was going to be flavour of the month if she produced him out of nowhere. But she knew that she would have to sooner or later. Her mum always phoned at least three times a week, and always had a chat with Oliver. Sarah wouldn't want her to find out via her grandchild that the heartbreaker and callous reprobate was now around.

'I'm getting the picture,' Raoul said slowly.

Sarah thought it better to move on quickly from that topic of conversation. 'I'm sure they'll be very happy.' She crossed her fingers behind her back. 'They're very conventional. They'll be delighted that Oliver will now have a father figure in his life.'

He stood up. 'I'll be in touch tomorrow. No—scrap that. I'll come by tomorrow afternoon so that I can be introduced to my son.'

The formality of that statement brought a rush of colour to Sarah's face, because it underlined his lack of enthusiasm for the place in which he now found himself.

'Should I buy him something special to wear?' she said tartly. 'I wouldn't want his appearance to offend you.'

'That's not helpful.'

'Nor is your approach to Oliver!' Tears stung the back of her eyes. 'How can you be so…so…*unemotional*? This wasn't how I ever thought my life would turn out. I always thought that I would fall in love and get married, and when a baby came along it would be a cause for celebration and joy. I never imagined that I would have a child with a man who wasn't even pleased to be a father!'

Raoul flushed darkly. What did she expect of him? He was here, wasn't he? Prepared to take on a task which had been sprung on him. Not only that, but she would be the recipient of a new house to replace her dismal rented accommodation, and also in the enviable position of never having to worry about money in her life again. Were hysterical accusations in order? Absolutely not!

He was very tempted to give her a checklist of all the things she should be thankful for. He settled for saying, in a cool voice, 'I've found that life has a funny way of not playing fair in the great scheme of things.'

'Is that all you have to say?' Sarah cried in frustration. 'Honestly, Raoul, sometimes I could...*hit you*!'

Her eyes were blazing and her hair was a tumbling riot of gold—and he felt a charge race through his system like an uncontrolled dose of adrenaline.

'I'm flattered that I still get you so worked up,' he murmured with husky amusement.

He couldn't help himself as he reached out and tangled his fingers in that hair. The contact was electric. He felt her response slam into him like a physical force and he revelled in the dark sexual hunger snaking through his body. *That* was something no amount of hard-headed logic or cool, calm reason could control.

Her lips had parted and her eyes were unfocused and half closed. Kissing her would halt all those crazy accusations in mid-flow. And he was hungry for her—hungry to remind himself of what her lips felt like.

'Don't you dare, Raoul...'

He pulled her towards him and noted, with a blaze of satisfaction, the unspoken invitation in her darkened eyes.

That first heady taste of him was intoxicating. Sarah moaned and pressed her hands against his chest. He had always been able to make her forget everything with a single touch, and her mind duly went blank. She forgot everything as her body curved sensuously against his, every bit of her melting at the feel of his swollen masculinity pushing against her, straining against the zipper of his trousers. Her breasts ached and she moved them against him, almost fainting at the pleasurable sensation of the abrasive motion on her sensitised nipples.

Raoul was the first to pull away.

'I shouldn't have done that.'

It took a few seconds for the daze in Sarah's head to clear, and then she snapped back to the horrified realisation that after everything she had been through, and hot on the heels of her really, *really* wanting to hit him, she had just *caved in*—like an addict who couldn't control herself. He had kissed her and all the hurt, anger and disappointment had disappeared. She had become a mindless puppet and five years had vanished in the blink of an eye.

'Neither of us should have…'

'Maybe it was inevitable.'

'What do you mean? What are you talking about?'

'You know what I'm talking about. This *thing* between us…'

'There's nothing between us!' Sarah cried, stepping back and hugging herself in an automatic gesture of self-defence.

'Are you trying to convince me or yourself?'

'Okay, maybe we just…just gave in to something *for the sake of old times*.' She took a deep breath. 'And now we've got that out of the way we can move on and…and…'

'Pretend it never happened?'

'Exactly! Pretend it never happened!' She took a few more steps back, but she thought that even if she took a million steps back and fled the country the after-effects of that devastating kiss would still be with her. 'This isn't

about *us*. This is about Oliver and your part in his life, so…
so…'

Raoul looked at her with a brooding intensity that made
her tremble. She didn't have a clue what was going on in
his head. He had always been very good at shielding his
thoughts when it suited him. She worked herself up into
a self-righteous anger, remembering how terrific he had
been at keeping stuff from her—like their lack of future—
until she had fallen for him hook, line and sinker. Never
again would she let him have that level of control!

'So just come here tomorrow. You can meet Oliver, and
we can work out some kind of schedule, and…then we can
both just get on with our own lives…'

CHAPTER THREE

By the time the doorbell went the following afternoon Sarah hoped that she had risen above her physical weakness of the day before and reached a more balanced place. In other words sorted her priorities. Priority number one was Oliver, and she bracingly repeated to herself how wonderful it was that his father would now be there for him, willing to take on a parental role, whatever that might be. A full and frank discussion of that was high on her agenda. Priority number two, on a more personal level, was to make sure that she kept a clear head and didn't get lost in old feelings and memories.

She opened the door to a casually dressed Raoul.

'Oliver's in the sitting room, watching cartoons,' she said, getting down to business straight away.

Raoul looked at her carefully, and noted the way her eyes skittered away from his, the way she kept one hand on the doorknob, as though leaving her options open just in case she decided to shut the door in his face. In fact she had only half opened the door, and he peered behind her pointedly.

'Are you actually going to let me in, or do you want me to forge a path past you?'

'I just want to say that we'll really need to discuss… um…the practicalities of this whole situation…'

'As opposed to what?'

'I've been thinking, Raoul…'

'Dangerous,' Raoul said softly. She was in a pair of jeans and a tight tee shirt that reminded him a little too forcibly of the mysterious physical hold she still seemed to have over him. He had spent the night vainly trying to clear his head of images of her.

'I've been thinking that we should have as little to do with one another as possible. I don't want anything to happen between us. Been there, done that and have the tee shirt. The important thing is that you get to know Oliver, and that should be the extent of our relationship with one another.'

'And have you told him who I am?'

Sarah was startled and a little taken aback at the speed with which he had concluded a conversation she had spent hours rehearsing in her head. Had she hoped that he would at least try and knock down some of her defences? Had she erected her *Keep Off* sign in the expectation that he might just try and steamroller through it? Had she secretly *wanted* him to steamroller through it?

'Not yet,' she said crisply. 'I thought it best that you two get to know one another first.'

'Okay. Well, there's some stuff I'd like to bring in.'

'Stuff? What kind of stuff?'

He nodded to his car, which was parked a few spaces along. 'Why don't you go inside? I'll be a few minutes.'

'You haven't bought him presents, have you?' she asked suspiciously, but when she tried to step outside to get a closer look, he gently but firmly prevented her.

'Now, how did I know that you would disapprove?'

'It's not appropriate to show up with an armful of gifts the very first time you meet him!'

'I'm making up for lost time.'

Sarah gave up. You couldn't buy affection, she conceded, but perhaps a small token might help break the ice. Oliver had had no male input in his short life so far aside from her own father, whom he adored. She had been too busy just trying to make ends meet to dip her toes in the dating pool, and anyway she had not been interested in trying to replace Raoul. To her way of thinking she had developed a very healthy cynicism of the opposite sex. So Oliver's sole experience of the adult world, to a large extent, had been *her*.

He was in the process of trying to construct a tower of bricks, with one eye on the manic adventures of his favourite cartoon character, when Raoul appeared in the doorway. In one arm there was a huge box, and in the other an enormous sack.

There was more in the boot of the car, but Raoul just hadn't had the arms to bring it all in. Now he was glad that he hadn't. Oliver appeared to be utterly bewildered, and Sarah… Her mouth had fallen open in what could only be described as an expression of horror. Couldn't she say something?

Feeling like a complete fool for the first time in as long as he could recall, Raoul remained standing in the doorway with what he hoped was a warm smile pasted to his face.

'Oliver! This is…this is my friend, Raoul! Why don't you say hi to him?'

Oliver scuttled over to Sarah and clambered onto her lap, leaving Raoul trying to forge a connection by introducing a series of massively expensive presents to his son.

An oversized remote controlled car was removed from the box. The sack was opened to reveal a collection of games, books and stuffed toys which, Raoul assured a progressively more alarmed Sarah, had come highly recommended by the salesperson at the toy shop. He stooped to Oliver's level and asked him if he would care to try out the car. Oliver, by way of response, shook his head vigorously, to indicate very firmly that the last thing he wanted was to go anywhere near the aggressive silver machine that took up a fair amount of their sitting room space.

The games, books and stuffed toys garnered the same negative response, and silence greeted Raoul's polite but increasingly frustrated questions about playschool, sport and favourite television programmes.

At the end of an agonising forty-minute question and no answer session, Oliver finally asked Sarah if he could carry on with his blocks. In various piles lay the items that Raoul had bought, untouched.

'Well, *that* was a roaring success,' was the first thing Raoul muttered venomously under his breath, once he and Sarah were in the kitchen, leaving Oliver in the sitting room.

'It's going to take time.'

Raoul glared at her. 'What have you told him about me?'

'Nothing. Just that you were an old friend.'

'Hence the friendly way with in I was greeted?'

His own son had rejected him. Over the years, in his inexorable upward march, Raoul had trained himself to overcome every single setback, because every setback could be seen as a learning curve. He needed to speak French to close a deal? He learnt it. He needed intimate knowledge of the gaming market to take over a failing computer company? He acquired sufficient knowledge to get him by, and employed two formidable gaming geeks to do the rest. He had built an empire on the firm belief that he was capable of doing anything. There were no obstacles he was incapable of surmounting.

Yet half an hour in the company of a four-year-old had

rendered him impotent. Oliver had been uninterested in every toy pulled out of the bag and indifferent to *him*. There was no past experience upon which Raoul could call to get him through his son's lack of enthusiasm.

'Most kids would have gone crazy over that toy car,' he imparted in an accusatory tone. 'At least that's what the salesperson told me. It's been their biggest seller for the past four years. That damned car can do anything except carry passengers on the M25. So tell me what the problem was?' He glared at her as she serenely fetched two glasses from the cupboard and poured them some wine. 'The boy barely glanced in my direction.'

'I don't think it was such a good idea to bring so many toys for him.'

'And how do you work that one out? I would have been over the moon if I had ever, as a kid, been given *one* new toy! So how could several new, expensive, top of the range toys fail to do the trick?'

With a jolt of sympathy that ran contrary to every defence mechanism she had in place, Sarah realised that he really didn't have a clue. He had drawn from his own childhood experiences and arrived at a solution for winning his son's affections—except he hadn't realised that there was more to gaining love and trust than an armful of gifts.

'Do you know,' Raoul continued, swallowing the contents of his glass in one gulp, 'that every toy I ever played with as a child had come from someone else and had to be shared? A remote controlled car like the one languishing in your sitting room would have caused a full-scale riot.'

'That's just awful,' Sarah murmured.

'Now you're about to practise some amateur psychology on me. Don't. You should have told me that he liked building things. I would have come armed with blocks.'

'You're missing the point. You need to engage him. Like I said, he's used to only having me around. He's going to view any other adult on the scene with suspicion. What happened on birthdays? Christmas?'

'What are you talking about?'

'With you? Didn't you get birthday presents? What about Father Christmas?'

Raoul looked at her with a crooked smile that went past every barrier and settled somewhere in the depths of her heart.

'I don't see what this has to do with anything, but if you really want to know Father Christmas was tricky. Frankly, I don't think I ever believed in the fat guy with the beard. My earliest memory is of my mother telling me when I was three years old that there was no such person. Thinking about it now, I suspect she didn't want to waste valuable money on feeding that particular myth when the money could have been so much better spent on a bottle of gin. Anyway, even at the foster home there wasn't much room to hold on to stories like that. Father Christmas barely rated a mention.' He laughed without rancour. 'So—you're going to give me a lesson on engagement. If Oliver has no time for anything I bought for him, then how do we proceed?'

'Are you asking for my help?'

'I'm asking for your opinion. If I remember correctly, you have never been short of those…'

'Why don't you go out there and build something with him?' she suggested. 'No. I'll get him to bring his bricks in here, and the two of you can build something on the kitchen table while I prepare supper.'

'Forget about cooking. I'll take you both out. Name the restaurant and I'll ensure the chef is only too happy to whip up something for Oliver.'

'No,' Sarah said firmly. 'This is what normal life is all

about with a child, Raoul. Spaghetti Bolognese, familiar
old toys, cartoons on television, reading books at night before sleep…' Except, she thought, suddenly flustered by
the picture she had been busy painting, that was the *ideal*
domestic situation—one in which two people were happily married and in love. It certainly wasn't *their* situation.
As she had told him—*and she had meant every word of
it*—they had no relationship outside the artificial one im-
posed by circumstance.

'Okay. I'll bring Oliver in and you can start chopping
some onions. They're in the salad drawer in the fridge.
Chop them really small.'

'You want me to *cook*?'

'Well, to help at any rate. And don't tell me that you've
forgotten how to cook. You used to cook on the compound.'

'Different place, different country.'

'So…you just eat out all the time?' Sarah asked, distracted.

'It's more time-efficient.'

'And what about with your girlfriends? Don't you want
to stay in sometimes? Do normal stuff?'

The questions were out before she had the wit to keep
her curiosity to herself, and now that she had voiced them,
she realised that it had been on her mind, poised just beneath the surface, ever since she had laid eyes on him
again. In fact, thinking about it, it was something she had
asked herself over and over again through the years. Had
he found someone else? Had another woman been able to
capture his interest sufficiently for him to make the commitment that he had denied her? He hadn't loved *her*, but
had he fallen in love with someone else? Someone prettier
or cleverer or more accomplished?

'Not that it's any of my business,' she added, and
laughed airily.

'It is now. Haven't you said that yourself? No women in Oliver's presence… Rest assured that the only woman in my life at the moment is *you*…'

'That's not what I was asking and you know it, Raoul!'

'No. You're just curious to know what I've been getting up to these past few years. There's nothing wrong with curiosity. Curiosity's healthy.'

'I don't *care* what you've been getting up to!' It was a lie. She cared. Who were these women he had dated? What had he felt for them? Anything? Had he preferred them to *her*? She was mortified just thinking about that particular question.

'I haven't been getting up to anything of interest,' Raoul replied drily. 'Yes, there have been women. But I've deterred them from doing anything that involved pots, pans, an apron, candlelight and home-cooked food.'

'Oh, Raoul, you're such a charmer.' But a tendril of relief curled inside her. She squashed it. 'Now, I'm going to fetch Oliver.'

'Hey, what about you? Don't I get the low-down on *your* life? No man at the moment, but any temptations? Do you cook your spaghetti Bolognese for anyone else aside from Oliver?'

His voice was light and mildly amused, and he wondered why he felt so tense when it came to thinking of her with another man. He, after all, had never been and would never be a candidate when it came to marriage and rings on fingers. He was now a father, and that was shocking enough, but that was the only derailment to his carefully constructed life on the cards as far as he was concerned.

'Maybe…'

'Maybe? What does *that* mean?' The amusement sounded forced. 'Am I in competition with someone you've got hidden in a cupboard somewhere?'

'No,' Sarah admitted grudgingly. 'I've been too busy being a single mum to think of complicating my life with a guy.' She sensed rather than saw the shadow of satisfaction cross his face, and continued tartly, 'But, as you've pointed out, life is going to get much easier for me now. It's going to make a huge difference with you around, playing a role in Oliver's life. I won't be doing it on my own. Also, it'll be nice not having to think about money, or rather the lack of it, all the time—and it'll be fantastic having a bit of time to myself…time to do what I want to do.'

'Which *doesn't* mean that you've now got carte blanche to do whatever you like.' Raoul didn't care for the direction in which this conversation was now travelling.

'You make me sound like the sort of girl who can't wait to pick someone up!'

She was wondering what right he had to lay down any kind of laws when it came to her private life. Raoul Sinclair didn't want his life encumbered with attachments. True, he had discovered that some encumbrances were beyond his control, but just as he had never contemplated committing to her, so he had never contemplated committing to anyone. It was small comfort. *He* might think that it was perfectly acceptable to lead a life in which he and his son were the only considerations, but it was totally unfair to assume that *she* felt the same way. *He* might want to pick up women and discard them when they were no longer of any use, but *she* needed more than that. For Raoul, a single life was freedom. For her, a single life would be a prison cell.

'I'm not going to suddenly start scouring the nightclubs for eligible men,' she expanded, with a bright, nervous laugh, 'but I *will* be able to get out a bit more—which will be nice.'

'Get out a bit more?'

'Yes—when you have Oliver.'

'I don't think we should start projecting at this point,' Raoul said deflatingly. 'Oliver hasn't even spoken to me as yet. It's a bit premature to start planning a hectic social life in anticipation of us becoming best friends. Let's just take one day at a time, shall we?'

'Of course. I wasn't planning on going clubbing next week!'

Clubbing? What did she mean by that? Other men? Sleeping around? While he kept Oliver every other weekend?

He pictured her dressed in next to nothing, flaunting herself on a dance floor somewhere. Granted, the women he went out with often dressed in next to nothing, but for some reason the thought of *Sarah* in a mini-skirt, high heels and a halterneck top set his teeth on edge.

'Good. Because it won't be happening.'

'Excuse me?'

'Think about it, Sarah. Oliver doesn't even know that I'm his father. Don't you think that he'll be just a little bit confused if *your friend*, who has mysteriously and suddenly appeared on the scene from nowhere, starts engineering outings without you? You're the constant in his life. As you keep telling me. For me to have any chance of being accepted we have to provide a united front. We have to get to a point where he trusts me enough to leave you behind now and again.'

'Exactly what are you trying to say, Raoul?'

'That you have to scrap any crazy notions of us having nothing to do with one another. You're living in cloud cuckoo land if you think that's going to work. The whole bedtime story, spaghetti Bolognese thing is going to have to involve both of us. Of course it'll be a damn sight easier when you get out of this place and move somewhere more

convenient. And less cramped. On the subject of which—
I have my people working on that.'

There were so many contentious things packed into that
single cool statement that Sarah looked at him, staggered.

'When you say *involve both of us*...'

Raoul flushed darkly and dealt her a fulminating look
from under his lashes.

'I don't know the first thing about being a parent,' he
told her roughly. 'You've witnessed my sterling performance out there.'

'I didn't know the first thing about being a parent either,' Sarah pointed out with irrefutable logic. 'It's just a
case of doing your best.'

The thought of doing things with Raoul and Oliver, a
cosy threesome, was enough to bring on the beginnings
of a panic attack in her. Already she was finding it difficult to separate the past from the present. She looked at
him, and who was she kidding when she told herself that
she was no longer attracted to him? Raoul was in a different place, and would be able to take her on board as just a
temporary necessity in his life, easily set aside once he had
what he wanted: some sort of ongoing relationship with
his son. But she was aghast at the prospect of having him
there in *her* life. How on earth was she ever going to get
to that controlled, composed place of detachment if she
was continually tripping over him in the kitchen as he attempted to bond with his son over fish fingers?

Perhaps he had exaggerated, she thought, soothing her
own restless, panicked mind. He was still smarting from
Oliver's less than exuberant reception of him. Right at this
very moment this was the only plan he could see ahead of
him, and Raoul was big on plans. He would not be taking
into account the simple fact that when children were involved plans could never really be made. In a day or two

he would probably revise his ideas, because she very much doubted that he wanted to spend quality time with *her* in the picture.

'And the whole house issue...' she continued faintly. 'You have your *people* working on it?'

'Here's one of the things I've discovered about having money: throw enough of it at a problem and the problem goes away. Right now they're in the process of drawing up lists of suitable properties. I will be giving them until the end of next week. So,' he drawled when she failed to respond, 'are we on the same wavelength here, Sarah?'

'I can't just move into a house *you* happen to choose. I know you probably don't care about your surroundings, but *I* care about mine...'

'Don't you trust me to find somewhere you'd like?'

He'd used to be amused at her dreamy, whimsical ideas. From where he had stood there had been little use for dreams unless you had the wherewithal to turn them into reality, and even then he had never made the mistake of confusing dreams with the attainment of real, concrete goals. What was the point in wishing you could own a small island in the middle of the Pacific if the chances of ever having one were zero? But her dreams of cottages and clambering roses and open fires had made him smile.

'True, the thatched cottage with the roses and the apple trees might be a little troublesome to find in London...'

Sarah blushed, unsettled by the fact that he had remembered her corny youthful notion of the perfect house. Which she recalled describing in tedious detail.

'But I've got them working on the Aga in the kitchen, the garden overlooking water, and the fireplaces...'

'I can't believe you remember that conversation!'

She gave a brittle laugh, and went an even brighter

shade of red when he replied softly, 'Oh, there's a lot I re-member, Sarah. You'd be surprised.'

He didn't miss the flare of curiosity in her eyes. She might have made bold statements about not wanting any-thing to do with him, about shoving that kiss they had shared into a box at the back of a cupboard in her head, where she wouldn't have to confront it, but every time they were in each other's company he could feel that undercur-rent of electricity—a low, sizzling hum that vibrated just below the radar.

'Well, I don't actually remember all that much,' Sarah responded carelessly.

'Now, I wonder why I'm not believing you...'

'I have no idea, and I don't care. Now, if you wouldn't mind getting to work on those onions, I'll go and fetch Oliver.'

She disappeared before he could continue the conver-sation. When he looked at her like that she would swear that he could see right down into the very depths of her. It was an uncomfortable, frightening sensation that left her feeling vulnerable and exposed. Once she had gladly opened up to him—had told him everything there was to know about herself. She had taken him at face value and turned a blind eye to the fact that while she had been fall-ing deeper and deeper in love with him, he had pointedly refused to discuss anything that involved a future between them. He had taken everything she had so generously given and then politely jettisoned her when his time on the com-pound was up.

Raoul was a taker, with little interest in giving back. When he looked at her with those lazy, brooding eyes she could sense his interest. Some of his remarks carried just that little hint of flirtation, of deliberately treading very close to the edge. He had possessed her once, much to her shame. Did he think that he could possess her again?

She returned with Oliver to find him at the kitchen counter, dutifully chopping the onions as instructed.

Oliver had brought in a handful of his blocks, and Sarah sat him on a chair and then called Raoul over. She made sure to keep her voice light and friendly, even though every nerve in her body tingled as he strolled towards them, a teatowel draped over one shoulder.

'Blocks...my favourite.'

She had sat at the table, next to Oliver, and now Raoul leaned over her, his strong arms trapping her as he rested his hands on the table on either side of her. Sarah could feel his breath whisper against her neck when he spoke.

'Did you hear that, Oliver? Raoul loves building things! Wouldn't it be fun for you two to build something for me? What about a tower? You love building towers! Do you remember how high your last tower was? Before it fell?'

'Twelve blocks,' Oliver said seriously, not looking at Raoul. 'I can count to fifty.'

'That's quite an achievement!' Raoul leaned a little closer to Sarah, so that the clean, minty smell of her shampoo filled his nostrils.

She shifted, but had almost no room for manoeuvre. Her eyes drifted compulsively to his forearm, to the fine sprinkling of dark hairs that curled around the dull matt silver of his mega-expensive watch.

'Why don't you sit down, Raoul?' she suggested stiltedly. 'You can help Oliver with his tower.'

'I don't need any help, Mum.'

'No, he really doesn't. I sense that he's more than capable of building the Empire State Building all on his own.'

Oliver glanced very quickly at Raoul, and then returned to the task in hand.

Sarah heard Raoul's almost imperceptible indrawn breath as he abruptly stood back, and when she turned to look at him he had removed himself to the kitchen sink, his expression one of frustrated defeat.

'Give it time,' she said in a low voice, moving to stand in front of him.

'How much time? I'm not a patient man.'

'Well, I guess you'll have to learn how to be. Good job with the onions, by the way.'

But she could feel his simmering impatience with the situation for the rest of the evening. Oliver was not so much hostile as wary. He answered Raoul's questions without meeting his eye and, dinner over, finally agreed to go outside with him to test drive the car which had been abandoned in the sitting room.

Through the kitchen window, Sarah watched their awkward interaction with a sinking heart.

She had planned on sitting Oliver down and explaining that Raoul was his father once a bond of trust between them had been accepted. To overload him with too much information would be bewildering for him. But how long was that going to take? she wondered. Raoul was obviously trying very hard.

She watched as Oliver sent the oversized car bouncing crazily into the unkempt bushes at the back of the tiny garden, losing interest fast and walking away as Raoul stooped down to deliver a mini-lecture on mechanics.

The consequences of him missing out, through no fault of his own, on those precious first four years hit her forcibly. Another man, with experience of growing up in a real family, might have had something to fall back on in a situation like this. Raoul had no such experience, and was struggling to find a way through his own shortcomings.

She abandoned her plans to have him read something to

Oliver before bed, which was their usual routine. Instead, she told him to wait for her in the kitchen while she settled Oliver.

'You can help yourself to…um…whatever you can find in the fridge. I know dinner was probably not what you're used to…'

'Because I'm such a snob?'

Sarah sighed heavily, 'I'm just conscious that we're… we're miles apart. When we were working out in Africa there wasn't this great big chasm separating us…'

'You need to move on from the past.'

'*You* haven't moved on from yours!'

'I'm not following you?'

'You thought you could buy Oliver with lots of presents because that's what your past has conditioned you to think! And then you got impatient when you discovered that it doesn't work that way.'

'And *you* can't move on from the fact that—okay… yes—I dumped you!' Raoul thundered. 'You want to find something to argue about—*anything at all*—because you've wrapped yourself up in a little world comprised of just you and Oliver and you can't deal with the fact that I'm around now! Dinner was disappointing because it was stressful! I didn't know how to deal with him.'

Hell, Oliver had played with his food, spread most of it on the table, and had received only the most indulgent scolding from Sarah! His childhood memories of mealtimes were of largely silent affairs, with rowdy behaviour at the table meriting instant punishment.

'I *don't* know how to deal with him.'

Dumbfounded by that raw admission, Sarah was overcome with regret for her outburst. He was so clever, so *all-knowing*, that she hadn't really stopped to consider that now he really was at a loss.

'I'm…I'm sorry, Raoul. I shouldn't have said that stuff about your past…' she mumbled.

'Look, we've found ourselves in this situation, and constantly sniping isn't going to get either of us very far.'

Mind made up, Sarah nodded in agreement. 'I'll take him up for a bath… Yes, you're right…it's difficult for both of us…' She managed a smile. 'I guess we both need to do some adjusting…'

She returned forty-five minutes later and looked as fresh as a daisy. He felt as though he had done ten rounds in a boxing ring.

'I think he's really beginning to warm to you!' she said cheerfully.

Raoul raised his eyebrows in an expression of rampant scepticism. 'Explain how you've managed to arrive at that conclusion?' He raked his fingers through his hair and shook his head with a short, dry laugh. 'There's no need to put on the Little Miss Sunshine act for me, Sarah. I may not know much when it comes to kids, but I'd have to have the IQ of a goldfish not to see that my own son has no time for me. You were right. All those toys were a complete waste of time and money.'

'You're just not accustomed to children. You don't know how they think. Sometimes it's hard to imagine you being a kid at all! Oliver enjoys pushing the boundaries. Most children do, Raoul. He'll fiddle with his food until I have to be firm, and he'll always go for *just another five minutes* or *one more story* or *two scoops of ice cream, please.*'

'Whatever happened to discipline?' Raoul scowled at her laid-back attitude.

'Oh, there's a lot of that. It's just knowing when to decide that it's really needed.'

She looked at Raoul thoughtfully. The man who could move mountains had discovered his Achilles' heel, and she was sure that he would never ask for her help. He was stubbornly, maddeningly proud. To ask for help would be to admit a weakness, and she knew that was something he would find it very hard to do.

But helping him was the only solution—and, more than that, helping him would give her a psychological boost, even out the playing field.

'Okay, well, he's now thrilled with the car. Tonight I'll pack away all the rest of the stuff you brought for him. I can bring bits out now and again as treats.' She folded her arms and braced herself to take control with a guy who was so used to having the reins that he probably had no idea relinquishing them was a possibility.

Raoul sat back and clasped his hands behind his head. He had thought for one crazy moment, when he had laid eyes on her again, that time hadn't changed her. He had been wrong. This was no longer the blindly adoring girl who had yielded to him with such abundant generosity. There was a steely glint in her eye now, and he realised that he had seen it before but maybe hadn't really recognised it for what it was. The molten charge between them was still there, whether she wanted to admit it or not, but along with that was something else…

Raoul felt a certain fascination, and a surge of raw, powerful curiosity.

'Am I about to get a ticking off?' he drawled, his eyes roving lazily over her from head to toe in a way that made it difficult for her not to feel frazzled.

'No,' she said sweetly. 'But I am going to tell you what you need to do, and you're going to listen to me.' She smiled a bit more when she saw his frown of incomprehension. 'You like to think you know everything, but you don't.'

'Oh? You're going to be my teacher, are you?'

'Whether you like it or not!'

Raoul shot her a slow, dazzling smile. 'Well, now,' he said softly, instantly turning the tables on her, 'it's been a while since anyone taught me anything. You might find that I like it a lot more than you expect…'

CHAPTER FOUR

SARAH looked at her reflection in the mirror and frowned. Her cheeks were flushed, and her eyes were glowing. She looked *excited*. Guilt shot through her, because this was just what she didn't want. She didn't *want* to find herself giddy with anticipation because Raoul was on his way over.

For the past four weeks she had kept her manner brisk and impersonal. She had pretended not to notice those occasional sidelong glances of his, when his fabulous dark eyes would rest speculatively on her face. She had taken extra care to downplay what she wore. Anyone would have been forgiven for thinking that the only components of her wardrobe were faded jeans, tee shirts, shapeless jumpers and trainers. Now that the weather was getting warmer, and spring was edging tentatively into summer, the jumpers had been set aside, but the jeans, the tee shirts and the trainers were still fully in evidence.

Sarah was determined to make sure that her relationship with Raoul remained detached and uninvolved. She knew that she couldn't afford to forget what had happened in the past.

She had thrown herself into the task of helping him get to know his son, and she had to admit that it was no longer the uphill struggle it had initially been. Oliver was gradually opening up and losing some of his restraint, and Raoul, in turn, was slowly learning how to relate to a child. Like a teacher struggling with troublesome pupils and finally seeing the light at the end of the tunnel, she could now cautiously tell herself that her role of mediator had been successful.

And *that* accounted for the glow in her eyes and her flushed cheeks.

Oliver was actually looking forward to seeing Raoul. In fact, he was dressed and ready to go.

She clattered down the stairs as the doorbell buzzed and smiled at the sight of Oliver in the sitting room, kneeling on the chair by the bay window, eyes peeled for Raoul's arrival. He had been treated to several rides in Raoul's sports car, and had gravely told her that he would buy *her* one just as soon as he had saved enough money. He had two pounds, and considered himself well on the way.

'Am I dressed correctly for a day out at a theme park, Miss?' Raoul laughed at her exasperated expression.

'You know I hate it when you call me that.'

'Of course you don't! It makes you feel special. And besides…I enjoy watching the way you blush when I say it.'

On cue, Sarah felt her cheeks pinken.

'You shouldn't say stuff like that.'

'Why not?'

'Because…because…it's not appropriate…'

And because it threatened her. She had been walking on thin ice for the past four weeks as he dug deeper and deeper under her defences with his easy charm, his wit, his willingness to tackle head-on a situation that must have rocked his world. She desperately wanted her one-dimensional memory of him back, because it was so much easier to deal with him as the man who had ruined her life.

'Now you really *are* beginning to sound like a school-teacher,' Raoul said softly. 'Should I expect to be punished any time soon?'

'Stop it!'

He held up his hands in a gesture of surrender and laughed, throwing his head back, keeping his velvety black eyes on her face.

Sarah glared at him. This couldn't continue. Raoul didn't know what he was doing to her, but she was mentally and emotionally exhausted. She would talk to Raoul today. Begin the process of sorting out visiting arrangements. She couldn't foresee any problem with Raoul now taking Oliver out for the day without her having to be there as chaperone.

In other words it was time to acknowledge that her brief stint at usefulness was over and Raoul had been right. It had been essential for them to present a united front to Oliver so that his confidence in Raoul could be built. Would it come as a shock for him to accept Raoul as his father? Certainly it would be a lot easier now than it would have been a month ago, when Raoul had been an intimidating stranger bearing expensive gifts who had landed in their midst from nowhere.

The gifts had all been stowed away and Raoul had not repeated his mistake—although he warned her he would definitely be christening the new house he had bought for them with something spectacular in the back garden.

When Sarah considered the speed with which her life had changed in a matter of a month, her head spun.

Raoul back on the scene. Oliver slowly beginning to bond with his father. A house which she and Oliver had seen only two weeks previously immediately purchased by Raoul on the spot, with enough money thrown at the deal to ensure that it closed with record speed.

'You like it. Why hang around?'

He had shrugged with such casual dismissal of the cost that Sarah had stared at him, open-mouthed. That had been the point when she had thought that the attainment of wealth was the most important thing to Raoul, and instinctively she had shied away from what that implied about his character. Very quickly, however, she had realised that the only thing wealth represented to him was freedom. Money gave him the ability to do as he liked without reference to anyone else. It was the opposite of the way he had grown up.

In fact, and only by accident, she had recently discovered that he gave large sums of his vast fortune to charity—including the very same charity which had originally brought them together all those years ago. She had been in his penthouse with Oliver, waiting for him while he finished a conference call in his office. Oliver had been wandering around, gaping at the high-tech television and then experimenting with the chrome and black leather stools at the granite-topped kitchen counter, swivelling round and round with childish enjoyment, and there on the table by the massive window that overlooked a private park had been a letter of gratitude, thanking Raoul for his contributions over the years.

Sarah had not mentioned a word of what she had inadvertently seen, but she had filed it away in her head, where it jostled for space with all the other bits and pieces she was unconsciously gathering about him. In every way he was the most complex man she would ever meet. He was driven, ambitious, and ferociously single-minded. But the way in which he had applied himself to the task of getting to know his son showed compassion, patience, and an ability to roll with the punches.

There was no question that he used women, and yet

there was nothing manipulative about him. He had big *Keep Out* signs all around him, and yet she couldn't help feeling that she had seen something of the boy who had become the man—even though when he talked about his past it was only through necessity, and in a voice that was utterly devoid of emotion.

Five years on and Raoul Sinclair still fascinated her. Although that was something that Sarah barely recognised. She just knew that she was becoming dangerously addicted to his visits, which were frequent, even though she kept telling him that she didn't want to disrupt his work schedule.

She felt as though she was seeing him through the eyes of an adult as opposed to the romantic young girl she had once been, and she wondered what life would be like when their relationship became normalised. When he popped over on a Wednesday evening and took Oliver out, leaving her behind, or when he had Oliver for a weekend and she had her much espoused free time to do as she liked.

She immediately told herself that it would be brilliant. She would be able to build some kind of life for herself! She no longer had the excuse of lack of money, lack of time and lack of opportunity.

Raoul had insisted on opening a bank account for her, and when she had tried to assert her independence he had turned her determination on its head by quietly telling her that it was the very least he could do, bearing in mind that she had been a single mother for all those years when he had been rapidly building his fortune. Had he been more aggressive she would have taken refuge in an argument. But, brilliant judge of character that he was, he had known the most efficient way to get exactly what he wanted.

Sarah sighed and tried not to think. Aside from the disturbing melee of her own feelings, there was the very simple reality that they would be moving soon, and Oliver would need to be told who Raoul really was.

Today they were going to a theme park. Oliver had never been to a theme park. Nor had Raoul. She had only learned this after a great deal of questioning, during which she had been determined to prise from him what he had longed for as a kid but never had. She had asked him in the crisp voice she made sure to use in order to reinforce that their relationship was entirely impersonal, and he had adopted the slightly sardonic, lazy drawl which he always used when referring to his past. But then he had said, in a voice that contained a certain amount of surprise—maybe because the memory had come from nowhere—that he had missed the big annual treat of the year when he had been nine years old and his age group were taken to a theme park. It had been a celebration of sorts, to mark the fiftieth anniversary of the place, but he had been laid up with flu and had spent the entire weekend cooped up in the sick quarters.

There and then Sarah had decided that a visit to the theme park was essential.

Lagging behind as Raoul and Oliver walked towards the car, Sarah mentally took in the picture they made. Raoul literally towered over his son, who had to walk at a smart pace to keep up with him. From behind, she noted the similarity of their hair colour and the trace of olive in Oliver's skin tone that would burnish and darken over time—just as Raoul's had. Oliver was proudly carrying his backpack, which was a new purchase, and wearing his jeans, also a new purchase.

Her eyes drifted across to Raoul and she felt suddenly dizzy, because he just continued to take her breath away. Without fear of being observed *watching him*, she feasted on the length of his muscular legs, the low-slung faded black jeans, the white shirt, sleeves slightly pushed up even though it was still quite cool. However good she was at being adult and detached when she was in his company, she still knew that her indifference was a long way from being secure.

Raoul popped the boot of his car and Sarah glanced in and said, surprised, 'What's all that?'

Raoul gazed down at her upturned face and shot her a crooked half-smile.

'What does it look like?'

'You've made a *picnic*?'

'*I* haven't made a picnic. My caterer has. I've been assured that there's an ample selection.'

The past few weeks had been a massive learning curve for Raoul. Having never seen himself in the role of father, he had found himself having to adapt in all sorts of ways that were alien to him. Defined through his staggering ability to work, he had had to sideline hours in front of his computer or at the office in favour of the soul-destroying task of trying to edge responses out of his son. Accustomed to having every word he spoke treated with respect, and every order he gave obeyed to the letter, he had had to dig deep and find levels of patience that were foreign to him— because small children frequently disobeyed orders and often lacked focus. Ferociously against ever asking anyone for help, he had found himself in the uncustomary position of having to take guidance from Sarah, so that his path to a relationship with Oliver was eased. He had had to learn how to jettison his very natural inclination to command. But it had all paid enormous dividends because Oliver was gradually warming to him.

And alongside that he'd been witness to a new side of Sarah, so wildly different from the impressionable young girl she had been years ago. There was a core of strength in her now that intrigued him.

'I'm impressed, Raoul,' Sarah murmured, staring down at the wicker basket and the requisite plaid rug, and the cooler which was full of ice-cold drinks.

She imagined that when he decided on a certain course of action he gave one hundred percent of his energy to it. His course of action, in this instance, was winning over the son he'd never known he had, and he had approached the task in hand with gusto. This elaborate picnic was evidence of that. All kids loved a picnic. *She* loved a picnic.

He slammed shut the boot on Sarah's dismayed realisation that in the process of charming Oliver Raoul inadvertently been doing exactly the same with her.

'Of course I would have been more impressed if you'd prepared it all yourself...' Her voice sounded forced.

'Never satisfied...' But he was grinning in a way that made her skin warm. 'You're a tough taskmaster.'

'You don't need a caterer to prepare food for you. I know that you're perfectly capable of doing it yourself.'

'I'll bear that in mind for next time,' Raoul murmured.

'Next time? There won't be a next time,' she told him in a fast rush. 'Don't forget that all of this is...you know... part and parcel of your learning curve.'

'Theme park—tick. Picnic—tick. Homecooked food eaten at the kitchen table—tick. Fast food restaurant— tick. When did you get so regimented?'

'I'm not regimented. I'm practical. And isn't it time we left? Oliver's already in the car. Have I told you how excited he was about today? He could hardly get to sleep last night!'

'I found sleeping pretty difficult myself.'

Sarah's eyes widened, and she sucked in a shaky breath

as he braced himself against the car, circling her so that she had to half sit on the bonnet.

'What are you doing?' she squeaked.

'I'm tired of trying to kid myself that I don't want you, Sarah.'

'You *don't* want me. I don't want *you*. I know we've been getting along, but it's all because of Oliver—because… because… Don't look at me like that!' But her body was betraying her protest. 'This isn't part of the plan. You *like* plans. Have you forgotten?'

'Which just goes to show what a changed man I'm becoming.'

'You haven't changed, Raoul.' She flattened her hand against his chest to push him back, but just touching him weakened her defences. 'I told you—we've been there. We're not good for one another. We just need to be…to be friends…'

'Okay.' He straightened, and his voice was mild, but there was a glitter in his eyes that made her pulses race. 'If you're sure about that…'

He let his hand slide over her shoulder in a caressing, assured move that made her stomach flip and her breath catch in her throat. Then he backed off, and she was gulping in oxygen like a drowning person breaking the surface of the water.

Her heart was beating madly as she slipped into the passenger seat and turned to make sure that Oliver was strapped into his car seat. Over the years, her memories of Raoul had taken on a static form. Faced once again with the living, breathing, charismatic, dynamic and unbearably sexy Raoul, who could make her laugh and make her want to grind her teeth together in frustration in the next breath, had undermined all her defences.

Had he intuited this? Was that why he had made that

move? With the confidence of a predator knowing that it
was just a matter of time?

The theme park was already packed by the time they
got there. Oliver's excitement had been a slow burn, but
his first sight of some of the rides, the chaos of the crowds,
and the roar of the machines flying through the air with
people dangling from them like rag dolls took his breath
away.

'Does this live up to expectations?' Sarah asked Raoul
halfway through, as he and Oliver descended from one of
the child and parent rides. She was determined to keep her
head and be as normal as possible. She *wouldn't* get in a
flap.

It had warmed up, and his polo shirt exposed strong,
muscled arms. She watched them flex and harden as he
stooped to lift Oliver in one easy movement.

'Are you asking whether I've managed to discover my
inner child yet? Nope,' he told her before she could say
anything. 'I'm not one of those losers who gets wrapped
up in that sort of thing.'

But, hell, he'd been doing quite a lot that was out of
character for him. A picnic? Since when had he ever been
the sort of guy who was interested in picnics? It was even
more disquieting to realise that he had done it *for her*.

'Well, you should be.' Sarah saw a golden opportunity
to strike out for independence and remind him that she
had a life outside his many visits—that he couldn't just re-
enter her life and take what he happened to want because
it suited him.

Or maybe, she decided uneasily, it was to remind *herself*
that she shouldn't be up for grabs, that she had a life outside his many visits. Although where exactly that life was
she wasn't quite sure. The teaching assistant job which she
had been due to start was now off the cards as they would

be moving from the area, and she was caught in a limbo of not really knowing when she should start looking for something else. Should she wait until they had settled in their new house before she began registering with agencies?

With nothing on the agenda, it had been easy to slip into a comfortable pattern of just Oliver and Raoul. Really, it wasn't healthy.

'I mean,' she continued, as they began walking towards the next bank of rides. 'I don't think it's so much about getting in touch with your *inner child*. I think it's more about just being able to relax and have fun. I know you've been around us a lot, but that's not going to last for ever, and when you resume your hectic work schedule... Well, I can't imagine that you won't be stressed out. Having fun and taking time out can't be shoved into a few weeks before normal life resumes...'

'Why are you trying to engage me in an argument?'

'I'm just saying that there's nothing loser-like about someone who knows how to have a good time. In fact, I think it's a great quality in a guy. I'd go so far as to say that the kind of guy I would be interested in dating would be someone who really knew how to let his hair down and enjoy himself...'

When she tried to imagine this fictitious person, the image of Raoul annoyingly superimposed itself in her mind.

Raoul frowned and cast her a quelling look from under his lashes. He'd thought the subject of this so-called single life she envisaged leading had taken a back seat. He'd concluded that the matter had been shelved because she had seen the obvious—which was that there would be no single life for her while they were trying to sort out things with Oliver. It was disconcerting to think that she might

have been biding her time, filling her head with thoughts
of climbing back on the dating bandwagon when she was
still attracted to *him*. He had *felt* it.

'Oliver's looking tired. I think we should have something to eat now,' he said coolly, turning abruptly in the
direction of where the car had been parked.

'In fact,' Sarah continued, because this seemed as good
a time as any to start talking about where they went from
here, 'I think we need to have a little chat later.'

They had eased themselves out of the crowds now, and
Raoul gently deposited Oliver on the ground. He had managed to win a stuffed toy at one of the stalls, and its furry
head poked out from the top of his backpack. Insistent on
having 'just one more ride', his attention was easily di-
verted at the promise of the chocolate cake which Raoul
told him was waiting in the wicker basket.

'There's a lot to discuss now that the house has been
bought. We have to talk about arrangements. I want to get
my life in order and really start living it.'

'"Really start living it"?' Raoul's voice had become several shades cooler, and he kept it low because even though
Oliver had yanked the stuffed panda out of his backpack
and was currently engaged in conversation with it, he was
fully aware that careless words could be picked up.

'Well, you have to admit that we've both been in a
kind of hiatus over the past few weeks, and I suppose that
might have led you to assume…well, the past few weeks
have been peculiar…' Sarah took a deep breath. 'I bet you
haven't had this much time off work since you started!'
She gave a bright laugh at his juncture, although Raoul
didn't seem amused. 'It's time for us *both* to come back
down to reality…'

They were at the car, and Raoul began hauling stuff out
of the boot. Having parked away from the main car park,

they found themselves in a private enclosed spot, with shady overhanging trees that seemed designed to indulge prospective picnickers.

His mood had nosedived, although he was at pains not to let Oliver have any inkling of that. He unpacked a quantity of food sufficient to feed a small army, and stuck the chilled wine in the ice bucket which had thoughtfully been provided.

Oblivious of the atmosphere, Oliver attacked the picnic with enthusiasm, and awkward silences were papered over with his chatter as he relived every experience of every ride and tried his best to elicit promises of a return visit.

So she wanted to get back to the land of the living? Why shouldn't she? She was still young, and already she was changing as the worry eased off her shoulders. When he had bumped into her again she had been cleaning floors, and the stress of her situation had shown plainly on her face. Now the contours were returning to her body, and her features had lost the gaunt look that had originally caught him off guard. Why *wouldn't* she want to have some kind of fun? Go to clubs? Lead the life most young people her age were leading and which she had had to sidestep because of the responsibility of having to look after a child?

In every single detail it was a situation that should have suited him perfectly. He had left her once with the best of all possible intentions, and he had never deviated from his resolution to steer clear of the murky waters of matrimony. He was not one of those people who had ever thought that despite coming from no family background to speak of, despite a childhood rife with disillusionment and disappointment, he could somehow turn the tide and become a fully paid up member of the happy-ever-after crew. He had always sworn that the one thing he had taken from his experiences would be his freedom, and although he now had one other person to consider, he certainly wasn't going to go the whole hog and do anything that he would regret. If you only lived life for yourself, no one else had the power to disappoint. It was a credo in which he fully believed.

Okay, so he was still attracted to her. Yes, he hadn't had so many cold showers late at night in his life before. And, sure, she was attracted to him—whether she wanted to believe it of herself or not. But that surely wasn't enough to justify the rising tide of outrage at the thought of her *getting out there*.

Above all else he was practical, and taking this sizzling sexual attraction one step further would just add further complications to an already complicated situation. In fact he should be *urging* her to get out there and live a little. He should be heartily *agreeing* that the very thing they need to do now was plot a clear line forward and get on with it.

Within the next few days he anticipated that Oliver would be told by them, jointly, that he was his father. At that point the domestic bubble which they had built around themselves for a very essential purpose would no longer be required. She was one hundred percent right on that score. Gradually Oliver would come to accept the mundane business of joint custody. It wasn't ideal, but what in life ever really was?

Except he was finding it hard to accept any of those things.

There was a distinct chill in the air as the picnic was cleared away, and on the drive back Oliver, exhausted, fell into a soft sleep. To curtail any opportunity for Sarah to embark on another lengthy exposé of what she intended to do with her free time, Raoul switched on the radio, and the drive was completed in utter silence save for the background noise of middle-of-the-road music.

Twenty minutes from home, Sarah began chatting nervously. Anything to break the silence that was stretching like a piece of tautly pulled elastic between them.

The day which had commenced so wonderfully had ended on a sour note, and the blame for that rested firmly on her shoulders. But the realisation that she had been sliding inexorably back to a very dangerous place—one which she had stupidly occupied five years ago—had made her see the urgency of making sure that her barriers were up and functioning. She would never have believed it possible that time with Raoul could lower her defences to such an extent, but then he had always had a way of stealing into her heart and soul and just somehow *taking over*.

There were some things that she wanted to do to the house as soon as contracts had been exchanged. She wanted to do something lovely and fairly colourful to the walls. So she heard herself chattering inanely about paints and wallpaper while Oliver continued to doze in the back and Raoul continued to stare fixedly at the road ahead, only answering when it would have been ridiculously rude not to.

'Okay,' Sarah said finally, bored by the sound of her own voice droning on about a subject in which he clearly had next to no interest. 'I'm sorry if you think I wrecked the day out.'

'Have I said anything of the sort?'

'You don't have to. It's enough for you to sit there in silence and leave me to do all the talking.'

'You were talking about paint colours and wallpapers. I can't even pretend to manufacture an interest in that. I've already told you that I'll get someone in to do it all. Paint. Wallpaper. Furniture. Hell, I'll even commission someone to buy the art to hang on the walls!'

'Then it wouldn't be a home, would it? I mean, Raoul, have you ever really looked around your apartment?'

'What's that supposed to mean?'

'You have the best of everything that money can buy and it *still* doesn't feel like a home. It's like something you'd see in a magazine! The kitchen looks as though it's never been used, and the sofas look as though they've never been sat on. The rugs look as though nothing's ever been spilled on them. And all that abstract art! I bet you didn't choose a single painting yourself!'

Anger returned her to territory with which she was familiar. The hard, chiselled profile he offered her was expressionless, which made her even angrier. How could she not get to him when he got to her so easily? It wasn't fair!

'I don't *like* abstract art,' she told him nastily. 'In fact I hate it. I like boring, old-fashioned paintings. I like seeing stuff that I can recognise. I like flowers and scenery. I don't enjoying looking at angry lines splashed on a canvas. I can't think of anything worse than some stranger buying art for me because it's going to appreciate. And, furthermore, I don't like leather sofas either. They're cold in winter and hot and sticky in summer. I like warm colours, and soft, squashy chairs you can sink into with a book.'

'I'm getting the picture.' Raoul's mouth was compressed. 'You don't want help when it comes to interior design and you hate my apartment.'

Not given to being unkind, Sarah felt a wave of shame and embarrassment wash over her. She would never normally have dreamt of criticising anyone on their choice of décor for their home. Everyone's taste was different, after all. But the strain of having Raoul around, of enjoying his company and getting a tantalising glimpse of what life could have been had he only wanted and loved her, was finally coming home to roost. For all his moods and failings, and despite his arrogance, his perverse stubbornness and his infuriating ability to be blinkered when it suited him, he was still one hell of a guy—and this time round she was seeing so many more sides to him, having so many more opportunities to tumble straight back into love.

'*And* we still have to talk,' she said eventually, but contented herself with staring through the window.

If she had hoped to spark a response from him then she had been sorely mistaken, she thought sourly. Because he just didn't care one way or another what opinions she had about him, his apartment, or any other area of his life.

'Yes. We do.'

In an unprecedented move Raoul had done a complete U-turn. Thinking about her with some other man—pointlessly projecting, in other words—had been a real turn-off, and even more annoying had been the fact that he just hadn't been able to get his thoughts in order. Cool logic had for once been at odds with an irritating, restless unease which he had found difficult to deal with.

But her little bout of anger and her petulant criticisms had clarified things in his head, strangely enough.

Sarah wasn't like all the other women he knew, and it went beyond the fact that she had had his child.

It had always been easy for him to slot the *other* women who had come and gone like ships passing in the night into neat, tidy boxes. They'd filled a very clearly defined role and there were no blurry areas to deal with.

Yes, Sarah had re-entered his life, with a hand grenade in the form of a child, but only now was he accepting that her role in his life was riddled with blurry areas. He didn't know why. Perhaps it was because she represented a stage in his life before he had made it big and could do whatever he liked. Or maybe it was just because she was so damned open, honest and vibrant that she demanded him to engage far more than he was naturally inclined to. She didn't tiptoe around him, and she didn't make any attempts to edit her personality to please him. The women he had dated in the past had all swooned at their first sight of his apartment, with its rampant displays of wealth. He got the impression that the woman sulking in the seat next to him could have written a book on everything she hated about where he lived, and not only that would gladly have given it to him as a present.

The whole situation between them, in fact, demanded a level of engagement that went way beyond the sort of interaction he was accustomed to having with other women. Picnics? Home cooked meals? Board games? *Way* beyond.

He pulled up outside her house, where for once there was a parking space available. Oliver was rousing slowly from sleep, rubbing his eyes and curling into Sarah's arms. Taking the key from her, Raoul unlocked the front door and hesitatingly kissed his son's dark, curly mop of hair. In return he received a sleepy smile.

'He's exhausted,' Sarah muttered. 'All that excitement and then the picnic…he's not accustomed to eating so late. I'll just give him a quick bath and then I think he'll be ready for bed.'

She drew in a deep, steadying breath and firmly trod on the temptation to regret the fact that she had lashed out at him, ruined the atmosphere between them, injected a note of jarring disharmony that made her miserable.

'Why don't you pour yourself something to drink?' she continued, with more command in her voice that she felt. 'And when I come down, like I said, we'll discuss…arrangements.'

She was dishevelled. They had both shared the rides with Oliver, but she had done a few of the really big ones on her own. Someone had had to stay with Oliver, and Raoul had generously offered to babysit, seeing it as a handy excuse to get out of what, frankly, had looked like a terrifying experience. He might have felt sorely deprived as a boy at missing out on all those big rides, but as an adult he could think of nothing worse.

Her hair was tousled and her cheeks were pink, and he noticed the top two buttons of her checked shirt had come undone—although she hadn't yet noticed that.

'Good idea,' he murmured blandly, with a shuttered expression that left her feverishly trying to analyse what he was thinking.

Raoul noted the hectic colour that had seeped into her cheeks, and the way her arms tightened nervously around a very drowsy Oliver. Arrangements certainly needed to be made, he thought. Though possibly not quite along the lines she anticipated.

She wanted to deal with the formalities, and there was no doubt that certain things had to be discussed, but he was running with a different agenda.

At long last he had lost that unsettling, disconcerting feeling that had climbed into the pit of his stomach and refused to budge. He liked having an explanation for everything and he had his explanation now. Sarah was still in his head because she was unfinished business. There were loose ends to their relationship, and he looked forward to tying all those loose ends up and moving on.

He smiled at her slowly, in a way that sent a tingle of maddening sensation running from the tips of her toes to the crown of her head.

'I'll pour you a drink too,' he said, his dark eyes arrowing onto her wary face, taking in the fine bone structure, the wide eyes, the full, eminently kissable mouth. 'And then we can…as you say…begin to talk about moving forward…'

CHAPTER FIVE

Sᴀʀᴀʜ took longer than she had planned. Oliver, for a start, had discovered a new lease of life and demanded his set of toy cars. And Raoul. In that order.

Determined to have a bit of space from wretched Raoul, in which she could clear her head and plan what she was going to say, Sarah had immediately squashed that request and then been forced to compensate for Raoul's absence by feigning absorption in a game of cars which had involved pushing them around the bed in circles, pretending to stop off at key points to refuel.

Forty minutes later she had finally managed to settle him, after which she'd taken herself off for a bath.

She didn't hurry. She felt that she needed all the time she could get to arrange her thoughts.

First things first. She would chat, in a civilised and adult fashion, about the impending necessity to talk to Oliver. She foresaw no problem there.

Secondly she would announce her decision to finally break the news to her parents that Raoul was back on the scene. She would reassure him that there would be no need to meet them.

Thirdly, they were no longer in a relationship—although they were *friends* for Oliver's sake. Just two people with a common link, who had managed to sort out visiting rights

without the interference of lawyers because they were both
so mature.

She would be at pains to emphasise how *useful* it had
been doing stuff together, for the sake of his relationship
with his son.

Downstairs, Raoul had removed himself to the sitting
room, and Sarah saw, on entering, that he had poured himself a glass of wine. Ever since he had been on the scene
her fridge had been stocked with fine-quality wines, and
her cheap wine glasses had been replaced with proper
ones—expensive, very modern glasses that she would
never have dreamt of buying herself for fear of breakages.

He patted the space next to him, which wasn't ideal as
far as Sarah was concerned but, given that her only other
option was to scuttle to the furthest chair, which would
completely ruin the mature approach she was intent on
taking, she sat next to him and reached for her drink.

'I think we can say that was a day well spent,' Raoul
began, angling his body so that he was directly facing her
and crossing his legs, his hand on his thigh loosely holding
his glass. 'Despite your rant about the state of my apartment.'

'Sorry about that.' She concentrated hard on sipping
her wine.

He shrugged and continued to look at her, his brilliant
dark eyes giving very little away. 'Why should you be?'

'I suppose it was a bit rude,' Sarah conceded reluctantly.
'I don't suppose there are very many people who are critical of you…'

'I had no idea you were being critical of *me*. I assumed
you were being critical of the décor in my apartment.'

'That's what I meant to say.'

'Because you have to agree that I've taken every piece

of advice you've given and done everything within my power to build connections with Oliver.'

'You've been brilliant,' Sarah admitted. 'Have you... have you enjoyed it? I mean, this whole thing must have turned your world on its head...'

She hadn't actually meant to say that, but it was something they hadn't previously discussed—not in any depth at all. He had accepted the situation and worked with it, but she couldn't help but remember how adamant he had been all those years ago that the last thing he wanted was marriage and children.

'You had your whole life mapped out,' she continued, staring off into the distance. 'You were only a few years older than the rest of us, but you always seemed to know just what you wanted to do and where you wanted to be.'

'Am I sensing some criticism behind that statement?' Raoul harked back to her annoying little summary of the sort of thing she looked for in a man. 'Fun-loving' somehow didn't quite go hand-in-hand with the picture she was painting of him.

'Not really...'

He decided not to pursue this line of conversation, which would get neither of them anywhere fast. 'Good.' He closed the topic with a slashing smile. 'And, to get back to your original question, having Oliver has been an eye-opener. I've never had to tailor my life to accommodate anyone...'

And had he enjoyed it? He hadn't asked himself that question, but thinking about it now—yes, he had. He had enjoyed the curious unpredictability, the small rewards as he began making headway, the first accepting smile that had made his efforts all seem worthwhile...

'If it had been any other kid,' he conceded roughly, 'it would have been a mindless chore, but with Oliver...' He shrugged and let his silence fill in the missing words. 'And, yes, my life had been disrupted. Disrupted in a major way. But there are times when things don't go quite according to plan.'

'Really? I thought that only happened to other people.' Sarah smiled tightly as she remembered all the plans he had made five years ago—none of which had included her. 'What other times have there been in your life when things didn't go according to your plan? In your adult life, I mean? Things don't go according to plan when you let other people into your life, and you've *never* let anyone into your life.'

Okay, so now she was veering madly away from her timetable, but the simmering, helpless resentment she felt after weeks of feeling herself being sucked in by him all over again was conspiring to build to a head. It was as if her mouth had a will of its own and was determined to say stuff her head was telling it not to.

'I mean, just look at your apartment!'

'So we're back to the fact that you don't like chrome, leather and marble…'

'It's more than that!' Sarah cried, frustrated at his polite refusal to indulge her in her histrionics. 'There's nothing personal anywhere in your apartment…'

'You haven't seen all of my apartment,' Raoul pointed out silkily. 'Unless you've been exploring my bedroom when I haven't been looking…'

'No, of course I haven't!' But at that thought she flushed, and shakily took another mouthful of wine.

'Then you shouldn't generalise. I expected better of you.'

'Very funny, Raoul. I'm being serious.'

'And so am I. I've enjoyed spending time with Oliver.

He's my son. Everything he does,' Raoul added, surprising himself with the admission, 'is a source of fascination.'

'You're very good at saying all the right things,' Sarah muttered, half to herself.

Where had her temper tantrum gone? He was refusing to co-operate and now she was reduced to glowering. It took her a few seconds before she brought her mind to bear on the things that needed discussion.

'But I'm really glad that everything is going so well with Oliver, because it brings me to one of the things I want to say.' She cleared her throat and wished that he would stop staring at her like that, with his fabulous eyes half closed and vaguely assessing. 'Oliver has come to like you very much, and to trust you. When he first met you I really thought that it would be a huge uphill struggle for you two to connect. He had no real experience of an adult male in his life, and you had no experience of what to do around young children.'

'Yes, yes, yes. You're not telling me anything I don't already know…'

Sarah's lips tightened and she frowned. She had laid out this conversation in her head and she had already deviated once.

'It's terrific that you haven't seen it all as a chore.'

'If you're hoping to get on my good side, then I should warn you that you're going about it the wrong way. Derogatory remarks about where I live, insinuations that I'm too rigid for parenting…anything else you'd like to throw in the mix before you carry on?'

She thought she detected an undercurrent of amusement in his voice, which made her bristle. 'I think we should both sit down with Oliver and explain the whole situation. I'm not sure if he'll fully take it in, but he's very bright, and I'm hoping that he'll see it as a welcome development.

He's already begun to look forward to your visits.' She
waited. 'Or, of course, I could tell him on my own.'

'No. I like the idea of us doing it together.'

'Good. Well…maybe we should fix a date in the diary?'

'"*Fix a date in the diary*"?' Raoul burst out laughing,
which made Sarah go even redder. 'How formal do we
have to be here?'

'You know what I mean,' she said stiffly. 'You're busy.
I just want to agree on a day.'

'Tomorrow.'

'Fine.'

'Shall I get my phone out so that I can log it in?'

'I'm trying to be serious here, Raoul. After we talk to
Oliver I can talk to my parents. I haven't breathed a word
to them, but Oliver's mentioned you a couple of times when
he's spoken to Mum.'

Nor had she visited her parents in nearly a month. She
was used to nipping down to Devon every couple of weekends, and she was guiltily aware that it had been easier to
fudge and make excuses because her mother would have
been able to eke the truth out of her, and she hadn't wanted
the inevitable sermon.

'But that's not your problem. You won't have to meet
them at all. I'll explain the situation to them…tell them
that we happened to bump into one another… They'll be
pleased because it's always worried them that you were out
there, not knowing that you had fathered a son. I'll have to
explain that I haven't mentioned anything earlier because
I wanted you to get to know Oliver, work through some of
the initial difficulties. I think they'll understand that…'

'And I won't meet them because…?'

'Why should you? You'll be involved in Oliver's life,
but you won't be in mine. Which is really what I want to
talk to you about. Visiting rights and such. I don't think

we have to go through lawyers to work something out, do we? I mean, the past few weeks have been fine. Of course I realise that it's not really been a normal routine for you, but we can work round that. I'm happy to be flexible.'

Raoul found himself recoiling from the deal on the table, even though it was a deal that suited him perfectly. Yes, he had taken a lot of time off work recently. In fact working late into the night, pretty much a routine of his, had been put on temporary hold, and even time catching up in front of his computer had been limited. Her willingness to compromise should have come as a relief. Instead, he was outraged at her easy assumption that he would be fobbed off with a night a week and the occasional weekend as Oliver's confidence levels in him rose.

'Visiting rights...' he repeated, rolling the words on his tongue and not liking how they tasted.

'Yes! You know—maybe an evening a week, whenever suits you. It would be good if you could set aside a specific day, although I know that's probably unrealistic given your lifestyle...'

Quite out of the blue she wondered when his lifestyle outside of work would recommence. His extra-curricular activities. Should she go over old ground? Repeat that she would prefer Oliver not to have to deal with any unfamiliar women? Or would Raoul be sensible enough to understand that without her having to spell it out in black and white?

It was all well and good, laying out these rules and regulations in a calm, sensible voice, but nothing could disguise the sickening thump of her heart when she thought about the longer term. The days when she would wave goodbye to Oliver and watch from the front door of her new house as Raoul sped him away to places and experiences of which she would be ignorant.

She had become accustomed to the threesome.

She had to swallow hard so that the smile on her face didn't falter. 'Aren't you going to say anything?' she prompted uncertainly.

'Let me get this straight,' Raoul intoned flatly. 'We arrange suitable days for me to pick Oliver up and drop him off a couple of hours later, and beyond that our relationship is severed...'

'I'd prefer it if you didn't call it a *relationship*.' She thought of the tingling way he made her feel, and tacking the word *relationship* onto that just seemed to make things worse.

'What would you like me to call it?'

'I'd like to think that we're *friends*. I never thought that I'd see the day when I could refer to you in that way, but I'm pleased to say that I can. Now.'

'Friends...' Raoul murmured.

'Yes. We've really worked well together on this...er... project...' That didn't sound quite right, and she lowered her eyes nervously, realising, with a start that she had managed to drink her glass of wine without even knowing it. She could feel his proximity like a dense, lethal force, and it was all she could do not to squirm away from him.

'And that's what you want, is it, Sarah?'

Dazed and confused, she raised her bright green eyes to his, and was instantly overwhelmed by a feeling of light-headedness.

The sofa was compact. Their knees were almost touching. The last rays of the sun had disappeared into grey twilight, and without benefit of the overhead light his wonderful face was thrown into half shadows.

'Yes, of course,' she heard herself mumble.

'Friends exchanging a few polite words now and again...'

'I think that's how these things go…'

'It's not what I want and you know that.'

A series of disconcerting images flashed through Sarah's mind at indecent speed. All the simple little things they had done together over the past few weeks…things that had shattered her confidence in her ability to keep a respectable distance from him. And now here he was, framing the very words she didn't want to hear.

'Raoul…' she breathed shakily.

Raoul homed in on the hesitancy in her voice with an unassailable feeling of triumph. It had shocked him to realise how much he still wanted her—until he had worked out the whole theory of unfinished business. With that explanation in his head, he could now easily see why he had been finding it difficult to concentrate at work—why images of her kept floating in his mind, like bits of shrapnel in his system, ruining his concentration and his ability to focus.

'I like it when you say my name.' Right now the lack of focus thing seemed to be happening big-time. His voice lacked its usual self assured resonance. He extended his arm along the back of the sofa and then allowed his hand to drop to the back of her neck, where he slowly caressed the soft, smooth skin.

Sarah struggled to remember the very important fact that Raoul Sinclair was a man who was programmed to get exactly what he wanted—except she didn't know why on earth he would want *her*. But she felt her body sag as she battled to bring some cool reasoning to the situation.

Her moss green eyes were welded to his, and the connection was as strong as a bond of steel.

'I really want to kiss you right now.' He sounded as unsteady as she looked.

'No. You don't. You can't. You mustn't…'

'You're not convincing me…'

She knew that he was going to kiss her, just as she knew that she should push him away. But she couldn't move. Her slender body was as still as a statue, although deep inside was a torrential surge of sensation that was already threatening to break through its fragile barriers.

The touch of his mouth against hers was intoxicating, and she fell back, weakened with fierce arousal. With an unerring sensual instinct that was uniquely his Raoul closed the small distance between them. Or maybe her treacherous body had done that of its own sweet accord. Sarah didn't know. She was ablaze with a hungry craving that had been building for weeks. She moaned softly, and then louder as he trailed an exploring hand underneath her top, sending electric shocks through her whole body.

The hand that had flattened against his chest, aiming to push him away, first curled into a useless fist and then splayed open to clutch the neck of his shirt, so that she could pull him towards her.

She was burning up, and her breasts felt tender, her nipples tightening in anticipation. She strove to stifle a shameless groan of pleasure as his hand climbed higher, caressing her ribcage, moving round to unhook her bra.

As sofas went, this sofa was hardly the most luxurious in the world, but Raoul didn't think he could make it up the stairs to her bedroom. He tugged the cotton top over her head, taking her bra with it in the process, and gazed at her, half undressed, her eyes slumbrous, her perfect mouth half parted on a smile while her breasts rose and fell in quick rhythm with her breathing.

He couldn't believe how much he wanted her. Pure, driven sensation wiped out all coherent thought. If the house had suddenly been struck by an earthquake, he wasn't sure he would have noticed.

The effect she had on him was instantaneous, and as he fluidly removed his clothes he marvelled at his incredible sense of recall. It was as if his memories of her had never been buried, as he had imagined, but instead had remained intact, very close to the surface. It proved conclusively that she was the one woman in his life he had never forgotten because what they'd shared had been prematurely concluded. He had never had time to get tired of her.

Sarah watched as his clothes hit the ground. For a businessman he still had the hard, highly toned, muscular body of an athlete. Broad shoulders narrowed to a six pack and...

Her eyes were riveted by the evidence of his impressive arousal.

'You still like looking at me,' Raoul said with a slow smile. 'And I still like you looking at me.'

The touch of her slight hand on his erection drew a shudder from him, and he curled his fingers in her hair as he felt the delicacy of her mouth and tongue take over from where her hand had been.

Sarah, in some dim part of her mind, knew that she should pull back, should tell him that this was now and not then. But she had always been achingly weak around him and nothing had changed.

The taste of him simply transported her. She found that she couldn't think. Everything had narrowed down to this one moment in time. Her body, which had spent the past five years in cold storage, roared into life and there was nothing she could do about it.

She wriggled out of the rest of her clothes.

She was barely aware of him moving to shut the sitting room door, then tossing one of the throws from a chair onto the ground. She *was* aware of him muttering something about the sofa not being a suitable spot for lovemaking for anyone who wasn't vertically challenged.

The fleecy throw was wonderfully soft and thick.

'This is much better,' Raoul growled, straddling her and then leaning down so that he could kiss her. At the same time he slid his hands under her back, so that she was arched up to him, her breasts scraping provocatively against his chest. 'There's no way that a five-foot sofa can accommodate my six foot two inches.'

'I don't recall you being that fussy five years ago,' Sarah said breathlessly. There was so much of him that she wanted to touch, so much that she had missed.

'You'll have to tell me if I've lost my sense of adventure,' he murmured. He felt her twist restlessly under him. It was a cause of deep satisfaction that he knew exactly what she wanted.

He reared back and began to caress her breasts, looking down at her flushed face as he massaged them, rolling his thumbs over the pouting tips of her nipples while she, likewise, attended to his throbbing erection.

This was a foreplay of mutual satisfaction between two people comfortable with each other's wants. It was like resuming the steps to a well-rehearsed dance.

He bent so that he could feather her neck with kisses— soft, tender nibbles that produced little gasps and moans— and then, taking advantage of the breasts offered up to his exploring mouth, he began to suckle the pink crests, drawing one distended nipple into his mouth, driving her crazy, and making her impatient for him to do the same to the other breast.

It was incredible to think that the body he was now touching had carried his child, and a wave of bitter regret washed over him. So the circumstances would have been all wrong, and he had never factored a child into his life plan, but he would have risen to the challenge. He would have been there right from the very start. He wouldn't have missed out on the first four years of his son's life. He wouldn't have been obliged to spend weeks playing catch up in the father stakes.

But regret was not an emotion with which Raoul was accustomed to dealing, and there was no value in looking at things with the benefit of hindsight.

He blocked out the fanciful notion of a different path and instead trailed his mouth over the flat planes of her stomach, maybe not quite so firm as it had once been, but remarkably free of stretch marks.

The taste of her, as he dipped his tongue to tease her most sensitive spot, was the most erotic thing he had ever experienced.

He smoothed his hands over the satin smoothness of her inner thighs and she groaned as he gave his full attention to the task.

Several times he took her so close to the edge that she had to use every ounce of will-power to rein herself back. She wanted him inside her. She found that she was desperate to feel that wonderful moment when he took one deep, final thrust and lost all his control as he came.

'Are you protected?'

Those three words penetrated her bubble, and it took a few seconds for them to register.

'Huh?'

'I haven't got any protection with me.' Raoul's voice was thick with frustration. 'And you're not on the pill. I can tell from the expression on your face.'

'No. I'm not.' It was slowly sinking in that, however wrapped up he was in the throes of passion, there was no way he would permit another mistake to occur. Look at what his last slip-up had cost him!

'Still, there are other ways of pleasing each other...'

'No, I can't... I'm sorry... I don't know what happened...'

She rolled onto her side, feeling exposed, and then sat up and looked around to where their clothes lay in random piles on the ground. Reaching out, she picked up her top and hastily shoved it on. This was followed by her underwear, while Raoul watched in silence, before heaving himself up on one elbow to stare at her with brooding force.

'Don't tell me that you've suddenly decided to have an attack of scruples now!'

'This was a mistake!' She backed away from him to take refuge on the sofa, drawing her knees up and hugging herself to stave off a bad bout of the shakes.

She dragged her eyes away from the powerful image of his nudity. She wished that she could honestly tell herself that she had just given in to a temporary urge that had been too strong. But the questions raining down on her were of an altogether more uncomfortable nature.

How far had she *really* come these past few years? Had she forgotten just how easily he had found it to dump her? To write her off as surplus to requirements when it came to the big plan of how he wanted to live his life?

A few weeks ago Raoul Sinclair had been the biggest mistake she had ever made. Seeing him again had been a shock, but she had risen above that and tried hard to view his reappearance in her life as something good for the sake of Oliver.

Yes, he had still been able to get to her, but her defences had been up and she had been prepared to fight to protect herself.

But he had attacked her in a way she had never planned for. He had won her over with the ease with which he had accepted what must have been a devastating blow to all his long-term plans. He had controlled his ego and his pride to listen to what she had to say, and he had thrown himself into the business of getting to know his son with enthusiasm and heart wrenching humility. Against her will, and against all logic and reason and good judgement, she had succumbed over the weeks to his sense of humour, his patience with Oliver, his determination to go the extra mile.

How many men who had never contemplated having a family, indeed had steadfastly maintained their determination never to go down that road, would have reacted to similar news with the grace that he had?

Sarah suspected that a lot would either have walked away or else would have contributed financially but done the absolute minimum beyond that.

He had reminded her of all the reasons she had fallen in love with him in the first place and more.

Was it any wonder that she had been a sitting target when he had reached out and touched her?

Sarah could have wept, because she knew that fundamentally Raoul hadn't changed. He might want her body, but he didn't want her dreams, her hopes or her romantic notions—which, it now seemed, had never abandoned her after all, because they were part and parcel of who she was.

'Of course this wasn't a mistake!' He raked impatient fingers through his hair and looked at her as he got dressed. Huddled on the sofa in front of him she looked very young—but then, of course, she *was* very young. Had he presumed too much? No. Of course he hadn't. Her signals had been loud and clear. She had given him the green light, and for the life of him he couldn't understand why she was backing away from him now. The past few weeks had been inexorably leading to this place. At least that was how he saw it.

It wasn't just that she still had the same dramatic effect

on his libido that she'd always had. It wasn't just that she could look at him from under those feathery lashes and make him break out in a sweat. No, they had connected in a much more fundamental area, and he knew that she felt the same way. Hell, he was nothing if not brilliant when it came to reading the signs.

And just then? Before she had decided to start back-tracking? She had been as turned on as him!

'In fact,' he said huskily, 'it was the most natural thing in the world.'

'How do you figure that?'

'You're the mother of my child. I happen to think that it's pretty damned good that we're still seriously attracted to one another.' He sat on the sofa, elbows on thighs, and looked sideways at her.

'Well, I don't think it's good. I think it just…complicates everything.'

'How does it complicate everything?'

'I don't want to get into a relationship with you. Oh, God—I forgot you don't like the word *relationship*. I forgot you find it too threatening.'

Raoul could feel her trying to impose a barrier between them and he didn't like it. It annoyed him that she was prepared to waste time dwelling on something as insignificant as a simple word.

'I want you to admit what's obvious,' he told her, turning so that he was facing her directly, not giving her the slightest opportunity to deflect her eyes from his. 'You can't deny the sexual chemistry between us. If anything, it's stronger than it was when we were together five years ago.'

It terrified Sarah that he felt that too—that it hadn't been just a trick of her imagination that she was drawn to him on all sorts of unwelcome and unexpected levels. In

Africa they had come together as two young people about to take their first steps into the big, bad world. They had lived in a bubble, far removed from day-to-day life. There was no bubble here, and that made the savage attraction she felt for him all the more terrifying.

'No...' she protested weakly.

'Are you telling me that if I hadn't interrupted our love-making you would have suddenly decided to push me away?'

Sarah went bright red and didn't say anything.

'I thought so,' Raoul confirmed softly. 'You want to push me away but you can't.'

'Don't tell me what I can and can't do.'

'Okay. Well, let me tell you this. The past few weeks have been...a revelation. Who would have thought that I could enjoy spending so much time in a kitchen? Especially a kitchen with no mod-cons? Or sitting in front of a television watching a children's programme? I never expected to see you again, but the second I did I realised that what I felt for you hadn't gone away as I had assumed it had. I still want you, and I'm not too proud to admit it.'

'Wanting someone isn't enough...' But her words were distinctly lacking in conviction.

'It's a damn sight healthier than self-denial.' Raoul let those words settle. 'Martyrs might feel virtuous, but virtue is a questionable trade off when it goes hand in hand with unhappiness.'

'You are just *so* egotistical!' Sarah said hotly. 'Are you really saying that I'm going to be unhappy if I pass up the fantastic opportunity to sleep with you?'

'You're going to be miserable if you pass up the opportunity to put this thing we have to bed. You keep trying to deny it. You blow hot and cold because you want to kid yourself that you can fight it.'

Sarah would have liked to deny that, but how could she? He was right. She wavered between wanting him to touch her, enjoying it madly when he did, and being repelled by her own lack of will-power.

'I don't like thinking of you going to clubs and meeting guys,' he admitted roughly.

'Why? Would you be jealous?'

'How can I be jealous of what, as yet, doesn't even exist? Besides, jealousy isn't my thing.' He lowered his eyes and shifted. 'You still have a hold over me,' he conceded. 'I still want you…'

'There's more to life than the physical stuff,' Sarah muttered under her breath.

'Let's agree to differ on that score,' Raoul contradicted without hesitation. 'And it doesn't change the fact that we're going to end up in bed sooner rather than later. I'm proposing we make it sooner. We're unfinished business, Sarah…'

'What do you mean?'

Raoul took her fingers and played with them idly, keeping his eyes locked to hers. 'Back then, I did what was right for both of us. But would what we had have ended had it not been for the fact that I was due to leave the country?'

'Yes, it *would* have ended, Raoul. Because you're not interested in long-term relationships. Oh, we might have drifted on for a few more months, but sooner or later you would have become tired of me.'

'Sooner or later you would have discovered that you were pregnant,' Raoul pointed out with infuriating calm.

'And how would that have changed anything? Of course it wouldn't! You would have stuck around for the baby because you have a sense of responsibility, but why don't you admit that there's no way we would have ended up together!'

'How do I know what would have happened? Do I have a crystal ball?'

'You don't need a crystal ball, Raoul. You just need to be honest. If we had continued our…our whatever you want to call it…would it have led to marriage? Some kind of commitment? Or would we have just carried on sleeping together until the business between us was finally finished? In other words, until you were ready to move on? I know I'm sometimes weak when I'm around you. You're an attractive guy, and you also happen to be the father of my child. But that doesn't mean that it would be a good idea to just have lots of sex until you get me out of your system…'

'What makes you think that it wouldn't be the other way around?'

'In fact,' she continued, ignoring his interruption, 'it would be selfish of us to become lovers because we're incapable of a bit of self-denial! I don't want Oliver to become so accustomed to you being around that it's a problem when you decide to take off! I'm sorry I've given you mixed signals, but we're better off just being…friends…'

CHAPTER SIX

SARAH wondered how she had managed to let her emotions derail her to such an extent that she had nearly ended up back in bed with Raoul. The words *unfinished business* rankled, conjuring up as they did visions of something disposable, to be picked up and then discarded once again the minute it suited him.

Had he imagined that she would launch herself into his arms in a bid to take up where they had left off? Had he thought that she would greet his assertion about still wanting her as something wonderful and complimentary? He didn't want her seeing anyone else—not because he wanted to work on having a proper relationship with her, but because he wanted her to fill his bed until such time as he managed to get her out of his system. Like a flu virus.

He was an arrogant, selfish bastard, and she had been a crazy fool to get herself lulled into thinking otherwise!

She had a couple of days' respite, because he was out of the country, and although he telephoned on both days she was brief before passing him over to Oliver, which he must have found extra challenging, given Oliver's long silences and excitable babbling.

'I think we'll tell him at the weekend,' she informed Raoul crisply, and politely told him that there would be absolutely no need for him to rush over the second he got back, because at that time of night Oliver would be asleep anyway.

On the other side of the Atlantic, Raoul scowled down the phone. He should never have let her think about what he had said. He should have kissed her doubts away and then just made love to her until she was silenced.

Except, of course, she would still have jumped on her moral bandwagon. What had been so straightforward for him had been a hotbed of dilemma for her. He told himself that there were plenty of other fish in the sea, but when he opened his address book and started scanning down the names of beautiful women, all of whom would have shrieked with joy at the sound of his voice and the prospect of a hot date, he found his enthusiasm for that kind of replacement therapy waning fast.

Whereas before he had been comfortable turning up at Sarah's without much notice, he had now found himself given a very definite time slot, and so he arrived at her house bang on five-thirty to find Oliver dressed in jeans and a jumper while she was in her oldest clothes, her hair wet from the shower and pinned up into a ponytail.

'I thought we could sit him down and explain the situation to him,' were her opening words, 'and then you could take him out for something to eat. Nothing fancy, but it'll be nice for him to have you to himself without me around. I've also explained the whole situation to Mum and Dad. They're very pleased that you're on the scene.'

Within minutes Raoul had got the measure of what was going on. She was making it perfectly clear that they would now be communicating on a need-to-know basis only. Her bright green eyes were guarded and detached, only warming when they had Oliver between them so that they could explain the situation.

Finally fatherhood was fully conferred onto him. He was no longer the outsider, easing himself in. He was a dad, and as she had predicted it was a smooth transfer. Oliver had had time to adjust to him. He accepted the news with solemnity, and then it was as though nothing had changed. Raoul had brought him back a very fancy but admirably small box of bricks and an enormous paint-box, both of which were greeted with enthusiasm.

'Take a few pictures when he starts painting in your living room,' Sarah said sarcastically. 'I'd love to see how your leather furniture reacts to the watercolours.'

'Is this how it's now going to be?' Raoul enquired coldly, as Oliver stuffed his backpack with lots of unnecessary items in preparation for their meal out.

Defiant pink colour suffused Sarah's cheeks. She didn't want to be argumentative. He was going to be on the scene, in one way or another, for time immemorial, and she knew that they had to develop a civil, courteous relationship if they weren't to descend into a parody of two warring parents. But she was truly scared of reaching the point they previously had, which had been one of such easy friendship that all the feelings she had imagined left behind had found fertile ground and blossomed out of control. She had let him crawl under her skin until the only person she could think about had been him, so that when he'd finally touched her she had gone up in flames.

'No. It's not. I apologise for that remark,' she responded stiffly, stooping down to adjust Oliver's backpack, whilst taking the opportunity to secretly remove some of the unnecessary stuff he had slipped in. 'Now, you're going to be a good boy, Oliver, aren't you? With your dad?' Oliver nodded and Sarah straightened back up to address Raoul. 'What time can I expect you back? Because I'm going out. I'll only be a couple of hours.'

'You're going out? Where?'

Raoul gave her the once-over. Sloppy clothes. Damp hair. She was waiting for them to leave before she got dressed.

'I don't think that's any of your business, actually.'

'And what if you're not back when I return?'

'You have my mobile number, Raoul. You could always give me a call.'

'Who are you going to be with?'

Raoul knew that it was an outrageous question. He thought back to his brief—very brief—notion that he might get in touch with another woman, go on a date. The idea had lasted less than ten seconds. So...who was *she* going out with? On the first evening he had Oliver? With a man? What man? She had claimed that there was no one at all in her life, that she had been just too busy with the business of trying to earn some money and be a single parent. She might not have had the time to cultivate any kind of personal life, but that didn't mean that there hadn't been men hovering on the periphery, ready to move in just as soon as she found the time.

The more Raoul thought about it, the more convinced he became that she was meeting a man. One of those sensitive, fun-loving types she professed to like. Had she made sure to appear in old clothes so that he wouldn't be able to gauge where she was going by what she was wearing?

He was the least fanciful man in the world, and yet he couldn't stop the swirl of wildly imaginative conclusions to which he was jumping. He was tempted to stand his ground until he got answers that satisfied him.

Sarah laughed incredulously at his question. 'I can't believe you just asked that, Raoul.'

'Why?'

'Because it's none of your business. Now, Oliver's beginning to get restless.' She glanced down to where he was beginning to fidget, delivering soft taps to the skirting board with his shoe and tugging Raoul's hand impatiently. 'I'll see you in a couple of hours, and you know how to get hold of me if you need to.'

Sarah thought that it was a damning indication of just how quickly their relationship had slipped back into dangerous waters—the fact that he saw it as his right to know what she was getting up to. They might not have become lovers, the way they once had been, but it had been a close call. Had she sent out signals? Without even being aware of doing so?

She was going out with a girlfriend for a pizza. Wild horses wouldn't have dragged the admission out of her. She would be gone an hour and a half, tops, and whilst she knew that she shouldn't care one way or another if he knew that her evening out was a harmless bit of catching up with a pal, she did.

So instead of her jeans she wore a mini-skirt, and instead of her trainers she wore heels. She wasn't quite sure what she was trying to prove, and she certainly felt conspicuous in the pizza parlour, where the dress code was more dressing down than dressing up, but she was perversely pleased that she had gone to the trouble when she opened the door to Raoul two and a half hours later.

Oliver was considerably less pristine than he had been when he had left. In fact, Sarah thought that she could pretty much guess at what they had eaten for dinner from the various smears on his clothes.

'How did it go?'

Raoul had to force himself to focus on what she was asking, because the sight of her tight short skirt and high black heels were threatening to ambush his thinking processes.

'Very well…' He heard himself going through the motions of polite chit-chat, bending down to ruffle Oliver's hair and draw him into the conversation. Crayons and paper had been produced at the restaurant, and he had drawn some pictures. Happy family stuff. There would be a psychologist somewhere who would be able to say something about the stick figure drawings of two parents and a child in the middle.

'Right… Well…'

Raoul frowned as she began shutting the door on him. He inserted himself into the small hallway.

'We need to discuss the details of this arrangement,' he told her smoothly. 'As well as the details of the house move. Everything's signed. I'll need to know what needs to be removed from this place.'

'Already?'

'Time moves on at a pace, doesn't it?'

Sarah fell back and watched him stride towards the sitting room. 'I'll get Oliver to bed and be back down in a sec,' she mumbled helplessly to his departing back.

Tempted to get out of her ridiculous gear, she decided against it. Whatever technicalities had to be discussed wouldn't take long, although she was surprised at how fast the house had become available. The last time she had seen it, it had been something of a derelict shell. At the time, she had confided in Raoul what she would like in terms of furniture, but that was the last she had heard on the subject, which had been a couple of weeks ago. She had assumed that the whole process would take months, and had deferred thinking about the move until it was more imminent.

'I can't believe the house is ready. Are you sure?' This as soon as she was back in the sitting room, where he was relaxed in one of the chairs, with his back to the bay window. 'I thought these things took months...'

'Amazing what money can do when it comes to speeding things up.'

'But I haven't really thought about what to fill it with. I mean, none of this stuff is mine...'

'Which is a blessing, judging from the quality of the furnishings.' Raoul watched as she nervously took the chair facing his on the opposite side of the tiny sitting room. She had to wriggle the short skirt down so that it didn't indecently expose her thighs and his lips thinned disapprovingly. The top was hardly better. A vest affair that contoured her generous breasts in a way that couldn't fail to arouse interest.

Sarah couldn't be bothered to react because she didn't disagree.

'It's going to be weird leaving here,' she thought out loud.

'Oliver's excited.' *Who had the short skirt and the tight top and the high heels been for?* 'He's looking forward to having a bigger garden. Complete with the swing set I promised him. Did you enjoy your evening?'

Sarah, who had still been contemplating the prospect of being uprooted sooner than she had expected, looked at Raoul in sudden confusion.

'You're dressed like a tart,' he expanded coolly, 'and I don't like it.'

Sarah gripped the arms of the chair while a slow burning anger rose inside her like red spreading mist.

'How *dare* you think that you can tell me how I can dress?'

'You never wore clothes like that when I was around. Yet the very first time you have a bit of free time without Oliver you're dressed to the nines. I'm guessing that you've used your time profitably by checking what's out there for a single girl.'

'I don't have to…to…*dignify* that with a response!'

No, she didn't, and her stubborn, glaring eyes were telling him that he was going to get nowhere when it came to dragging an explanation of her whereabouts out of her.

Hot on the heels of her rejection, her self-righteous proclamation that their sleeping together wasn't going to be on the cards, her strident reminders to him that she wanted commitment, Raoul finally acknowledged what had been staring him in the face.

When it came to Sarah he was possessive, and he wanted exclusivity. He didn't want her dipping her toe into the world of dating and other men. Seeing her in that revealing get-up, he realised that he didn't even want her dressing in a way that could conceivably attract them. If she had to wear next to nothing, then he wanted it to be for his benefit and his benefit only.

He had never been possessive in his life before. Was it because she was more than just a woman to him? Because she was the mother of his child? Did he have some peculiar dinosaur streak of which he had hitherto been unaware? He just knew that the thought of her trawling the clubs made his blood run cold.

So he had never been moved by the notion of settling down with anyone? Well, life wasn't a static business. Rules and guidelines made yesterday became null and void when situations changed. Wasn't flexibility a sign of a creative mind?

He wondered that he could have been disingenuous enough to imagine his perfectly reasonable proposition that they take what they had and run with it might be met with enthusiasm. Sarah would never settle for anything less than a full-time relationship. And would that even be with him? he wondered uneasily. It was true that the sexual chemistry between them was electrifying, but it certainly wouldn't be the tipping point for her.

'Let's just talk about the practicalities,' she continued firmly. 'If you give me a definite date as to when we need to be out of here… I haven't given notice to the landlord,' she said suddenly. 'I need to give three months' notice…'

'I'll take care of that.'

'And I suppose we should discuss what days suit you to come and see Oliver. Or should we wait until we're settled in the new place? Then you can see how easy it is for you to get to where we are. Public transport can be a little unreliable. Oops, sorry—I forgot that you wouldn't be taking public transport…'

Raoul was acidly wondering whether she was eager to get her diary in order, so that she knew in advance when she would be able to slot in her exciting single life. What the hell was going on here? He was *jealous*!

He stood up, and Sarah hastily followed suit, bemused by the fact that he seemed to be leaving pretty much as fast as he had arrived. Not only that, but he had somehow managed to make her feel like a cheap tart. Although she knew that he had no right to pass sweeping judgements on what she wore or where she went, she still had to fight the temptation to make peace by just telling him the truth.

'The house will be ready by the middle of next week.'

'But what about my things?'

'I'll arrange to have them brought over. If all this furniture is staying, then I can't imagine that what's left will amount to much.'

'No, I suppose not,' she said in a small voice, perversely inclined to dither now that he was on his way out.

Raoul hesitated. 'It's going to be fine,' he said roughly.

'The house will be entirely in your name. You won't have to be afraid that you could lose the roof over your head, and really, it's just a change of location.'

'It'll be great!' She tried a bright smile on for size. 'I know Mum and Dad are really thrilled about it. They haven't been too impressed with our rented house, what with the busy street so close to the front door and not much back garden for Oliver.'

'Which brings me to something I haven't yet mentioned. Your parents.'

'What about them?'

'I want to meet them.'

'Whatever for?' Sarah asked, dismayed. Try as she had, she couldn't stop feeling deeply suspicious that neither of them had really believed her when she had told them that Raoul was back on the scene but that it was absolutely fine because she had discovered that she felt nothing for him.

'Because Oliver's my son and it makes sense for me to know his grandparents. There will be occasions when they visit us in London and vice versa.'

'Yes, but…'

'I also don't want to spend the rest of my life with your parents harbouring misconceptions about the kind of man I am.'

'They don't have misconceptions,' Sarah admitted grudgingly. 'I told them how much time you'd spent with Oliver, and also about the house.'

'I'd still like to meet them, so you'll have to arrange that and give me a few days' advance notice.'

'Well, maybe when they're next in London…'

'No. Maybe within the next fortnight.'

With the house move a heartbeat away, and a date set in the diary for the three of them to visit her parents in

Devon, Sarah had never felt more like someone chucked onto a rollercoaster and managing to hang on only by the skin of her teeth.

Her possessions, once she had packed them all up, amounted to a few cardboard boxes, which seemed a sad indictment of the time she had spent in the rented house. Nor could she say, with her hand on her heart, that there was very much that she would miss about where she'd lived. The neighbours were pleasant enough, although she knew them only in passing, but the place was wrapped up in so many memories of hardship and trying to make ends meet that she found herself barely glancing back as the chauffeur-driven car that had been sent for them arrived to collect her promptly on Wednesday morning.

Oliver could barely contain his excitement. The back of the opulent car was strewn with his toys. Of course Raoul's driver knew who they were, because from the start Raoul had flatly informed her that he couldn't care less what other people thought of his private life, but she could see that the man was curious, and amused at Oliver's high spirits. Sarah wondered whether he was trying to marry the image of his boss with that of a man who wouldn't mind a four-year-old child treating his mega-expensive car with cavalier disrespect.

Sarah was charmed afresh at the peaceful, tree-lined road that led up to the house, which was in a large corner plot. Anyone could have been forgiven for thinking that London was a million miles away. It was as far removed from their small rented terraced house on the busy road as chalk was from cheese. Whatever her doubts and anxieties, she couldn't deny that Raoul had rescued them both from a great deal of financial hardship and discomfort.

Hard on the heels of that private admission she felt a

lump in her throat at the thought of them being *friends*. She had been so offended by his suggestion that they become lovers for no other reason than they were still attracted to one another, and so hurt that he only wanted her in his bed as a way of exorcising old ghosts... She had positively done the right thing in telling him just where he could take that selfish, arrogant proposal, and yet...

Had she reacted too hastily?

Sarah hurriedly sidelined that sign of weakness and scooped Oliver's toys onto her lap as the car finally slowed down and then swept up the picturesque drive to the house.

Raoul was waiting for her inside.

'I would have brought you here,' he said, picking up Oliver, who demanded to be put down so that he could explore, 'but I've come straight from work.'

'That's okay.' Sarah stepped inside and her mouth fell open—because it bore little resemblance to the house she had last seen.

Flagstone tiles made the hallway warm and colourful, and everywhere else rich, deep wood lent a rustic, cosy charm. She walked from room to room, taking in the décor which was exactly as she would have wanted it to be, from the velvet drapes in the sitting room to the restored Victorian tiles around the fireplace.

Raoul made a show of pointing out the bottle-green Aga which took pride of place in the kitchen, and the old-fashioned dresser which he had had specifically sourced from one of the house magazines which had littered her house.

'You had a crease in the page,' he informed her, 'so I took it to mean that this was the kind of thing you liked.'

Oliver had positioned himself by the French doors that led from the small conservatory by the kitchen into the garden, and was staring at the swing set outside with eyes as round as saucers.

'Okay,' Sarah said on a laugh, holding his hand, 'let's have a look outside, shall we?'

'I don't remember the garden being this well planted,' she said, looking around her at the shrubs and foliage that framed the long lawn. There was even a rustic table and chairs on the paved patio, behind which a trellis promised a riot of colour when in season.

'I had it landscaped. Feel free to change anything you want. Why don't we have a look upstairs? I can get my driver to keep an eye on Oliver,' he added drily. 'We might have a fight on our hands if we try and prise him off the swing.'

Raoul had had considerable input with the furnishings. He had hired the very same mega-expensive interior designer who had done his own penthouse apartment, but instead of handing over an enormous cheque and giving her free rein he had actually been specific about what he wanted. He knew that Sarah hated anything modern and minimalist. He'd steered clear of anything involving leather and chrome. He had stopped short of buying artwork, although he had been tempted by some small landscapes that would have been a terrific investment, but he had done his utmost with a bewildering range of colour options and had insisted that everything be kept period.

'I can't believe this is going to be our new home,' Sarah murmured yet again, as she ran her hands lovingly over the Victorian fireplace in what would be her bedroom. A dreamy four-poster bed dominated the space, and the leaded windows overlooked the pretty garden. She could see Oliver on the swing, being pushed by Raoul's very patient driver, and she waved at him.

'Did you choose all this stuff yourself?'

Raoul flushed. How cool was it to have a hand in choosing furnishings for a house? Not very. Especially when there had been a million and one other things clamouring for his attention at work. But he had been rattled by her rejection, and had realised that despite what he saw as an obvious way forward for them he could take nothing for granted.

'I think I know what you like,' he prevaricated, and received a warm smile in response.

Sarah squashed the temptation to hug him. He did things like this and was it any wonder that her will-power was all over the place? She had expected to find a house that was functioning and kitted out in a fairly basic way. Instead there was nothing that wasn't one hundred percent perfect, from the mellow velvet curtains in the sitting room to the faded elegant wallpaper in the bedroom.

Oliver's room, next to hers, was what any four-year-old boy would have dreamt of, with a bed in the shape of a racing car and wallpaper featuring all his favourite cartoon characters.

Yet again she had to remind herself that she had done the right thing in turning her back on what had been on offer. Yet again she forced herself back onto the straight and narrow by telling herself that, however good Raoul was at being charming, going the extra mile and throwing money at something with a generosity that would render most people speechless, he was still a man who walked alone and always would. He was still a man with an in-built loathing of any form of commitment, which in his head was the equivalent of a prison sentence.

Yet again she was forced to concede that his invitation to be his lover would have sounded the death knell for any ongoing amicable relationship they might foster, because she would have been the one to get hurt in the end. She knew that if she got too close to him it would be impossible to hold any of herself back.

But the steps he had taken to ensure that she walked into a house that was brilliant in every way moved her.

'We'll have to sit down and talk about visiting.' She strived to hit the right note of being convivial, appreciative but practical.

Raoul looked at her with veiled eyes. Had he hoped for a more favourable reaction, given the time and effort he had expended in doing this house up for her? Since when did *quid pro quo* play a part in human interaction? Was this the legacy that had been willed to him courtesy of his disadvantaged background?

He thrust aside that moment of introspection, but even so he knew that she was sliding further and further away from him.

'I don't want to have weekly visits,' he told her, lounging on the ledge by the window and surveying her with his arms folded.

'No…well, you can come as often as you like,' she offered. 'I just really would need to find out exactly when, so that Oliver isn't disappointed…I know your work life makes you unpredictable…'

'Have I been unpredictable so far?'

'No, but…'

'I've come every time I said I would. Believe me, I understand how important it is to be reliable when there's a child involved. You forget I have intimate experience of kids waiting by windows with their bags packed for parents who never showed up.'

'Of course…'

'I know how damaging that can be.'

'So…what do you suggest? He'll be starting school in September…maybe weekends might be a good idea. Just to begin with. Until he gets used to his new routine. Kids can be tetchy and exhausted when they first start school…'

'I'm not in favour of being a part-time father.'

'You *won't* be.'

'How am I to know that would be a continuing state of affairs?'

'I don't understand…'

'How long before you find another man, in other words?' He thought of her, dressed to kill, on the hunt for a soulmate.

Sarah stared at him incredulously. Slowly the nuts and bolts cranked into gear and she gave a shaky, sheepish laugh. 'Okay. I know what you're getting at. You think that I went somewhere exciting the last time you took Oliver out. You think that I got dressed up and decided to…I don't know…paint the town red…'

Raoul flushed darkly and kept his eyes pinned to her face.

'Do you really think that I'm the type of person who keeps her head down, bringing up a child, and then hits the clubs the very second she gets a couple of hours out of the house?'

'It's not that impossible to believe. Don't forget you were the one who made a big song and dance about wanting to be free to find your knight in shining armour! If such a person exists!'

'Oh, for heaven's sake!' She walked towards him, angry, frustrated, and helplessly aware that the only contender for the vacancy of knight in shining armour was standing right in front of her—the very last man on whom the honour should ever be conferred because he wasn't interested in the position. 'Look, I didn't go *anywhere* last Saturday. Well, nowhere exciting at any rate. I met my friend and we went out for a pizza. Are you satisfied?'

'What friend was this?'

'A girlfriend from Devon. She moved to London a few months ago, and we try to get together as often as we can. It's not always possible with a young child, and so I took advantage of having a night off to have dinner with her.'

'Why didn't you tell me at the time?'

'Because it was none of your business, Raoul!'

'Did it give you a kick to make me jealous?'

It was the first time he had ever expressed an emotion like that. Many times he had told her that he just wasn't a jealous person. His admission now brought a rush of heady colour to her cheeks, and she could feel her heart accelerate, beating against her ribcage like a sledgehammer. Suddenly conscious of his proximity, she widened her eyes and heard her breaths come fast and shallow. She feverishly tried to work out what this meant. Did he feel more for her than he had been willing to verbalise? Or was she just caving in once again? Clutching at straws because she loved him?

'You're telling me that you were *jealous*?'

Having said more than he had intended to, Raoul refused to be drawn into a touchy feely conversation about a passing weakness. He looked at her with stubborn pride.

'I'm telling you that I wasn't impressed by the way you were dressed.' He heard himself expressing an opinion that would have been more appropriate had it come from someone three times his age. 'You're a mother...'

'And so short skirts are out? I'm *not* getting all wrapped up in this silly business of you thinking that you can tell me what to wear or where to go or what to think!' Her temporary euphoric bubble was rapidly deflating. 'And I'm *not* about to start clubbing. I have too much on my plate at the moment,' she admitted with honesty, 'to even begin thinking about meeting a guy.'

'And I'm not prepared for that time to come,' Raoul said with grim determination. 'I don't want to be constrained to two evenings a week, and I don't want you telling me that this is about you. It's not. It's about Oliver, and you can't tell me that it's not better for a child to have both parents here.'

Sarah looked at him with dazed incomprehension. 'So…?'

'So you want nothing short of full time commitment? Well, you've got it. For Oliver's sake, I'm willing to marry you…'

CHAPTER SEVEN

For a few seconds Sarah wondered whether she had heard right, and then for a few more seconds she basked in the bliss of his proposal. Now that he had uttered those words she realised that this was exactly what she had wanted five years ago. His bags had been packed and she had been hanging on, waiting for him to seal their relationship with just this indication of true commitment. Of course back then his response had been to dump her.

'You're asking me to marry you,' she said flatly, and Raoul titled his head to one side.

'It makes sense.'

'Why now? Why does it make sense now?'

'I'm not sure what you're getting at, Sarah.'

'I'm guessing that the only reason you've asked me to marry you is because you don't like the thought of being displaced if someone else comes along.'

'Oliver's my son. Naturally I don't care for the thought of another man coming into your life and taking over my role.'

But would he have asked her to marry him if he hadn't happened to see her in a short skirt and a small top, making the most of what few assets she possessed, and jumped to all the wrong conclusions? He hadn't asked her to marry him when she had told him that she wanted the opportunity to meet someone with whom she could have a meaningful relationship, that there was more to life than sex...

Sarah reasoned that that was because, whatever she said, he had believed deep down that his hold over her was unbreakable. Historically, she had been his for the asking, and he knew that. Had he imagined that it was something she had never outgrown? Had he thought that underneath all her doubts and hesitation and brave denials she was really the same girl, eager and willing to do whatever he asked? Until it had been brought home to him, silly and mistaken though he was, that she might actually have *meant* what she said?

For Sarah, it all seemed to tie up. Raoul enjoyed being in control. When they had lived together on the compound all those years ago he had always been the one to take the lead, the one to whom everyone else instinctively turned when it came to decision making. Had the prospect of her slithering out of his reach and beyond his control prompted him into a marriage proposal?

'I didn't think that you ever wanted to get married,' she pointed out, and he gave an elegant shrug, turning to stare out of the window to where Oliver's appetite for the garden appeared to be boundless.

'I never thought about having children either,' he returned without hesitation, 'but there are you. The best-laid plans and so on.'

'Well, I'm sorry that Oliver's come along and messed up your life,' she said in a tight voice, and he spun round to look at her.

'Don't ever say that again!' His voice was low and sharp and lethally cold, and Sarah was immediately ashamed of her outburst because it hadn't been fair. 'I may not have planned on having children but I now have a child, and there is no way that I would wish it otherwise.'

'I'm sorry. I shouldn't have said that. But...look, it would be a disaster for us to get married.'

'I'm really not seeing the problem here. There's more than just the two of us involved in this...'

'So what's changed from when you first found out about Oliver?'

'I don't understand this. Are you playing hard to get because you think that I should have asked you to marry me as soon as I found out about Oliver?'

'No, of course not! And I'm not playing *hard to get*. I know that this isn't some kind of game. You don't *want* to marry me, Raoul. You just want to be in a position of making sure that I don't get involved with anyone else and jeopardise your contact and influence with Oliver, and the only way you can think of doing that is by putting a ring on my finger!'

She spun round on her heels and made for the door, but before she could reach it she felt his fingers on her arm and he whipped her back round to face him.

'You're not going to walk out on this conversation!'

'I don't want to carry on talking about this. It's upsetting me.'

Raoul shot her a look of pure disbelief. 'I can't believe I'm hearing this! I ask you to marry me and you're acting as though I've insulted you!'

'You want me to be grateful, Raoul, and I'm not. When I used to dream of being married it was never about getting a grudging proposal from a man who has an agenda and no way out!'

'This is ridiculous. You're blowing everything out of proportion. Oliver needs a family and we're good together.' But Raoul couldn't deny that the idea of her running around with other men had, at least in part, generated his urgent decision. Did that turn him into a control freak? No!

'In other words, all things taken into account, why not? Is that how it works for you, Raoul?' She couldn't bring herself to look at him. His hand was a band of rigid steel on her arm, even though he actually wasn't grasping her very hard at all.

Silence pooled around them until Sarah could feel herself beginning to perspire with tension. Why was it such a struggle to do what she knew was the right thing? Why was it so hard to keep her defences in place? Hadn't she learnt anything at all? Didn't she deserve more than to be someone's convenient wife, even though she happened to be in love with that *someone*? What sort of happy future could there be for two people welded together for the wrong reason?

'Look, I know that the ideal situation is for a child to have both parents at home, but it would be wrong for us to sacrifice our lives for Oliver's sake.'

'Why do you have to use such emotive language?' He released her to rake an impatient hand through his hair. 'I'm not looking at it as a *sacrifice*.'

'Well, how *are* you looking at it?'

'Haven't we got along for the past few weeks?' He answered her question with a question, which wasn't exactly an informative response.

'Yes, of course we have…' Too well, as far as Sarah was concerned. So well, in fact, that it had been dangerously easy to fall in love with him all over again—for which foolishness she was now paying a steep price. A marriage of convenience would have been much more acceptable were emotions not involved. Then she could have seen it as a business transaction which benefited all parties concerned.

'And I know you don't like hearing this particular truth,' Raoul continued bluntly, 'but we get along in other ways as well…'

'Why does it always come down to sex for you?' Sarah muttered, folding her arms. 'Is it because you think that's my weakness?'

'Isn't it?'

Suddenly he was suffocatingly close to her. Her nostrils flared as she breathed in his heady, masculine scent. Unable to look him in the face, she let her eyes drift to the only slightly less alarming aspect of his broad chest. The top two buttons of his shirt were undone, and she could glimpse the fine dark hair that shadowed his torso.

'There's nothing wrong with that,' Raoul murmured in a velvety voice that brought her out in goosebumps. 'In fact, I like it. So we get married, Oliver has a stable home life, and we get to enjoy each other. No more having to torture yourself with pointless Should we? Shouldn't we? questions…no more wringing of hands…no more big speeches about keeping our hands off one another while you carry on looking at me with those hot little eyes of yours…'

Although he hadn't laid a finger on her, Sarah felt as though he had—because her body was on fire just listening to the rise and fall of his seductive words.

'I don't look at you…that way…'

'You know you do. And it's mutual. Every time I leave you I head home for a cold shower.' He tilted her mutinous head so that she was looking up at him. 'Let's make this legal, Sarah…'

The sound of Oliver calling them from downstairs snapped Sarah out of her trance and she took a shaky step back.

'I can't drag you kicking and screaming down the aisle,' Raoul said softly as she turned to head down the stairs.

Sarah stilled and half looked over her shoulder. 'But think about what I've said and think about the consequences if you decide to say no.'

'Is there some sort of threat behind what you're saying, Raoul?'

'I have never used threats in my dealings with other people. I've never had to. Instead of rushing in and seeing everything insofar as it pertains to *you*, try looking at the bigger picture and seeing things insofar as they pertain to everyone else.'

'You're telling me that I'm selfish?'

'If the cap fits…'

'I'm just not as cynical as you, Raoul. That doesn't make me selfish.'

Raoul was stumped by this piece of incomprehensible feminine logic, and he shook his head in pure frustration. 'What's cynical about wanting what's best for our child? You need to think about my proposition, Sarah. Now, Oliver's getting restless, but just bear in mind that if *I* am not impressed by the thought of some guy moving in with you and taking over my role, how would *you* feel when some woman moves in with me and takes over *your* role…?'

Leaving her with that ringing in her head was the equivalent of a threat, as far as Sarah was concerned. Furthermore, for the rest of the day he treated her with a level of formality that set her at an uncomfortable distance, and she wondered whether this was his way of showing her, without having to spell it out, what life would be like should they go their separate ways, only meeting up for the sake of their child.

She resented the way he could so effectively narrow everything down in terms that were starkly black and white. Oliver needed both parents at home. They got along. There was still that defiant tug of sexual chemistry there between them. Solution? Get married. Because she had rejected his original offer: *Become lovers until boredom sets in.* Marriage, for Raoul, would sort out the thorny problem of another man surfacing in her life, and also satisfy his physical needs. It made such perfect sense to him that any objection on her part could only be interpreted as selfishness.

Ridiculous!

But, whether he had intended it that way or not, his point was driven home over the next few days, during which he came at appointed and prearranged times so that he could take Oliver out. He had asked her advice and laughed when she had told him that any restaurant with starched white linen tablecloths and fussy waiters should be avoided at all costs, but there was a patina of politeness he now exuded which Sarah found horribly unnerving.

Of course she wondered whether she was imagining it. His marriage proposal was still whirring around in her head. Had that made her hyper-sensitive to nuances in his demeanour?

She had tried twice to raise the topic, to explain her point of view in a way that didn't end up making her feel as if she was somehow *letting the side down*, but in both instances his response had been to repeat that she had to think it through very carefully.

'Wait and see how this arrangement works,' he had urged her, 'before you decide to rush headlong into a decision that you might come to bitterly regret.'

In a few well-chosen words he had managed to sum her up as reckless, irresponsible, and incapable of making the right choices.

Again Sarah had tried to get a toe hold into an argument, but he had expertly fielded her off and she had been left stewing in her own annoyance.

And at the bottom of her mind crawled the uncomfortable scenario of Raoul finding someone else. Now that he had taken on board the concept of marrying someone, would it prove persuasive enough for him to actually consider a proper relationship? He had had a congenital aversion to tying himself up with someone else. His background had predicated against it. But then Oliver had come along and a chip in the fortress of his self-containment had been made. Then he had taken the step of asking her to marry him.

Of course for all the wrong reasons as far as she was concerned! But he *had* jumped an enormous hurdle, even if he *did* see it only as a logical step forward, all things considered.

What if, having jumped that hurdle, he now allowed himself to finally open up to the reality of actually taking someone else on board? What if he *fell in love*?

When Sarah thought about that, she found herself quailing in panic. *She* could give him long, moralising speeches about the importance of not getting married simply for the sake of a child. *She* could scoff at the idea of entering into a union as intimate as marriage without the right foundations in place, because she was scared that she would not be able to survive the closeness without wanting much, much more. But how thrilled would she be if he took himself off to some other woman and decided to tie the knot?

It could easily happen, couldn't it? Having a child would have altered everything for him, even if he barely recognised the fact. She wondered whether he had been changed enough to consider the advantages of having a permanent woman in his life—someone who could be a substitute mother. Sarah felt sick at the prospect of having a *step-*

mother in the mix, but on the subject of things *making sense* it certainly would make sense, down the road, for him to get married.

He would surely find it difficult to continue playing the field, always making sure that Oliver and whatever current woman of the day didn't overlap. Would he want to live the rest of his life like that? And what about when Oliver got older and became more alert to what was happening around him? Would Raoul want to risk having his private life judged by his own child? No, of course he wouldn't. If there was one thing she had learnt, it was that Raoul was capable of huge sacrifices when it came to Oliver. He would never countenance his own son seeing him as an irresponsible womaniser.

Sarah found herself frequently drifting off into such thoughts as they settled into their new house and began turning it into a home.

There was absolutely nothing to be done, décor-wise, because everything was of an exquisite standard, but the show home effect was quickly replaced with something altogether more cosy as family pictures were brought out of packing boxes and laid on the mantelpiece in the sitting room. The fridge became a repository for Oliver's artwork as she attached his drawings with colourful little magnets, and the woven throws her mother had given her when she had first moved to London turned the sofa in the conservatory into a lovely, inviting spot where she and Oliver could watch television. They went on short forays into the nearby village, locating all the essentials.

On the surface, everything was as it should be. It was only her endlessly churning mind that kept her awake at night and made her lose focus when she was in the middle of doing something.

Raoul continued to behave with grindingly perfect, gentlemanly behaviour, and Sarah found herself wondering on more than one occasion what he was getting up to on the evenings when he wasn't around.

She hadn't realised how accustomed she had become to seeing him pretty much every day, or at least being given some explanation of where he was and what he was doing on those days when he hadn't been able to make it. On the single occasion when she had tried fishing for a little information he had raised his eyebrows, tutted, and told her that really it wasn't any of her business, was it?

Two days before they were due to go to Devon to visit her parents Raoul returned Oliver to the house after their evening at a movie and, instead of leaving, informed her that the time had come to have a chat.

'I'll wait for you in the kitchen.' He had given her two weeks, and two weeks was plenty long enough. He wasn't used to hanging around waiting for someone else to make their mind up—especially when the matter in question should really have required next to no deliberation—but Raoul had taken a couple of steps back.

Although she was attracted to him, she had refused to become his mistress, and he didn't think that she had done so because she had been holding out for a bigger prize. The plain and simple truth was that she was no longer his number one adoring fan. He had hurt her deeply five years ago, and that combined with the hardship of being a single mother without much money to throw around had toughened her.

Raoul knew that there was no way he could push her into marrying him. He was forced to acknowledge that in this one area, he had no control. But biding his time had driven him round the bend—especially when he kept remembering how easy and straightforward things had been between them before.

She returned to the kitchen forty-five minutes later. She had changed into a pair of loose, faded jeans that sat well below her waist and a tee shirt that rode up, exposing her flat belly, when she stretched into one of the cupboards to get two mugs for coffee.

'So…' she said brightly, once they were both at the kitchen table with mugs of coffee in front of them. This kitchen, unlike the tiny one in the rented house, was big enough to contain a six-seater table. He sat at one end, and Sarah deliberately took the seat at the opposite end. 'You wanted to talk to me? I know I've said this a thousand times, but the house is perfect. I can't tell you what a difference it makes, and there's so much to do around here. I've already found a morning playgroup we can go to! It's just so leafy and quiet.'

Raoul watched her and listened in silence, waiting until she had rambled on for a while longer before coming to a halting stop.

'Two weeks ago I asked you a question.'

Having spent the entire two weeks thinking of nothing else *but* that question he had posed, Sarah now looked at him blankly—and received an impatient click of his tongue in response.

'I'm not going to hang around for ever waiting for you to give me an answer, Sarah. I've waited so that you have had time to settle into the house. You've settled. So tell me—what's the answer going to be?'

'I…I don't know…'

'Not good enough.' Raoul contained his mounting anger with difficulty.

'Can I have a few more days to think about it?' Sarah licked her lips nervously. 'Marriage is such a big step,' she muttered, by way of extra explanation.

'Likewise having a child.'

'Yes...but...'

'Are we going to go down the same monotonous route of self-sacrifice?'

'No!' Sarah cried, stung by his bored tone of voice.

'Then what's your answer to be?' He looked at her fraught face and thought that he might have been sentencing her to life in prison—and yet five years ago she would have exploded with joy at such a proposal. 'If you say no then I *walk away*, Sarah.'

'Walk away? What do you mean walk away? Are you saying that you're going to abandon Oliver if I don't agree to marry you?'

'Oh, for God's sake! When are you going to stop seeing me as a monster? I will never abandon my own flesh and blood!'

'I'm sorry. I know you wouldn't,' Sarah said, ashamed, because sudden panic had driven her to say the first stupid thing in her head. 'So what *are* you saying?'

'I'll find someone else,' Raoul told her bluntly, 'and we will get in touch with lawyers, who will draw up papers regarding settlement and visiting rights. You will see me only when essential, and only ever when it is to do with Oliver. Naturally I will have no control over who you see, don't see, or eventually become seriously involved with, and the same would apply to me. Am I spelling things out loud and clear for you?'

The colour had drained from Sarah's face. Presented with such a succinct action-and-consequence train of events, she felt her wildly scattered thoughts finally crystallise into one shocking truth. She would lose him for ever. He really would meet another woman and the question of love wouldn't even have to arise. He would regulate his love-life because he would have to, and she would be left on the outside...watching.

She wouldn't conveniently stop loving him just because he'd removed himself from her.

He might not love her, but he would be a brilliant father—and she would be spared the misery of *just not having him around*. Who had ever said that you could have it all?

She was sadly aware that she would settle for crumbs. She wanted to ask him what would happen when he got bored with her. Would he begin to conduct a discreet outside life? It was a question to which she didn't want an answer.

She had thought that any marriage without love would be doomed to failure. She had never imagined herself walking down the aisle knowing that the guy by her side was only there because he had found himself in the unenviable position of having no choice. Duty and responsibility were two wonderful things, but she hadn't ever seen them as sufficient. Raoul, on the other hand, had moved faster towards the inevitable—and she had to catch up now, because the stark alternative was even more unpalatable and she hated herself for her weakness.

'I'll marry you,' she agreed, daring to steal a look at his face.

Raoul smiled, and realised that he had been panicked at the thought that she might turn him down. He *never* panicked! Even when he had been confronted with a child he hadn't known existed, when he had realised that his life was about to be changed irrevocably for ever, he hadn't panicked. He had assessed the situation and dealt with it. But watching her, eyes half closed, he had been aware of a weird, suffocating feeling—as if he had stepped off the edge of a precipice in the hope that there would be a trampoline waiting underneath to break his fall.

He stood up, thinking it wise to cover the basics and

then leave—before she could revert to her previous stance, reconsider his offer and tell him that it was off, after all. She could be bewilderingly inconsistent.

'I'm thinking soon,' he said, feeling on a strange high. 'As soon as it can be arranged, to be perfectly honest. I'll start working on that straight away. Something small…' He paused to look at her pinkened cheeks. Her hair was tumbling over her shoulders and he wanted nothing more than to tangle his fingers into it and pull her towards him.

'Although you are the one who factored marriage into your dreams of the future,' he murmured drily, 'so it's up to you what sort of affair you want. You can have a thousand people and St Paul's Cathedral if you like…'

Sarah opened her mouth to tell him that anything would do, because it wouldn't really be a *true* marriage, would it? Yes, they had known each other once. Yes, they had been lovers, and she had been crazy enough to think that he had loved her as much as she had loved him, even if he had never said so. But he hadn't intended marrying her then, or even setting eyes on her again once he had left the country. He hadn't wanted her then and he didn't want her now, but marriage, for him, was the only way he could be a permanent and daily feature in his son's life. Because she had rejected the first offer on the table, which had been to be his mistress.

Approaching the whole concept of their union in the way he might a business arrangement, maybe he had thought that living together would be the lesser of two evils. They would have learned to compromise without the necessity of having to take that final, psychologically big step and commit to a bond sealed in the eyes of the law. Or maybe he had just thought that if what they had fizzled out it would just be a whole lot easier to part company if they had merely been living together. And by then

he would have had a much stronger foothold in the door—
might even have been able to fight for custody if he'd chosen to.

Racked with a hornets' nest of anxieties, she still knew
that it would be stupid to open up a debate on the worth
of a marriage that had yet to happen. What would that get
her? Certainly not the words she wanted to hear.

'Something small,' she said faintly.

'And traditional,' Raoul agreed. 'I expect you would
like that, and so would your parents. I remember you saying something about a bracelet that your grandmother had
given your mother, which she had kept to be passed on to
you when you got married? You laughed and said that it
wasn't exactly the most expensive trousseau in the world,
but that it meant a lot to both of you.'

'Isn't there *anything* that you've forgotten?' Sarah asked
in a tetchy voice. All her dreams and hopes were being
agonisingly brought back home to her on a painful tide of
self-pity. She thought that she might actually have been
hinting to him at the time when she had said that. 'Anyway,
I think she lost that bracelet.'

'She *lost* it?'

'Gardening. She took it off, to…er…dig, and it must
have got all mixed up with soil and leaves…' Sarah
shrugged in a suitably vague and rueful manner. 'So, no
bracelet to pass on,' she finished mournfully.

'That's a shame.'

'Isn't it?' She suddenly frowned. 'So…we get married
and live here…'

'In this house, yes.'

'And what will you do with your apartment?'

Raoul shrugged. His apartment no longer seemed to
have any appeal. The cool, modern soullessness of the
décor, the striking artwork that had been given the nod by

him but bought as an investment, the expensive and largely unused gadgets in the kitchen, the imposing plasma screen television in the den—all of it now seemed to belong to a person with whom he could no longer identify.

'I'll keep it, I expect. I don't need to sell it or rent it, after all.'

'Keep it for what?'

'What does it matter?'

'It doesn't. I was just curious.'

They were going to be married. It wouldn't be a marriage made in heaven, and Sarah knew that her own suspicious nature would torpedo any hope of it being successful. As soon as Raoul had told her that he would keep the apartment she had foreseen an unpalatable explanation. An empty apartment would be very handy should he ever decide to stray.

She tried her utmost to kill any further development on that train of thought. 'I suppose you have some sort of sentimental attachment to it?' she prompted.

Raoul shook his head. 'Absolutely none. Yes, it was the place I bought when I'd made my first few million, but believe it or not it's been irritating me lately. I think I've become accustomed to a little more chaos.' He grinned, very relaxed now that he could see a definite way forward and liked what he saw.

Suddenly the reality of Raoul actually *living* with them made her giddy with apprehension. Would there be parameters to their marriage? It wouldn't be a *normal* one, so of course there must be, but was this something she should talk about now? Were there things she should be getting straight before she entered into this binding contract?

'Er…we should really talk about…you know…'

He paused and looked down at her. She had one small hand resting on his arm.

'What your expectations are…' Sarah said stoutly.

Raoul's brows knitted into a frown. 'You want a list?'

'Obviously not *in writing*. That would be silly. But this isn't a simple situation…'

'It's as simple or as difficult as we choose to make it, Sarah.'

'I don't think it's as easy as that, Raoul. I'm just trying to be sensible and practical. I mean, for starters, I expect you'd like to draw up some kind of pre-nup document?' That had only just occurred to her on the spur of the moment—as had the notion that laying down guidelines might confer upon her some sort of protection, at least psychologically. The mind was capable of anything, and maybe—just maybe—she could train hers to operate on a less emotional level. At least to outward appearances. Besides, he would be mightily relieved. Although, looking at his veiled expression now, it was hard to tell.

'Is that what you want?' Raoul asked tonelessly—which had the instant effect of making Sarah feel truly horrible for having raised the subject in the first place.

In turn that made her angry, because why should *he* be the only one capable of viewing this marriage with impartial detachment? What was so wrong if she tried as well? He didn't know what her driving motivation for doing so was because he wasn't in love with her, but why should that matter? He didn't have the monopoly on good sense, which was his pithy reason for their marriage in the first place!

'It might be a good idea,' she told him, in the gentle voice of someone committed to being absolutely fair. 'We don't want to get in a muddle over finances later on down the road. And also…' She paused fractionally, giving him an opportunity for encouragement which failed to materialize. 'I think we should both acknowledge that the most we can strive for is a really good, solid friendship…'

Her heart constricted as she said that, but she knew that she needed to bury all signs of her love. On the one hand, if he knew how she really felt about him the equality of their relationship would be severely compromised. On the other—and this would be almost worse—he would pity her. He might even choose to remind her that at no point, *ever*, had he led her to believe that lust should be confused with something else.

It would be a sympathetic let-down, during which he might even produce a hankie, all the better to mop up her overflowing tears. She would never live down the humiliation. In short, she would become a guilty burden which he would consider himself condemned to bear for the rest of his life. Whereas if she feigned efficiency she could at least avert that potential disaster waiting in the wings.

That thought gave her sufficient impetus to maintain her brisk, cheery façade and battle on through his continuing unreadable silence.

'If you think that we're embarking on a sexless marriage…' Raoul growled, increasingly outraged by everything she said, and critical of her infuriating practicality— although he really shouldn't have been, considering it was a character trait he firmly believed in.

Sarah held up one hand to stop him in mid-flow. This would be her trump card—if it could be called such.

'That's not what I'm saying…' Released from at least *that* particular burden—of just not knowing what to do with this overpowering attraction she felt for him—Sarah felt a whoosh of light-headed relief race through her. 'We won't take the one big thing between us away…'

The hand on his arm softened into a caress, moved to rest against his hard chest, and she stepped closer into him, arching up to him, glad that she no longer had to try and fight the sizzling attraction between them.

Raoul caught her hand and held it as he stared down at her upturned face,

'So tell me,' he drawled softly, 'why didn't you just agree to be my lover? It amounts to the same thing now, doesn't it?'

'Except,' Sarah told him with heartfelt honesty, 'maybe I just didn't like the notion of being your mistress until I went past my sell-by date. Maybe that's something I've only just realised.' She hesitated. 'Do you...do you want to reconsider your proposal?'

'Oh, no...' Raoul told her with a slow, slashing smile, 'this is exactly what I want...'

CHAPTER EIGHT

A WEEK and a half later and Raoul wasn't sure that he had got quite what he had wanted—although he was hard pressed to put a finger on the reason *why*.

Sarah's histrionics were over. She no longer vacillated between wanting him and turning him away. She had stopped agonising about the rights and wrongs of their sleeping together.

In fact, on the surface, everything appeared to be going to plan. He had moved in precisely one week previously. For one day the house had been awash with a variety of people, doing everything it took to instal the fastest possible broadband connection and set up all the various technologies so that he could function from the cosy library, which had been converted into a study complete with desk, printer, television screens to monitor the stock markets around the world and two independent telephone lines. Through the window he could look out at the perfectly landscaped garden, with its twin apple trees at the bottom. It was a far more inspiring view than the one he had had from his apartment, and he discovered that he liked it.

The wedding would be taking place in a month's time.

'I don't really care when it happens,' Sarah had told him with a casual shrug, 'but Mum's set her heart on something more than a quick register affair, and I don't like to disappoint her.'

Thinking about it, that attitude seemed to character-ise the intangible change Raoul had uneasily noticed ever since she had accepted his marriage proposal.

True to her word, they were now lovers, and between the sheets everything was as it should be. Better. He touched her and she responded with fierce, uninhibited urgency. She was meltingly, erotically willing. With the lights turned off and the moonlight dipping into the room through a chink in the curtains they made love with the hunger of true sexual passion.

Just thinking about it was enough to make Raoul half close his eyes and stiffen at the remembered pleasure.

But outside the bedroom she was amicable but re-strained. He came through the front door by seven every evening, which was a considerable sacrifice for him, be-cause he was a man accustomed to working until at least eight-thirty most days. Yes, she asked him how his day had been. Yes, she would have cooked something, and sure she had a smile on her face as she watched him go outside with Oliver for a few minutes, push him on the swing, then return to play some suitably childish game until his son's bedtime beckoned. But it was almost as though she had manufactured an invisible screen around herself.

'Right. Have you got everything?' They were about to set off for Devon for their postponed visit to her parents. There was more luggage for this two-night stay than he would have taken for a three-week long-haul vacation. Favourite toys had had to be packed, including the over-sized remote controlled car which had been his first and much ignored present for Oliver, but which had risen up the popularity ladder as the weeks had gone by. Drinks had had to be packed, because four-year-olds, he'd been assured, had little concept of timing when it came to long car journeys. Several CDs of stories and sing-a-long nursery rhymes had been bought in advance, and Sarah had drily informed him that he had no choice when it came to listening to them.

She had made a checklist, and now she recited things from it with a little frown.

'Is it always this much of a production when you go to visit your parents?' he asked, when they were finally tucked into his Range Rover and heading away from the house.

'This is a walk in the park,' Sarah told him, staring out of the window and watching the outskirts of London fly past. 'In the past I've had to take the train, and you can't believe what a battle *that's* been with endless luggage and a small child in tow.' She looked round to make sure that Oliver was comfortable, and not fiddling with his car seat as he was wont to do, and then stared out of the window.

Weirdly, she always felt worse when they were trapped in the confines of a car together. Something about not having any escape route handy, she supposed. With no door through which she could conveniently exit, she was forced to confront her own weakness. Her only salvation was that she was trying very hard, and hopefully succeeding, to instil boundaries without having to lay it on with a trowel.

She was friendly with him, even though under the façade her heart felt squeezed by the distance she knew she had to create. She couldn't afford to throw herself heart and soul into what they had, because she knew that if she did she would quickly start believing that their marriage was real in every sense of the word—and then what protection would she have when the time came and his attention began to stray? He didn't love her, so there would be no buffer against his boredom when their antics in the bedroom ran out of steam.

Daily she told herself that it was therefore important to get a solid friendship in place, because that would be the glue to hold things together. But at the back of her mind she toyed with the thought that friendship might prove more than just glue. Maybe, just maybe, he would become reliant on a relationship forged on the bedrock of circumstance. He had proposed marriage as a solution, and how much more he would respect her if she treated it in the same calm, sensible, practical way he did.

She was determined to starve her obsession with him and get a grip on emotions that would freewheel crazily given half a chance.

The only time she really felt liberated was when they were making love. Then, when he couldn't see the expression on her face, she was free to look at him with all the love in her heart. Once she had woken up to go to the bathroom in the early hours of the morning, and she had taken the opportunity, on returning to bed, to stare. In sleep, the harsh, proud angles of his beautiful face were softened, and what she'd seen wasn't a person who had the power to damage, but just her husband, the father of her child. She could almost have pretended that everything was perfect…

As they edged out of London, heading towards Devon along the scenic route rather than the motorway, Oliver became increasingly excited at the sight of fields and cows and sheep, and then at his favourite game of counting cars according to their colour, in which her participation was demanded.

After an hour and a half his energy was spent, and he fell asleep with the abruptness of a child, still clutching the glossy cardboard book which she had bought earlier in the week to occupy him on the journey down.

'I expect you're a bit nervous about meeting my parents…' Sarah reluctantly embarked on conversation rather than deal with the silence, even though Raoul seemed perfectly content.

Raoul gritted his teeth at the ever-bland tone of voice which she had taken to using when the two of them conversed.

'Should I be?'

'I would be if I were in your shoes.' Sarah's eyes slid over to absorb the hard, perfect lines of his profile, and then she found it was a task to drag them away.

'And that would be because…?'

'I'm not sure what they'll be expecting,' she told him honestly. 'I haven't exactly blown your trumpet in the past. In fact when I found out that I was pregnant… Well, put it this way: wherever in world you might have been, you ears would have been burning.'

'I'm sure that will be history now that I'm around and taking responsibility for the situation.'

'But they'll still remember all the things I said about you, Raoul. I could have held everything back, but finding out that I was pregnant was the last straw. I was hormonal, emotional, and a complete mess. I got a lot off my chest, and I doubt my mother, particularly, will have forgotten all of it.'

'Then I'll have to take my chances. But thank you for being concerned on my behalf. I'm touched.' His mouth curved into a sardonic smile. 'I didn't think you had it in you.'

'There's no need to be sarcastic,' Sarah said uncomfortably.

'No? Well, I hadn't intended on having this conversation, but seeing that you're up for a bit of honesty… I go to bed with a hot-blooded, giving, generous lover, and wake up every morning with a stranger. You'll have to excuse me for my assumption that you wouldn't be unduly bothered one way or another what your parents' reaction to me is.'

Hot-blooded, giving, generous... If only he knew that those words applied to her in bed and out of it, by night and by day.

'I hardly think that you can call me a *stranger*,' Sarah protested on a high, shaky laugh. 'Strangers don't... don't...'

'Make love for hours? Touch each other everywhere? Experiment in ways that would make most people blush? No need to worry, Sarah. We're not exactly shouting, and Oliver's fast asleep. I can see him in my rearview mirror.'

Sarah could feel her cheeks burning from his deliberately evocative language.

What do you want? she wanted to yell at him. Did he want her to be the adoring, subservient wife-in-waiting, so that he could lap up her adulation safe in the knowledge that she had been well and truly trapped? When he certainly didn't adore *her*?

'Well, aren't you pleased that you were right?' she said gruffly. 'I can't deny that I find you very attractive. I always have.'

'Call me crazy, but I can smell a *but* advancing on the horizon...'

'There *is* no but,' Sarah told him, thinking on her feet. 'And I really don't know what you mean when you accuse me of being a stranger. Don't we share all our dinners together now that we're living under the same roof?'

'Yes, and your increasing confidence in the kitchen continues to astound me. What I'm less enthusiastic about is the Stepford Wife-to-be routine. You say the right things, you smile when you're supposed to, and you dutifully ask me interested questions about my working day... What's happened to the outspoken, dramatic woman who existed two weeks ago?'

'Look, as you said yourself, what we're doing is the right thing and the sensible thing. I've agreed to marry you and I don't see the point in my carrying on arguing with you...'

'I'm a firm believer that sometimes it's healthy to argue.'

'I'm tired of arguing, and it doesn't get anyone anywhere. Besides, there's nothing to argue about. You haven't let us down once. I'm surprised no one's sent men in white coats to take you away because they think you've lost the plot—leaving work so early every evening and getting in so late every morning.'

'I'd call it adjusting my body clock to match the rest of the working population.'

'And how long is *that* going to last?' She heard herself snipe with dismay, but there was no reaction from him.

After a while, he said quietly, 'If I had a crystal ball, I would be able to tell you that.'

Sarah bit down on the tears she could feel welling up. There was a lot to be said for honesty, but since when was honesty *always* the best policy?

'Maybe I'm leaving work earlier than I ever have because I have something to leave for...'

Oliver. Paternal responsibility had finally succeeded in doing what no woman ever had or ever would. Sarah diplomatically shied away from dragging that thorny issue out into the open, because she knew that it would lead to one of those arguments which she was so intent on avoiding. Instead she remained tactfully silent for a couple of minutes.

'That's true,' she said noncommittally. 'I should tell

you, though, before we meet my mum and dad, that they'll probably guess the reasons behind our sudden decision to get married...'

'What have you told them?' Raoul asked sharply.

'Nothing...really.'

'And what does *nothing...really* mean, Sarah?'

'I may have mentioned that you and I are dealing with the situation like adults, and that we've both reached the conclusion that for Oliver's sake the best thing we can do is get married. I explained how important it was for you to have full rights to your son, and that you didn't care for the thought of someone else coming along and putting your nose out of joint...'

'That should fill them with undiluted joy,' Raoul said with biting sarcasm. 'Their one and only daughter, walking down the aisle to satisfy *my* selfish desire to have complete access to my son. If your mother hadn't lost that heirloom bracelet she'd been hoping to pass on to you she probably would have gone out into the garden, dug a hole and buried it just to save herself the hypocrisy of a gesture for a meaningless marriage.'

'It's not a *meaningless marriage.*'

Sarah knew she had overstepped the self-assertive line. It was one thing being friendly but distant. It was another to admit to him that she was spreading the word that their marriage was a sham. Not that she had. She hadn't had the heart to mention a word of it to her parents. As far as she knew they thought that her one true love had returned and the ring soon to be on her finger was proof enough of happy endings. They had conveniently forgotten the whole dumping saga.

Raoul didn't trust himself to speak.

An awkward silence thickened between them until

Sarah blurted out nervously, 'In fact, as marriages go, it makes more sense than most.'

More uncomfortable silence.

She subsided limply. 'I'm just saying that there's no need to pretend anything when we get to my parents.'

'I'm not following you.' Raoul's voice was curt, and for a brief moment Sarah was bitterly regretful that she had upset the apple cart—even if the apple cart *had* been a little wobbly to start with.

She was spared the need for an answer by the sound of little noises from the back seat as Oliver began to stir. He needed the toilet. Could they hurry? Their uncomfortable conversation was replaced by a hang-on-for-dear-life panic drive to find the nearest pub, so that they could avail themselves of the toilets and buy some refreshments by way of compensation.

Oliver, now fully revived after his nap, was ready to take up where he had left off—with the addition of one of the nursery rhyme tapes. He proceeded to kick his feet to the music in the back, protesting vehemently every time a move was made to replace it with something more soothing.

He was the perfect safeguard against any further foolhardy conversations, but as the fast car covered the distance, only getting trapped in traffic once along the way, Sarah replayed their conversation in her head over and over again.

She wondered whether she really *should* have warned her parents about the reality of the situation. She questioned why she had felt so invigorated when they had been arguing. She raged hopelessly against the horrible truth— which was that maintaining a friendly front was like drinking poison on a daily basis. She asked herself whether she had done the right thing in accepting his marriage proposal, and then berated herself for acknowledging that she had because she couldn't trust herself ever to be able to deal with the sight of him with another woman.

But what if he *did* stray from the straight and narrow? What if he found marriage too restrictive, even with Oliver there to keep his eyes firmly on the end purpose? She had attempted to give that very real possibility house room in her head, but however many times she tried to pretend to herself that she was civilised enough to handle it, she just couldn't bring herself to square up to the thought. Should she add a few more ground rules to something that was getting more and more unwieldy and complex by the second?

She nearly groaned aloud in frustration.

'I think I'm getting a headache,' she said tightly, running her fingers over her eyes.

Raoul flicked a glance in her direction. 'I sympathise. I'm finding that "The Wheels on the Bus" can have that effect when played at full volume repeatedly.'

Sarah relaxed enough to flash him a soft sideways smile. She was relieved that the atmosphere between them was normal once again. It was funny, but although her aim was to keep him at a distance the second she felt him really stepping away from her she panicked.

'We'll be there before the headache gets round to developing.'

Sure enough, twenty minutes later she began to recognise some of the towns they passed through. Oliver began a running commentary on various places of interest to him, including a sweet shop of the old-fashioned variety which they drove slowly past, and Sarah found herself pointing out her own landmarks—places she remembered from when she was a teenager.

Raoul listened and made appropriate noises. He was

only mildly interested in the passing scenery. Small villages in far-off rural places did very little for him. If anything they were an unwelcome reminder of how insular people could be in the country—growing up as one of the children from the foster home in a town not dissimilar to several they had already driven through had been a sure-fire case of being sentenced without benefit of a jury.

Mostly, though, Raoul was trying to remain sanguine after her revelation that she had already prejudiced her parents against him.

His temper was distinctly frayed at the seams by the time he pulled up in front of a pleasant detached house on the outskirts of a picturesque town—the sort of town that he imagined Sarah would have found as dull as dishwater the older she became.

'Don't expect anything fancy,' she warned him, as the car slowed to a halt on the gravelled drive.

'After the build-up you've given your parents, believe me—I'm not expecting anything at all.'

Sarah flinched at the icy coldness in his voice.

'I did you a favour,' she whispered defensively, because she could think of no way of extricating herself from her lie. 'It saves you having to pretend.'

'There are times,' Raoul said, before launching himself out of the car, 'when I really wonder what the hell makes you tick, Sarah.'

He moved round to the boot, extracting their various cases, and slammed it shut—hard—just as Oliver, released from the restrictions of his car seat, flew up the drive towards the middle-aged couple now standing on their doorstep to throw himself at them. Sarah was following Oliver, arms wide open to receive their hugs.

Raoul took it all in through narrowed eyes as he began walking towards the house. Her father was stocky, his hair thinning, and her mother was an older version of Sarah, with the same flyaway hair caught in a loose bun, tendrils escaping all over the place just as her daughter's did, and wearing a long flowered skirt and a short-sleeved top with a thin pink cardigan. She was as slender as her husband was rotund, and she had Sarah's smile. Ready, warm, appealing.

So, he thought grimly, these were the people she had decided to disabuse. Two loving parents who had probably spent their entire lives waiting for the day their much loved only daughter would get married, settle down...only to hear that the getting married and settling down wasn't quite the kind they had had in mind.

Making his mind up, he walked towards them. The smile on his face betrayed nothing of what was going through his head.

'So nice to meet you...' He slung his arm over Sarah's shoulder and pulled her against him, feeling the tension in her body like a tangible electric current. Very deliberately, he moved his hand to caress the back of her neck under the tumble of fair hair. 'Sarah's told me so much about you both...' He looked down at her and pressed his thumb against the side of her neck, obliging her to look up at him. Her big green eyes were wary. 'Haven't you, sweetheart...?'

What was he playing at? Whatever it was, he was managing to blow a hole in her composure.

The gestures of affection hadn't stopped at the front door.

Yes, there had been moments of reprieve during the course of the afternoon, when Oliver had demanded attention and when she'd gone into the kitchen to help prepare the dinner with her mother, but the rest of the time...

On the sofa he was there next to her, his arm along the back, his fingers idly brushing her neck, while he played the perfect son-in-law-to-be by engaging her parents in all aspects of conversation which he knew would interest them.

She realised how much she had confided in him about her background, because now every scrap of received information had come home to roost. He quizzed them about her childhood. He produced anecdotes about things he remembered having been told like a magician pulling rabbits from a hat. He recalled something she had said in passing about her father always wanting to do something with bees, and much of their time, as they sat at the dinner table, was taken up with a discussion on the pros and cons of bee-keeping, about which he seemed to be indecently well informed.

Even if she *had* told her parents the truth about their relationship they would have been hard pressed to believe her based on Raoul's performance.

He engaged them on every level, and when she showed signs of taking a back seat he made sure to drag her right back into the conversation—usually by beginning his remark pointedly with the words, 'Do you remember, darling…?'

Every reminder brought back a fuzzy familiarity that further undermined her composure. He talked at length about the compound in Africa, and revealed what she had known from that random communication she had glimpsed ages ago—that he contributed a great deal to the compound. He listed all the improvements that had been made over time, and confided that he had actually employed someone to oversee the funding.

'Those were some of the most carefree months in my

entire life,' he admitted, and she knew that he was telling the absolute truth.

The complex, three-dimensional, utterly wonderful man she had fallen deeply in love with was well and truly out of the box in which she had tried, vainly, to shove him. Holding back the effect he had on her was like trying to shore up a dam with a toothpick.

The bedroom in which they had been put—her old bedroom newly revamped, but with all the mementoes of childhood still in evidence—did nothing to repair her frayed nerves.

She was as jumpy as a cat on a hot tin roof when, at a little after ten, they were shuffled off upstairs—because surely they must be exhausted after that long drive from London?

'And don't even *think* about getting up for Oliver,' her mother carolled as Sarah was leaving the kitchen. 'Your dad and I want to spend some time with him, so you just have yourselves a well-deserved lie-in! Lots planned for the weekend!'

Sarah crept upstairs to find Raoul already showered and waiting for her on the bed, where he was sprawled, hands folded under his head, wearing nothing but for a pair of dark boxer shorts. Instantly all thought left her head. Her body reacted the way it always did: liquefying and melting, and already anticipating the feel of his fingers on it.

But her emotions were all over the place, and she informed him that she was going to take a shower.

'I'll be waiting for you when you return,' Raoul told her, following her with his eyes as she disappeared into the adjoining shower room, which was small but perfectly adequate.

She reappeared twenty minutes later. He watched her

walk towards him, wearing nothing, and swiftly whipped the duvet over him—because a man could lose his mind at the sight of that glorious body, with its full, pouting breasts and smooth lines, and his mind was precisely what he needed at this very moment.

Sarah slid under the covers and turned towards him, covering his thigh with hers and splaying her fingers across his broad chest.

The shower had helped cool her down, but there was still a desperation in her as she slid further on top of him and felt the rock-hardness of his erection press against her. With a soft moan she parted her legs and moved sinuously against the shaft, her body aching and opening up for him. As the sensitised, swollen bud of her clitoris rasped against him she had to stop herself from groaning out loud.

Raoul shuddered, fighting the irresistible impulse to spin her onto her back and sate his frustration by driving into her.

'No,' he said unevenly.

Sarah wriggled on top of him. 'You don't mean that,' she breathed, panicked by that single word.

She dipped her head, covered his mouth with hers, felt him groan as he kissed her back. Hard. He flipped her onto her back and straddled her so that he could carry on kissing her.

Sarah arched away. Her breasts ached and tingled. She wanted the wetness of his mouth on her nipples, suckling them, driving her crazy. She desperately needed to feel his mouth licking and exploring between her legs, sending her to greater and greater heights until she needed him to thrust into her. She wanted the fragile balance she had forced onto their relationship restored, because without it she was all at sea, lost and struggling to find a foothold in stormy waters.

'*No*, Sarah! God!' Raoul sprang back from her, literally leapt off the bed and walked tensely towards the window, to stare outside until his body began to damn well do as it was told. 'Cover yourself up,' he told her harshly, because the distraction of her nudity was doing his head in.

Sarah squirmed until she was sitting up and drew her knees up, pulling the covers right the way to her chin while he continued to loom over her in the semi-darkness like a vengeful god.

She felt cheap and dirty, and the ramifications of how she had tackled her own wayward emotions slammed into her with the savagery of a clenched fist.

How could she ever have thought that she could separate herself? Peel away her emotions and leave intact the deep craving of her body to be satisfied under cover of darkness? She wasn't built like that. She was engulfed with a sudden sense of shame.

'This isn't working,' he told her with harsh condemnation.

'I don't know what you're talking about.'

'You know damn well what I'm talking about, Sarah!' He raked his fingers through his hair. He wanted to punch something.

'No, I don't! I thought today went really well! I mean, they like you…'

'Against all odds?' His mouth curled cynically.

'I didn't exactly *say* all those things I told you,' Sarah confessed in a small voice. 'I didn't really tell them about the state of our relationship. Of course they know how it ended between us five years ago, but I didn't tell them that we were only together now because of Oliver. I just couldn't face telling them the truth—at least not just yet…'

'Why are you only now coming clean on that score?'

'What difference does it make whether they know or

not? It's true, isn't it? One chance meeting,' she said bitterly, 'and both our lives changed for ever. What's that they say about the butterfly effect? Half an hour later and I would have finished cleaning that part of the office. Half an hour later and you would have left without even knowing that I was only metres away from you, in another part of the building…'

'I prefer not to dwell on pointless *what if?* scenarios.'

Sarah gazed down at her interlinked fingers. Raoul's reappearance in her life might have turned her world upside down, but for Oliver it had been nothing but the best possible outcome.

Her heart was beating so furiously inside her that she could scarcely breathe.

'That bracelet…'

Sarah looked up at him quickly, so aggressively dominant in the small bedroom. 'What about it?'

'Gold rope? With some kind of inscription on the outside? Your mother was wearing it. Looks like the gardening accident wasn't quite as terminal for the piece of jewellery as you imagined.'

'I…I… Maybe I was mistaken…'

'No,' Raoul told her coldly, 'maybe *I* was mistaken. I stupidly thought that you were willing to give this marriage a try, but you're not.'

His lack of anger was terrifying.

'I *am* giving it a try…'

'Really? Because you're sleeping with me?'

Sarah felt the slow boil of anger thread its way through her panic and confusion. Suddenly he was dismissive of the fact that they were sleeping together? What a noble guy! Anyone would have thought that making love was way down on his agenda, when it was the *only* thing he had placed any value on! The only thing he had *ever* placed any value on. How dared he stand there, like a headmaster in front of a disappointing and rebellious student, and preach to her that he wasn't satisfied?

'Weren't *you* the one who made such a great big deal about our *mutual attraction*? Our *sexual chemistry*?' she flung at him. 'Didn't you tell me that we had *unfinished business* and the only way we could possibly sort that out was by *jumping into bed together*? You have a very convenient memory when it comes to things you don't want to remember, Raoul!'

'Am I to be forever punished for being honest when we first reconnected, Sarah?'

'And am *I* to be punished for being honest now?' she returned just as quickly. '*You* made it clear what this marriage was going to be all about, didn't you?'

She hated the shard of hope inside her that still wanted to give him the chance to say something—to tell her that she was wrong, that it wasn't just about the fact that they had a child together.

His silence shattered her.

'I'm playing by *your* rules, Raoul, and I'm finding that they suit me just fine! In fact, I think you were right all along! Having sex and lots of it is really working wonders at getting you out of my system!'

She sensed his stillness and wanted to snatch the words back. But they were out in the open now, and she didn't know what to do with his continuing lack of response. She tried to recapture some of her anger but it was disappearing fast, leaving in its wake regret and dismay.

'So the sex is all that matters to you, I take it?'

'Yes, of—of course it is…' she stammered, bewildered by that remark. 'Just like it is to you. And responsibility too, of course… We're doing this for Oliver, because it's always better for a child to have both parents at home. We're being sensible...practical...'

'What story are you going to spin your mother when it comes to the heirloom bracelet?'

'Wha...?'

'I one hundred percent agree with you. Heirlooms to be handed over are for brides who actually *want* to be married.'

'You're not being fair, Raoul.'

'I'm being perfectly fair. I had actually thought we had more going for us than just physical attraction, but I was wrong.' He began walking towards the door.

Sarah watched him, frantically trying to process what he had said.

His voice was flat and composed and as cold as ice. 'I've got your message loud and clear, Sarah. It's always good to have the rules laid bare...'

CHAPTER NINE

SARAH lay frozen for a few minutes. Now that she wanted to recall everything he had said, so that she could sift through his words and get them to make sense, she found that her thoughts were in a jumble. Her heart was beating so furiously that she could scarcely catch her breath, and she had broken out in a film of perspiration. Her nakedness was a cruel reminder of how she had attempted to drown her misery in making love.

She could get herself worked up at the thought of Raoul using *her*, but only now was she appreciating that she had been equally guilty of using *him*—even if she had tried to tell herself that that couldn't possibly be the case, because wasn't sex all he had wanted from her from the very start?

Where had he gone?

His self-control was such a part and parcel of his personality that to see him stripped of it had shaken her to her core.

Or had she been mistaken? Was he just angry with her?

With a little cry of horror and shaky panic, Sarah flung the covers off her and scrambled around the room to fling on a pair of jogging bottoms and an old long-sleeved jumper—a left-over reminder of her teenage years, when she had been in the school hockey team.

The house was dark and quiet as she tiptoed into the

hall. Her parents had never been ones to burn the midnight oil, and they would be fast asleep in their bedroom at the far end of the corridor. Oliver's door was ajar, and she peeped in, through habit, to see him spread flat on the bed, having kicked off his quilt, a perfect X-shape, lightly snoring.

Just in case, though, she made sure not to turn on the lights, and so had to grope her way down the stairs until her eyes adjusted to the darkness and she could move more quickly, checking first the kitchen, then the sitting room.

It wasn't a big house, so there was a limited number of rooms she could check, and her anxiety increased with each empty room. After twenty minutes, she acknowledged that Raoul just wasn't in the house.

The temperature had dropped, and she hugged herself as she quietly let herself outside.

At least his car was still there. She hurried down to the road and glanced in both directions. Then, as she headed back towards the house, a faint noise caught her ears and she stealthily made her way to the back of the house.

The garden wasn't huge, but it backed onto fields so there was an illusion of size. To one side was her mother's vegetable plot, and towards the back, through a wooden archway that had been planted with creeping wisteria, was a gazebo. Her father's potting shed was right at the very bottom of the garden. Trees and shrubbery formed a thick perimeter.

Walking tentatively through the archway, she spotted Raoul immediately. He was in the gazebo, sitting with his head in his hands. She paused, and then walked quietly towards him, feeling him stiffen as she got nearer although he didn't look up at her.

'I'm really sorry,' she said helplessly.

Just when she thought that he wasn't going to reply at all, he looked up and shrugged his broad shoulders.

'What for? You were being honest.'

'I was just trying to be mature about the whole thing...'

Raoul flung his head back and stared up, away from her, and in the fierce, proud, stubborn set of his features she could see the little boy who'd grown up in a foster home, learning young how to hide himself away and build a fortress around his emotions.

She rested her hand on his forearm and felt him flinch, but he didn't pull it away and for some reason that seemed like a good sign.

'I gave you what you wanted,' Raoul said, his eyes still averted. 'At least I gave you what I thought you wanted. Don't you like the house?'

'I love it. You know I do. I've told you so a million times.'

'I've never done that before, you know. I've never let myself be personal when it comes to choosing things for another person, but I made it personal this time.'

'I know. You wanted Oliver to have the very best.'

'I very much doubt whether Oliver cares that there's a bottle-green Aga in the kitchen or not.'

Her heart skipped a beat. 'What are you trying to say?'

'Trying? I thought it had been obvious all along.' He glanced across at her and her breath caught painfully in her throat. 'I wanted you to marry me. Maybe at the beginning I didn't think it was necessary. Maybe at the beginning I was still clinging to the notion that I was a free, independent guy who happened to have found himself with a child. It took me a while to realise that the freedom I'd spent my life acquiring wasn't the kind of freedom I wanted after all.'

'I don't want to tie you down,' Sarah said quietly. 'I did.

Once. When we were out there. I thought you were just the most wonderful thing that had ever happened to me in my entire life. I built all sorts of castles in the air, and then when you dumped me my whole world fell to pieces.'

'I did what I thought was right at the time.'

'And I understand that now.'

'Do you? Really? I look at the way you are with your family, Sarah, and I see how badly you must have been affected by our break-up. You've grown up with security and a sense of your own place in the world. I grew up without either. I never allowed myself to get too close to anyone, and even when we met again, even after I found out that I was a father, I kept holding on to that. It was different with Oliver. Oliver is my own flesh and blood. But I still kept holding on to the belief that I wasn't to let anyone else in.'

'I know. Why do you think it's been so hard for me, Raoul? You've no idea what it's been like, standing on the side, wondering if the time will ever come when I can just get inside that wall you've spent a lifetime building around yourself.' She sighed and dragged her eyes away from him. The moon was almost full and it was a cloudless night. 'Look, you're not the only one who was afraid of getting hurt.'

Raoul opened his mouth to protest that he wasn't scared of anything, and then closed it.

'I know you hate the thought of anyone being able to hurt you.'

'God, it's ridiculous how well you seem to know me.'

There was wry, accepting amusement in his voice and, heartened by that, Sarah carried on.

'I spent so many years thinking of you as the guy who broke my heart that when we met again I *still* wanted to think of you as the guy who broke my heart. Yes, there was Oliver, and there was never any question that I would tell you about him and accept the consequences, but it was so important for me to keep you at a distance. And you kept looking at me and reminding me how much I still wanted you.'

'And yet you could never come right out and say it,' Raoul inserted gruffly. 'You were driving me crazy. I wanted to sleep with you and I knew you wanted to sleep with me, and you carried on fighting it. Every time I looked at you it was as though we had never been separated by five years. I didn't even know it at the time, but I let you into my life five years ago, Sarah, and you shut the door behind you and never left. I only thought you did.' He groped for her hand and linked her fingers through his. 'Asking you to marry me was a very big deal for me, Sarah.'

'You said that we were unfinished business…'

'If that's all you were to me I would never have asked you to marry me, because it wouldn't have bothered me if eventually you found another man.'

'You were worried about losing Oliver.'

'I think I knew, deep down, that that wouldn't happen. You would have allowed me all the access I wanted—and, let's face it, it's not as though children of parents who don't live together end up forgetting who the absent parent is. No, I asked you to marry me because I wanted you in my life and I couldn't envisage life without you in it.'

'Oh, Raoul.' Tears gathered in the corners of her eyes and she smiled at him, a smile of pure joy.

'I love you, Sarah. That's why I asked you to marry me. Like a fool, I'm only now admitting it to myself. I loved you five years ago and I never stopped. I love you and want you and need you, and when you retreated into that shell of yours and only came out at night when we were making love, it was as though the bottom of my world had dropped out.'

Sarah flung her arms around him, almost sending them both toppling off the narrow seat, and buried her head in the crook of neck.

'Are you telling me that you love me too?'

She heard the broken quality of his voice and knew that underneath the self-assurance there was still uncertainty– a legacy that he hadn't yet left behind.

'Of *course* I love you, Raoul!' She kissed his cheeks, his eyes, and her hands fluttered across his harshly beautiful face until he captured them and kissed the tips of each of her fingers. 'I was so scared of getting hurt all over again,' she admitted, with a catch in her voice. 'I thought I'd be able to handle our relationship, *us*, without getting involved. I mean, I was so shocked when I saw you again. But I told myself that I'd grown up and learnt lessons from the way things had turned out between us. I told myself that I was free of whatever influence you had over me...'

She thought back to those many weeks when he had infiltrated her life and shown her flimsy notions up for the nonsense they had been from the very beginning.

She lay back against him and stared up at the bright constellations. 'When Oliver met you and the two of you didn't...um...'

'Exactly hit it off?' It seemed like a very distant memory now.

'Yes... Well, I realised that the two of you would have to learn to interact, and I knew that the only way that would happen would be if I intervened. I just didn't take into account how devastating it would be to have you back in my life, virtually full-time... We were both older...somehow it felt like I'd started seeing the real you...and I fell in love with you all over again.'

'Was that why you broke my heart by pushing me away?'

'Stop teasing. I didn't really break your heart...'

'You did. Into a thousand pieces. I came here intending to give you everything. I wasn't going to let you get away with being my woman by night and a person I barely recognised by day.'

'And you thought I'd rejected you...'

'Somehow just wanting me for my body didn't work.' He laughed with incredulity. 'I can't believe I've just said that.'

'Of course,' Sarah breathed, in a lingering, seductive voice, 'wanting you for your body isn't *such* a terrible thing...especially now that you know that I want you for so much more...'

They were married a month later, at the little village church. It was a quiet affair, with friends and family mingling easily and getting to know one another, and Sarah had never felt happier than when Raoul slipped that ring on her finger and whispered how much he loved her.

And then her parents had Oliver for ten days while they had a blissful honeymoon in Kenya. For their last three days they went back to the compound in Mozambique where they had first met, so that they could both see the changes that had taken place over the five years. And there were many changes, thanks to Raoul's generous contributions over the years, although the house with all the steps, which they had shared along with the other gap year students, was still there, and a moving reminder of where it had all begun.

Even the log was still there—the very same log she had sat on, filled with misery and despair. It had survived the punishing weather, and she wondered who else had sat on it and thought about their loved ones.

The new batch of students working there seemed so young that it made her laugh.

They finally returned to London, and the very first thing Raoul said, on walking through the front door, was that they needed a house in the country.

'I never thought I'd step outside London again,' he confessed as they lay in bed on their first night back. 'But I'm beginning to think that there's something quite appealing about all that open space…'

He gently smoothed her hair back from her face, and she smiled at him with such tenderness and love that he felt, once again, that feeling of safety and a sense of completion.

'We could go there on weekends…somewhere in Devon…it's not that far…'

'Yes,' Sarah replied seriously, 'that might not be a bad idea. I mean, it would be great to see more of Mum and Dad—especially now that you've managed to convince Dad that he should take up the bee-keeping thing, with lots of help from you—and the children would like it…'

'Already planning an extension to our family?' Raoul laughed softly, and slipped his hand underneath her lacy top.

They had made love less than an hour ago, but just the feel of her swollen nipple between his fingers was sufficient to rouse him to an instant erection. He pushed the top up, licked the valley between her breasts, which was still salty and damp with perspiration, and settled himself to suckle on the sweet pink crests.

'I thought we were talking,' Sarah laughed.

'Fire away. I'm all ears.'

'I can't talk…when…' She gave up, arching her body to greet his eager mouth as he sucked and teased her breasts, then moved lower down to torment the little bud already swollen in anticipation.

The flicking of his tongue stifled all hope of conversation, and it was a long time before she whispered drowsily, 'Not so much *planning* an extension to our family as thinking there might be one arriving in the next few months or so…'

Raoul propped himself up and looked at her with urgent interest.

'You're pregnant?'

'I was going to tell you as soon as I did a test—but, yes, I think I am. I recognise all the signs…'

And she *was* pregnant.

She had almost stopped believing in fairytales, but now she had to revise that opinion—because whoever said that fairytales *didn't* come true…?

* * * * *

THE NANNY'S
SECRET

ELIZABETH LANE

For Tiffany

Elizabeth Lane has lived and travelled in many parts of the world, including Europe, Latin America and the Far East, but her heart remains in the American West, where she was born and raised. Her idea of heaven is hiking a mountain trail on a clear autumn day. She also enjoys music, animals and dancing. You can learn more about Elizabeth by visiting her website, www.elizabethlaneauthor.com.

One

Dutchman's Creek, Colorado

> *HELP WANTED*
> *Live-in nanny for newborn. Wolf Ridge area. Mature.*
> *Discreet. Experience preferred.*
> *Start immediately. Email résumé and references to*
> *wr@dcsentinel.com*

Wyatt Richardson glared at the stack of résumés on the borrowed desk. So far he'd interviewed three teenagers, a Guatemalan woman who barely spoke English, a harried mom with her own two-year-old and a grandmotherly type who confessed she got heart palpitations at high altitudes. His need for a qualified nanny bordered on desperation. But so far not one of the applicants was right for the job.

At least none of them had seemed to recognize him in his faded baseball cap. But that didn't solve his problem.

Maybe he should have gone through an agency instead of placing that blind ad through *The Dutchman's Creek*

Sentinel. But agencies asked questions, and this was a personal matter, demanding privacy. Not even his staff at the resort knew that his sixteen-year-old daughter, Chloe, had shown up on his doorstep almost nine months pregnant—or that she'd just given birth to a baby boy at the local hospital.

With a weary sigh he scanned the final résumé. Leigh Foster, 26. At least her age was in the ballpark he'd wanted to see. But the journalism degree from the University of Colorado wouldn't be much help. And her experience handling children was limited to some babysitting in high school. Glancing down the page he noticed she'd edited a defunct travel magazine and was currently working part-time for the local paper. He'd bet she was scrambling for money. Why else would an educated woman apply for this job?

Never mind. Just get it over with. He buzzed the receptionist, a signal to send in the next applicant.

High heels clicked down the tiled hallway, their cadence brisk and confident. An instant later the door of the small interview room opened. Wyatt's gaze took her in at a glance—willowy figure, simple navy blue suit, dark chestnut hair worn in a sleek pageboy. An Anne Hathaway type. He liked what he saw—liked it a lot. Unfortunately he was looking for a nanny, not a date.

"Mr. Richardson." Her long legs flashed as she strode toward the desk, hand extended. Her use of his name put Wyatt on instant alert. She worked for the *Sentinel* and would have known who placed the ad, he reminded himself. But the woman was a journalist. Did she really need a job or was she scoping out some juicy gossip for a story?

Either way, his first priority had to be protecting Chloe.

Rising, he accepted her proffered handshake. Her fingers felt the way she looked—slim and strong but surprisingly warm. Her tailored jacket had fallen open to reveal a coppery silk blouse. The fabric clung to her figure enticingly.

Yanking his gaze back to her face, Wyatt nodded toward the straight-backed chair opposite the desk. She settled onto the edge, one shapely knee crossed over the other in her narrow little skirt.

Sitting again, he perused her résumé, giving him a reason to take his eyes off her. "Tell me, Miss Foster. You appear well qualified for work in your own field. Why would you want a job as a nanny?"

Her lush mouth twitched in a sardonic smile. "I may be qualified, but times are tough. Right now I'm working twenty hours a week and camping out in my mother's guest room. She sells real estate, so she's struggling, too—and she has my younger brother to support. I'd like to contribute instead of feeling like a burden."

"So it's all about money."

"No!" She stared down at her hands. When she looked up again he noticed her eyes for the first time. Framed by thick, black lashes, they were the color of aged whiskey with intriguing flecks of gold.

"There are many factors involved. Most of my friends have children." The words sounded rehearsed. "I've been thinking that down the road a few years from now, if I don't get married, I might try adoption, or even have a child by a donor. Meanwhile, I'd love the experience of caring for a little baby. Of course I can't promise to stay for a long time...." Her husky voice trailed into a breath. "If you're still interested, could you tell me more about the job? Otherwise, I'll just leave now."

She clasped her hands on her knees, looking so vulnerable that Wyatt almost melted. He was interested all right—interested in getting to know this woman better. But he couldn't do or say anything that might make her hesitate to take the job. He needed a nanny for Chloe's baby, and right now Leigh Foster was his only option.

On the other hand, he had to make sure she wasn't out to exploit the situation.

Clearing his throat, he reached for the briefcase he'd left under the desk. "I'll need to run a background check, of course," he said, lifting out a manila folder. "But before we pursue this any further, would you be willing to sign a confidentiality agreement?"

Her eyes widened. "Of course. But why—?"

"You're a journalist." He slid a single page across the desktop. "And even if you weren't I'd demand your signature on this document. Protecting the privacy of my family is incredibly important to me. You must agree that whether you take the job or not, nothing you see or hear will be carried away—starting right now. You're not to publish it or share gossip with anyone, not even your own mother. Do I make myself clear?"

She leaned forward to scan the page—a boilerplate document outlining the legal consequences of sharing information in any form. The open neck of her blouse gave him a tantalizing glimpse of creamy flesh and black lace before he tore his eyes away. If he wanted her to take the job, it wouldn't do to be caught ogling her cleavage or any other delicious part of her. Especially since she'd be sharing his home.

"Any questions?" he asked her.

She straightened, impaling him with her stunning eyes. "Just one, Mr. Richardson. Could you spare me a pen?"

Leigh scrawled her name along the blank line at the bottom of the page. Maybe if she did it fast enough, he wouldn't notice that her hand was shaking.

The confidentiality agreement was no problem. Even without that piece of paper there was no way she'd reveal what she hoped to learn. But that didn't ease her nervous jitters. If Wyatt Richardson knew why she was really here, she'd be up to her ears in you-know-what.

The truth was she knew a lot more about the man than she was letting on. Even under that silly baseball cap she'd have recognized the local celebrity who'd put Dutchman's Creek on the map. In his younger days he'd been a daredevil downhill skier, winning several Olympic medals and enough product endorsements to make him rich. Coming home to Colorado he'd bought Wolf Ridge, a run-down resort that was little more than a hangout for local ski bums. Over the past fifteen years he'd built the place into an international ski destination that rivaled Aspen and Vail in everything but size.

That much was public knowledge. Discovering the details of his private life had taken some digging. But what Leigh learned had confirmed that she needed to be here today. There was no guarantee she'd be hired for the nanny job. But either way, she had to take this masquerade as far as it would go.

Right now, everything depended on her playing her cards carefully.

"Satisfied?" She slid the signed contract back across the desk. "I'm not looking for a story. I'm looking for a job."

"Fine. Let's see how it goes after we've talked." He slid the baseball cap off his head and raked a hand through his thick, gray-flecked hair. He'd be a little past forty, she calculated. His athlete's body, clad in jeans and a gray sweatshirt, was taut and muscular, his strongly featured face scoured by sun and wind. His eyes were a deep, startling Nordic blue. The year he'd won Olympic gold, a popular magazine had named him as one of the world's ten sexiest men. From the looks of him, he hadn't lost that edge.

It was public record that he'd been divorced for more than a decade. He looked as virile as a bull and, along with that, was certainly rich enough to have women falling at his feet, but he'd managed to keep his sex life out of the public eye—though, of course, in a small community like Dutchman's Creek there was always talk. Not that it mattered. She wasn't here to become one more notch on Wyatt Richardson's bedpost.

Although the notion did trigger a pleasant sort of tingle between her thighs.

"Tell me about the baby," she said.

"Yes. The baby." He exhaled slowly, as if he were about to wade into battle. "My daughter's. She's sixteen."

"You have a daughter?" Leigh feigned surprise.

"Her mother and I divorced when she was young. I didn't see much of her growing up, but for reasons I won't go into now, Chloe and the baby will be staying with me."

"What about the father?" Her pulse shot to a gallop, the pressure hammering against her eardrums. She willed her expression to remain calm and pleasant.

"Chloe won't give me a name. She says he's history. I take it he's just some boy she met while she and her mother were living here. But if I ever get my hands on the little bastard…"

One powerful fist crumpled the baseball cap. He released it with a muffled sound that could have been a sigh or a growl.

"That's the least of my worries now. Chloe insists she wants to keep her baby. But she doesn't know the first thing about being a mother. Lord, she's barely more than a baby herself." His cerulean eyes drilled into Leigh's.

"The nanny who accepts this job will be taking care of *two* children—the baby and his mother. Do you understand?"

Leigh had begun to breathe again. "I believe I do, Mr. Richardson."

"Fine. And please call me Wyatt." He rose, catching up the briefcase and jamming the cap back onto his head. "Let's go."

"Go where?" She scrambled to her feet as he strode around the desk.

"I'm taking you to the hospital to meet Chloe. If she thinks you'll do, I'll be willing to hire you for two weeks' probation. That should give me time to find someone else if things don't work out. We can discuss salary on the way back here."

Two weeks. High heels teetering, she struggled to keep pace with his strides. Next to a long-term job it was the best she could hope for. And even if he didn't hire her she'd at least get to see the baby.

"My vehicle's around back." He paused to hold the door for her. The October sun was blinding after the dim hallway of the small office building. Beyond the town, the mountain slopes were a riot of green-gold aspen, scarlet maple and dark stands of pine. The light breeze carried a whisper of winter to come—the winter that would bring snow to the mountains and skiers flocking to the high canyon runs.

"Careful." His hand steadied her elbow, guiding her around a broken piece of the asphalt parking lot. She could feel the power in his easy grip—a grip that remained even after they'd passed the danger spot.

She'd half hoped he'd be driving a sports car. But the only vehicle in the back parking lot was an elephant-sized black Hummer with oversized snow tires. "Sorry about the behemoth," he muttered. "This is my snow vehicle. My regular car's getting a brake job."

When he opened the passenger door for her, Leigh realized that the floor was thigh-high. There was no step, just a grip handle on the frame inside the door. There was no way she could climb up without making a spectacle of herself in the pencil skirt and high heels she'd worn to look professional for the interview. Maybe she should've worn jeans and hiking boots.

He stood behind her, saying nothing. For heaven's sake, was the man waiting for her to hitch up her skirt and give him a show?

Glancing back, she shot him an annoyed look. "If you wouldn't mind…"

His chuckle caught her off guard. "I was waiting for you to ask. If I were to just grab you, I'd be liable to end up getting slapped."

With that, he scooped her up in his arms as if she weighed nothing. Her breath stopped as his strong hands lifted her high and lowered her onto the leather seat. The subtle heat of his grip lingered as she fastened her safety belt. Her pulse was racing. As he strode around the vehicle and swung into the driver's seat, she willed herself to take deep breaths. Wyatt Richardson was a compellingly attractive man, capable of making her hormones surge with a glance from those unearthly blue eyes. But Leigh knew better than to go down that road. Let him get close enough to discover the truth about her, and she'd be up the proverbial creek.

And she wouldn't be the only one in trouble.

As the engine purred to life, she settled back into the seat. "So your daughter's in the hospital. When did she have the baby?"

"Yesterday morning. An easy birth, or so I was told.

She and the baby are doing fine. They should be ready to leave sometime tomorrow."

"What about the girl's mother? Is she in town to be with her daughter and see her grandchild?"

He winced as if she'd stuck him with something sharp. "Her mother's in Chicago with her new husband. Evidently the marriage is on shaky ground. That's why she chartered a plane for Chloe last week and sent her to me."

"I'm sorry, but that's monstrous."

"Don't judge her too harshly. The situation has us all thrown. I didn't even know Chloe was pregnant till the girl climbed out of a taxi and rang my front doorbell. Frankly, I'm still in shock."

And what about your poor daughter? Leigh thought it but she didn't say it. For now, at least, she'd be wise to tread lightly.

He turned onto the side road that led to the county hospital. "I didn't mean to dump all this on you before you met the girl. But at least you'll know what you could be getting into. Chloe's been through a devil of a time. And aside from taking her in and hiring somebody for the baby, I don't know how to help her through this."

"It sounds as if you care, at least. That should count for something."

A bitter laugh rumbled in his throat. "Say that to Chloe. She'll tell you that my caring's come about fifteen years too late."

He swung the Hummer into the parking lot and pulled into an empty space. After walking around to open the door on Leigh's side, he held up his arms. Taking her cue from him, she placed her hands on his muscled shoulders. His grip around her waist was brief as he lowered her to the ground. But as he released her, their eyes met. His were sunk into weary shadows—the eyes of a man who'd spent some sleepless nights. A worried man, unsure, perhaps, for the first time in his life.

For the space of a breath his big hand lingered on her hip. As if suddenly aware, he pulled it away and took her arm. "Let's go inside," he said.

Leigh was familiar with the hospital, a sprawling one-story maze of wings and hallways. Having visited several friends there, she knew her way to the maternity ward. "Were you here when the baby was born?" she asked as Wyatt walked beside her.

"I was wrapping up a meeting and missed the delivery, but I saw Chloe in recovery. They'd given her an epidural for the birth. She was still groggy when I left. She probably won't even remember I was there."

Leigh glanced down a side hall where the nursery windows were located. She was hoping to see the baby for a moment, but Wyatt kept walking on down the corridor, checking the room numbers. He paused outside a door that was slightly ajar. "I guess this is it."

"Go on in," Leigh said. "I'll wait out here until you're ready to introduce me."

Murmuring his thanks, he squared his shoulders, knocked lightly on the door and stepped into the room.

Chloe was sitting up in bed, peering into a small, round mirror as she dabbed mascara onto her eyelashes. With her mop of auburn curls, she looked like a little girl playing with her mom's makeup. How could this child be a mother?

"Hello, sweetheart," he said.

"Hello, *Daddy*." Her voice was edgy. The bouquet of pink roses he'd sent earlier had been shoved into a space above the sink.

Wyatt cleared his throat. "I'm told you have a beautiful little boy. How are you feeling?"

"How do you think?" She twisted the top onto the mascara tube. "I texted my friends. They're coming by to see the baby. His name's Michael, by the way. Mikey for now."

"Did you call your mother?"

She shrugged. "I sent a text. She's on her way to New York with *Andre*. He has some kind of gallery show."

"So she's not coming to see the baby?"

"Why should she? Mom's still in denial about being a grandma. Anyway, who needs her?" Chloe fished a lipstick out of her purse and swiped the burgundy hue onto her cupid's bow mouth.

Wyatt lowered himself onto a handy chair. "We need to talk, Chloe."

"What's to talk about?" She looked at him warily, as if bracing herself for a fight. "You already know I'm going to keep him."

Yes, she'd made that completely clear, despite his many arguments against it. But he wouldn't rehash that now, not when he could see how tired she looked. "I understand. And I hope you know that you and Mikey will have a home with me for as long as you need it. But what about the rest? Have you ever taken care of a baby?"

Her sky-blue eyes cast him a blank look.

"For starters…" He wrestled with the delicate question that needed to be asked. "How are you going to feed him?"

Her eyes widened. "You mean, am I…? OMG, no way! I'm not going around with saggy boobs for the rest of my life—and I do plan to have a life, Daddy. I want my baby, but you can't expect me to sit home with him all the time. As soon as you buy me a car, I'm going to—"

"The car can wait." It was all Wyatt could do to keep from snapping at her. "Meanwhile you've got a child to take care of. Do you even know how to change a diaper?"

She stared at him as if he'd just climbed out of a flying saucer.

"Goodness, Daddy. What do you think we're getting a nanny for?"

Waiting outside the half-opened door, Leigh heard everything. Wyatt had given her an inkling of what to expect. Now the impact of what she'd be dealing with smacked her full in the face. She could see what he'd meant when he'd said she'd have two children in her care. And Chloe sounded like a handful. Only the thought of the baby kept her from turning around and walking out of the hospital.

Seconds later he reappeared in the doorway, his face a mask of frustration. "Sorry you had to hear that," he muttered.

"It's just as well that I did." Following his lead, she allowed him to usher into the room. Chloe was sitting up against the pillows. Even in the drab hospital gown she looked like a petite little doll with Shirley Temple curls and china-blue eyes—almost as blue as her father's.

"Chloe," Wyatt said, "this is Miss Foster. Unless you have some objection, I plan on asking her to become your son's nanny."

The girl scrutinized her carefully. Leigh wondered what she was looking for. Chloe seemed to be wondering the same thing as uncertainty passed over her face. She stole a glance at her father, but he seemed to be replying to a message on his phone. "Fine," the girl said, clearly trying too hard to sound authoritative. "She'll do."

"Thank you." The less said, the better, Leigh resolved.

Chloe glanced toward the door, where the nurse had appeared with a blue-wrapped bundle. "I hope you're not staying much longer," she said. "My friends are coming over to see Mikey, and they'll be here any minute."

"We were just about to leave." Wyatt eased toward the door as the nurse entered.

"Wait!" Leigh said, seizing the moment. "Since I'll be helping with your baby, Chloe, would you mind if I held him for a minute?"

"Whatever."

Leigh felt her heart drop as the nurse placed the warm bundle in her arms. He felt so tiny, almost weightless. Scarcely daring to breathe, she pulled down the edge of the blanket to reveal the small, rosebud face. Little Mikey was beautiful, with his mother's blue eyes and russet curls. But it was his other features she looked for and found—the aquiline nose and square chin, the ears that didn't quite lie flat, the dark, straight brows—all coming together in one perfect package.

Leigh fought back welling tears. There could be no more doubt. She was holding her brother's child.

Two

With her emotions on the brink of spilling over, Leigh turned toward Wyatt. "Time for you two to get acquainted," she said, thrusting the blue bundle toward him.

He seemed to hesitate. Then his big hands took the slight weight, holding the child away from his body like a jar of live honeybees. His expression was a stoic mask. Leigh stifled her dismay. Wyatt hadn't asked for this little boy to come into his life, she reminded herself. Still it wouldn't hurt for him to show some affection. How could anyone with a soul not love a baby?

Leigh noticed that Chloe was focused on the sight of her son in her father's arms as well, but Chloe's expression was difficult to read. Sadness? Wistfulness? Worry? Envy? Dismay? Maybe all of the above—or maybe none of them. Whatever she was feeling, she didn't say a word. Leigh sighed, the task before her looming like a mountain. It wouldn't be easy, maybe not even possible. But in the time allowed, she would do her best to help these people become a family.

* * *

Wyatt gazed down at the tiny face. The eyes that looked up at him were blue like Chloe's, but with an openly trusting quality to them that Chloe's hadn't held in years. He saw his daughter in the wispy amber curls and full, heart-shaped mouth. But some features were unfamiliar. The unknown boy, who'd taken what he wanted without a second thought, had left traces of himself, too.

The boy who'd derailed Chloe's young life.

If Wyatt had known about the pregnancy early on, would he have discouraged her from having this baby? Chloe was his only child, and he'd had such plans for her—college, maybe a career and a good marriage with children born at the right time. But it was too late for questions and regrets. The baby was here and she seemed determined to keep it. They would have to make the best of a bad situation.

But Lord, where would he find the wisdom? Where would he find the patience to be there for his daughter and grandchild? It just wasn't in him.

Sensing his tension, perhaps, the baby broke into a plaintive wail. The knot in Wyatt's stomach jerked tight. Now what? He didn't know anything about babies, especially how to deal with crying ones.

"You take him." He shoved the mewling child into Leigh's arms. Out of the corner of his eye, he saw Chloe flinch. Something here didn't seem right. But whatever it was, Wyatt didn't know how to fix it. As a man, he'd taken pride in his ability to handle any situation. But right now he felt just plain lost.

Leigh cradled the baby close. He stopped crying and snuggled into her warmth, his rosebud mouth searching instinctively for something to suck. Aching, Leigh brushed a fingertip over the satiny head. He was so tiny, so sweet and so helpless. How could she do this job without losing her heart?

From the open doorway, delighted teenage squeals shattered the stillness.

"Chloe! Is that your baby?"

"OMG, he's so little!"

"Let me hold him!"

Three pretty, stylish girls swarmed into the room, laden with wrapped gifts and shopping bags, which they piled on the foot of the bed. With a sigh of relief, Leigh surrendered little Mikey to one of them. Her eyes met Wyatt's across the crowded room. He nodded toward the door. It was time for the grown-ups to leave.

"You look rattled. How about some coffee?" Wyatt's hand brushed the small of Leigh's back, setting off a shimmer of awareness as he guided her into the corridor.

"Thanks, that sounds good. I'd guess we're both rattled." Leigh's knees were quivering. Only the arrival of Chloe's girlfriends had saved her crumbling composure.

Kevin's baby. Her own little nephew. And she couldn't risk telling a soul.

Leigh and her teenage brother had always been close. Last spring Kevin had confided to her that he'd gotten a girl pregnant. *Chloe Richardson—her dad owns Wolf Ridge and she goes to that snooty private school. She texted me that she was pregnant. I offered to...you know, man up and be responsible. But she said to forget it because she planned to get rid of the kid. She was moving away and never wanted to hear from me again. Promise me you won't tell Mom, Leigh. It would kill her.*

Leigh had kept her promise, believing the issue would never surface again. Then a few days ago, as she was proofing the ads for the paper, she'd discovered that Wyatt

Richardson needed a nanny. Some simple math and a discreet call to the hospital had confirmed all she needed to know.

Telling Kevin was out of the question. After a long phase of teenage rebellion he was finally thinking of college and working toward a scholarship. The news that he had a son could fling the impulsive boy off course again. Worse, it could send him blundering into the path of a man angry and powerful enough to destroy his future. Leigh couldn't risk letting that happen. But she wanted—needed—to know and help Kevin's baby.

"Here we are." Wyatt opened the door to the hospital cafeteria. "Nothing fancy, but I can vouch for the coffee." Finding an empty table, he pulled out a chair for Leigh. She waited while he went through the line and returned with two steaming mugs along with napkins, spoons, cream and sugar.

Seating himself across from her, he leaned back in his chair and regarded her with narrowed eyes. "Well, what do you think?" he demanded.

Leigh took her time, adding cream to her coffee and stirring it with a spoon. "The baby's beautiful. But I get the impression your daughter is scared to death. She's going to need a lot of help."

"Are you prepared to give her that help?"

Leigh studied him over the rim of her mug. She saw a successful man, a winner in every way that mattered to the world. She saw a tired man, his jaw unshaven and his eyes laced with fatigue. She saw a father at his wits' end, and she knew what he wanted to hear. But if she couldn't be honest in everything, she would at least be honest in this.

"Assuming the job's mine, I'll do my best to give her some support. But make no mistake, Wyatt, it's the baby I'll be there for. Chloe's *your* child. If you think you can step aside and leave her parenting to me, we'll both end up failing her. Do I make myself clear?"

For an instant he looked as if she'd doused him with a fire hose. Then a spark of annoyance flared in his deep blue eyes. One dark eyebrow shifted upward. Had she said too much and blown her chance? As he straightened in his chair, Leigh braced herself for a storm. But he only exhaled, like a steam locomotive braking to a halt.

"Good. You're not afraid to speak your mind. With Chloe, that trait will come in handy."

"But did you *hear* what I said?"

"Heard and duly noted. We'll see how things go." He whipped a pen out of his pocket and wrote something on a napkin. "This is the weekly salary I propose to pay you. I trust it's enough."

He slid the napkin toward her. Leigh gasped. The amount was more than twice what she'd anticipated. "That's very…generous," she mumbled.

"I expect you'll earn every cent. Until Chloe and the baby settle into a routine, you'll be needed pretty much 24/7. After things calm down we'll talk about schedules and time off. In the next few days, I'll have a formal contract drawn up for you. That nondisclosure document you signed will be part of it. Agreed?"

"Agreed." Leigh felt as if she'd just consigned away her soul. But it was all for Kevin's baby. She took a lingering sip of her coffee, which had cooled. "So when do you want me to start?"

"How about now? The nursery needs to be set up. I'd intended for that to happen before the baby was born, but Chloe couldn't make up her mind on what she wanted. It can't wait any longer—you'll just have to decide for her. Earlier today I called Baby Mart and opened an account. After I take you back to your car, you can go there and pick out whatever the baby's going to need—clothes, diapers, formula, a crib, the works. Everything top-of-the-line. I've arranged for special delivery by the end of the day." He rose from his chair, all energy and impatience. "After that, you should have a couple of hours to resign from the paper, pack your things and report to my house."

"You want me there *tonight?*"

"If the baby's coming home tomorrow, we've got to have the nursery ready and waiting. Will you need directions to the house?"

"No. I know where you live." No one who'd been to Wolf Ridge could miss the majestic glass-and-timber house that sat like a baron's castle on a rocky bluff, overlooking the resort. Finding her way shouldn't be a problem, even in the dark. But Leigh couldn't ignore a feeling of unease, as if she were being swept into a maelstrom.

Wyatt Richardson was a man who'd started poor and achieved all he had through force of will. Mere moments after she'd agreed to work for him, he was taking over her life, barking orders as if he owned her—which to his way of thinking, he probably did.

Since he was her employer, she would put up with a certain amount of it. But if the man expected her to be a doormat he was in for a surprise. She would be little Mikey's advocate, speaking up for his welfare, even if it meant bashing heads with Wyatt.

Kevin's child had been born into a family with an immature teenage mother, an uncaring grandmother and a reluctant grandfather, whose idea of family duty was to turn everything over to the hired help. In the hospital room, when she'd given Wyatt the baby, he'd handled the tiny blue bundle like a ticking bomb. He seemed to be in denial about his grandson's very existence, never referring to him by name, only calling him "the baby."

Changing things would be up to her. She could only hope she was wise enough, and tough enough, for the challenge.

Wyatt boosted Leigh into the Hummer, struggling against the awareness of his hands sliding over her warm curves. Her fragrance was clean and subtle, teasing his senses to the point of arousal. Her long legs, clad in silky hose, flashed past his eyes as she climbed onto the seat. What would she do if she knew he was imagining those legs wrapping his hips?

She'd probably kick him halfway across the parking lot.

What had gotten into him? Didn't he have enough trouble on his hands with Chloe and the baby? Did he really need to complicate things with an attraction toward the woman he'd hired to be the nanny?

He'd never had trouble getting bed partners. All he needed to do was stroll through the resort lodge and make eye contact with an attractive female. If she was available, the rest would be easy.

So why was he suddenly craving a woman who came with a hands-off sign?

Maybe that was the problem. With Chloe and the baby sharing his house, an affair with the nanny would be a dicey proposition. For that matter, with Chloe in residence, bringing any woman to his bedroom would be a bad idea—just one of the ways his life was about to change.

But right now, that was the least of his worries.

Closing the door, he walked around the vehicle and climbed into the driver's seat. Leigh had fastened her safety belt and was attempting to tug her little skirt over her lovely knees. Wyatt willed himself to avert his eyes.

"Just for the record," he said, starting the engine, "we

don't hold with formal dress at the house. Pack things you'll be comfortable in, like jeans and sneakers."

Or maybe you should dress like a nun, to remind me to keep my hands off you.

"Jeans and sneakers will be fine." Her laugh sounded strained. "I don't suppose your grandson will care what I'm wearing."

"My grandson. Lord, don't remind me. I'm still getting used to that idea."

"This isn't about you. It's about an innocent baby who'll need a world of love—and a young girl learning to be a mother. You'll need to be there for both of them."

Isn't that where you come in? Wyatt knew better than to voice that thought. Leigh had expressed some strong notions about family responsibility. But wasn't he doing enough, taking Chloe and her baby under his roof, buying everything they needed and hiring a nanny to help out?

Back when he was married, Tina had complained that he was never home—but blast it, he'd been busy working to support his wife and daughter. He'd been determined to give them a better life than he'd had growing up.

Even after the divorce he'd taken good care of them. He'd given Tina a million-dollar house, paid generous alimony and child support and always remembered Chloe's birthday and Christmas with expensive gifts—gifts he'd never have been able to afford if he hadn't poured so much time and energy into the resort.

Hadn't he done enough? Was it fair that he was expected to finish raising a spoiled teenager with a baby so Tina could run off with her twenty-seven-year-old husband?

"There's my car." Leigh pointed to a rusting station wagon parked outside the office he'd used for the interviews. One look was enough to tell him that the car would never make it up the canyon on winter roads. He would need to get her something safe to drive before the first snowfall.

Wyatt pulled the Hummer into a nearby parking place. Steeling himself against her nearness, he climbed out and opened the door on the passenger side. Leigh was waiting for him to boost her to the ground. She leaned outward, her hands stretching toward his shoulders. Wyatt was reaching for her waist when her high heel caught on the edge of the floor mat. Yanked off balance, she tumbled forward on top of him.

He managed to break her fall—barely. For a frantic instant she clung to him, her arms clasping his neck, her skirt hiked high enough for one leg to hook his waist. But his grip wasn't secure enough to hold her in place. Pulled by her own weight, she slid down his body. Wyatt stifled a groan as his sex responded to the delicious pressure of her curves pressed against him so intimately.

Her sudden gasp told him she'd felt his response. He glimpsed wide eyes and flaming cheeks as she slipped downward. Then her feet touched the ground and she stumbled back, breaking contact. They stood facing each other, both of them half-breathless. Her hair was mussed and one of her shoes was missing. She tugged her skirt down over her thighs.

"Sorry," she muttered. "I didn't hurt you, did I?"

Wyatt tried his best to laugh it off. "No, I'm fine. But that maneuver could've gotten us both arrested."

Her narrowing gaze told him she didn't appreciate his humor. It appeared that, despite her naughty little skirt, Miss Leigh Foster was a prim and proper lady. All to the good. He'd be wise to keep that in mind.

"Excuse me, but I need my shoe." She teetered on one high-heeled pump. Wyatt retrieved the mate from the floor of the SUV, along with her brown leather purse. She took them from him, wiggling her foot into the shoe.

"You'll be all right?" he asked her.

"Fine. I'll be going straight to Baby Mart from here, then home. I should be knocking on your door by nightfall."

"Plan on dinner at the house, with me. And remember you're to say nothing about Chloe and her baby. All the people at Baby Mart need to know is who's paying for the order and where it's to be delivered." He fished a business card out of his wallet and scribbled his private cell number on the back. "Any questions or problems, give me a call."

"Got it." She tucked the card in her purse, pulled out her keys and walked away without a backward glance. He watched her go, her deliberate strides punctuating the sway of her hips. Her clicking heels tapped out a subtle code of annoyance. Could she be upset with him?

Wyatt watched the station wagon shudder to a start, spitting gravel as it pulled into the street. No, he hadn't read her wrong. The woman was in a snit about something.

Maybe she thought he'd pushed her too hard, giving her orders right out of the starting gate. But since he was paying her salary, it made sense to let her know what he expected. After all, he was her employer, not her lover.

And that, he mused, was too damned bad.

Returning to his vehicle, he pulled into traffic and headed toward the road that would take him out of town. He'd gone less than two blocks when he saw something ahead that hadn't been there earlier. City workers were digging up the asphalt to fix what looked like a broken water main. Neon orange barricades blocked the roadway. A flashing detour sign pointed drivers to the right, down a narrow side street.

He'd made the right turn and was following a blue Pon-

tiac toward the next intersection before he realized where
he was. A vague nausea congealed in the pit of his stomach. He never drove this street if he could help it. There
were too many memories here—most of them bad.

Most of those memories centered around the house part-
way down the block, on the left. With its peeling paint and
weed-choked yard, it looked much the same as when he'd
lived there growing up. Wyatt willed himself to look away
as he passed it, but he'd seen enough to trigger a memory—one of the worst.

He'd been twelve at the time, coming home one summer night after his first real job—sweeping up at the corner grocery. The owner, Mr. Papanikolas, had paid him
two dollars and given him some expired milk and a loaf
of bread to take home to his mother. It wasn't much, but
every little bit helped.

His mouth had gone dry when he'd spotted his father's
old Ranchero parked at the curb. Pops had come by, most
likely wanting money for the cheap whiskey he drank. He
didn't spend much time at home, but he knew when his
wife got paid at the motel. If she gave him the cash, there'd
be nothing to live on for the next two weeks.

Wyatt was tempted to stay outside, especially when
he heard his father's cursing voice. But he couldn't leave
his mother alone. Pops would be less apt to hurt her if he
was there to see.

Leaving the bread and milk by the porch, he mounted
the creaking steps and pushed open the door. By the light
of the single bulb he saw his mother cowering on the
ragged sofa. Her thin face was splotched with red, her
eye swollen with a fresh bruise. His father, a hulking man
in a dirty undershirt, loomed over her, his hands clenched
into fists.

"Give me the money, bitch!" he snarled. "Give it to me now or you won't walk out of this house!"

"Don't hurt her!" Wyatt sprang between them, pulling the two rumpled bills out of his pocket. "Here, I've got money! Take it and go!"

"Out of my way, brat!" Cuffing Wyatt aside, he raised a fist to punch his wife again. Wyatt seized a light wooden chair. Swinging it with all his twelve-year-old strength, he struck his father on the side of the head.

The blow couldn't have done much damage. But it hurt enough to turn the man's rage in a new direction. One kick from a heavy boot sent the boy sprawling. The last thing Wyatt remembered was the blistering whack of a belt on his body, and his mother's screams....

Forcing the images from his mind, Wyatt turned left at the intersection and followed the detour signs back to the main road. His father had taken the money that night. And while his mother rubbed salve on his welts, he'd vowed to her that he would change their lives. One day he'd be rich enough to buy her all the things she didn't have now. And she would never have to change another bed or scrub another toilet again.

He'd accomplished his goals and more. But his mother hadn't lived to see his Olympic triumph or the successes that followed. She'd died of cancer while he was still in high school.

His father had gone to prison for killing a man in a bar fight. Years later, still behind bars, he'd dropped dead from a heart attack.

Wyatt had not attended the burial service.

He'd put that whole life behind him—had made himself into a new man who was nothing at all like his dad.

So why did he feel so lost when it came to dealing with his daughter?

Not that he didn't love Chloe. He'd never denied the girl anything that might make her happy. He'd been the best provider a man could be and not once—not ever—had he raised a hand against her. But now it slammed home that in spite of all the work he'd done and the things he'd bought, he still didn't know the first thing about being a father.

Three

Turning onto the unmarked side road, Leigh switched her headlights on high beam. Until now, she hadn't been worried about finding Wyatt's house. But the moonless night was pitch-black, the thick-growing pines a solid wall that shut off the view on both sides.

She hadn't planned on arriving so late. But everything back in town had taken longer than she'd expected. When the clerk at Baby Mart had helped her make a list of furniture and supplies, Leigh had been staggered at how much it took to keep one little baby in comfort—and how long it took to choose each item. By the time she'd left the store her head was pounding, her feet throbbing in her high-heeled pumps.

She'd stopped at the paper to tell her boss she was quitting, then headed home. Kevin and her mother had hovered around her bed as she threw clothes and toiletries into her suitcase. They'd demanded to know what was going on. Leigh had mumbled something about a secret assignment, assuring them that she'd be fine, she'd keep in touch, and they could always reach her on her cell phone. They probably suspected she'd gone to work for the CIA, or maybe that she was running from the Mafia.

She hated keeping secrets from her family. But there was no other way to make this work. Kevin's baby son needed her help; whatever it took, she would be there for little Mikey.

A large, pale shape bounded into her headlights. Her foot slammed the brake. The station wagon squealed to a stop, just missing the deer that zigzagged across the road and vanished into the trees.

Shaken, she sagged over the steering wheel. What was she doing, driving up a dark mountain road to move in with a man she barely knew—a man who made her pulse race every time his riveting indigo eyes looked her way?

The memory of that afternoon's encounter, when she'd tumbled out of the SUV and into his arms, was still simmering. The clumsy accident must have been no more than a simple embarrassment for Wyatt. But the brief intimate contact had flamed through *her* like fire through spilled gasoline. Wyatt Richardson was a good fifteen years her senior. But never mind that—the man exuded an aura that charged the air around him like summer lightning. How was she going to keep her mind on work if her pulse ratcheted up every time he came within ten feet of her?

Right now Wyatt should be the least of her worries. Tucked into her purse was the one item she'd bought with her own cash at Baby Mart—a thick paperback on infant care. Truth be told, her experience with babies consisted of a few bottles and diaper changes. What she didn't know about umbilical cords, fontanels, bathing and burping would fill…a book.

Once the nursery was set up, she planned to spend the rest of the night reading. She'd always been a quick study.

This time she would have to be. She couldn't fake it with a baby—it was become an expert before tomorrow or risk doing something wrong and possibly harming the child.

Braking for the deer had killed the engine and left her badly spooked. Starting the car again, she drove at a cautious pace up the winding road. An eternity seemed to pass before the trees parted and she found herself looking up a rocky slope. From its top, light shone through towering windows.

Minutes later she pulled up in front of the house. She stepped out of the car to see Wyatt standing on the broad stone porch, his arms folded across his chest.

"What kept you? I was about to send out a search party. Why didn't you call?" He sounded like the parent of a teen who'd missed curfew.

"Sorry. My phone died. And everything took longer than I'd expected. I didn't even take time to change." She glanced down at her rumpled suit, then down further to where her feet had swollen to the shape of her pumps. Opening the back of the station wagon, she reached for her suitcase, but Wyatt was there ahead of her. He snatched up the heavy bag and carried it into the front hall.

"Did the order from Baby Mart get here?" she asked.

"It arrived a couple of hours ago. I had the delivery man put the crib together, but everything else is still in boxes. You'll have your work cut out for you."

"There's no one here to help?" She'd expected to see a servant or two but there wasn't another soul in sight.

His eyebrow quirked upward. "Just you—and me. Dinner's warming in the oven if you're hungry."

"I'm starved." And she was, even though she hadn't given food a thought until now. "Don't tell me you cook," she said.

"Lord, no. I keep snacks and breakfast food in the

kitchen, but when I want a real meal, I have it delivered from the restaurant at the lodge. Tonight it's lasagna." He lowered the suitcase to the floor. "You can leave your things here till we've eaten."

He ushered her into the great room, its cathedral roof shored by massive, rough-hewn beams. The north wall, overlooking the resort, was floor-to-ceiling glass. No blinds were needed. Seeing inside from below would be next to impossible.

The logs in the huge stone fireplace had burned down to coals, leaving the space pleasantly warm. After kicking her shoes off her swollen feet, Leigh slipped off her jacket, tossed it back over her suitcase and followed Wyatt. Off to her right she glimpsed a formal dining area, but it appeared they'd be eating in the brightly lit kitchen, where the steel-topped table had been set for two.

Wyatt seated her and used a padded glove to lift the foil-wrapped pan out of the oven. There was a fresh salad on the table, along with a baguette, a bottle of vintage claret and two glasses.

"I'll pour and you dish." He handed her a spatula. "It might be overcooked."

"My fault for being late. Sorry." Leigh scooped two squares of lasagna onto the plates. It didn't look over-cooked, and it smelled heavenly.

"Eat hearty. We've got plenty work ahead of us, getting that nursery set up."

"You said *we*. Does that mean you're planning to help?"

"With the heavy lifting, at least. But you'll be the one organizing things. I hope you plan to change into something more comfortable."

"Of course." Leigh's face warmed as his cobalt eyes lingered on her. The silk blouse she'd worn with the suit had always been a little snug. She'd forgotten that problem when she'd taken off her jacket. She scrambled to change the subject. "I still find it hard to believe you don't have help in this big house—in addition to me, of course."

"You mean like a butler and a chauffeur and a cook?" His eyes twinkled, an unexpected surprise. "You've been watching too many episodes of *Masterpiece Theatre*. A gaggle of servants hanging around would drive me crazy. I can load the dishwasher, answer my own doorbell and drive my own car. And I have a cleaning crew up from the lodge every Wednesday to keep the place looking ship-shape. Believe me, I like my peace and quiet."

She took a sip of wine and speared a sliced mushroom from her salad. It would be a waste of words, reminding him now, but Wyatt's precious peace and quiet was about to be shattered.

Leigh's room was on the second floor. Like the rest of the house, its decor was rustic and masculine with an eye to comfort. The queen-sized bed featured a decadent European-style featherbed and duvet. A hand-woven Tibetan rug covered much of the hardwood floor. Wooden shutters masked the tall windows.

One wall was decorated with framed black-and-white photos of the Himalayas. Among them was an image of a grinning, bearded Wyatt between two Sherpa porters. As Leigh stripped off her blouse, skirt and pantyhose, it was as if his mocking eyes watched her every move.

She would have to do something about that picture.

A side door opened into the nursery, which was piled with bags and boxes from Baby Mart. Zipping her jeans and tugging her sweatshirt over her head, she prepared to do battle with the mess. It was going to be a long night. And her tortured feet would feel every step she took.

Wyatt had just unpacked a solid oak rocker and was

situating a cushion on the seat. He glanced up as she padded barefoot into the nursery.

"That's more like it," he said, taking in her outfit. "But where are your shoes?"

Leigh wiggled her swollen toes. "Too many hours in stilettos. I'm so footsore I can't even wear my sneakers."

"That's no good." He rose, gesturing toward the chair. "Maybe I can help. Sit down."

She hesitated. "We really need to get started here."

"Sit. That's an order."

Leigh sank onto the padded seat. Being bossed rankled her, but she was on his clock, and if he could do something for her feet, who was she to argue?

Dropping to a crouch, he cradled her left foot between his hands. "Trust me. I've dealt with enough sports injuries to pick up a few tricks."

His strong hands began kneading her foot, fingers pressing the arch as his thumbs massaged the bones and tendons between her toes. Leigh could feel herself relaxing as the pain eased. Delicious sensations trickled up her leg. She closed her eyes. A moan escaped her lips.

He chuckled. "Feels good, does it?"

"Mmm-hmm. You could do this for a living." Her mind began to wander forbidden paths, imagining how those skilled hands would feel in other places. She hadn't been in a physical relationship since breaking her engagement, eleven months ago. Now she felt her body awakening to Wyatt's masculine touch. And she couldn't help remembering that they were alone here, with a bed in the next room....

But what was she thinking? Sleeping with Wyatt was a crazy idea. Any intimacy between them would just make it that much harder for her to hold on to her secrets.

With a mental slap, Leigh shocked herself back to reality. When she opened her eyes, Wyatt was looking up at her as if he'd detected something in her face. Her cheeks warmed. Had he guessed what she'd been thinking?

"How's your room?" He broke the awkward silence. "Will it be all right?"

"It's lovely—although I may not be able to roll myself out of that bed in the morning."

"Chloe chose that room for you. She wanted you next to the nursery, where you could hear the baby at night."

"And where will Chloe be?"

"Her room's downstairs. She says she doesn't want his crying to wake her up."

So, what's wrong with this picture? Leigh bit back an acerbic comment. She'd known she was getting into a prickly situation. That was why she'd taken the job in the first place. But this was no time to climb on her soapbox— especially since the issue would need to be addressed with Chloe, not the girl's father.

"I can guess what you're thinking." He switched to her other foot, skilled fingers kneading away the soreness. "But for now I want you to cut the girl some slack—give her time to get back on her feet, physically and emotionally. When her mother had to choose between her husband and her pregnant daughter, Chloe found herself on her way to the airport with her bags. As if she hadn't been through enough already, dealing with the pregnancy on her own." Wyatt's fingers pressed harder against Leigh's arch, almost hurting. "So help me, if I ever find the irresponsible jerk who took advantage of a young girl's trust and then just walked away...."

"I think we'd better get to work." Leigh pulled free and scrambled to her feet, uncertain she could trust herself not to rise to her brother's defense if Wyatt continued in that vein. It wasn't as if Kevin hadn't offered to stand by

Chloe. As for what had happened—Kevin had told her it had been after a party, with both of them more than a little drunk. No trust—or even love—involved. No one taking advantage. Just two reckless kids being stupid.

But the result of their thoughtless act was the little miracle she'd held for the first time today.

Not that she could explain any of that to Wyatt. Not now, and probably not ever.

Reaching for a box of linens, she began unwrapping crib pads, sheets and towels. "These will all need to be washed and dried before we use them," she said. "There's baby soap here somewhere. If you'll point me toward the laundry room, I'll get started."

"It's just off the kitchen—you'll see it when you go downstairs. Meanwhile, I'll unpack more of these boxes and recycle the cardboard. You can put everything away when you get back here."

"Thanks." Leigh found the pink soap box, bundled up the linens and headed for the stairs. She needed a break from Wyatt's overpowering presence, and the laundry gave her an excuse. His drive had won Olympic glory and built one of the finest ski resorts in the state. But up close and personal, his magnetism could be an emotional drain. Her physical attraction to him only complicated things.

It would be easier after tomorrow, with the baby here. She'd have something to focus on, something to love—*no, not to love*. She was here to give Kevin's son a good start in life. Sooner or later she would have to let go and walk away. If she allowed herself to fall in love with little Mikey, the final break would rip her heart out.

Wyatt stood alone on the second floor balcony. He'd expected to be worn out after helping Leigh set up the nursery. But they'd finished a couple of hours ago, and he was still too restless to sleep.

Leigh had been a whirlwind of efficiency—all business. There'd been no more sign of the chemistry that had flared between them when he'd rubbed her feet. But he hadn't forgotten it. He'd always maintained that the sexiest thing about a woman was her face. The sight of Leigh's face, her eyes closed, her lips parted in a blissful moan, had jolted his imagination into overdrive. He'd pictured that lovely dark-framed face on a pillow, her entranced expression deepening as he pleasured her....

Wyatt took a moment to enjoy the memory, then closed the door on it. For now, at least, a foot massage was as intimate as he planned to get with Miss Leigh Foster. Bed partners were a dime a dozen. But he'd already learned that a suitable nanny was worth more than gold.

A sliver of moon had risen above the canyon. Far below, beyond the trees, the lights of the resort spread like a jeweled carpet. The summer concert season was over, but the autumn color drew hikers to the slopes and sightseers flocking to the hotels, shops and restaurants. And the cold season was coming soon. Already his crews were inspecting every inch of the runs and lifts, getting ready for the first big snowstorm.

A light breeze, smelling of winter, cooled his face. He always savored this time of year and the changes it brought. But the changes happening now were like nothing in his experience.

Leigh was right. Chloe was going to need him. But how could he even begin to nurture her, discipline her and give her the support she needed? From his own father, Wyatt had inherited a legacy of neglect and abuse. What if the traits that made a good parent were simply missing in him? It was that fear that had made him keep his distance when she was a baby, herself. He'd missed the chance to get to know her, to build the kind of relationship that would help him understand how to be there for her. Could he trust himself to build that relationship now? Where did he even begin?

As for the baby... He couldn't begin to wrap his brain around that reality. Not tonight. But if he wasn't sure how to be a father after all these years, then he couldn't believe that Chloe was prepared to be a mother when she was barely more than a child herself. Having a child could destroy her future. Since she'd arrived, he'd tried over and over again to help her realize that the best thing for all of them would be to give the little boy up to a good family. The message hadn't gotten through, but perhaps things would change now that the baby was here. Once she realized that having a baby wasn't like having a new doll, the girl might come to her senses.

Meanwhile, there was Leigh. He was depending on her to maintain a level of sanity he could live with. So far, she'd proved as efficient, hardworking and practical as she was pretty. He could only hope she had the skill to care for the baby and the patience to deal with the red-haired hellion that was Chloe at her worst.

The weariness he'd been holding back too long crashed in on him. Time he got some rest. It was late, and tomorrow he'd be bringing Chloe and the baby home from the hospital. The day was bound to be trying.

Stepping back inside, he headed toward the stairs. That was when he glanced down the dark hallway and noticed the sliver of light under the closed door of Leigh's bedroom. Discretion told him to ignore it. But it was one-thirty in the morning. What if something was wrong? What if she was sick or in some kind of trouble?

Outside the door he paused to listen. Hearing nothing, he rapped lightly on the rough-hewn wood. When there was no answer, he pressed the latch and inched the door open.

Lamplight glowed on Leigh in bed, propped against two oversized pillows. She was dead asleep, her eyes closed, her head drooping to one side. The thin strap of her silky black nightgown had slipped off one shoulder to reveal the upper curve of a satiny breast.

Had she been waiting up for *him?* But that notion wasn't worth the time it took to kick it to the curb. Nothing in tonight's behavior could've been read as an invitation.

So why hadn't she just turned off the light and rolled over? In the next instant he found the answer. On the duvet, where it could have fallen from her hand, lay a thick paperback book. Drawing closer, Wyatt could make out the title—*Baby Care for the New Mother*.

Leigh had fallen asleep cramming for her job.

So her claim to be experienced in childcare was something of a stretch. A smile teased the corners of Wyatt's mouth. He wasn't ready to fire Leigh. But he wanted to let her know, in a subtle way, that he was wise to her little fib.

Tired as she was, she'd probably sleep until morning. If she woke to find the book on the nightstand and the lamp switched off that should be enough to give her a clue.

Leaving his shoes in the hallway, he stole across the carpet to the bed. Close up, her lush beauty was even more tempting—ripe lips softly parted, lashes like velvet fringe against her satiny cheeks, and a fragrance that stirred his senses like a seductive night breeze.

As he leaned over her to pick up the book, she shifted against the pillow. The black ribbon strap slipped lower on her shoulder, giving him a glimpse of one rosebud nipple peeking above the lace trimming the neckline.

His sex rose like a flagpole, straining against his jeans. Wyatt cursed silently as his fingers closed around the open book. They were alone in the house. If Leigh opened her eyes, what would he do? Would he mumble an excuse and leave like a gentleman, or would he be true to his manly nature?

Silly question. But never mind. Leigh had shown him her proper side. Nothing she'd said or done had indicated that she'd take kindly to being awakened with a man bending over her bed.

Giving in to his better judgment, Wyatt laid the book on the nightstand, switched off the lamp and, with a last regretful glance, left the room.

Four

Leigh opened one eye, found the bedside clock and groaned. Seven-thirty. Of all mornings to oversleep, she had to pick this one.

When she swung her legs off the bed, she noticed something on the nightstand. The baby book. How many chapters had she gotten through before she fell asleep? And how many of those pages could she actually remember? She could only hope she'd have time for a refresher while Wyatt was picking up Chloe and the baby.

She was walking away from the bed when it struck her—she had no memory of closing the book and laying it on the nightstand. And she certainly hadn't switched off the bedside lamp before dropping off. Somebody had looked in on her in the night. And that somebody was wise to her lack of experience.

She stifled a groan. Not a great way to start a new job.

The aroma of fresh coffee wafted under the door and into her nostrils. Her shower would have to wait. Right now she needed to get herself downstairs and convince Wyatt she had everything under control.

Yanking on her jeans and a black turtleneck, she splashed her face, brushed her teeth and ran a hasty comb through her hair. For now, that would have to do.

Still barefoot, she followed her nose, padding down the stairs and into the kitchen. Wyatt sat sipping coffee at the table, dressed in jeans and a dark blue cashmere sweater that matched his eyes. Those eyes took her measure, from her bare toes to her still-tousled locks. "Coffee's on the counter," he said pleasantly. "I put out a mug for you. How did you sleep?"

"Too well. That featherbed is decadent."

"And your feet? You're going to need your shoes today."

"They'll be fine." Leigh inhaled the fragrant steam as she poured the coffee. "Cream?"

"In the fridge. If there's anything you'd like for the kitchen, you can order it through the lodge by phone or email. The number and email address are on the contact list by the phone. It'll usually be delivered by the end of the day."

"Thanks. I'll make a list after I find out what Chloe would like. How soon will you be picking her and the baby up?"

"They should be ready any time after ten. But I changed my mind about going. I'm sending you instead."

"Me?" A reflexive grab barely saved Leigh's mug from crashing to the floor.

"Since I've already paid the hospital there's no reason for me to be there. And I've got an important phone conference scheduled for ten o'clock." He pulled a chair out from the table. "Sit down, Leigh. We need to talk."

She sat, perching on the edge of the chair like a child about to be punished. What now?

He turned his seat to face her. "When I hire someone I usually give them a written job description. I've never hired a nanny before, but we both need to know what's expected."

Leigh nodded, holding her tongue. Better to keep still than to speak and make a fool of herself.

"You've made it clear that your first priority will be the baby. That's fine. But you need to be aware of my other concerns."

"Of course." She willed herself to meet his gaze. His eyes were the color of a deep mountain lake—and at this moment, just as cold, she thought.

"One concern, a big one, is my family's privacy. Chloe's friends know about the baby, of course. So does the hospital staff. All of them have been warned to keep the matter under wraps. I won't have my daughter falling prey to gossip, especially if the press gets involved. And I won't have her future reputation tainted by one careless mistake."

How could anyone look at that beautiful boy and call him a mistake? Keeping that thought to herself, Leigh nodded her understanding.

"Is that why you want me to drive her home—so she and the baby won't be seen with you and recognized?"

"In part." He rose to put his empty cup in the sink. "That will be one of your prime responsibilities—keeping a lid on things. For now, at least, Chloe's not to take the baby out in public—for safety reasons as well as privacy. You're to track her online activity, Twitter, Facebook, anything that could be seen by the wrong people—"

"No."

He stared in surprise as she rose. "No?"

"I'm a nanny, not a spy. I understand your wanting to protect her, Wyatt, but the one who monitors her computer and phone should be her father."

His scowl darkened. She plunged ahead before he could interrupt.

"Think about it. I'm here in a nurturing role, to care for the baby and help Chloe learn to be a mother. She needs to trust me. If that's to happen I can't wear two hats. I can't support her and police her at the same time."

"So you're saying I should be the bad guy."

"If that's what you want. You must have surveillance people at the resort. You'll find a way."

He took his time rinsing his mug and stowing it in the dishwasher. "All right, you win—for now. But there's one more thing."

"I'm listening." Leigh remained on her feet, as did he.

"Chloe's young and she's bright. If she could put this incident behind her, she could still have a promising future."

Incident? A baby?

"If she sticks with her choice to raise the boy, I'll respect her decision," he continued. "But you and I both know it will change her life, and not for the better. What I'm hoping is that soon she'll be sensible and give him up for adoption—to a good family, of course. I trust you'll do your best to steer her in that direction. In the long run it would be better for her and for the baby. Don't you agree?"

Leigh stood rooted to the floor as his words sank in. *Sensible? Yes. But oh, so cold.* She found her voice.

"You're Chloe's father, and I can see where you're coming from. I'll give the matter some thought."

"Then let me give you something else to think about. I'm sure you're aware that if Chloe gives up the baby it will mean the end of your job here. In the spirit of fairness, if that becomes her decision and you support her in it, I'm willing to offer you a severance package of twenty-five thousand dollars. I'll have it written into your contract."

Leigh willed herself to appear calm. Inside, she was

reeling—not so much because of the amount, but because of his icy determination, and his assumption that her help could be bought.

"That's a generous offer," she replied. "I'll keep it in mind. But right now it's getting late. If I'm to be at the hospital by ten, I need to get ready...."

With her voice threatening to break, she turned and headed out of the kitchen.

"Leigh, one more thing."

She froze but didn't turn around.

"I just thought you should know. You have your shirt on inside out."

Stifling a groan, she fled up the stairs.

Wyatt stood on the balcony, watching the black sport wagon disappear behind the trees. He'd had the vehicle brought up from the resort for Leigh's temporary use. The Hummer would be hard for Chloe to climb into, and the girl would turn up her pretty nose at that rust bucket Leigh had driven here.

Later today he'd contact his supplier for a sturdy wagon with all-wheel drive. Chloe would be pestering him for a sports car but she wasn't getting it before spring, and only then if she showed some responsibility. For now, she and Leigh could share the new vehicle.

Wyatt could afford as many luxury cars as he wanted; but the mountain property didn't have enough level ground to waste on a big garage. The one at the rear of his house had room for just three vehicles—the Hummer, the new SUV he planned to buy and the Bentley that was his one indulgence, a vintage 1976 Corniche that he'd restored himself after his divorce. He'd be getting it back from the mechanic later today with new brakes. He also owned a couple of snowmobiles, which he kept in a shed, mostly for emergencies.

A scrub jay fluttered onto a nearby pine branch, cocked its head and regarded him with curious eyes. The bird's presence reminded Wyatt why he'd chosen to live in this remote spot overlooking the canyon. The place was wild and clean, and he'd done his best to keep it that way with solar panels on the roof and state-of-the-art recycling technology. For the past ten years he'd enjoyed his privacy here. Now all that was about to change.

Maybe it wouldn't be all bad. He'd enjoyed seeing Leigh come into the kitchen this morning, fresh-faced, rumpled and hastily dressed, as if she'd just tumbled out of bed. The warm, pleasant feeling had lingered like an aura—until they'd started talking.

Leigh had barely spoken while he helped secure the baby carrier in the car's backseat; and she'd driven off without even saying goodbye. Her silence had spoken volumes about his offer and what she thought of it.

Wyatt didn't take well to being denied. In fact, if he'd known how headstrong Leigh was, he might not have hired her in the first place.

Not just headstrong, he mused. There was something unsettling about the woman. Something that didn't add up. She was too sophisticated, too self-assured to settle for a job like this one. So why had she taken it? Her reasons from the interview didn't hold water. If she was as experienced with babies as she'd implied, why had she been reading that baby book in the middle of the night?

Who was she? What did she really want?

Leigh managed to hold herself together until she was sure the car couldn't be seen from the house. Then she pulled off the road, pressed her shaking hands to her face and allowed reality to sink in.

Wyatt Richardson didn't want his precious grandson. And he expected *her* to talk Chloe into giving the boy up. He'd even offered her money.

How was she supposed to deal with that?

She knew that Wyatt was thinking of Chloe's future. As far as he was concerned, the baby was an unlucky accident to be hushed up and sent away for the good of all concerned. Her heart rebelled at the thought of it…but she forced herself to take a deep breath and think with her head.

Was he right? Would little Mikey be better off with two adoptive parents than with an unmarried teenage mother and a grandfather who only wanted him gone? Maybe. But even if Chloe decided to take the adoption route today, Leigh was certain it would still take time to find the right parents and get through the paperwork. And in the meantime, the baby was going to need someone on *his* side, to fight for his rights and his welfare. For now, she would be that someone. And she would do everything in her power to see that whatever choice was made would be driven by love, not by expediency.

But she couldn't be there forever. When the time came, and she'd done all she could…

Unable to finish the thought she started the car and pulled back onto the road.

She arrived at the hospital thirty minutes later to find Chloe sitting on the bed, wearing sweats, flip-flops and an impatient pout. "Where's Daddy?" she demanded.

"Home waiting for you." Leigh fixed her face in a determined smile. "You're all checked out. As soon as the nurse gets here with Mikey we'll be on our way."

As if on cue, the nurse appeared with the baby, tightly

wrapped in a new white blanket. Chloe brightened. "Put him down. I want to see him in his new outfit!"

With her son on the bed, she unwrapped the blanket to reveal what looked like a puppy costume—a white stretch jumpsuit with brown spots and a matching hat that sported droopy brown ears. "Isn't that precious?" she cooed. "My BFF Monique gave him that. Got to send pictures." Fishing her cell phone out of her purse, she leaned over the baby and began snapping photos.

Leigh took advantage of the delay to feast her gaze on her nephew. Even since yesterday he'd changed. His cheeks were rounder, his features more defined. Delicate golden lashes fringed his eyelids, framing dark blue eyes, like his grandfather's. Baby expressions flickered across his face— a frown, a look of wide-eyed wonder, and then something that could almost have been a smile. Even in that silly dog costume, his beauty took Leigh's breath away.

While Chloe was busy texting, Leigh folded back the cuffs that covered his hands. They were oversized like Kevin's, the digits long and thin. When she brushed his palm, his baby fist closed around her finger. She felt the strong clasp all the way to her heart.

"Away we go!" The nurse, who'd left the room, returned with a wheelchair. Still texting, Chloe took her seat, leaving Leigh to wrap the baby and grab the take-home bag the hospital had provided.

With a no-nonsense manner, the nurse picked up the baby and thrust him at Chloe. "Put away that phone, dearie, and take your little boy," she snapped. Chloe did as she was told, though she stuck out her tongue when the nurse turned away. Watching, Leigh took a mental note. She had a lot to learn about the girl.

Minutes later they were on their way, with Mikey in the backseat, buckled into his carrier. Chloe had chosen to sit in front with Leigh. She took her phone out of her purse and checked her messages.

"Can we stop for a Coke?" she asked.

Leigh kept her eyes on the road. "Your father wanted me to bring you straight back. There'll be sodas in the fridge."

Chloe fell into a pouting silence, playing with her phone and finally putting it back in her purse. "What did Daddy say your name was?" she demanded.

"It's Leigh Foster. You can call me Leigh."

"Leigh Foster." There was a long pause before she asked, "Are you by any chance related to a jerk named Kevin Foster?"

Leigh's pulse lurched. She took a few breaths to collect herself before she answered. "There are a lot of Fosters in Dutchman's Creek. We take up half a page in the phone book."

The answer seemed to satisfy the girl—for now. But she was far from finished. "So what made you want to be a nanny? Why would anybody want a job changing poopy diapers?"

Leigh feigned a shrug. "I needed the work. The pay is good. What's more, I happen to like little babies, diapers and all."

"And my rich, handsome, single daddy had nothing to do with it?"

"Nothing at all." Like the rest of Leigh's answers, that was—technically—true.

"Plenty of women have tried to land him, even a couple of movie stars who came here. You'd recognize them if I told you who they were. They were pretty in person. A lot prettier than you."

Wyatt's daughter was testing her, Leigh realized. She was probing for weak spots that could be exploited later to get what she wanted. It wasn't going to work.

"How are you feeling, Chloe?" she asked, changing the subject. "Still pretty sore, I imagine."

"Are you kidding? I hurt all over! Especially my boobs! The nurse said my milk was coming in. Gross! Don't they have some pills I can take for that?"

"They used to. Then they found out the pills increased the chance of breast cancer. So you'll just have to tough it out till the swelling goes away—unless, of course, you decide to nurse your baby. It's not too late."

"No way! That would be so gross!"

"Then I'll see about getting you some ice packs at the house." Leigh swung the car onto the private road. "But don't expect to jump right back into your life. It'll take you a few weeks to get back to normal."

Chloe winced as a tire jounced over a fallen rock. "How come you know so much? Have *you* ever had a baby? You certainly look old enough."

"I'm twenty-six. And the answer is no, I haven't had a baby. But most of my friends have children. I've talked with them about what it's like."

If only she could talk to them now. But even if she didn't name names, confiding in her friends that she was taking care of a baby would be skating the edge of the agreement she'd signed. If Wyatt Richardson had the means to monitor his daughter's emails and phone calls, he could, and likely would, do the same with hers.

"Ever been married?" Chloe asked.

"Never."

"Ever lived with a guy?"

"In Denver, for about a year. We were engaged." Leigh didn't like talking about her past, but if it would help her build rapport with the girl, she was willing to open up a little.

"And you didn't get married? What happened?"

"The usual." Leigh managed a wry laugh. "He cheated on me."

"Guys can be such douche bags." Chloe sounded more like a world-weary forty-year-old than a girl barely out of middle school.

"What about your father?" The question popped out before Leigh could think the better of it.

"Daddy is who he is. He likes his privacy and his women. And he likes being in control. He's pretty generous. He'll give you anything you ask for—except his time. Anything else you want to know, ask the people he works with—they see more of him than I ever did. I can't say he'd win many prizes as a father. But at least he doesn't pretend to be somebody he isn't."

Leigh hesitated, weighing her response.

"I wouldn't get involved with him if I were you," Chloe said. "He doesn't let anybody get too close, even when he is around. That's part of why my mother left him, I think. Maybe—"

The jangle of her cell phone cut off whatever she'd been about to say. "Hi, Daddy…Yes, we're on the mountain road…Mikey's in the back. He's fine. We're all fine… See you in a few minutes." She ended the call with a sigh. "Such a control freak! I swear he checks on every breath I take!"

Leigh held her tongue and kept on driving. The task ahead of her loomed like Pike's Peak. Could she do enough to mend this dysfunctional family for Mikey's sake—and still keep her heart intact?

She'd never been much of a churchgoer. But as they rounded the last steep curve, her lips moved in a silent prayer for wisdom.

Five

Wyatt came outside as the car pulled up to the porch. After opening the door on Chloe's side, he reached in to help her stand. With a muttered "I'm not an invalid," she waved him away and climbed out by herself. For a young woman who'd just given birth she looked all right. But imagining what she'd been through was like a kick in the gut—or a bad dream.

Lord, she was a mother now—his little girl, who wasn't much more than a child herself.

Leigh had opened the back door and lifted the baby carrier off its base. "Mikey must've liked the car ride," she said, beaming down at Chloe's son. "He's fast asleep. Just look at him, Wyatt. Isn't he beautiful?" Moving deftly, she blocked Wyatt's path to the house, and thrust the baby carrier into his line of vision.

Wyatt sensed what the woman was up to. He'd made no secret of his feelings toward the baby or his hope that Chloe would give the child up, and it was clear that Leigh disapproved. He wanted to ignore her question, and the baby she was holding out toward him. The last thing he wanted was to become attached to the little mite. But there was no mistaking the steel in Leigh's eyes and the set of her jaw. She wouldn't step aside until he'd taken a good look at his grandson.

Tilting the carrier toward him, she folded back the blanket to reveal a miniature face as perfect as a flower. Wyatt's throat went dry. Yesterday, holding the baby, he'd been focused on his own discomfort and his anger toward the unknown father. Now he saw an innocence that threatened to wrap around his heart and crush it like a root tendril crushing a stone.

Whatever he was feeling, it hurt. And it wasn't what he wanted to feel.

"Well, what do you think of him?" Leigh asked.

"He's a handsome boy, all right." The words came with effort. "But I can't say much for the dog outfit. A gift from one of Chloe's friends, I take it."

At the sound of his voice, the baby yawned adorably and opened calm, curious eyes. His cheek dimpled as he smiled—not a real smile, of course. Not yet. But it was a good imitation.

Something tightened in Wyatt's chest. He sensed the closing of a trap.

"I'm starved!" Chloe called from the doorway. "What's to eat around here?"

"Pizza's in the oven." He was grateful for the diversion. "Double cheese supreme, your favorite. Are you up to eating in the kitchen or can we bring a tray to your room?"

"Kitchen." She sounded cranky, probably hurting. "After that I'm going to sleep. That hospital bed sucked, and the food sucked even worse."

At least she seemed glad to be home. Wyatt held the door so Leigh could carry the baby inside. "The pizza's for you, too, Leigh. In fact, you're welcome to share the table at all our meals. We're family here, for whatever that's worth."

Her smile was like the sun coming out. "Thanks. As the hired help, I was wondering about that."

"You shouldn't. Like I said, you've been watching too many episodes of *Masterpiece Theatre*."

"Then I hope you won't mind my wanting to cook now and then. You have a great kitchen. It's a shame to waste it."

"Knock yourself out." He followed his daughter into the kitchen where the table was already set for three. Chloe didn't even glance his way as she pulled the pizza pan out of the oven. Things were bound to be prickly with Chloe for a while. He could only hope having Leigh as a buffer would ease the tension.

Chloe took her seat, scooped two pizza slices onto her plate and popped the tab on a can of diet soda. Leigh placed the baby carrier on the far end of the table before she sat down. The baby was awake and doing his best to suck on his fist.

"Shouldn't you put him to bed?" Chloe asked.

"Mikey's part of your family now," Leigh said. "As long as he's not fussing, it's good for him to be here, listening to friendly voices."

"Whatever." Chloe shrugged and went on eating. "You're the expert."

Wyatt cast her a frown as he took his seat. In open defiance of his wishes, Leigh was doing all she could to bond the baby into the family. What he couldn't understand, given the offer he'd made her, was *why*.

He found himself watching the little fellow. Darned if that fist wasn't a real challenge. When he couldn't get it into his mouth, he became visibly frustrated. But he kept on trying—at least he wasn't a quitter. His hands flailed at his face until—*ouch*—he hit himself in the eye.

The blow must've hurt, or at least surprised him. He flinched sharply and began to cry—not a mewling whimper, but a full-blown howl. What a pair of lungs.

Leigh was out of her chair like a shot, scooping him up and gathering him against her shoulder. Rocking him gently, she made little soothing sounds until his cries faded to baby hiccups.

Chloe watched with anxious eyes. "Is he all right, Leigh?"

"He's fine. But he might be hungry. The hospital gave us a few bottles of prepared formula. Keep an eye on him. I'll go get one."

She lowered Mikey into the carrier, but she'd no sooner let him go than he started to bawl again. Chloe stared at her son with a pained look. "Why is he yelling like that? Isn't there something you can do to stop it?"

"Sorry, but I'm afraid you'll have to get used to it. We all will." Leigh picked up the infant and thrust him toward the girl. "He likes to be held. Give it a try. I'll be right back."

Wyatt didn't miss the panic that flashed across his daughter's face. Chloe was feeling overwhelmed—and he couldn't say he blamed her. "Give the boy to me," he heard himself saying. "I can hold him for a minute."

With a look of surprise, Leigh passed him the squirming bundle. Making a cradle with his arms, Wyatt gathered the little squalling creature against his chest. How could anything so small be so demanding? Young Mikey was already bossing the adults around as if he owned the place.

"Hello, Mikey." The words emerged as a growl from Wyatt's tight throat. Startled by the unfamiliar voice, the baby stopped crying and gazed up at him with those stunning eyes. Acting on instinct, Wyatt began to rock him gently, singing the first song that popped into his head—a timeworn ditty about the fate of a daredevil skier.

"He was headed down the slope doin' ninety miles an hour…"

He looked over to see that Chloe was watching with an enraptured expression on her face. "OMG, Daddy, look at him. He loves it. Did you ever sing that song to me?"

Wyatt replied with a shrug. As busy as he'd been when Chloe was small—and as nervous as he'd been about turning into his own father—he hadn't spent much time with her. Maybe if he had, they'd have a better relationship now. But it was too late to change the past. He could only hope to salvage her future—a future without a fatherless baby in it.

Leigh had found one of the bottles in the bag the hospital had provided. The formula was room temperature. That had to be all right. By tomorrow she'd have to be up to speed on how to prepare the bottles herself. So much to learn. How long could she keep faking it before she got herself in trouble?

Walking back to the kitchen, she paused in the doorway. Wyatt was cradling Mikey in his arms, his head bent over the baby. She could hear his rumbling song, and although she couldn't make out the words, she could tell that both he and his grandson were having a good time. Listening to his playful voice and watching the fall of sunlight on his hair, she felt something soften inside her. Maybe there was hope for this man—and this family—after all.

As she entered the room, Wyatt glanced up and stopped singing. "Take this little rascal," he said. "I wasn't cut out to be a nursemaid."

Reaching from the side, Leigh lifted the baby to her shoulder. "Want to try feeding him, Chloe?"

"You do it. I'm tired, and you're the expert."

Leigh took a seat at the far end of the table and settled Mikey in her arms. She hadn't bottle-fed an infant since her high school babysitting days, but how hard could it be?

Mikey had been fed in the hospital, so he knew the ropes. As soon as the nipple brushed his lips, he latched on and began chomping like a hungry piglet.

"Quite an appetite the boy's got." Wyatt was frowning but he couldn't disguise the note of pride in his voice. So far he was proving an easy conquest. Chloe, on the other hand, seemed to be going out of her way not to look at them. Maybe the girl just needed time.

Or maybe she was scared to death of being a mother.

Mikey had already downed half the small bottle. Was he drinking too much? Leigh slipped the nipple out of his mouth. The baby let out a howl of protest, keeping it up until she replaced it. "He seems to be strong-willed," she said. "Now, how do you suppose he came by that?"

She glanced from father to daughter. Chloe was eating and still refusing to look their way. Wyatt's only response was a deepening scowl. So much for her lame attempt at humor.

In the next few minutes Mikey finished off the formula and seemed satisfied. Now, if Leigh remembered right, he'd need to be burped to get rid of any air he might have swallowed. Raising him against her shoulder she began patting his back. Nothing. And now he'd started fussing. Was she doing something wrong?

She was about to change tactics when she heard a startling belch. She began pulling him back off her shoulder a little to see if he was all right when something warm and wet washed over the shoulder of her black turtleneck, soaking the ends of her hair and trickling down her chest and back.

"OMG!" Chloe was staring, goggle-eyed. Wyatt was struggling to keep a straight face. When Leigh lifted the baby fully away from her shoulder, she saw that the dog outfit was drenched in spit-up formula.

If Mikey was upset about the mess, he didn't show it. In fact his attention seemed to be focused on something else. As Leigh held him at arm's length, a bubbling sound rose from his diaper, along with an unmistakable aroma.

Wyatt cocked an eyebrow. "I think it's time for Mikey to be excused, Leigh. We'll save you some pizza."

Clutching her wet, smelly nephew, Leigh fled toward the stairs.

By the end of the day Leigh was worn out. She'd peeled off Mikey's reeking clothes, wiped, sponge bathed and changed him, fed him a small amount, burped him, this time with a protective cloth, and put him down for a blessed nap. While he was sleeping she'd put his soiled garments and hers to soak in cold water, tidied herself up, rigged a couple of makeshift ice packs for Chloe's swollen breasts, and sterilized the unused bottles and nipples she'd bought at Baby Mart.

She'd barely had time to wolf down two slices of warmed-over pizza before Mikey woke up again, fussing and wanting to be held. Babies learned fast how to get what they wanted.

With Chloe deep in exhausted slumber and Wyatt gone off in the car without saying where, the house was quiet. Snuggling the warm little body in her arms, she sank into the rocking chair. Mikey seemed to like the rocking motion. She could feel him relaxing against her. His eyes were calm and alert. If only her mother could see him. Once she got over the shock, she would fall in love with the little boy.

It was a shame that that could never happen, especially

since Leigh's mother had voiced her yearning for a grandchild many times. She'd been so happy about Leigh's engagement to Edward and so dejected over the breakup. Leigh had never told her the whole story—how she'd walked into the apartment to find Edward in bed with a coworker, and learned that he'd been cheating on her all along.

Would she ever trust a man again? But the answer to that question was on hold. Right now, and for the foreseeable future, the most important male in her life was the one in her arms.

The room darkened into twilight. Mikey had closed his eyes. His even breathing told her he'd fallen asleep. Carrying him as if he might break, Leigh tiptoed to the crib and eased him down on his back. He was as limp as a worn-out puppy, arms flung outward, hands curled into tiny fists.

With a last tender look, she picked up the receiver for the baby monitor, made sure it was working and slipped out of the room.

At the far end of the hallway was a cozy sitting area with a gas fireplace, well-stocked bookshelves and a state-of-the-art TV. It would be bliss, Leigh thought, to sink into the sofa and spend a mindless hour staring at whatever was on the screen. But right now she needed fresh air.

Double glass doors opened onto the upstairs balcony. Stepping outside, she set the monitor on a handy chair, leaned on the rail and inhaled the cool, piney fragrance of an October night. Far below, the lights of the resort glimmered in the dusk, climbing the ski runs and flowing down the bed of the canyon. This was Wyatt's kingdom, which he'd built over the years into a mecca of glamour.

Having done her homework, Leigh knew that Wyatt was vastly rich. The resort with its hotels and businesses, lodge, ski runs and surrounding properties, along with some major investments and holdings, had to be worth well over a billion dollars. But she'd seen firsthand how modestly he lived. Even this house—beautiful as it appeared—was built more for comfort than for display. It struck her that in placing it on this lonely bluff, overlooking the resort, Wyatt had set up his own private world—a world apart from the lavish milieu below. Did that private world have room in it for a pair of new additions?

She remembered how she'd seen him earlier today, singing to Mikey as he cradled the tiny boy in his arms. Behind the domineering, hard-driving facade he showed the world, the man had a tender side—a side she wouldn't mind seeing more of. Besides, there was something sexy about a man holding a little baby.

Even without the baby, Wyatt was one of the most compelling men she'd ever met. Last night, when he'd massaged her feet, she'd been close to panting. It wouldn't have taken much to push her past the limits of common sense. And if she didn't get herself under control, it wouldn't take much again....

A stray breeze, smelling faintly of wood smoke, cooled her damp hair. The night had turned chilly, but she wasn't ready to go inside. The stars were coming out, so many, so bright, undimmed by the lights of town. Far below, through the pines, she could make out the glow of headlights coming up the road. Her pulse quickened.

It had to be Wyatt.

Wyatt had picked up the Bentley at the resort, where the only mechanic he trusted had delivered it. He savored the feel of the vintage auto as he drove it up the mountain road, flying around the curves for the fun of it. With the first heavy snow, the car would be stored in the heated garage. Until then he could enjoy having it back in good repair.

As he drove, he kept a sharp eye out for deer. Leigh had mentioned almost hitting one last night. Her near miss was a reminder for him to be careful.

His thoughts circled back to Leigh—as they'd been circling all day. The woman puzzled, intrigued and frustrated him. She had the kind of classy sex appeal that made him want to fling her over his shoulder and haul her into his bed. But why would such a woman apply for a nanny job? What was she after?

Her background check had come back squeaky clean—not so much as a parking ticket. No bankruptcies. No pressing debts. Her education and work record exactly matched her résumé. She appeared to be smart and capable, and anyone with eyes could see how she felt about little Mikey.

But when it came to baby care, Leigh was obviously flying blind.

Catching her with that baby book had roused his suspicions. Today's incident had confirmed them. Anyone experienced with babies would have known Mikey might spit up. Hellfire, even *he* knew better than to burp an infant without putting a towel on his shoulder. But he'd seen the shock on Leigh's face. She'd been totally unprepared for the drenching she got.

Whatever else she might be, she definitely wasn't an experienced nanny. Not that he was planning to fire her. She was conscientious, hardworking and damned easy on the eyes. But he meant to discover Leigh's hidden agenda—by any means it took.

Earlier, he'd resolved not to lay a hand on his new employee. But getting up close and personal might be the only way to pry out her secret. A little pillow talk could accomplish wonders. Besides, it was bound to be fun.

Whistling under his breath, he rounded the last curve in the road and swung the Bentley toward the garage.

* * *

Leigh was still on the balcony when the car pulled up to the house. She heard the garage close, then the sound of Wyatt's footsteps crossing the porch. There was no reason to think he'd be coming upstairs. His bedroom, which she'd never seen, was on the main floor, flanked by his office and a private den. After today, he was likely ready for solitude.

The baby monitor was still silent, the night sky so glorious that she couldn't bring herself to go back inside. Standing at the rail, her eyes tracing the path of the Milky Way, she felt alone in the darkness. The last thing she expected was to feel a soft weight settle around her shoulders.

"Take my jacket," Wyatt's voice murmured in her ear. "Can't have you freezing out here."

"Thanks." She snuggled into his alpaca coat, her heart thundering as his arms wrapped it around her. "I haven't seen a sky like this in years. Too much light in town."

"I know. It's one of the reasons I built up here." His arms tightened, drawing her back against his chest. Against her better judgment she sank into his warm strength. His nearness was deliciously comforting.

"How's Chloe?" he asked. "I brought Chinese in case anybody's hungry."

"We can warm it up tomorrow. Chloe took a pain pill and went to bed. She was fast asleep when I last checked."

"And the baby?"

"He's asleep, too. But I have the monitor in case he wakes up."

A chuckle vibrated in his throat. "You've had quite the day yourself."

"I know. I took a few minutes to shower and change but I wouldn't be surprised if I still smell like baby spit."

He nuzzled her hair, taking his time. A thread of heat

uncurled in the secret depths of her body, shimmering upward. She felt her nipples pucker inside her bra. Oh, this wasn't smart. She should make her excuses and go inside. But her feet refused to move.

"Can't smell a thing. Just soft, clean, lovely hair." His lips brushed the tip of her ear. Her breath eased out in a long, whispered sigh. Common sense told her that Wyatt Richardson was up to something. But she'd been too long alone, too long angry and hurting, to pull away from the comfort he was offering.

And—Leigh forced herself to face the truth—she'd been thinking about this man all day. She'd wanted him from the moment she'd fallen out of his Hummer and into his arms.

Six

"I have a question for you, Leigh." His breath stirred her hair. His voice was bedroom husky; but something in his tone told her romance wasn't the upmost thing on his mind. "I'm hoping we can talk this over and come to an understanding."

Leigh had been careening toward the brink of surrender. But she gave herself a mental splash of cold water. "Go ahead."

"I've told you where I stand on Chloe's keeping her baby. But you've made it equally clear you don't agree."

She stiffened, her defenses prickling. A moment ago he'd seemed bent on seduction. Now she feared she was about to be fired. What kind of game was he playing?

"You have every right to feel as you do," he continued. "But what I don't understand is your motive—for shoving Mikey into the middle of the family and making sure Chloe and I interact with him. You must know that I don't *want* to get attached to the little mite. And I'm not sure I want Chloe to get too attached to him, either. That's why

I offered you a bonus to help her make a sensible decision. If it's more money you want—"

"You think this is about *money?*" She pulled away and spun to face him. "This is about Mikey! He's not some stray puppy you're trying to give away. He's a baby, Wyatt! He's Chloe's son and your grandson—your own flesh and blood. True, he might be better off with the right adoptive parents. But if Chloe makes that decision it should be because she *loves* him enough to want what's best for him instead of what's easiest for her. And the same goes for you! That innocent little boy deserves better than to have you turn your back on him!"

Wyatt stood frozen, looking as if she'd slapped him. Had she said too much? Was she about to get her walking papers?

"I see." His voice was expressionless. "That leaves me with another question. As a nanny, you've been winging it pretty well. But I'd bet my Bentley you're no more qualified for this job than I am. Why are you so passionate about a baby you didn't know existed until yesterday? What's your stake in all this?"

Dread congealed in the pit of Leigh's stomach. She'd revealed too much; and now Wyatt was within a sliver of stripping away her subterfuge.

Should she come clean and tell him everything, exposing her brother to Wyatt's fury and possible ruin?

Or should she risk a bluff—the only one that came to mind?

There was no way she was going to get Kevin in trouble and cause pain to her mother. The bluff was her only remaining choice.

"Leigh, I asked you a question." Wyatt's voice was as stern as his expression.

"Yes, I know…" With time running out, she had to act

fast. Flinging her arms around his neck, she pulled his head down and pressed her mouth to his in a desperate, devouring kiss.

Wyatt went rigid. A growl of surprise escaped his throat. Then his reflexes kicked in. Whatever game the woman was playing, he'd be only too happy to play along.

His arms caught her close, molding her curves against his solid body. A quiver went through her as he took control, his kiss utterly possessing her. Her lips parted, welcoming the playful thrust of his tongue. When his hands slid under her shirt, unclasping her bra in a single deft motion, she made no move to stop him. If this was an act, it was a good one, Wyatt told himself. He could feel the surging heat of her response. He knew his women, and this one showed every sign of wanting what he had to give.

His coat slipped off her shoulders to fall around their feet. She moaned as his hand moved over her bare back. His thumb skimmed the satiny edge of her breast, lingering just long enough for a tease. His mouth nibbled down her throat.

She was delicious, like hot buttered rum on a winter night.

Her chest arched against him in a clear invitation for more. Wyatt's fingers slid under one cup of her lacy bra to stroke her breast—small, but so firm, so perfect.... She gasped as he brushed her taut nipple, and then, as his palm cupped her, she made a little melting sound and pressed against him. His sex was hot and hard, threatening to rip out the rivets in his jeans. He knew she could feel it.

He kissed her again, taking time to savor those ripe, swollen lips. "So *this* is why you applied to work here?" he muttered half-teasingly.

"Mm-hmm...I've had a crush on you for years, and this

was my chance." She strained upward for another kiss with what appeared to be sincere eagerness. Not that he was fooled. She was probably lying through her pretty teeth about having planned this all along, but he believed she truly did want him at this moment and, besides, he was enjoying this too much to care. Sooner or later he'd get to the truth. Right now he had more urgent things on his mind.

Leigh was losing control. She'd meant to distract Wyatt from his line of questioning, maybe even convince him that she'd come here because of him. But the man had taken charge and was sweeping her along like a twig in an avalanche.

His lips nibbled hers with an easy restraint that made her ache for more. His hand rested on her bare breast, his thumb stroking her nipple to a throbbing, exquisitely sensitive nub. Heat streamed through her body, driven by her pounding heart. Where her hips pressed the solid ridge of his erection, the contact triggered spasms of need. She hadn't asked to want him like this, hadn't expected to. But the sensations that pounded through her body were too powerful to deny.

"You're so damnably sexy, Leigh." His free hand moved down the hollow of her back to dip below the waistband of her jeans. His fingers invading her panties, stroking the diamond shape at the base of her spine. "I've wanted you from the moment you walked into that interview in that hot little skirt of yours. Those legs…"

His touch was driving her to a frenzy. She whimpered and shifted her hips. Nuzzling her mouth again he let his hand glide around to rest on the flat of her belly. Somewhere in her brain, alarm sirens blared a warning. But Leigh was past hearing. His touch felt so good….

Breathless, she waited for his fingertips to glide lower.

Wetness soaked the crotch of her panties. She pressed against his hand, anticipating…

"We're in the wrong place for this," he muttered. "Come on." Keeping her in the circle of his arm, he propelled her back inside and down the hall toward her room.

"Chloe…the baby…" she whispered anxiously.

"They're asleep, and we can be quiet." He pulled her inside and closed the door. His mouth caught hers in a powerful kiss that sent whorls of heat pulsing through her body. His tongue probed hers, thrusting, caressing in an unmistakable pantomime of what he had in mind as he guided her toward the bed. His borrowed jacket, along with her shirt, bra, jeans and panties, left a trail across the floor.

Her arms wrapped his neck, fingers raking his hair as his kisses grazed her face, her throat, her breasts. The hollow between her hips had gone molten. Heaven help her, she wanted this man. She'd wanted him from the first instant their eyes locked.

"Tell me to leave, and I'll leave," he muttered in her ear. "But you'd better tell me now."

"Wyatt, I'm a big girl. And as the saying goes, this isn't my first rodeo. I know tonight isn't forever. I just want to enjoy it—and enjoy you. No strings attached."

One dark eyebrow quirked upward. "Well, now, that's refreshing. So we'll leave it at that—for the present, at least."

Leigh's hands found the hem of his cashmere sweater and underneath it, the chiseled contours of his athlete's body—the rippling back, the rock-solid abs, the tender, sensitive nipples that triggered a moan when she skimmed them with her fingertip.

With a murmur of impatience, he lowered her to the bed, then stripped off his clothes and added protection to his jutting arousal. There would be no tender words between them, no wooing, no promises, nothing between them but pure, pleasurable lust. And right now that was enough.

Climbing into the bed he caught her in his arms. Leigh could feel his length and bulk along her belly. She could almost imagine him inside her, filling the hungry, hidden place that had been empty too long. Her need deepened to an ache.

His hand readied her, stroking the moist, tender folds. As his finger slid into her, riding on her slickness, she came with a little gasping shudder.

"Yes…" she whispered. "Now. Please."

Laughing softly, he mounted between her eager legs and entered her with one long, gliding push. Her breath eased out in a sigh of bliss. The feel of him was pure heaven.

Neither of them was in the mood to take things slowly. As her legs wrapped him, their thrusts became a wild ride, fast and hard and joyous. She met each push with her hips, deepening the contact as her climax swirled and burst like a sky full of Independence Day fireworks.

He grunted, quivered and then relaxed against her. "Not bad for the first time," he chuckled.

With a gentle kiss he rolled off her, stood and padded into the bathroom, leaving Leigh curled blissfully in bed.

A wail arose from the crib in the adjoining room. Yanked back to reality, Leigh stumbled to her feet and flung on her robe. Mikey's plaintive cries tore at her heart.

Flinging open the door, she burst into the nursery. In the glow of the night-light, Mikey lay in the crib, fussing and waving his fists. As soon as Leigh picked him up and gathered him close, his cries stopped. He snuggled against her, making little smacking sounds.

"Is he all right?" Wyatt stood in the doorway, his jeans pulled up over his hips.

"He's fine. Just lonesome and hungry—and wet." Her hand felt the dampness on the seat of Mikey's pajamas. "As long as you're here, could you do me a favor? His formula bottles are downstairs in the fridge. Could you warm one a little in some hot water and bring it up here?"

When he hesitated, she added, "Or I can do it if you'd rather stay here and change him."

She glanced down at Mikey, who was sucking on his fist. When she looked up again, the doorway was empty.

So much for romance. Wyatt found the bottles in the refrigerator. The prepared formula was cold. Running some hot water in a pan he set one bottle in it and waited. How warm was the blasted formula supposed to be? He could've sworn they'd unpacked a bottle warmer last night. But Leigh was still organizing things in the nursery. It could have been put away and forgotten. After all, she'd had plenty on her mind.

As he'd just learned tonight…

Was this really what she'd planned all along? Taking the job to seduce him? He found that hard to believe, but as long as he could have her in bed he wasn't complaining about her motives.

Still, he'd be smart to keep a cool head. This wouldn't be the first time a woman had tried to use him for her own purposes.

Another thing—was she right about including the baby in the family? Lord knows he'd meant well. But was ignoring an innocent child to spare his own feelings—and perhaps the baby's—the moral choice? The humane choice?

Leigh had given him a lot to think about—more than he was fit to process tonight. It was easier to dwell on what had happened at the *end* of their conversation.

Leaning against the counter, he relived those frantic moments in her bed. She'd been so sweet, so pliant and ready. And he'd been wild with the smell and taste and feel of her. The thought of having her again had him aching like a hormone-crazed high school sophomore.

He wanted her—plain and simple. Any way he could have her. But the next time he got intimate with his sexy nanny, he wanted to make sure there'd be no distractions. He wanted the time and privacy to drive her mad with pleasure.

With Chloe and the baby in the house, that was going to take some planning.

When the bottle felt lukewarm he carried it back upstairs. From the dark hall he could see through the open doorway to where Leigh sat in the rocker with Mikey cradled in her arms. Her head was bent over him, the nightlight casting her in a soft glow. She was singing, her voice so low that he could barely hear it, let alone make out the words. But the expression on her face was one of pure love.

The emotion that stirred in him had nothing to do with lust. Seeing her in that light with the baby was like looking at a Renaissance painting—beautiful and strangely moving. For a moment he stood spellbound. Then she glanced up and saw him.

"Did you bring the formula? This little guy is hungry."

"Right here." He held up the bottle. "But I don't know if it's the right temperature."

"You test it like this." She held out her free hand, palm up. "Dribble a few drops on my wrist…. Yes, that's it. It feels about right." She gazed up at him. "Why don't you try feeding Mikey?"

Wyatt caught the challenge in her eyes. He didn't relish the idea. But something told him he'd be smart to stay on this woman's good side.

"Here, sit down." Before he could argue, she moved

out of the chair and might have shoved him into it if he hadn't taken the seat on his own. The next thing he knew the baby was in his arms. Mikey was dressed in clean yellow pajamas and wrapped in a fresh receiving blanket printed with ducklings. The eyes that gazed up at Wyatt were so pure and clear that they seemed to see into the depths of his soul.

Leigh lowered herself to the stool at his feet. "Prop him up a little. Then just brush his lips with the nipple. He'll do the rest."

Wyatt followed her suggestion. Mikey latched on to the rubber nipple as though it was the real thing. He drank with small gulping sounds, his eyes closing with pleasure. "Ease him off a little," Leigh cautioned. "You've seen what can happen if he drinks too fast. That's it...."

She was smiling up at him, the night-light soft on her face. Wyatt cursed under his breath. Damn it, but she was beautiful.

"It's a shame you don't have children of your own," he said, making conversation. "You strike me as a natural."

"Maybe someday." She glanced down at her clasped hands. "Wyatt, what happened tonight...I'm aware that I made the first move. And I can't say I didn't enjoy it. But it wasn't very smart—especially with Chloe in the house."

Wyatt nodded, reluctant to speak and startle Mikey, now a warm, sleepy bundle of contentment in his arms.

"We can't be sneaking around behind her back, hoping she won't overhear us or walk in on us," Leigh continued. "My main reason for being here is to give Mikey a loving start, and to help Chloe any way I can. None of that will work if she can't trust me."

"So what about your so-called crush?"

"Oh, it's still there." She gave him a hint of a smile. "But it might have to wait for a better time. I've been burned before, and I know better than to think either one of us is looking for a serious relationship. We had a good time, and I certainly wouldn't mind a return engagement. But first things first."

Wyatt looked down at his sleeping grandson. Mikey's eyes were closed, his lashes golden feather spikes against his rosy cheeks. Leigh was right. What mattered most was doing the right thing for Chloe and for this precious new life. Other concerns could wait.

But not forever. True, after doing the marriage thing once, Wyatt knew he wasn't husband material, or even long-term boyfriend material. But the chemistry with Leigh was too delicious to put on hold for long. He meant to get her to himself—and he wasn't a patient man.

Leigh woke to the sound of a car backing down the drive. She flew to the window to see the Bentley swing onto the road and disappear behind the trees. She glanced at the clock. Six-thirty, not even sunup. Did Wyatt have pressing business this early or was he running away from pressures on the home front?

After feeding Mikey last night, he'd made his excuses and gone downstairs. She'd known better than to go after him. He'd had an emotional day and so had she. And they could hardly spend the night together with Chloe in the house. His distance from her had only been sensible. But today was different. Wyatt had gone off and left her to deal with the teen on her own—a whole new set of challenges.

Mikey was awake in the nursery making little cooing noises in his crib. Flinging on her robe, she hurried through the connecting doorway. His eyes brightened as she leaned over to pick him up. "Hello, big boy." She kissed the soft curve of his neck, inhaling the sweet baby aroma she'd already come to love. His diaper was soaked. He'd need changing and sponging before she went downstairs. Putting him back in the crib she pulled on her jeans and a fresh shirt. By the time she'd brushed her teeth and hair he was crying. Probably hungry. Maybe she should feed him first, then get him cleaned up.

Leigh was beginning to understand why some new mothers looked so frazzled. She felt like a wreck, and she hadn't even given birth.

The soggy diaper couldn't wait. She used a wipe on his bottom, being careful to keep his cord dry, and taped a fresh disposable into place. That done, she zipped him into dry pajamas, put him in his carrier and took him down to the kitchen. He was fussing and sucking on his fist. The poor little guy was really hungry.

She put a bottle in hot water and snuggled him while she waited. When she had a minute she would find that bottle warmer she'd put somewhere. And while she was at it, she'd organize the whole process of making formula. For the sake of her own sanity, she needed to become more efficient.

She'd just begun feeding Mikey when Chloe wandered into the kitchen. Dressed in her blue sweats, she was tousled and yawning but still managed to look pretty. "What's to eat?" she mumbled, sitting down.

Leigh glanced up from feeding the baby. "Tell me what sounds good and I'll do my best."

"French toast—with bacon. I'm starved."

Leigh had seen bread, eggs, bacon and some condiments in the fridge. "That sounds doable. Take your boy. By the time you've finished feeding him, I should have it ready."

Something akin to panic flashed in Chloe's cornflower eyes. "That's all right. I can wait till you're done."

Leigh knew she couldn't back off now. "You didn't feed him in the hospital?" she asked.

She shook her russet curls. "I told the nurses I wanted to rest. I've never fed him. I thought that was your job."

"It is. But I'll eventually have a day off. If you really want to keep this baby, you need to know how to take care of him when I'm not here. Feeding him's easy. Your father did it last night."

"Daddy fed Mikey?"

Leigh nodded. "If he can do it, anybody can. Here, take him." She held the baby toward the girl.

"What if I do it wrong? What if I hurt him?" Chloe shrank away, eyes wide with what appeared to be genuine fear.

"What is it, Chloe?" Nestling Mikey against her once more, Leigh took a seat at the table. "Why did you decide to keep your baby if you don't want to take care of him?"

Tears welled in the girl's eyes. "I wanted something to love, something that was all mine. Before he was born, loving him was easy. But now that he's here, he's so little and helpless, I don't know what to do with him. I'm so scared…."

"But you're his mother. Why should you be scared?"

Chloe stared down at her hands. The nails, bitten to the quick, were painted baby-blue. "I don't know. But I remember something that happened when I was little. Mom took me to see my aunt, who'd just had a baby girl. She was so pretty, like a little doll. While Mom and Aunt Trudy were talking I tried to pick her up. I…dropped her on the hard floor. She wasn't moving. Mom called the paramedics."

"Oh, no! Was she all right?"

"She was, after a trip to the hospital. But I was so scared. I remember my aunt screaming at me, 'If she dies, it'll be your fault! Don't you ever touch a baby again!'"

"Oh, Chloe!" Leigh could have wept. What an awful thing for a girl to live with—and then to have a baby of her own while she was still too young to have the confidence to overcome the past. If she wanted Chloe to be comfortable with Mikey, she would have to take things slowly.

Mikey's bottle was almost empty. "I'll tell you what," she said. "I'll burp him, and then you can sit and hold him while I make breakfast. After that you can watch me sponge bathe him and choose a cute outfit for him to wear. Okay?"

"Okay. I think." She still looked hesitant. Leigh finished burping the baby and placed him gently in Chloe's arms. Chloe held him as if he were made of porcelain. But when he looked up at her and cooed, she smiled.

"Hi, Mikey," she whispered. "Hey, I'm your mom. How about that?"

Seven

Wyatt had weighed the wisdom of leaving Leigh to deal with Chloe by herself. In the end he'd decided to spend a busy day at the resort.

True, it was the coward's way out. But he had his reasons. He and Chloe tended to rub each other the wrong way, especially when she wasn't feeling well. Without him around, Leigh's day might be more agreeable. Besides, it was Wednesday. For years he'd made it a tradition to spend Wednesdays in his office at the Wolf Ridge Lodge. While he was there any resort employee, from the managers to the lowliest dishwasher, could drop by to air a grievance, ask a question or make a suggestion. The practice paid dividends in efficiency and employee morale. It also got him out of the house while the cleaning crew did their work.

But today Wyatt's thoughts weren't just on business. The memory of Leigh in his arms was a smoldering reminder of where he wanted to take this relationship. She'd been right about the pitfalls of a secret affair while Chloe was in the house. Sooner or later the girl was bound to find out. And the discovery that her father was sleeping with the nanny would be a calamity for all concerned.

But there had to be ways around that. After all, he owned a resort with a hotel. The trick would be getting Leigh out of the house for a night. Between her duties with Mikey and Chloe's raised eyebrows, that was going to be a challenge. But Wyatt had never been one to let difficulties stand in his way. Somehow he would manage this. He wanted some leisurely time to make love to Leigh. And one way or another, he would find it.

He might not be good for the long haul. But at least he knew how to make a woman happy in bed.

"I'm bored!" Chloe flipped through the TV channels and tossed the remote on the floor. "Why can't I go out with my friends?"

"It's Wednesday. Your friends are in school." Leigh glanced up from folding the basket of baby clothes she'd just laundered. "Maybe you can have them here this weekend. Why don't you ask your father when he gets home?"

"He'll say no. He wants to keep me locked up like a prisoner."

"That's nonsense. He wants to keep you and Mikey safe, that's all."

"Well, I don't need protecting. I'm going crazy in this house. And I don't have anything to wear! I want to go shopping!"

Leigh sighed. "Give it time, Chloe. Your body's still getting back to normal. Besides, it's probably too soon to take Mikey out. He could get sick."

Muttering, Chloe dragged herself off the sofa and wandered down the stairs. She was probably going to spend some time on the computer in her room. Would Wyatt's security team be monitoring her internet activity? But that was Wyatt's problem, Leigh reminded herself. She'd made it clear she wasn't going to police the girl.

Mikey had gone down for his nap an hour ago. Soon he'd be awake and needing attention. Leigh brushed a stray lock out of her eyes. Her nephew was a precious angel, but tending to his needs was wearing her down.

Chloe hadn't moved much beyond holding him. When she'd watched Leigh bathe the baby, she'd taken one look at the shriveling umbilical cord and declared that it was "gross." Maybe Wyatt had the right idea. Chloe still had so much growing up to do—was it fair to Mikey to keep him from an adoptive mother who'd be better prepared to give him everything he needed? But it was too soon to give up. In spite of her immaturity, Leigh could see that Chloe truly did love her baby. For the sake of everyone involved, Leigh knew she had to keep trying.

From Chloe's room, rap music blasted up the stairs. The noise was loud enough to wake Mikey. Hearing him fuss, Leigh raced down the hall to the nursery. She'd just picked him up when the front doorbell rang.

Tucking the baby into her arms, she made her way downstairs to the entry. As the bell jangled a second time, she reached the door and cautiously opened it.

A middle-aged woman stood on the front porch with two young men behind her. All three were dressed in maroon and silver Wolf Ridge Resort uniforms, complete with ID badges.

"Cleaning crew." The woman was short and huskily built, with wiry gray curls and a smile that lit her round moon of a face. The smile broadened as she caught sight of the baby. "So that's the little man! Hello there, Mr. Mikey!"

Leigh's jaw dropped. Clearly the woman had been talking to Wyatt. "Please come in and get started," she said, stepping back. "We'll do our best to stay out of your way."

"No, it's our job to stay out of *your* way." The woman stepped inside and motioned the two younger men toward the back of the house where the cleaning supplies were kept. "My name's Dora. And since your eyes are popping out of your head, I'll explain. I've been coming here to clean this house for the past nine years. Mr. Richardson trusts me like family. And he knows I keep my mouth shut."

Glancing at the woman's badge, Leigh read the words Housekeeping Supervisor. "I'm happy to meet you, Dora," she said. "Mikey may not be at his best right now. He just woke up, and I can smell his messy diaper."

"Oh, never mind that!" Dora reached out and scooped Mikey into her arms. "I've smelled plenty of diapers. Raised four kids on my own after my husband left—all girls, and they turned out fine. Mr. Richardson says you're pretty new at this. Would you like my phone number? You can call me anytime you have a question about babies."

"Thank you." Leigh felt as if she'd been drowning and the woman had tossed her a life preserver. "I really mean that, I just hope I won't bother you too much."

"No such thing as too much." Dora lifted Mikey to eye level, making little clucking sounds as she bounced him in her arms. Young as he was, Mikey responded, cooing in unmistakable delight. "Look at this handsome boy," she murmured. "And those blue Richardson eyes! This one's going to break hearts, just like his grandpa!"

She broke off, as if realizing she'd said too much. In the stillness Leigh could hear the two young men cleaning the kitchen.

"Where's the new mother?" Dora asked.

The rap music blaring from the hallway answered her question. Dora frowned and shook her head. "Oh, mercy, this won't do."

The next thing Leigh knew, Dora was striding down the hall with Mikey in the crook of her arm. Her free hand knocked sharply on Chloe's door.

The music stopped. Seconds passed before the door opened.

"Here you are, Miss Chloe," Dora said. "Since your so-called music woke this baby, he's all yours—and right now he needs his diaper changed."

Chloe's pert nose wrinkled. "That's not my job. It's the nanny's."

Dora's scowl deepened. "You're his mother. A nanny's job is to *help* you, not take your place." She glanced back at Leigh, who was watching wide-eyed. "Miss Foster, if you wouldn't mind bringing us some clean diapers and wipes, and maybe a towel."

The woman's voice rang with authority. Leigh raced to the nursery and returned with what was needed. Dora, who'd raised four girls, was giving her a lesson in how to handle a surly teen mother—a lesson Leigh badly needed to learn.

"Daddy, I changed Mikey's diapers today."

"Oh?" Wyatt glanced up from his plate of braised chicken, potatoes and gravy.

"They were gross. But I did it. I gave him a bottle, too."

"That's nice."

Sitting across the candlelit dinner table, Leigh glanced from father to daughter. Chloe seemed to crave her father's approval. But Wyatt was too preoccupied to notice. Seeing Chloe's disappointment at his nonresponse, Leigh thought of praising the girl herself, but decided against it. Dora had told her not to make too much of a fuss over Chloe for helping with Mikey's care—the teenager needed to see tending her baby as part of her normal routine, not something deserving special recognition.

Dora had made more progress with Chloe than Leigh had believed possible. In past years she'd served as Chloe's babysitter and was firmly in charge. Chloe had obeyed her without a murmur of argument.

Leigh felt she'd gained a friend as well, someone she could turn to when she needed advice. Dora had already given her some helpful hints on getting Mikey to sleep and organizing his things for more efficiency. His portable bassinet was now in Chloe's room, along with extra diapers, wipes and pajama outfits.

Dora was bound to know a lot about Wyatt. But Leigh had known better than to bring him up. The woman's first loyalty would be to her boss. Discussing his personal life would cross a forbidden line.

Leigh watched the play of candlelight on his rugged features. Remembering their plunge into passion the night before, a slow heat stirred inside her. Despite their constraints, she was eager for the next time. But tonight he seemed withdrawn. Maybe he was accustomed to sex partners who were gone the next morning. A woman who was waiting when he came home to dinner might be too much of an intrusion into his life.

"I'm having a new car delivered tomorrow," Wyatt said. "It's a Mercedes SUV with all-wheel drive and good snow tires. Leigh, it's to be your transportation while you're here. You can use it for errands and to drive Chloe and the baby where they need to go."

Chloe's fork clattered to the table. "What about me? Where's my sports car?"

Wyatt sighed. "You can't drive a sports car on these roads in wintertime, Chloe. Besides, I have yet to see that driver's license you told me you had."

"I know how to drive!" Chloe snapped.

"Maybe you do. But without that license, you're not getting behind the wheel."

Chloe's lower lip jutted outward in a little girl pout. "That's not fair, Daddy. I never finished driver training because I got pregnant and had to quit school. But Mom let me drive anyway. Ask her. I can drive just fine!"

"Not without your license, young lady. There should be a copy of the driver's handbook online. After you've studied it, you can go and take your test."

"And then you'll buy me a sports car?"

"We'll see—in the spring when the snow's gone."

"No! You promised! Two years ago, you said—" She broke off as she met his steely eyes. "Forget it! I can't believe anything you say!"

Bolting out of her chair, she stormed down the hall. The slam of her bedroom door reverberated through the house, waking Mikey in his upstairs crib.

"I'll get him." Leigh jumped up from the table and darted toward the stairs. Chloe had made a lot of progress today, but she was still sixteen years old, teetering between maturity and childhood.

Wyatt watched her rush out of sight. With a weary exhalation he pushed away his half-finished dinner. The clash with Chloe had pretty much destroyed his appetite. He was trying to do right by the girl. Why did she have to test him at every turn?

And what about Leigh? She'd told him she wanted Chloe to bond with her baby. But it was his lovely nanny who seemed to be doing most of the bonding. She couldn't be more attached to the little boy if she'd given birth to him herself. What would she do when the time came to let Mikey go?

Thinking of that sweet, innocent infant nestling in his arms last night, he found he was uncomfortable with the thought of Mikey leaving, too. And not just because he didn't know what he'd do when Leigh no longer had a reason to stay in his home.

Leigh returned moments later with Mikey snuggled against her shoulder. He was chomping hungrily on the collar of her shirt. "I think he wants his bottle," she said. "Do you mind holding him while I warm it?"

"Not a bit." Wyatt held out his arms for the baby. It amazed him how fast he was getting used to the little fellow. Holding him now seemed as natural as breathing.

Mikey was no longer fussing. His clear gaze took Wyatt in. Wyatt had heard somewhere that newborns couldn't focus their eyes. But in Mikey's case he didn't believe it. Those big blues seemed to be seeing everything.

"Hello, Mikey," he said using the gruff voice the baby seemed to like. "How's your day been? Want to tell me about it?"

Expressions flickered like sunbeams across the tiny face—surprise, amazement, a fearsome scowl—or was Mikey just passing gas? Wyatt found himself wondering what the boy would be like in years to come. Would he take to skiing? Would he be quick to learn in school? Would the girls chase after him?

But if things went as planned, he would never know, Wyatt reminded himself. How could Chloe raise a child when she was still a child herself?

Leigh had brought the bottle warmer downstairs and was waiting for the formula to heat. She stood by the kitchen counter, watching him with the baby. The tenderness in her eyes almost did him in. But it was little Mikey who'd put it there, he'd told himself. Even though they'd had a great time in bed, she had no reason to look at her grumpy, over-the-hill employer with so much love.

Face it, he wasn't good at relationships. Building a business, making money and providing generously for those in his care—that had been his way of showing love, the only way he knew how. The rest of it—the tenderness, the involvement, the sharing of time and emotion, was like a closed door to him.

"Mikey is so contented with you," she said. "You've got just the right touch."

He had to say it. "You're wrong, Leigh. I've been a decent provider. But when it comes to nurturing, I haven't got a clue. Experience has taught me that I just don't have what it takes to be a family man."

"I'm not sure I believe that. Look at you." Testing the formula on her wrist, Leigh walked back toward the table. Just watching her move was a pleasure. The sway of her jeans-clad hips and the flowing stride of her long legs teased his senses. Wyatt imagined her gliding naked across a candlelit room, the soft glow bathing her skin, her delicious breasts rising and falling with each breath, while he lay on his bed, waiting for her....

Damn, this wasn't helping!

"Since you're holding Mikey, would you like to feed him?"

Had she heard a word of what he'd just told her? Or was she trying to convince him he was wrong? Wyatt shook his head. "You can have him back. But I can't believe how much he changes from day to day. Tonight he's really been looking me over."

Leigh's breast brushed the peak of his ear as she reached past him to lift the baby. Choosing a nearby chair, she settled him in her arms and offered him the bottle. Mikey took it like a pro. She smiled.

"I'm remembering something Dora said—that Mikey seems to be one of those babies who come into the world knowing just how to get on with their lives. She called him an old soul."

Wyatt tried to ignore the tightness in his throat. "Dora's a gem," he said.

"She truly is. I can't believe how well she handled Chloe."

"Yes. Chloe." Wyatt exhaled. "Tonight you got a glimpse of her dark side. After seeing that little tantrum, do you still think the girl is ready to be a mother?"

"I never said she was," Leigh replied gently. "But she's capable of loving her baby and taking some responsibility for him. You should have seen her after she changed his diaper and fed him. She was so proud of herself. But when she told you about it tonight, all you said was 'That's nice.' It was like you hadn't even heard her."

"Maybe I didn't know what else to say. Am I supposed to be proud that my sixteen-year-old daughter can change and feed her—" He bit back the ugly, unthinkable word.

"Oh, Wyatt!" Her stricken look was like an ice pick in his chest. "She's still your little girl. And right now you're all she's got. She wants to know that you're on her side, that you believe in her. She needs you—and she loves you."

"She's got a funny way of showing it."

"I'm guessing it's the only way she knows." Leigh glanced down at the baby, then back at Wyatt. Her eyes were amber in the light of the burning candle. "I was about Chloe's age when I lost my father in a plane crash. We'd had an argument that morning because he wouldn't let me go to a party. As he went out the door with his suitcase the last words I said to him were 'I hate you.'"

The emotion in her voice was so wrenching that Wyatt couldn't reply.

"Of course I didn't mean it. And I have to think he knew that. But over the years…" She shook her head. "I'd give anything, even now, to have him back long enough to tell him I love him."

Wyatt found his voice. "Have you told Chloe that story?"

"I've never told anyone. Not until tonight."

His gaze caressed her—the softness of her features, the glimmer of tears in her eyes, the stray lock of dark hair that fell across her face. He'd known some stunning women in his time. But Leigh was beautiful to the marrow of her bones.

She glanced down at Mikey, as if overcome by sudden regret. Was she sorry she'd been so open with him?

For the flicker of a moment he was tempted to tell her about his own father. But he'd never shared that part of his past with anyone. And the story was so ugly it would only repel her. What he really wanted right now was to get her into his arms—and his bed—again. There, he'd know exactly what to do, exactly how to please her. But that would have to wait for a better time and place.

Since she was holding the baby, he had to settle for rising, stepping behind her and placing his hands on her shoulders. His thumbs gently massaged the tension from her taut muscles. She responded with a little purring sound that triggered wicked images in his mind.

"Thank you," he said, reining in his thoughts. "It means a lot, your sharing that story. It helps me put Chloe's issues in perspective."

"I wasn't so different myself at that age. I had to grow up fast after my father died. Chloe will grow up, too."

"I know," he said. "And I'm sure your father must've known you loved him."

Mikey stirred and began to fuss, breaking the quiet spell that had fallen over them.

"That reminds me," she said. "I haven't called my mother since I got here. I'd like to take Mikey upstairs, get him settled and phone her now, before it gets too late. Do you mind?"

"Of course not." Wyatt willed himself not to sound disappointed.

"Don't worry." She rose, still cradling Mikey in her arms. "I haven't forgotten the paper I signed. I won't disclose a thing."

He watched her turn away. Had it been overkill, asking her to sign the nondisclosure agreement? Now that he knew her, the whole idea seemed ludicrous. He could no longer imagine distrusting her. Though he still felt she was keeping something from him, he was sure it was nothing harmful or malicious—she would never do anything to hurt him or his family.

But trust wasn't the only thing on his mind as she walked toward the door. She moved like a dancer, her fluid hips whispering seduction. Wyatt cursed under his breath. Didn't the woman know what she was doing to him? If she hadn't been holding the baby, and if Chloe hadn't been nearby, he'd have been tempted to go after her, spin her against him and kiss her all the way to his bedroom. In the days before his life turned upside down that might have been possible. But Leigh was only here because Chloe and the baby were here—an irony that was driving him crazy. For now he had no choice except to wait.

Once they finally had time to explore each other thoroughly, surely this aching attraction would become manageable. The draw he felt toward her, the need to be close—nothing more than the symptoms of delayed gratification at work.

A physical relationship was all he had to offer her, so he had to believe that that was all he wanted.

Leigh changed Mikey, laid him in the crib and turned on the musical duck mobile. He wasn't sleepy but the sound and motion might at least keep him quiet while she made her phone call.

It was Kevin who answered on the second ring. "Hey, sis! How's the secret agent business? Where're you calling from, Bangladesh?"

"Silly!" Leigh made a show of laughing off his question. What would Kevin do if he knew she was less than an hour away, taking care of his baby son? "I'm just calling to check in with Mom. Is she around?"

"She's right here, fighting me for the phone—hey!" His laughter faded into the background as Leigh's mother came on.

"Is everything all right, dear?" Leigh could picture her, dressed in the black pantsuit she wore for selling real estate, her makeup in place, her chestnut hair meticulously dyed and curled. Diane Foster was a survivor, a woman who hid her vulnerability beneath the tough exterior it took to get ahead in the world.

"Everything's fine, Mom. I just wanted to say hello. How are things at home?"

"We're managing. I think I may have sold that old Meriwether house down the block. And Kevin's made the midterm honor roll. But we miss you. I just wish you could tell me more about your new job."

"So do I. But I had to sign a nondisclosure agreement. Just know that I'm safe, and I'll be in touch. As I said before, you can always reach me on my cell."

"I know. But I hate to bother—" She broke off. "Heavens to Betsy, what's that noise?"

Leigh's pulse lurched as she turned back to face the crib. For whatever reason, Mikey had started to fuss. As she leaned over him, his whimpers rose to a full-blown baby howl.

Eight

"What am I hearing?" Leigh's mother demanded again. "It sounds like a baby crying."

"It…*is* a baby." Leigh sagged against the side of the crib. A blatant lie, she knew, would make her mother even more suspicious. "I'm not supposed to tell you this, but I'm babysitting for a celebrity family. I'm not allowed to say who it is or where they are. It has to be kept a secret. You can't even tell Kevin. Is he still there with you?"

"No, he's gone up to his room."

"Good. He can't know, Mom. If he does, he might tell someone or try to find out more. If that happens, I'm out of a well-paying job."

In truth, the job was the least of her worries, but Leigh had already said more than she should.

"I understand, dear," her mother said sweetly. "Don't worry, I won't breathe a word. But I don't want to worry about you. Promise to keep in touch, all right?"

"I promise. And now I have to go. This baby needs my attention. We'll talk later, okay? Love you."

Ending the call, Leigh gathered Mikey into her arms. He stopped crying as soon as she picked him up. The little mischief clearly wanted to be held. He was already getting spoiled. Tomorrow she would ask Dora if it was all right to let him cry a little. For now she would just snuggle him. She enjoyed it as much as he seemed to.

"What's up, Mikey?" She brushed a kiss across the top of his silky head. "What do you think of the world so far? How about the people in it? Do you think we're a pretty loony bunch?"

He cooed and butted his head against her shoulder. Laughing, she pressed her nose against his neck, inhaling his clean, milky baby smell. "You're my sweet boy," she whispered. "And I love you. Never forget that."

"Lucky little man." Wyatt stood in the doorway. "What do *I* need to do for that kind of treatment?"

Leigh stifled a gasp. How long had he been there? How much had he heard?

"I hope you weren't eavesdropping," she said.

"Nothing of the kind. Just feeling the quiet a bit too much. I was about to turn on the news and wondered if you wanted to share some hot cocoa and watch it with me."

"I'll pass on the cocoa, thanks. But if you don't mind my bringing Mikey, I'll watch the news with you. Being up here is like being on the moon. I could use a reminder of the real world."

Still apprehensive, she followed him into the cozy lounge area at the top of the stairs. He'd dimmed the lights and switched on the gas-fueled fireplace. Wyatt's invitation had sounded harmless enough. But what was he up to? Did he suspect something? Did he want to pry more secrets out of her?

If only things were simpler! Aside from the complications, snuggling on the couch with Wyatt and the baby sounded like a little bit of heaven.

Still cradling Mikey, she settled against the cushions. Wyatt sat down beside her. His arm lay across the back of the couch, not quite touching her. He was probably thinking of Chloe, who could wander out of her room at any time.

Clicking the remote, he switched on a local channel. "I wanted to get the weather report," he said. "We might be getting snow—and snow is our business here. Do you ski?"

Leigh shook her head. "By the time I was old enough I had a part-time job. With that and school, there was no time to learn."

"I could give you some personal lessons."

She forced a laugh. "Trust me, I'm not the queen of co-ordination. I'd probably break something. How would I take care of Mikey, dragging around in a cast?"

"Maybe later, then." His fingertips brushed her shoulder. "The other night wasn't enough, Leigh. I want some serious time with you."

His meaning was clear. Leigh glanced down at Mikey, fearful that Wyatt might read the truth in her face. She craved the chance for more intimacy with him. But every encounter would raise the risk she was taking. If he were to learn the truth, he'd want nothing more to do with her.

"Leigh? Have I misread some signals?"

She forced herself to meet his gaze. Golden flames reflected in the blue depths of his eyes. She remembered those eyes blazing down at her in the lamplight of her bedroom as he filled her with his heat. Wyatt's lovemaking had made her want to beg for more. But would deepening their involvement only lead to more bitterness in the end?

She shook her head, willing herself to be as honest as she dared. "You haven't misread anything, Wyatt. I'd welcome more time together if we could find it. But things are a bit…overwhelming right now. I have all I can handle with Mikey and Chloe."

"Fine. For now…but not for long, Leigh. As you know, I'm not a patient man." Tilting her chin with a finger he brushed a feathery kiss across her lips. The brief contact sent a jolt of sensual need through her body. She ached with wanting him—his arms around her, his skin naked against hers. But was she willing to risk the consequences?

Mikey made a little whimpering sound, like a puppy wanting attention. Reaching out, Wyatt nudged the baby's hand. The tiny fist closed around his finger and held on tight. He laughed.

"He's a precious little guy, isn't he? I can see why you've become so attached to him."

Leigh braced herself for a lecture on why Chloe shouldn't keep her baby. But the weather forecast had come on the TV. With Mikey still clasping his finger, Wyatt gave it his full attention.

By the time the forecast ended, he was grinning like a schoolboy. "Snow! Not a big storm but maybe enough to open early—even if we have to bring out the snow machines. And it's already moving in. What do you say to that, Mikey?"

But Mikey had fallen asleep in Leigh's arms.

Easing his finger free, Wyatt gazed down at his slumbering grandson. "He's beautiful, isn't he?"

"Yes. I see a lot of Chloe in him. And now that he's asleep, maybe I can put him back to bed." Fighting emotion, she rose with the baby and turned away.

"Leigh." His voice caught her as she moved toward the hall.

"Is there something you need?"

"Yes. After you've put him down, come back."

Leigh retreated without a reply. Coming back to him could open the door to disaster. She'd be a fool to trust herself with the man. But deeper instincts told her that nothing could keep her away.

Mikey was sound asleep. He didn't even whimper as she laid him on his back. All the same, she lingered beside the crib, watching him as she battled the urge to race back to Wyatt—a battle she had no wish to win.

She could no longer hear the TV. Had he given up on waiting and gone downstairs? Pulse racing, she hurried back to where she'd left him. The lights and TV were off and the couch was empty.

She was about to turn and go back to her room when the door to the balcony opened and Wyatt walked in. His cobalt eyes were sparkling, his cheeks flushed with cold. "Come outside with me. You've got to see this," he said.

Lifting a knitted afghan from the back of the couch, he held it like a wrap. "Come on. This'll keep you warm. Now close your eyes."

Enfolded in the thick wool, Leigh allowed him to lead her out through the door. Shutting it behind them, he led her to the rail. "Now look!" he said.

Leigh opened her eyes. It was snowing—a world of fluffy, white flakes drifting down through the darkness. Far below, veiled by snowfall, she could see the lights of the resort. But here where they stood, snow and darkness were all around them. "It's magical," she whispered. "Like being in the middle of a giant Christmas card!"

His laugh tickled her ear as he drew her close. And then he was kissing her—with tender passion, the way she'd always dreamed of being kissed. She stretched on tiptoe, responding to the night, the snow and the fairy-tale kiss that went on and on.

Heaven save her, was she falling in love?

* * *

Two weeks had passed. Mikey was growing every day, becoming more alert and even more adorable. Mikey's mother, however, was climbing the walls. Chloe's strong young body had made a remarkable recovery from the birth. She was squeezing herself into her old jeans and clamoring for a trip to town, to buy new clothes and hang out with her friends.

Wyatt, who'd been spending most of his time at the resort, had turned a deaf ear to her constant whining. Only after Leigh took the girl's side and offered to drive her had he given in. Even then, he'd insisted that Leigh keep an eye on his daughter and have her back by dinnertime.

Mikey was to be left home. Wyatt had arranged for Dora to tend him, but she'd come down with a cold at the last minute. In the wake of Chloe's tears, Wyatt had agreed to take time from the resort and watch the boy himself. He had plenty to do, but he could always work from his office while the baby slept.

Standing on the balcony, with Mikey swathed in blankets, he watched the Mercedes vanish behind the trees. It was time to let Chloe go out, he told himself. The girl needed some freedom and he couldn't protect her forever. But it felt strange, being left here with the baby. He could have asked one of his other employees to come. But there was no one other than Dora who he trusted alone in the house with his precious grandson.

Chloe, during one of her rants, had accused him of being overprotective. And he supposed he was. But there were people on the outside who wouldn't stop at exploiting his family or even harming them. He wanted—needed—to keep them safe. In spite of his plans not to get attached, Mikey was on that list.

And what about Leigh? Standing on the spot where he'd

last kissed her, Wyatt felt the familiar yearning. Between his work, her work and family pressures, time alone with her had become a rare commodity. A tender glance across the table, a brush of hands when passing on the stairs... Damn, it was better than nothing. But it wasn't enough. He wanted her in his arms, in his bed. And he was losing patience.

He could only hope Leigh was, too.

Mikey stirred, fussing in his arms. He'd just awakened and wasn't likely to nap anytime soon. Wyatt brushed a kiss across the russet curls. "Hey, big guy," he murmured. "What do you say we go inside and watch some football?"

While Leigh drove, Chloe texted, her thumbs a blur of movement over the face of her cell phone. Wyatt's daughter was excited to see her friends, and a Saturday afternoon with them at the mall was probably her idea of heaven.

It would be Leigh's job to tag along at a discreet distance and pretend she wasn't really with them. Chloe had her own credit card and could buy whatever struck her fancy. Her friends, all from well-off families, probably had the same.

For teens, the new Dutchman's Creek Mall was the social center of town. Chloe's three friends were waiting by the fountain inside the main entrance. They raced toward her, squealing and jumping up and down as they came together. Standing back, Leigh felt like an aging duenna. Fragments of conversation drifted to her ears—boys, dates, clothes and a little about the baby. Chloe had never seemed happier. Maybe it was time Wyatt thought about sending his daughter back to the exclusive private school she'd attended last year. Leigh resolved to mention it the next time they had a chance to talk.

Not that those chances came often. Wyatt was very

much a hands-on owner. With the resort opening early, he was busy from morning to night checking the equipment, interviewing new staff and seeing that everything was in perfect order. She remembered what Chloe had told her on the way home that first day—that Wyatt was generous with money and things, but not with his time. Now she understood the truth of that. How could any woman compete with his work?

Leigh had seen so little of him that she'd begun to wonder if she'd imagined that breathless kiss in the snow. But then, she'd been equally busy with Chloe and Mikey.

Still, the work hadn't kept her from dreaming up some luscious fantasies....

Chloe's friends were crowding around her, exclaiming over the baby photos on her cell phone. It pleased Leigh to see that she'd snapped some. Unprepared as the girl was to be a mother, she did appear to love her little boy. The question of giving up Mikey was no longer being asked. Even Wyatt had stopped mentioning it.

Laughing and chattering, the four girls headed into the main part of the mall. Leigh kept pace with them, hovering as they trooped into exclusive shops to try on the kind of clothes she hadn't even dreamed of wearing as a teen. Chloe's purchases—two cashmere sweaters, a leather jacket, designer jeans, boots, a five-hundred dollar purse, and several sets of panties and bras, went into shopping bags. Leigh, who'd offered to carry them, was soon loaded down like a pack animal. She was grateful she'd worn her walking shoes, but she was getting tired.

Ahead of them, the sounds and smells of the food court drifted down the mall. "Who's hungry?" Chloe demanded. "Burgers and shakes for everybody, my treat!"

Like a flock of colorful birds, the girls circled and descended on a corner table. A snap of Chloe's fingers summoned a waiter. Wyatt's daughter was clearly in her element. "Want anything, Leigh?" she asked.

"Just a Coke, thanks." Leigh seated herself in a nearby chair. Ignoring her, the girls buzzed away, laughing and checking their phones for text messages. Tuning them out for the moment, Leigh rested her feet and let her thoughts drift back to Wyatt. Today was the first time he'd taken care of Mikey alone. By now he seemed at ease with his tiny grandson; but what if something unplanned were to happen? Could he handle it?

A hush had fallen over the girls' table. Following their gazes, Leigh saw three nice-looking high school boys strolling into the far end of the food court.

Her heart dropped.

One of them was Kevin.

Wyatt had moved the bassinet from Chloe's room to his office and set it on the floor by his desk. After feeding Mikey a warm bottle, he laid him on his back, tucked a blanket over his legs, and switched on his computer. With luck, the baby would sleep for several hours, allowing him to get some needed planning done for the resort. In this busy season, he couldn't spare time away from work.

He'd just brought up the spreadsheet for the restaurant when Mikey started to whimper. Remembering Leigh's mention that he sometimes fussed before going to sleep, Wyatt willed himself to ignore the little fellow. But as minutes passed, the cries became more insistent. Turning in his chair, he looked down. The small, tear-streaked face tore at his heart.

"What is it, Mikey? Are you okay?"

At the sound of his voice, Mikey's cries grew louder. Giving in to the inevitable, Wyatt picked the baby up and lifted him against his shoulder. Usually being held was all he wanted. But this time Mikey kept on crying. His body was rigid, as if he were in pain.

"What is it, big guy?" Wyatt rubbed the bony little back, growing more worried by the minute. Maybe he should call Dora and ask her what to do.

He was reaching for the phone when Mikey gave a little hiccup and spit a stream of sour formula down Wyatt's shoulder. Only then did Wyatt remember he hadn't burped the baby before putting him down. Spitting up seemed to take care of the problem. He'd stopped crying and was gazing at Wyatt with those dazzling eyes.

"If you could talk, I suppose you'd say this served me right!" Wyatt muttered. Rising, he carried Mikey into his room and laid him on a towel while he changed his shirt. Mikey's pajamas hadn't escaped the mess, and his diaper smelled suspiciously rank. He would need changing, too.

Upstairs in the nursery Wyatt managed to get his grandson out of his dirty clothes, wipe him down and dress him again. Mikey seemed to enjoy the process, cooing and kicking his feet the whole time. "You know, for such a little fellow, you're a lot of work," Wyatt said. "But something tells me you're here to stay."

As he spoke the words, Wyatt knew he meant them. This baby had become part of the family, and he would do everything in his power to help Chloe raise him. And maybe this time, he could take a more active role. He had to set an example for Chloe, and with Leigh there to make sure he got everything right, he might be able to handle being a good parental figure after all.

Looking down at the happy baby, he felt the now-familiar tightening in his chest. Something told him it was love.

Kevin and his friends John and Mark had paused in the entrance to the food court and were surveying the place, maybe looking for friends. Seized by panic, Leigh ducked her head and nudged Chloe's shoulder. "Going to the rest-room," she whispered. "Keep an eye on your bags."

Chloe paid her scant attention as she slunk off, weaving among the crowded tables in an effort to keep her back to the boys. She hated to leave the girl unawares, but there was no way to warn Chloe without giving herself away. She could only hope Kevin wouldn't notice the mother of his child, sitting across the food court with her girlfriends.

But what chance was there of that, when Chloe's flame-hued curls stood out like a beacon? Leigh reached the open L-shaped entrance to the ladies' room and flattened herself inside the barrier wall. Peering around it, she could see most of the food court. The boys were moving in the di-rection of the table, the girls watching them, giggling with anticipation—all except for Chloe. She sat frozen, staring down at her clenched hands. If only Leigh could have res-cued the poor girl from her awkward situation. But there was nothing she could do without giving herself away.

The boys passed the entrance to the ladies' room, so close that Leigh could almost have reached out and touched her brother. They were moving on when Kevin halted as if he'd slammed into an invisible wall.

"Hey, man, what's wrong?" Mark asked.

"Nothing. Just remembered something I need to do for my mom." Kevin sounded as if he'd seen a ghost.

"Now? When we're about to go talk to those hot girls?"

"You two go on. I'll call you later." Kevin did an about-face and strode hastily out of the food court, the way the boys had come in.

His two friends stared after him. "What was that all about?" John asked. Mark just shrugged.

Leigh began to breathe again. But she still wasn't out of the woods. Kevin's two friends had been to their house.

They would recognize her, too. What if they joined the girls? What would she do if the bunch of them went off somewhere together?

The boys had gone a few more steps toward the girls' table when Mark stopped with a muttered oath. "Hey, I know those chicks. They go to Bramford Hill. They're so snooty rich they won't even talk to common trash like us. Let's go before they put us down. We'll have better luck someplace else."

Leigh sagged against the wall in relief as the boys turned and left. She'd come so close to having everything blow up in her face—Kevin, Chloe, the baby…and Wyatt, who'd never speak to her again unless it was in court.

This time she'd had a narrow escape. But in many ways Dutchman's Creek was still a small town. There were bound to be more encounters, and next time she might not be so lucky. There was no getting around it—sooner or later the truth would come out. And when it did, the consequences would crush her.

Nine

By early November the snow was four feet deep on the runs. Wyatt had hoped for more but, with the help of the snow machines, there was enough to start the season. The lodge and hotel were booked, the restaurants and shops teeming with visitors.

Things were calm enough on the home front, as well. Mikey was growing into a robust, bright-eyed cherub. Chloe had started some online classes and would be going back to school spring semester, after the worst of the snow was gone. Meanwhile, she'd wheedled a promise from her father that during Christmas vacation she could have her friends up to the house for a ski holiday.

But as for Leigh…

Wyatt stood on the balcony gazing out at the leaden sky. The weather matched his mood. Ever since her trip with Chloe to the Dutchman's Creek Mall, he'd sensed a cooling in her demeanor toward him. She almost seemed to be avoiding him. Something had happened, and he didn't know what it was.

The frustration did nothing to dampen his desire. If anything, it made him want her even more. When misunderstandings or mixed messages had gotten between him and women before, he'd always worked it out in bed. He was confident he could do the same with Leigh, if they could just find an opportunity. There was no way he was going to let this woman escape without some serious lovemaking. He'd already waited too long. It was time he made his move.

One way or another, before the week was out, he was determined to get his beautiful nanny in bed. At the moment, she'd opted to visit her family for a couple of days. Some time off was written into her contract and she was ready for a change of scene. Wednesday night she'd be back.

She'd planned on driving her station wagon, which was in storage at the resort. But Wyatt had insisted she take the new Mercedes SUV. The canyon roads were slick with snow and he wanted her safe. Or maybe he was worried that she'd take her old rust bucket and disappear for good.

"What are you doing out here, Daddy? It's cold." Chloe stood in the doorway. Her sweet-as-pie smile told him she had a favor to ask. Steeling himself, he followed her inside and sat down.

"Tell me, have I been a good girl?" she asked. "Have I done my schoolwork and taken care of Mikey with Leigh gone?"

"You have." His eyebrow quirked. "I do believe there's hope for you yet."

She giggled charmingly. "Well, here's the thing, Daddy. Friday's Monique's birthday, and she's having a slumber party at her house. All my girlfriends will be there. Leigh won't even have to drive me. Amy says she can pick me up and bring me home the next day. Please say I can go."

She looked as appealing as a puppy. Wyatt had to admit she'd earned a break. "You can go on one condition," he said. "I want to make sure Monique's parents will be there to keep an eye on things. Give me their phone number and I'll make the call."

"Thank you, Daddy! You're the best! I'll text Monique and get the number for you." She jumped up, gave him a peck on the cheek and raced down the stairs to her room.

Watching her go, Wyatt felt a prickle of uncertainty that made him want to retract his permission. Maybe he was being overprotective. But this was a girl who'd had unprotected sex after a bout of underage drinking and Lord knows what else. He couldn't be too careful.

Then again, Chloe did deserve a treat…and besides, he couldn't ignore that other voice in his head—the one reminding him that, with Chloe gone overnight, he might finally get some time alone with Leigh. The timing of the annual winter reception gave him the perfect excuse to ask her out. If he could arrange for Dora to tend Mikey overnight, he could put the rest of his plan in motion.

He kept a secluded room at the lodge where he could stay if he needed to work late. The well-appointed suite also came in handy for entertaining female guests. Now, as he pictured the sitting room with its adjoining bedchamber, he realized it wasn't what he wanted for Leigh.

Too many memories, for one thing. Women from college students to models and movie stars had shared that bed over the years. Something told him Leigh would know, and it wouldn't bode well for setting a romantic mood. Even though they'd agreed that they weren't looking for a long-term relationship together, Leigh deserved better than to be treated like another one-night stand. He wanted a special setting—no, a perfect setting, the best that money could buy.

Adjacent to the rustic-style lodge was a fifteen-story luxury hotel. Much of the topmost floor was taken up by a penthouse suite complete with a hot tub on the terrace, a private elevator and a glorious view of the mountains. Reserved for visiting celebrities, royals and millionaires, the suite rented for ten thousand dollars a night.

As the owner, he would have no problem reserving the suite. He wanted Leigh to be impressed. Even more, he wanted her to know how important she was to him. And he wanted to make glorious, unbridled love to her in a sumptuous place where they wouldn't be disturbed.

Leigh had taken her mother to lunch while Kevin was in school. That night the three of them had devoured a pizza and seen a movie at the nearby dollar theater. The mall had a megaplex showing all the current releases. But Leigh had made excuses not to go there. Better not to risk running into Chloe's friends.

She was beginning to feel like a fugitive.

Her mother and brother had been curious about the expensive car. But it was easy enough to explain that she'd borrowed it from her employer. When Kevin pumped her for more information, Leigh had simply refused to answer his questions.

Around ten o'clock, their mother went to bed, leaving the two of them alone in the kitchen. Kevin poured a tall glass of milk, added a squirt of chocolate syrup and sat down at the table. His handsome young face looked troubled.

"What is it?" Leigh asked. "You know you can tell me."

He sighed, stirring his milk with a spoon. "I should probably just forget this. But I saw Chloe a couple of weeks ago. She was at the mall with her girlfriends."

"Did you talk to her?" Leigh hated faking ignorance, but she had little choice.

"No. I turned around and walked out. I thought she was gone for good. Now she's back, like nothing ever happened."

"And that bothers you?"

"Maybe it shouldn't. But there was a baby, Leigh. My baby. She said she was going to get rid of it. I don't know if she meant to give it away or just get an abortion. But it's gone, and I guess I'll never know what became of it." He shook his dark head. "There's no way I'd ask her. I'm the last person on earth she'd talk to. But I can't seem to get past it. I keep wondering if it was a boy or a girl, and how it would have looked."

"Oh, Kevin." Leigh ached to tell him about Mikey—how sweet he was, how bright and how loved. But knowing the truth would turn her brother's whole life upside down.

How long could she keep it from him? Her secret was like a ticking bomb that threatened to blow up at any moment, wounding all the people she held dear.

"All you can do is move on," she said. "You have a good life ahead of you. Make the most of it." Platitudes, she thought; empty words to mask the biggest secret she'd ever kept.

Maybe she should quit her nanny job and leave town—do it before Wyatt, Kevin or Chloe learned the truth. It would tear her apart to leave Mikey, but better now than later, under bad circumstances.

The more she thought about quitting, the more sense the idea made. Mikey was off to a good start with people who'd grown to love him. Chloe, too, would be all right, although Leigh had grown fond of the spunky teen and would miss her.

As for Wyatt…

She had to face it—the reality of never seeing him again. She'd built a world of fantasies around the man—loving him and being loved, sharing his bed, sharing his life. But even without her secret, none of those fantasies had stood a chance of coming true. And with the secret, sooner or later Wyatt was bound to find out how she'd played him. He would be hurt and angry. In all likelihood he would never forgive her.

Better to leave now, with her secret intact. Learning the truth after she was gone would, at least, lessen the blow to his pride.

By the next afternoon, with the Mercedes pulling out of the driveway, Leigh had made up her mind. According to the terms of her contract she was still on probation. That meant she could leave without notice. She would spend a couple of days putting things in order. Then she would walk out the door and never look back.

Leaving wouldn't be easy. But Chloe was competent with Mikey by now, and Dora was available if needed. They would manage fine until Wyatt could hire a new nanny.

Their lives would go on. So would hers. But she couldn't remain in Dutchman's Creek. A girlfriend in Denver had invited her to visit. That would give her a chance to do some job hunting. There had to be something for an unemployed journalist, even if it turned out to be waiting tables.

She was doing the right thing, she told herself. She would make this work for all concerned. She had to.

By the time she pulled up to the house it was getting dark. Powdery snowflakes, fine as sand, drifted down from the twilight sky. Wyatt was waiting on the front porch, lamplight silvering his thick hair. Dressed in jeans and a bulky ski sweater, he looked so strong and handsome that he almost stopped her heart.

Hurrying down the stone steps, he opened the car door for her, then took the keys and strode around to retrieve her suitcase from the back.

"Come in and get warm," he said. "I'll put the car away later. I was getting worried about you."

"Traffic was bad. A fender bender at the turnoff." Leigh stomped the light snow off her boots. As he opened the door, the smell of warm chili and cheese biscuits enfolded her like a welcome.

Chloe was waiting in the entry with a fussing Mikey in her arms. As Leigh shed her jacket, the girl thrust the baby toward her. "Thank goodness you're back, Leigh. Mikey's been a little stinker. I think he missed you."

As Leigh gathered him close, Mikey stopped crying and nestled against her shoulder. Leigh kissed the top of his downy head, her heart flooding with love. She'd felt so resolute in the car. But leaving these people was going to be the hardest thing she'd ever done.

"Are you hungry, Leigh?" Wyatt asked. "We kept some supper warm for you."

"Famished. I just hope Mikey will let me eat."

"I'll hold him." Wyatt took his grandson and made a cradle with his arms. Mikey fussed a moment before he found a fist to suck on.

The table had been cleared except for one place setting. While Leigh dished up chili and biscuits, Wyatt took a seat on the opposite side. "Don't you have schoolwork, Chloe?" he asked.

She pulled a face at him and disappeared in the direction of her room. "She's a smart girl," he said, giving Leigh a look that triggered a flutter in the pit of her stomach. She took her place at the table, deliberately avoiding eye contact with his penetrating gaze. What was he about to say to her? Had he already discovered what she was hiding?

Maybe she should quit now and spare herself the humiliation of being fired.

"I've been waiting to talk to you. But now that you're here, I feel like a schoolboy asking a girl to his first prom. I'd like to take you out on a Friday night date, Leigh."

At that, she finally looked up. "A date?"

"A real one. Every year I host a charity reception at the lodge to celebrate the opening of the winter season. We could spend an hour there, then sneak off and have a nice, private dinner at the hotel."

"What about...?" She nodded in the direction of Chloe's room.

"She's going to a slumber party at her friend's house. I've arranged for Dora to watch Mikey. So what do you say?"

Leigh fixed her gaze on the woven place mat. She understood what his invitation implied. They would have time alone, all the time they needed.

Did she want it to happen? But why ask? She'd wanted Wyatt Richardson from the first day they'd met. And ever since he'd made love to her, she'd burned to do it again.

Leigh knew it wouldn't be forever. Wyatt wasn't a forever kind of man. He was too driven, too focused on building his empire. In any case, she planned on leaving before he learned her secret. So why not? Why shouldn't Cinderella enjoy a night at the ball with Prince Charming before the clock struck twelve?

"Leigh?"

She looked up. In his lake-blue eyes she caught a glint of vulnerability. That alone gave her courage. Forcing a mischievous smile, she replied with a question.

"How could a girl refuse a man with a baby in his arms?"

* * *

Leigh had nothing to wear to a fancy-dress reception. But the resort's trendy boutiques stocked everything from ski clothes to formal wear. A delighted Chloe organized a Thursday shopping expedition. With Mikey bundled into his carrier, they trudged the heated boardwalks, looking, commenting, trying and comparing. Wyatt had told Leigh to charge her purchase to the resort. But she'd insisted on paying out of her own pocket. When she finally found the perfect dress, she was grateful for the generous salary that allowed her to splurge.

The one-shouldered cocktail-length gown was a dark, subtly iridescent emerald-green. On the hanger it looked like nothing more than a limp tube of fabric. But when Leigh stepped out of the fitting room the salesgirl gasped and Chloe cheered.

Their search was over. Almost. Leigh had planned to make do with her black pumps, but Chloe insisted on treating her to a spectacular pair of lattice-cut, high-heeled gold boots. They were the sort of footwear Leigh would never have picked for herself, but they added an elegantly funky touch to the simple gown.

It hadn't escaped Leigh's notice that she and Chloe wore the same shoe size. When the evening was over she would give the expensive boots to Wyatt's daughter—something Chloe may have had in mind all along.

After downing mugs of hot chocolate with whipped cream, they packed Mikey and their purchases into the Mercedes. It had been a good afternoon. Feeling relaxed and pleasantly tired, Leigh drove the canyon road. Her mind had begun to wander when Chloe's question jerked her back to the present.

"Leigh, are you in love with my father?"

With effort, Leigh found her voice. "Why do you ask?"

"I can tell he likes you a lot. I was just wondering if you feel the same about him. Do you?"

"Do I like him? Yes, very much."

"But do you love him?"

This was getting tough. "I could," Leigh said, "if I thought things might work out for us. But I'm afraid that's not going to happen."

"Why not, if you like each other so much?"

Leigh sighed. "I want a family. That's something your father doesn't seem to have time for. Besides, he's had a lot of beautiful girlfriends. You said so yourself. Why should he settle for me?"

"Because you're smart. Because you're clearly not after his money. And because you get along with Mikey and me." Chloe's hands clasped on her knees. "Why don't you stay? You and Daddy could even get married."

Leigh's stomach had tightened into a knot. Why was it becoming so painful to leave these people? "It's not that simple, Chloe," she said. "Maybe your father likes me, but I can't imagine he loves me."

"How do you know?"

"How does anybody know? By the things people say—by the way they treat you."

Chloe slumped a little. "I don't think anybody's ever loved me. For sure not my mother. And maybe not my dad, either."

"Chloe, I know your father loves you."

"Then why hasn't he ever spent time with me? All he's ever done is work—and buy me stuff!"

Leigh turned onto the narrow road that led up to the house. "Maybe that's his way of showing love—being a good provider."

"Well, it sucks!"

"What if it's the only way he knows?"

"Still sucks."

"Well, Mikey loves you. You're his mother."

She brightened. "Yes, he does! Don't you, Mikey?" She reached back over the top of the car seat and ruffled her baby's hair. "You're my own little baby. And I'm going to love you forever. I'll never kick you out like my mother kicked me out!"

As the car turned up the drive, Leigh reached over and patted the girl's arm. "You're just beginning to learn about love, Chloe. All of us—your father, me, even your mother—we're all still learning."

Had she said the right thing? Leigh pulled up to the house and saw Wyatt waiting on the porch. He'd been shoveling snow, and his cheeks were ruddy with cold. Leigh's heart softened at the sight of him. Why was love such a confusing emotion? What if she didn't know any more about it than Chloe did?

On Friday the afternoon sun was warm enough to melt the snow on the plowed roads. Late in the day, Chloe's friend Amy showed up in a red convertible. Blowing a kiss to Mikey, Chloe grabbed her overnight bag and skipped out the door like a newly freed prisoner. Wyatt scowled as he watched the car flash around the first curve. "Kids," he muttered to himself. "They drive like they think they're immortal."

Tearing his gaze away from the road, he carried Mikey back inside. He'd offered to tend the baby while Leigh showered and washed her hair. It pleased him that she and Chloe had gone shopping together. They'd kept her dress a secret, but Leigh would look ravishing in a gunnysack. He looked forward to walking into the ballroom with her on his arm.

"What do you think, big guy?" he asked Mikey. "Will this old man be around when you learn to drive a car?"

Mikey cooed and blew a bubble. He was growing so fast, changing day by day. Before long he'd be sitting up and crawling, then walking and talking. Every day brought its own small miracles. How many more of those days would he get to share? Wyatt wondered. Would Chloe stay here and raise her son, or would she spread her wings and take him far away? She'd most likely marry in a few years. What would become of Mikey then? Time passed so fast.

Speaking of time… He glanced at the clock. He was anxious to get Leigh where he could have her to himself. From her bathroom upstairs the sound of running water stirred a fantasy. He imagined himself stripped down, stepping into the spacious shower with her and running his soaped hands over the delicious curves of her body—her breasts, her hips, her thighs…maybe before the night was over even better things would happen.

Mikey sneezed. Looking down at his grandson, Wyatt chuckled. "What would you say if you knew what your old man was thinking? Would you be shocked?"

The eyes gazing up at him were as pure as the sky. The band of love around Wyatt's heart jerked tight—tight enough to hurt.

The reception was scheduled to start at seven-thirty with cocktails, a lavish buffet and a silent charity auction to raise funds for scholarships for needy students. Wyatt's staff was handling the arrangements, but he needed to be there on time to greet the guests.

Dora arrived at the house a few minutes early. She fussed over Mikey and kidded Wyatt about his tuxedo. "Don't you look gorgeous!" she exclaimed. "If I was ten years younger I'd have a hard time keeping my hands off you. Where's Leigh?"

"She'll be down in a minute. You know enough about this place to make yourself at home. There's plenty to eat in the kitchen, and Leigh says you can stretch out on her bed after Mikey goes down for the night."

"I take it you might be late." Wyatt's longtime head of Housekeeping was no fool.

"We'll see. In any case, I'll have my cell phone with me. If you have concerns about Mikey or anything else, don't hesitate to call."

"I've got you on speed dial." Dora lifted Mikey out of his carrier and kissed his plump cheek. "Come on, Mr. Mikey. You and I are gonna party tonight!"

Wyatt glanced up at the sound of clicking heels overhead. Seconds later Leigh appeared at the top of the stairs. His heart stalled at the sight of her.

The first thing he noticed was the dress. Modest but incredibly sexy, it clung to every curve, exposing one creamy shoulder, defining her slim waist and skimming the tops of her knees. Its glowing green color brought out the gold flecks in her eyes. Her hair was twisted loosely at the crown of her head, with stray tendrils framing her glowing face. Gold hoops, the only jewelry she wore, dangled from her earlobes.

But the pièce de résistance was the gold boots. So outrageous that only Chloe could have chosen them, they clung to Leigh's magnificent legs, their open-cut design showing glimpses of porcelain skin beneath.

Teetering slightly on five-inch stilettos, Leigh clung to the banister as she negotiated each step. Wyatt sprinted up the stairs to take her arm. Only then did he notice that her free hand clasped her black pumps. "Just in case my feet don't last," she muttered. "We can leave them in the car."

He laughed. "You'll be fine. Just hang on to me. You look stunning, by the way."

"Thanks. Chloe was a lot of help. And you clean up nicely yourself."

Wyatt steadied her until they reached the bottom landing. He found himself wishing they could just skip the reception and go straight to the penthouse. He wanted this woman all to himself.

Finding her woolen coat in the closet, he held it while she slipped her arms into the sleeves. "I'd like to wrap you in ermine," he murmured, pulling it around her.

She laughed. "That would be a waste. I don't wear little furry animals."

"That doesn't surprise me. You're a very gentle person, Leigh." He put on his own coat and led her outside where the Mercedes was parked next to Dora's sedan. With Leigh on his arm, he felt a foot taller and ten years younger. He could hardly wait to show her off.

Pulse humming with anticipation, he helped her into the car. Her fragrance teased his nostrils as he started the engine. He inhaled, filling his senses. Tonight was going to be good, he told himself. Not just good. If he had his way it would be perfect.

Ten

Willing herself to not appear nervous, Leigh waited for Wyatt to check their coats. The guests were just beginning to arrive. She recognized a few of them from her work at the newspaper. Most were strangers. But all of them looked rich. Heaven help her, they even *smelled* rich.

Most of the women were older and more conservatively dressed than Leigh. Clad in designer gowns, their ears, hands and throats sparkling with real jewels, they made her feel like some sort of disco queen. Why had she let Chloe help choose her outfit—especially those ridiculous boots?

Wyatt joined her, his hand resting beneath her elbow. "You look like a goddess," he whispered, bending his head to her ear. "Every man in the room is going to be jealous of me."

And the women? They could be pecking her apart like clucking hens—probably thinking she was some gold-digging tart after Wyatt's money.

But never mind. She was with the most important man

here, and she wasn't an idiot. She knew how to be gracious and personable, and she would do her best.

"Hang on to me," she whispered as Wyatt walked her across the freshly waxed floor. "I don't want to fall down—or embarrass you in any other way."

"You'll do fine." He chuckled and squeezed her arm. "Just relax and be your beautiful self."

The rustic ballroom was decorated for the holidays with garlands of evergreen that filled the room with fragrance. Bows of plaid satin, trimmed with pine cones and brass sleigh bells, anchored the greenery in place. Chandeliers glittered overhead. Behind a wrought iron screen, logs blazed in the huge stone fireplace.

Soon Wyatt was mingling with his guests, introducing her as "Ms. Leigh Foster." Teetering on her five-inch heels, Leigh greeted each one with a smile and what she hoped was a nice personal comment. Some of the men practically bowed over her hand. The more common reaction from the women was a frosty glare, but Leigh quickly got used to that. She was actually beginning to have a good time.

At the far end of the room was a bar and a long, lavishly set buffet table. Liveried waiters, balancing trays of drinks and hors d'oeuvres, circulated among the guests. On a dais in one corner, a jazz trio played classic Gershwin. The female singer who stepped up to the microphone was one of Leigh's mother's favorites. Her warm, husky voice wafted through the crowd. Leigh sighed. How her mother would have loved to share this evening.

By now the ballroom was filling up. Some of the new arrivals were younger women in short, glittering dresses and high platform shoes. Their presence made Leigh feel less of a sore thumb. She even caught a few admiring glances at her boots. She was going to be all right.

"Can I get you something, Leigh?" Wyatt asked.

"You mentioned dinner. If we're still on for that, I can wait. I don't want to spoil my appetite." And, truth be told, she didn't want to lose her balance and drop her food.

"Some champagne, maybe?"

She shook her head. "I'm fine. Alcohol makes me tipsy." And being tipsy, Leigh reminded herself, was the last thing she needed tonight.

The other guests seemed to have no such concerns. Most of them were drinking, some heavily, but everyone seemed to be in a jolly mood. Hopefully they'd be writing generous checks for charity.

"How long are we planning to stay?" she whispered to Wyatt.

"Not much longer." His sexy, secret smile sent a shimmer all the way to her toes. "I've got a few more people to greet. After that we can sneak out early. Are you getting tired?"

She returned his smile. "I'm fine. Take your— *Oh!*" She staggered sideways as a linebacker-sized man bumped her shoulder on his way to the bar. Wyatt's quick reflexes saved her from a fall, but as he pulled her upright, she felt a stabbing sensation in her left ankle. She bit back a cry.

"Are you all right?" His eyes probed her face. "No, you aren't. I can tell."

"I'll be fine," Leigh said. "Just gave my ankle a little twist. We don't need to leave." As if to prove her words, she took a step on her injured leg. The pain made her gasp.

"We are leaving. Now." In one motion he swept her up in his arms and strode to the passageway that connected the lodge and the hotel. Leigh curled against his chest, feeling every eye in the ballroom on them.

"Is this what you call sneaking out?" she asked. "We're going to be the talk of the party."

"Who cares?" As they approached the hotel lobby, he

took a turn toward a hidden elevator, punching a code on the panel next to the door. The door slid open and closed behind them without a sound. Inside, the elevator was paneled in aromatic cedar wood and floored with a rich Persian carpet. There were no floor stops. It carried them straight up, like a rocket rising into space.

"Wyatt, where is this taking us?" Leigh whispered in hushed wonder.

"You'll see." His laugh tickled her ear. "How's your ankle?"

"Hard to tell. It just feels numb."

"I'll check it when we stop. If it looks like anything serious, the resort keeps a paramedic on call. Not quite what I'd planned, I'll confess."

"What had you planned? Tell me the truth."

"The perfect evening in the perfect place."

"With the very imperfect Miss Foster? You had to know something would go wrong."

"Not imperfect in my book. I've waited a long time for this night, Leigh." His lips brushed her hair. "And I'm not giving up on it yet."

The elevator had come to a stop. The door glided open to reveal a suite so elegant that Leigh was struck speechless. Three of the walls were floor-to-ceiling glass, the lights kept low to reveal a vast panorama of the stars, the moon and the snow-crested peaks above the resort. Outside the far wall was a terrace, its landscape of shrubs and trees festooned with a hundred thousand tiny white lights. Tendrils of steam rose from a heated pool, glowing like a flawless turquoise among the rocks.

What she could see of the shadowed parlor area appeared to be furnished with massive dark chairs and a long couch arranged on a white rug. Flames in a copper fire pit with filigreed sides lent warmth and soft, golden light.

Wyatt lowered her into one cushiony chair. Switching on a table lamp, he knelt at her feet and unzipped the back of her boot. Leigh hadn't bothered with panty hose tonight. His touch sent delicious tingles up her bare leg.

Very gently he freed her foot. "I don't see any swelling. How does this feel?" He rotated the foot slightly.

She winced. "I can feel it. But it's not too bad."

"I'd say it's nothing to worry about. Maybe a mild sprain. Give it some rest and you should be fine."

"I'm sorry to have been such a baby."

"You weren't a baby." He unzipped her other boot and slipped it off her foot. "But you did give me a good excuse to get you out of that party."

Leigh's breath caught as his hand slid up her leg to her thigh. She'd been aching to be touched by him, but she hadn't counted on the deep well of emotion he'd opened up. Wyatt's touch wasn't enough. She wanted his love. But what was she thinking? She might as well want the moon.

Rising on his knees he leaned into her, his mouth capturing hers in a deep, intimate kiss. Letting go of her doubts, she let her response flow—her lips parting, her tongue mingling with his, her unbridled fingers furrowing his hair. She'd allow herself this one night with him. She would make every second count. Then tomorrow she would quit her job and walk away.

To stay longer would only break hearts—hers and others'.

His hand moved higher, his touch sure and confident. She opened to him, her head spinning as he found her lacy panties and pushed the crotch aside. She was already wet enough for his fingers to glide over her moisture-slicked folds. She moaned as he found their center, pressing against his hand to heighten the exquisite feeling. "I've wanted you, Leigh," he muttered. "Wanted you so damned much I could hardly stand it...."

Stroking her with his thumb, he slid a finger inside her. Already aroused, she came fast, exploding to a climax against his hand. She gave a little cry, her body shuddering.

As the rapture ebbed, her head fell against his shoulder.

He chuckled in her ear. "More to come. Meanwhile, I believe I promised you dinner."

Rising, he clicked what looked like a remote control. The elevator door slid open to reveal a white-draped cart holding champagne in a bucket of ice, several covered dishes and a bouquet of two dozen red roses in a crystal vase. "Just in time, I see." Wyatt rinsed his hands and wheeled the cart into the room. There was no waiter. Evidently he'd requested that the cart be sent up alone.

Glancing around, Leigh noticed a dining alcove with the table set for two. Whisking the food and flowers onto the table, Wyatt lit a pair of candles, popped the champagne cork and filled two crystal flutes with the sparkling liquid. "Back in the day, I earned my ski passes at Vail by working as a waiter," he said, helping Leigh to her chair. "Still haven't lost my touch."

"You've come a long way," Leigh said.

"Yes, I have. And I like where I am. Especially tonight." He took his seat. His hand moved across the tablecloth to rest on hers. "You take my breath away, Leigh. You have from the moment you walked into that interview."

"I still can't believe you hired me. You must've been desperate."

"I was. But I know a good thing when I see it. You and Mikey have turned my solitary world upside down. And, believe it or not, I've come to like it." Raising his champagne flute, he held it toward her. "To one lovely night."

What was he trying to do to her? Had he guessed that

she was going to quit? Was he twisting the blade, making everything more painful?

"One lovely night." She repeated the toast, touched her glass to his and drained it.

Dinner was delicious—Rock Cornish game hens with mushroom stuffing, cooked in wine sauce and served on a bed of fresh kale from the resort's organic greenhouse. For dessert there were rum-flavored miniature cream puffs garnished with slivers of chocolate—decadent but not too filling.

Keeping the champagne and the two crystal flutes, Wyatt whisked the dishes back onto the cart, rolled it into the elevator and clicked the remote. As the doors closed, his gaze wandered to the blue pool on the terrace. "A nice warm soak might be good for your ankle," he said.

"It might. But it's cold outside."

"No problem." He clicked another button on the remote. Heat lamps surrounding the pool began to glow. "There's a robe for you on the back of the bathroom door."

"I don't suppose there's a bathing suit. I didn't bring one."

He grinned impishly. "Neither did I."

The robe was a cloud of plush white terry cloth. It felt heavenly against Leigh's bare skin as she wrapped it around her body and tied the sash. There were cushiony white spa slippers, as well. Limping a little she made her way back to the parlor. The glass door to the terrace slid open at her approach. More tricks with the remote, she surmised.

Wyatt was already in the pool, his own robe draped over a chair. Even blurred by the bubbling water jets, the lights below the surface left little to the imagination. "If you're nervous, I can close my eyes," he teased.

"I'll take that as a challenge." Locking her gaze with

his, she stepped out of her slippers and untied the sash of her robe. As the garment fell open, she slipped it off her arms and laid it on a bench outside the circle of heat lamps. A chilly breeze struck her body.

"You've got goose bumps," Wyatt said. "Come on in and get warm."

Leigh needed no more urging. Finding the stone steps she lowered herself into the pool and sank in up to her shoulders. The heated water was lightly scented with rosemary. "This feels…marvelous," she breathed.

"Told you." Wyatt was chest deep on the opposite side of the bed-sized pool. In the glow of the heat lamps he looked tanned, fit and stunningly virile.

"Come here, Leigh." His husky voice was almost a growl. As she moved toward him through the bubbling water he reached out, caught her arm and pulled her against him. Naked, it was obvious that he still had the body of a champion athlete—solid muscle, strong and hard.

"I take it we aren't here for a deep, serious talk," she murmured as his arms tightened around her.

"Uh-uh." His kiss was long and deep and sensual. Their legs tangled under the water. She felt his arousal jutting like a rock against her belly. Reaching down, she clasped him. His size dwarfed her hand. As her fingers tightened, he groaned. "Watch it, lady, if you want to save the best for last."

"Are we going to stay here?"

"Lovemaking underwater is overrated. I have a better place in mind. Meanwhile just lie back and relax."

Turning her back to him, he cupped his hands beneath her breasts, and eased her head into the hollow of his shoulder. Her feet floated outward in the bubbling water. "Lovely," she whispered.

"So are you." His hands fondled her breasts, lightly

thumbing the nipples. A slow, sweet ache tightened between her legs. "When you're nice and warm let me know and we'll get out," he said.

"I may go to sleep right here."

"That's fine as long as you let me wake you up."

She closed her eyes, luxuriating in the bubbles and the caressing strokes of his strong but gentle hands. A man who put a woman's pleasure before his own was her kind of man. Too bad this one wasn't for keeps.

She could feel her body respond to him. Heat shimmered from her breasts into her limbs and down into her pulsing core. She wanted him in every way a woman could want a man. And she couldn't stand to wait any longer.

Turning in the water she seized his head and kissed him, not timidly but with all the stops out. He seized her with a rough laugh, no longer gentle as he lifted her out of the water and mounted the steps. Setting her down, he flung her robe around her and reached for his own. The thick fabric soaked up the moisture.

Without a word he scooped her into his arms again and strode inside. The bedroom was dark. She glimpsed a vast turned-down bed before he slipped off her robe and lowered her onto the silk sheets. She sank into the featherbed, cradled by its sumptuous warmth, while he paused to add protection. As he leaned over the bed her arms reached up, pulling him down to her. He laughed. "Eager little thing, aren't you?" he teased. "Just hold on."

He began kissing her—her eyelids, her lips, her throat. She whimpered as his skilled mouth worked downward to her breasts, flicking and suckling the nipples until her body burned. Still he gave her no mercy, no blessed release. His kisses skimmed her belly, blazing a trail to her hot, moist center, parting the petal-like folds with a flick of his tongue. She came in a flash, whimpering as she arched against him. But it wasn't enough. "Wyatt...now..." she pleaded.

Pushing forward, he entered her in a single gliding thrust.

As his hard-swollen sex filled the length of her, she felt herself tighten around him. His slightest movement set off fire bursts that rippled through her body. She moved with him, knowing he was lost in her now, and lost in the wild, primal urge that drove their bodies in a frenzy of need. Her head fell back. Indescribable sensations coursed through her veins. She gave a little cry as, with one hard final thrust, he shuddered like a stallion and slumped over her...laughing.

Heaven help her, she could get used to this.

They made love again, then again, until they lay in each other's arms, utterly exhausted. Cradled against him, Leigh inhaled the manly aroma of his damp skin. She loved the smell of him, the feel of him, the husky timbre of his voice. She couldn't ask for more than to spend every night of her life with this man.

But it wasn't going to happen. Wyatt only wanted a fling, and if she stayed until he learned the truth, he wouldn't even want that. Once he uncovered what she'd kept from him, he would hate her—and his vengeance on her brother could destroy Kevin's life.

Tomorrow, come what may, she would resign from her job and resolve to never see him—or Mikey—again.

Opening one eye, she glanced at the bedside clock. It was 1:15 a.m. They hadn't planned to stay the night. Before long it would be time to get home to Mikey so Dora could leave. But the bed was so soft and warm, Wyatt's nearness so sweet. She would rest a few more minutes. Then, if Wyatt hadn't stirred, she would wake him up to leave.

Closing her eyes, she drifted off. The next thing she

heard was the ringing of Wyatt's cell phone on the night-stand.

The sound startled her awake. Glancing at the clock again she saw that it was after two o'clock. Wyatt muttered groggily, sat up and reached for the phone.

"Hello?…Yes, what is it, Dora?"

Leigh was suddenly wide-awake. As the conversation continued she reached for her clothes and began getting dressed.

"He's *what?*…How high?…Yes, that's a good idea. We'll meet you there." He hung up the phone and turned to Leigh with a somber expression.

"What is it?" She stared at him, cold fear closing around her heart.

"It's Mikey." His voice was flat. "He's running a fever, seems to have a lot of congestion. Dora's taking him to the hospital. We'll meet her there. She thinks he might have pneumonia."

Eleven

A valet was waiting at the hotel entrance with the Mercedes and their coats. Leigh, who'd chosen to wear the spa slippers downstairs and carry her gold boots, was grateful she'd thought to leave her pumps in the car. But her feet were the least of her worries now. She imagined her precious baby desperately sick and struggling to breathe. What if Dora didn't make it to the hospital in time?

Wyatt drove as fast as the wheels could take the curves, his mouth set in a grim line. Beside him, Leigh kept a lookout for deer. "What do you know about pneumonia?" she asked him.

"Next to nothing. But I trust Dora's judgment. She was concerned enough to take Mikey right to the hospital." He handed her his cell phone. "We'd better let Chloe know. She'll want to be there."

Leigh scrolled down to Chloe's number and speed dialed. She heard the phone ring on the other end. It rang again, then again until Chloe's message voice came on, followed by a beep.

"Chloe, this is Leigh. Mikey's sick. He's on his way to the hospital. Call your dad when you get this."

"She's not answering?" Wyatt shot her an anxious look as she ended the call.

Leigh shook her head. "I'll try again in a few minutes. She might be asleep with the phone turned off."

"Asleep? This early? At a slumber party? That would be a first." Wyatt was trying to make light of things, but Leigh could tell he was worried. Not only about his grandson but about his daughter.

Even at high speed, with no traffic on the road, the ride down the canyon seemed to take forever. Leigh tried to call Chloe again, then again. There was no answer.

"What about the girl having the party?" she asked Wyatt. "Do you know where she lives?"

"No, but I called her mother before I agreed to let Chloe go. I may have put the number in my wallet. I'll look when we get to the hospital."

They pulled onto the main road and sped through the sleeping town. Leigh's pulse quickened when she spotted Dora's car in the hospital parking lot. At least she'd made it here with Mikey.

Leaving Wyatt to park the Mercedes, she leaped out and raced into the emergency entrance. She found Dora in the waiting room. The two women embraced. "They took him in a few minutes ago," Dora said. "We can go back once they've got him stabilized."

"Will he be all right?"

"Let's hope so. One of my babies had pneumonia so I know the signs. He's one sick little boy."

Wyatt rushed in through the double doors. Dora updated him on Mikey's condition.

"You said you were going to look for that phone number," Leigh reminded him.

He thumbed through his wallet and came up with a scrap of paper. "This is it. Let's hope they can rouse Chloe."

He'd found his cell phone and was about to dial the number when a nurse came into the waiting room. "We've got your baby on oxygen and an IV. You can go back and be with him if you'd like." She glanced at Leigh. "Are you his mother?"

"No, I'm—"

"She might as well be," Dora interrupted. "Just go, Leigh."

The nurse asked no more questions. Leaving Dora in the waiting area, Leigh and Wyatt followed her back along a hallway to a small room. Mikey lay in an incubator wearing nothing but a disposable diaper. An IV tube was attached by a needle to one tiny foot. His eyes were closed, his skin slightly blue. He looked so small and pathetic that Leigh wanted to weep. Her cold hand crept into Wyatt's.

Wyatt tightened his fingers around hers, taking and giving comfort. Looking down at his helpless little grandson, he felt a surge of love so powerful that it seemed to crush his heart. This little boy, neither expected nor wanted at first, had become the most precious thing on earth. Wyatt could no longer imagine life without him.

A bespectacled young man—presumably the doctor—stood beside the table making notes on a clipboard. "We've got your son on an antibiotic and we've suctioned him as best we can," he said. "I've seen worse cases pull through, and I'd say his chances are good. But the next few hours will be critical."

Your son. The doctor had assumed he and Leigh were Mikey's parents.

"Can I stay here with him?" Leigh asked.

"Sure." He nodded toward a chair in the corner. "There's coffee at the nurses' station. Restroom's across the hall."

Her hand slipped out of his. "You need to find Chloe. I'll call you if anything changes."

He nodded, taking a few more seconds to look down at Mikey. "Hang in there, big guy," he whispered. Then he tore himself away and walked back to the waiting room.

Dora was thumbing restlessly through a magazine. She rose as she saw him. "Thanks for getting Mikey here so fast," he told her. "He's not out of the woods yet, but the doctor seems optimistic."

"Thank goodness!"

"Leigh's going to stay with him. You're welcome to go home and get some rest."

She shook her head. "I won't rest till I know Mikey's all right. Where's Chloe?"

"That's what I'm trying to find out." Wyatt found his cell phone again and punched in the number his daughter had given him earlier. After several rings, a woman's sleepy voice answered.

"Sorry to wake you, Mrs. Winslow. This is Wyatt Richardson. I need to speak with Chloe. It's an emergency."

There was a pause on the other end of the line. "Chloe isn't here."

"What?"

"She was here for a while. But around ten she said she was feeling sick. Amy drove her home. Isn't she there?"

Wyatt felt his nerves clench. "Did Amy come back?"

"No. I assumed she'd stayed with Chloe or gone home."

Wyatt exhaled, forcing himself to speak calmly. "It's urgent that I find her. I'll need to speak to the other girls. One of them might know where she's gone. Do you mind if I come to your house?"

There was a beat of hesitation. "Of course not. I'll make some coffee."

"That won't be necessary." Wyatt got the address, jotted it down and ended the call.

Dora gazed at him in dismay, clearly having grasped what had happened from overhearing his side of the call. "That little pill ought to be locked up till she's twenty-one! I'll stay out here in case she shows."

"Thanks." Wyatt was out the door, racing to his car. He'd hoped motherhood was making Chloe more responsible. But he should have known better.

He recognized the neighborhood. The Winslow home wasn't far from the house he'd bought for Tina. The porch light was on, as was a lamp in the front room. Evidently the girls had been alerted that he was coming.

Mrs. Winslow, a petite blonde of Tina's vintage, answered the front door. She was dressed in a black silk robe and he noticed she'd put on fresh makeup. If there was a Mr. Winslow, he was nowhere to be seen. Not that it mattered.

After listening to his brief apology, she ushered him into the living room. Five girls in pajamas sat huddled on the sectional sofa looking like suspects in a police lineup.

Wyatt frowned at them. "Let's make this fast. Chloe's baby is in the hospital, very sick, and I need to find her. If any one of you can tell me where she's gone I'll be grateful—and so will she."

In the silence, the girls looked at each other. Finally one of them raised her hand. "Chloe and Amy went to Jimmy McFarland's house. His folks are out of town for the weekend so he's having a party. They said we'd be in big trouble if we told."

Wyatt exhaled. "You did the right thing. Now I need Jimmy's address."

The girls buzzed among themselves. Mrs. Winslow handed them a pen and notebook. One of them wrote down some directions. "It's a big house like the ones in England," she said. "You can't miss it."

Thanking the girls and Mrs. Winslow, who told him her name was Eve and that he could call her anytime, Wyatt returned to his car. It took him fifteen minutes to find the street.

No, he surmised as he turned the corner, there was no missing the oversized, rambling Tudor. Not with three flashing police cars pulled up in front.

His pulse quickened, pumping a rush of adrenaline. He could deal with Chloe's misbehavior later. Right now all that mattered was finding her and getting her safely to the hospital.

Passing in front of the house he noticed Amy's red convertible in the drive. Wyatt made a U-turn at the next corner and parked the Mercedes down the block on the opposite side of the street. Climbing out, he kept to the shadows as he approached the house.

The police officers were still in their cars, talking on their radios. Wyatt saw a half-dozen boys sneak around the side of the garage and disappear up the street at a dead run. If they'd come out a back door it should still be unlocked.

Slipping back the way the boys had come, Wyatt emerged on the patio. The outdoor pool had been drained and covered for the winter. There was nobody outside. But he found one of the French doors ajar. Mindful of the risk, he stepped inside. The air reeked with the smell of weed. If the police caught him here he'd have some tall explaining to do. But he had to find his daughter.

Anger roiled in the back of his mind. For the stunt she'd pulled, Chloe deserved to be arrested and maybe spend a night in jail. The experience might even teach her a lesson. But with her baby in the hospital, he knew he couldn't let that happen.

With the police outside, he'd wondered why there weren't more people fleeing the house. As he stepped into the living room he saw the reason. Teenagers were sprawled on the floor and draped over the furniture, most of them too drunk or too stoned to get up and leave. Heartsick, he scanned the dimly lit room for Chloe. He didn't see her.

A boy came out of the kitchen. At least this one was on his feet. He stared at Wyatt with glazed eyes.

"Chloe Richardson," Wyatt growled. "Where is she?"

The boy nodded toward a hallway. "Bathroom. Puking her guts out."

Plunging down the hall, Wyatt saw a door ajar and recognized the sounds coming from the other side. Chloe was hunched over the toilet, in the last stages of being violently sick. She looked up at him, her eyes huge in her chalky face.

"Oh, Daddy, I'm sorry!" she whimpered.

"Never mind. We're getting out of here." He pulled her to her feet and grabbed a towel to wipe her damp face. "Mikey's in the hospital. You need to be with your baby."

"Mikey? Oh, no…." She began to cry. Wyatt dragged her half stumbling out the back door as the police came in the front. Moments later they were safely in the car. Wyatt pulled away from the curb and headed back toward the hospital.

Chloe was sobbing. Wyatt pulled into an all-night driveup and bought her some coffee. It seemed to calm her a little. "What's wrong with Mikey?" she asked.

"Pneumonia. They've got him in an incubator."

"Will he be okay?"

"I hope so. We'll know for sure in a few hours. Leigh's with him. Dora's there, too. But a baby needs his mother."

"I'm not much of a mother, am I, Daddy?"

Wyatt shot her a dark look. "Don't play the sympathy game with me. You messed up big-time, and there *will* be consequences. For starters, don't plan on having your own car anytime soon. And you're grounded, starting now."

"Oh, please, don't do that," she whined. "I'll never drink again. Cross my heart."

Wyatt sighed, feeling old and tired. "Just be still, Chloe. We'll be at the hospital in a few minutes. Try thinking about Mikey for a change, instead of yourself."

She was mercifully silent for the rest of the drive. Wyatt knew he was partly to blame for what she'd done. He'd never been much of a father to the girl, substituting expensive gifts for what she'd really needed—his time and attention. How could she not grow up spoiled and demanding? How could she not act out in ways that would hurt him and herself?

True, part of the fault was Tina's. What kind of mother would choose her younger husband over her daughter and grandchild? But, looking back now, would Wyatt's ex-wife have evolved into a man-chasing cougar if he'd put more effort into their marriage? Tina's need had been to feel desirable and sexy and loved. When he was too busy to fill that need, she'd looked elsewhere.

At the time neither of them had given much thought to their daughter. Now they were paying the price.

Sadly, so was Chloe.

After an hour on oxygen, Mikey's color had improved and his breathing seemed easier. But the nurse had warned Leigh that it might take several days to kill off the bacteria and clear his lungs. "It doesn't take much to trigger these infections," she'd said. "It can be pretty scary. But if there's one thing I've learned, it's that these little guys want to live, and they're tougher than they look."

Leigh remembered those words as she sat next to the incubator, watching Mikey's every breath and silently praying. Except for a brief trip to update Dora in the waiting room, she hadn't left his side. It was as if, as long as she was there, she could will her love to wrap around his tiny body and keep him safe.

The hospital staff had been more than kind. Taking stock of her skimpy dress and bare legs, they'd found her some scrubs to wear. They'd even brought her coffee and a warm blanket for the chilly room. At least she was more comfortable now. But her gaze kept wandering to the clock on the wall. More than an hour had passed since Wyatt left to look for Chloe. Talons of worry clawed at her strained nerves.

Their passionate night in the hotel penthouse seemed like a faraway dream. Right now only Mikey was real. As she watched the rise and fall of his breathing, Leigh realized that the plan to quit her job wasn't going to happen anytime soon. As long as Mikey was sick she would be here for him. The risk of being found out would rise with each day. And her uncertain relationship with Wyatt would only complicate things. But that was a chance she'd have to take.

Where in heaven's name was he? Were he and Chloe all right?

She'd begun to imagine twisted wreckage and ambulance sirens by the time the door opened. Relief washed over her as Wyatt ushered Chloe into the room. They were both safe.

Then she noticed the girl's pale face and wasted expression. Her clothes reeked of vomit, alcohol and pot fumes.

Wyatt kept a hand at her back as she stumbled toward the incubator and stared down at her helpless baby.

"Oh, Mikey," she whispered, tears streaming down her face. "I'm so sorry."

Leigh patted her clammy hand. "The oxygen is helping him breathe. But the antibiotic may take a while to work. You can thank Dora for getting him here right away."

Chloe's face had paled. She clapped a hand to her mouth. "Gonna be sick," she muttered, staggering toward the door.

"The bathroom's across the hall. I'll go with you." Leigh sprang out of her chair to guide the girl in the right direction, leaving Wyatt in the room.

They made it in the nick of time. Leigh supported Chloe over the bowl as she lost whatever was left in her stomach. "I'm so sorry, Leigh," she whimpered over and over. "So sorry."

Leigh helped her wash her face and hands and dry them on a paper towel. "Why don't you rest in the waiting room with Dora till you feel better? I'll get you a warm blanket and some coffee. Mikey isn't going anywhere."

After getting Chloe settled with Dora, Leigh returned to Mikey's room. She found the door ajar and was about to walk in when she heard Wyatt's voice. He was standing next to the incubator, barely speaking above a whisper. She couldn't resist pausing outside to listen.

"Hang in there, big guy, you hear? Your grandpa has lots of plans for you. He wants to teach you to hike and fish and ski and ride a horse. He wants to get you a puppy and take you to ball games, and send you to college so you can become whatever you want to. But first you need to get better so you can grow up...."

His voice broke. Leigh wiped the wetness from her cheek and opened the door.

His glance swung toward her. Her gaze took in his naked face—the shadows of exhaustion and worry, the glint of vulnerability in his eyes. Here was a man who survived by being in control of everything and everyone around him. Tonight life had yanked that control away, leaving him adrift with nowhere to turn.

Without a word she walked toward him and wrapped her arms around his waist. He held her with all his strength, both of them trembling, both of them scared and needing comfort.

Heaven help her, what a disaster.

She loved him.

Twelve

A few days later Mikey was well enough to go home. His lungs were clear, his cheeks pink and his appetite like a little tiger's.

Wyatt bundled his grandson and, with Leigh at his elbow, carried him to the Mercedes. Leigh looked exhausted. During Mikey's illness she'd scarcely left the boy's side, even spending her nights in the hospital room where he'd been transferred from Emergency. Wyatt had ordered a cot for the room and spelled her when she allowed it, but she'd never left for more than an hour or two, taking time only to shower, change and grab a meal. And she was always there at night.

For a salaried nanny she'd shown an extraordinary measure of devotion. Wyatt might have suspected some ulterior motive, but he'd seen the way she looked at his grandson. What he read in those haunting eyes couldn't be mistaken for anything but love.

In the parking lot he opened the front passenger door for Leigh and handed the baby to Chloe, who sat in back with his carrier. "Hi, Mikey," she chirped as she buckled him in. "I've missed you!"

Along with the expected hangover, Chloe had come down with a nasty cold the morning after her escapade. It had given Wyatt an excuse to keep her at home, but it had also forced him to be there with her instead of spending more time at the hospital. Sadly, he could no longer trust his daughter to behave on her own.

Was Chloe a budding alcoholic who needed to be in rehab, or just a wild teen going through a phase? Tina had been a drinker, he recalled. Alcohol had contributed to her infidelity and their divorce. No way would he allow their daughter to go down the same road. Something had to be done, but what?

Inwardly he sighed. There was no getting around it. He would have to talk the situation over with her mother.

What had happened to him? Not that long ago he'd thought he had everything under control. Then Chloe had shown up on his doorstep, followed by Mikey and Leigh. Now his personal world was in chaos.

But the chaos wasn't entirely bad, Wyatt reminded himself. Leigh and Mikey had opened new windows of light and love in his heart. And fate had given him one last chance to get it right with his little girl. So far, on that front, he wasn't doing so well, but he wasn't going to stop trying—with Chloe or with Leigh and Mikey.

He glanced at Leigh, where she sat beside him. She'd given her all to be there for Mikey. Now she was worn-out. When they got home he was going to insist that she go to bed and get some rest. Chloe was well enough to tend Mikey for the rest of the day.

Once Leigh was feeling better he planned to have a serious talk with her. She wasn't just the nanny anymore. She'd become an important part of his life. Whatever happened with Chloe and Mikey, he wanted her to stay with him—and he'd make it clear that sharing his bed would be part of the bargain. He'd never been good at relationships, but he didn't want to lose this wonderful woman—and lose her he would if he didn't have the courage to take a chance.

Chloe might find the arrangement startling at first. But she liked Leigh and she'd get used to the way of things, especially if he let her know what to expect.

His spirits rose as he swung the Mercedes around the steep mountain curves. Downy snowflakes—always welcome—were drifting from the clouds. He switched on the wipers. He'd called his staff to make sure the house would be warm with a hot lunch waiting and someone to serve. It would be a small celebration of sorts, bringing Mikey home.

He could see the house as they came around the last bend. Parked in the driveway, next to the Wolf Ridge van from the hotel, was an unfamiliar white Cadillac with gold trim. Wyatt's instincts prickled. He wasn't expecting company, especially at home and especially today. But the car was empty, which meant his uninvited guest would be waiting inside the house.

Something wasn't right.

He'd planned to let Leigh, Chloe and the baby out at the front door, then park the Mercedes in the garage. Changing his mind, he pulled up to the porch and went in ahead of them.

As soon as he opened the door, Wyatt knew. It was the perfume, the distinctive, imported scent that filled the air like a miasma.

The petite redhead rose from the couch—movie star hair, chiseled porcelain face, spectacular curves—some of which he'd paid for. She smiled. "Hello, Wyatt."

He felt the day caving in on him. "Hello, Tina," he said.

* * *

Chloe had unfastened the car seat. With Mikey still buckled in, she carried it across the porch and through the front door. Bringing up the rear, Leigh almost bumped into the girl when she halted as if she'd hit a wall.

"Mom!" Chloe's voice blended surprise and a note of what might have been anger. Looking past her, Leigh's weary gaze took in the petite, elegant woman in the clinging black pantsuit.

Wyatt's ex-wife was an older version of her daughter, except that where Chloe's pretty features were natural, her mother's appeared to have been refined by the best cosmetic surgeons in the country. She was too sculpted, too perfect to be real.

But that didn't mean she wasn't beautiful. The woman's polished perfection made Leigh all the more aware of the stringy hair she'd washed in a hurry and air-dried on the way back to the hospital, of her bare face, bloodshot eyes and slept-in clothes.

"What are you doing here, Mom?" Chloe's tone was sullen. "Where's Andre?"

"Let's just say that Andre and I had a…parting of the ways." Her voice was low and sexy, like a blues singer's. "As for what I'm doing here, why shouldn't I want to see my only daughter and her darling baby?"

Chloe stood her ground, gripping the handle of the baby carrier. "Mikey's been sick in the hospital. He mustn't be around strangers yet."

"But I'm not a stranger, dear! I'm little Mikey's… *grandma*." She spoke the word as if she'd just bitten into a bad strawberry.

Leigh gulped back a rush of emotion, thinking how Mikey's *other* grandma would love to see him. Life was so unfair.

Wyatt stepped away from the fireplace where he'd been standing, a glint of steel in his eyes. "Chloe, why don't you take Mikey up to the nursery and put him to bed? Your mother can see him later."

Chloe wheeled and headed for the stairs. Her mother turned on her ex-husband. "You can't do this to me, Wyatt! I have every right to see my own grandchild!"

"Later, Tina." Wyatt shook his head. "The boy's getting over pneumonia and shouldn't be exposed to anything you may have picked up traveling. As for your so-called right, you gave that up when you kicked your pregnant daughter out of the house. How much you see of Mikey now won't be up to me. It will be up to his mother."

"We'll see about that." Turning away from him, she seemed to notice Leigh for the first time. "And who's this? If she's your latest girlfriend, you must be getting desperate."

Torn between following Chloe upstairs and giving the woman her due, Leigh hesitated. She was worn to a frazzle and in no mood to take insults. But she had no wish to worsen the situation by jumping into a catfight.

"Please come here, Leigh." Wyatt's voice held a note of subdued ferocity. Head high, Leigh crossed the room to his side. His hand reached out and came to rest on the small of her back.

"Leigh, my former wife needs no introduction," he said. "Tina, this is Leigh Foster, Mikey's wonderful nanny. She was with him in the hospital day and night. I don't know how we'd have managed without her. As for you, if you can't at least be civil, you're welcome to leave."

In the silence that followed, Tina cocked her head like an elegant bird. Her eyes were jade-green, not blue like Chloe's. "Well…" she said. "My sincere apologies, Miss Foster. I should have realized you weren't Wyatt's type."

With effort, Leigh held her tongue. From the kitchen came the rattle of pans and the drifting aroma of roast beef.

"Lunch is waiting," Wyatt said. "Tina, I don't turn visitors away hungry. You're welcome to stay and eat with us."

"I'll go up and tell Chloe," Leigh offered. "Then, if you don't mind, I'll excuse myself for a nap in a real bed." She hoped Wyatt wouldn't try to argue with her. She was hungry, but the last thing she needed was a tension-filled meal with three people whose issues shouldn't concern her.

"I'll keep a plate warm for you," Wyatt said.

"Sleep tight," Tina called as Leigh mounted the stairs and trudged down the hall to her room. At least meeting the woman had helped her understand the dynamics of Wyatt's family. Chloe might be impulsive and strong-willed, but compared to her mother she was a sweet little lamb.

What was going to happen now that Tina was separated from her husband and back in her daughter's life? Would she stay in Dutchman's Creek? Would Chloe move back with her mother, taking Mikey with her?

Would they want Leigh to go with the baby, or was her time with Kevin's son about to end? Right now she was too tired to reason it out.

After sending Chloe downstairs to eat, she checked on the sleeping Mikey, shed her rumpled clothes, pulled on an old T-shirt and tumbled into bed. The moment her head touched the pillow she fell asleep.

She opened her eyes to a late-day sun casting long shadows across the bed. She felt groggy and disoriented. How long had she slept? Three hours? Four?

Dragging herself out of bed she pattered into the bathroom, where she relieved herself, splashed her face and brushed her teeth. A glance in the mirror showed bloodshot eyes and tangled hair. What now? Should she throw on some clothes? Check on Mikey? Crawl back into bed?

Maybe it was her turn to get sick.

She was still dithering when she heard a polite knock on her door. "Leigh, are you up?" The voice was Wyatt's.

Leigh's T-shirt barely covered her hips. She scrambled back into bed and pulled the covers to her chest before she answered, "Come on in."

Wyatt opened the door. He was carrying a tray with a hot beef sandwich and potato salad on a plate. The food smelled delicious. Her stomach growled. Maybe she wasn't sick after all.

"I heard the water running and thought you might be ready to join the living," he said. "How are you feeling?"

"Better than I look." She fluffed the pillows to support her back. "Where's Mikey?"

"Asleep in Chloe's room. She's on her computer."

"And Tina?"

"Gone for now. Long story. Are you hungry?"

"Starved. And that tray looks good. You're spoiling me, you know."

"I like spoiling you." He set the tray on her lap, unfolded a cloth napkin and tucked it under her chin. "Something tells me you haven't had enough spoiling in your life."

He'd cut the toasted sandwich into neat quarters. Leigh nibbled one. It was succulent and tasty. She took a sip of cold milk. "Careful, I could get used to this," she joked.

"I'd like it if you did." He sat on the foot of the bed, his gaze disturbingly warm. "You've been my rock these past few days. Between Chloe's troubles and the baby, I don't know what I'd have done without you. You've become family, Leigh. I want you to know that. And I want you to stay—with me."

Leigh's appetite fled. Under different conditions, hearing those words from him would have thrilled her. But not now—not when every day she remained here was a betrayal of his trust.

Now would be the time to tell him she was leaving. But he would demand to know why. And then what? How could she go on lying to him? How could she tell him the truth?

"What about your ex-wife?" she asked, groping for a diversion.

"Tina has nothing to do with this. She's rented a house in Denver. At lunch she demanded that Chloe and Mikey move in with her and that you go along to take care of him. Chloe told her, in so many words, to take a hike."

"How can Chloe do that? Tina *is* her mother. And in spite of everything, she must love her daughter."

"She also loves the child support she was getting when Chloe lived with her, especially since her new marriage meant she was no longer entitled to alimony. But we won't go there. I know better than to pass judgment on another parent."

"Who has legal custody of Chloe?"

"We have joint custody. I've always felt that a young girl needed to be with her mother. But now—"

Breaking off, he frowned. "Why are we even talking about this? It's not the reason I'm here."

Leigh waited, bracing herself. She loved this man. But showing her feelings now would be the worst thing she could do.

"I came to tell you that I need you in my life, Leigh. I want more nights like the one we had. I want to spoil you the way I can afford to. And I want to know, that whatever happens with Chloe and Mikey, you and I will be here for each other."

Leigh stared down at the tray on her lap. He hadn't mentioned love. And there'd certainly been no hint of marriage.

But what difference did it make? Even if he'd offered his heart and soul, even if he'd offered her a lifetime, she still couldn't say yes. She couldn't even say maybe. She had to say no and make it stick.

"You're saying you want to promote me from nanny to live-in lover?" The sarcasm would sting. She needed it to. She shook her head. "I've been there. Next time I play that game, I'm playing for keeps—and you're not a 'for keeps' kind of man, Wyatt. You can have any woman you want. After a while you'd get bored with me and start looking around for some excitement."

His expression had turned stony. "I take it that's a no."

"In twenty-two-point, bold caps. *N-O.*"

Leigh knew she'd wounded him. Though he hid it well, she'd seen the flicker of hurt in his eyes. It had been all she could do to keep from flinging her arms around him and telling him she'd changed her mind. But no, this had to be done, and now she'd done it.

Wyatt was a proud man. He wouldn't be asking her again. But she needed to make sure.

"Consider this my two-week notice," she said. "I'll stay long enough to make sure Mikey's all right. Meanwhile you can start looking for a new nanny."

As long as he lived, Wyatt swore, he would never understand women. He'd been so sure that Leigh returned his feelings. But when he'd pushed for a long-term relationship, she'd thrown up a wall of resistance and announced she was quitting her job.

Chloe had mentioned earlier that Leigh had been engaged, and that her fiancé had cheated on her. Had the experience soured her for life on the idea of a lasting relationship? Or was she hiding something even deeper?

Wyatt had hoped to talk to her, at least. But she was

making every excuse to avoid him, hanging out in her room with Mikey and only showing up for meals when she knew Chloe would be there. Meanwhile, the days were ticking by like some grim clock. Would she really leave when the two weeks were up? He was determined—make that frantic—to stop her. Leigh Foster was the best thing that had ever happened to him. He couldn't let her walk out of his life without understanding why.

As if his worries about Leigh weren't enough, Tina was haranguing him daily by phone from Denver, threatening legal action if he didn't deliver Chloe and Mikey to her house. Wyatt's lawyer had assured him he had every right to keep his daughter and grandson. But that did little to ease his concerns. His ex-wife was an insecure, frightened woman, alone for the first time in her life. Right or wrong, he still felt some responsibility for her.

Chloe had declared that she would take Mikey and run away before she'd go back to her mother. Since Wyatt had no plans to send her, that wasn't a serious threat. But with Chloe, there were always other issues.

He'd stuck to his guns about punishing her for the drunken party escapade. Both the car and the ski holiday with her friends were on hold, and she was grounded to the house for the next month.

A grounded Chloe was like a caged wildcat. She whined and pouted from morning till night, locking herself in her room with her computer while blasting rap music through the house. If she was going to be miserable, so was everyone else.

The one ray of sunshine in the house was Mikey. He had blossomed into a plump, cooing, cuddling bundle of joy. Wyatt couldn't get enough of him when he was home. And when he was away from home, at least he had his work running the resort.

Today he stood on the side porch of the lodge, watching skiers glide down the powdery runs. It was a beautiful afternoon, the fresh-fallen snow glittering like diamond dust on the slopes. The lifts were full, the restaurants and coffee shops teeming, the lodge filled with the glow of a crackling fire. It cheered him to see what his efforts had built. And he was definitely in need of some cheering.

Last night Chloe had been impossible. It had been the evening of the annual winter carnival at her old school, a party that included a huge outdoor bonfire, hot dogs and s'mores, and a stag dance in the gym. She'd begged to be allowed to go. But Wyatt had stood firm. He knew for a fact that older boys often smuggled liquor into the event. Besides, she was grounded, and that was that.

But Chloe hadn't let up. "I just want to go to the carnival," she'd whined. "You can even take me there and bring me home if you want to."

When Wyatt had stood his ground, she'd railed at him. "You don't care about me! You never have! All you've ever done is buy me off with presents! Well, not anymore! If you don't let me go tonight, I'll take Mikey and go live with Mom!"

When that threat hadn't worked she'd stormed into her room and slammed the door, something she'd been doing a lot of lately. Wyatt wasn't looking forward to going home and facing her again.

Meanwhile, the snow was calling to him. With so much happening at home, he'd been too busy to ski this season. But some time on the slopes would do him a world of good today. Wyatt kept his own ski gear at the resort. He found himself whistling as he hauled it out of storage. Twenty minutes later he was riding the lift to the top of Breakneck, the resort's steepest run. Pushing off the summit, he flew downhill through the fresh powder, negotiating each

rise and turn with the skill that had won him a chestful
of Olympic medals. Even after months off, skiing felt as
natural to him as walking.

Maybe if Chloe behaved he could bring her along next
time. Or, if Leigh chose to stay he could give her lessons.
So many *if*s. And they all mattered so much.

The run felt so good that he did it again, and then went
down Blackrock, another favorite of his. By the time he
finished the sun was low above the mountains and storm
clouds were rolling in.

He hadn't meant to stay so late. He would put his gear
away and then call Leigh to tell her he was on his way.
She'd said something about making spaghetti and garlic
bread tonight, so she'd likely be waiting dinner for him.

His office staff had gone home for the day, but the message light was blinking on his phone. He'd call Leigh first,
then pick it up.

She answered on the second ring. "Sorry I'm late. I
decided to ski," he said. "I'll be home in a few minutes.
How's Chloe?"

"I haven't seen her since lunchtime, but I can hear the
music blasting in her room. I'm guessing she'll come out
when she smells dinner. It'll be ready to dish up when
you get here."

"Thanks for waiting. I won't be long." Wyatt wanted
to say more, but he knew she wasn't ready to hear it. Instead he ended the call and punched the message button.

"Mr. Richardson." It was Sam Gastineau, head of Security. "There's something you need to be aware of. You
can call me on my cell."

Sensing trouble, Wyatt dialed the number. "Sam, what
is it?"

"You asked us to monitor your daughter's internet and
phone. So far it's been mostly girl talk. But she's been chat-

ting online with an unknown male, and they've arranged a meeting in town."

Wyatt's stomach clenched. "An unknown male? Who?"

"We did some tracing. The name we found is Eric Underhill, which doesn't tell us much. All we've been able to find out so far is that he's not a student at any local high school."

Wyatt's knees threatened to buckle but he knew he had to stay calm. "I'll find out what I can and get back to you," he said.

Hanging up the phone, he dialed his home number again.

Thirteen

Leigh was taking the garlic bread out of the oven when the phone rang a second time. The voice on the line was Wyatt's, but he sounded nothing like the man she'd spoken with a few minutes earlier.

"Leigh, is Chloe there?"

"She's in her room. I can hear—"

"Go and look! If she's there, bring her to the phone!"

Alarmed by the urgency in his voice, she rushed down the hall to Chloe's room. She could hear music through the closed door but there was no reply to her knock. Heart pounding, she turned the knob, swung the door open and froze. The speakers on the computer were blaring. Chloe was nowhere to be seen.

Panic rising, Leigh checked the adjoining bathroom and found it empty. She plunged upstairs and raced from room to room—the nursery where Mikey was sleeping, the guest suites, even the porch. Returning to Chloe's room, she looked for the girl's purse. It was gone. So was her down jacket from the front hall closet.

By the time she got back to the phone she was out of breath. "Wyatt, she's gone! I can't find her anywhere!"

"What about Mikey?" His voice was calm now. Too calm.

"Asleep in his crib. I just saw him." Leigh thought she heard a breath of relief but couldn't be sure. "What is this? What aren't you telling me?"

"I'll explain later. Right now I need you to do one more thing. Open the center drawer in my office desk. In the right front corner you should see a pair of car keys on a black ring. I'll hold on."

She was back in less than a minute, her throat so tight she could barely speak. "No keys. I checked the drawer to make sure they hadn't been moved. They're gone."

After a beat of silence, he muttered something under his breath. "At least I can tell the police what to look for," he said. "Chloe's taken the Bentley."

When Wyatt came outside to the Hummer it was dark. Big, slushy snowflakes tumbled out of the sky, the kind that would freeze on the roads and turn them icy. The Bentley was no good for winter driving. That was why he'd put it away until spring. But Chloe wouldn't have thought of that.

Hellfire, he should've had somebody up to drain the fluids for the winter. That was what he usually did. But with so much on his mind he'd put it off. Now Chloe was driving the vintage sports car and there were so many ways this could end badly.

Not that the Bentley mattered so much. It was just a machine, after all. But his precious daughter wasn't safe in that car. He could only pray that the police would stop her before she hit a patch of icy road.

After talking with Leigh, he'd phoned Sam Gastineau

again and told him to give the police everything they asked for, including the description and license number of the car. According to their emails, Chloe and Eric Underhill, whoever the hell he was, had planned to meet in the school parking lot at the dance. When that hadn't worked out, they'd agreed to try the same place tonight. The whole idea gave Wyatt chills. Who was this person, and why would he want to meet Chloe alone? None of the answers he could think of were good.

Leigh came out on the porch when she heard the Hummer pull up. Wyatt swung out of the vehicle. "Any news?" he asked.

"Nothing. I've been trying to call her cell but she's not answering. Come on inside, it's freezing out here."

"Any idea how long she's been gone?" The glow of the porch light made his haggard face look gray.

Leigh shook her head. "Wyatt, I'm so sorry. If I'd checked on her more often, or tried to get her to talk—"

"It's not your fault." His voice was hoarse with tension. "If anything, it's mine. I should've been more of a father to her over the years. If I had we wouldn't be in this mess." He allowed Leigh to pull him inside and close the door. His hair and sheepskin coat were speckled with wet snow. Leigh suppressed the impulse to wrap her arms around him and hold him. He was too upset for that.

He slumped against the back of the sofa. "My security team's been screening her email. She left to meet someone named Eric Underhill. Have you ever heard the name?"

"Never. It almost sounds made-up."

"I keep trying to sort this out. One thing that's occurred to me is that this Eric Underhill might be Mikey's father."

Leigh flinched as if she'd been struck. Wyatt was guessing, that was all. But what if he was right? What if Kevin had contacted Chloe under another name?

"What if he *is* Mikey's father?" she forced herself to ask. "What would you do?"

"Ask me that after my little girl is safe. The police know where they're supposed to be meeting. They're on their way to pick him up." He raked a hand through his damp hair. "I can't stay here and wait, Leigh. Chloe's out there in the storm in a car that wasn't made for winter roads. And she's on her way to meet a man I know nothing about. I need to be out there looking for her."

Wyatt could be putting himself in danger, too; but Leigh knew better than to argue. "I'll stay here with Mikey," she said. "I've got your cell number. If I hear any news I'll call you. Will you do the same for me?"

"If I can." He pulled her against him in a hard embrace that lasted no more than a heartbeat. Then he turned and strode out the front door. Leigh heard the engine roar and watched the Hummer disappear through the falling snow. With a silent prayer for Wyatt's safety and for Chloe's, she turned and went back into the house.

Fumbling in her purse, she found her cell phone and speed dialed her brother's number. If Kevin was meeting Chloe she had to warn him. A rendezvous between two teenagers wasn't illegal, but once the police learned Kevin's real name, they would surely alert Wyatt, who could be capable of anything tonight.

Her brother's phone rang several times before his voice mail came on. She left a message asking him to call her, then tried her mother's phone. Again, there was no answer.

By now Mikey was awake. Leigh could hear him fussing as she hurried up the stairs. Lifting him from the crib she snuggled him close. His small, warm body was a comfort in her arms.

Kevin could be anywhere, she told herself. Maybe he was at the movies and had turned his phone off. Maybe the battery was low, or he'd left the phone where he couldn't hear it. He probably had nothing to do with Chloe's disappearance. But the two teens had seen each other at the mall. Either of them could have decided to make contact.

Whatever had happened, Leigh sensed that things were about to change. She'd depended on luck to keep her secret. But if Kevin and Chloe were in touch that luck was running out. Wyatt would soon learn the truth—and when he did, the world of love she'd found here would crumble like a sand castle.

The road down the canyon was like an ice rink, so slick that even the Hummer's oversized snow tires found little purchase. Wyatt drove slowly, peering through the thick snowfall for any sign of a wrecked vehicle. With luck the Bentley might just spin off the road. He would find it stuck on the shoulder with Chloe inside, cold and scared but uninjured. Other scenarios that flashed through his mind were much grimmer. She could hit another vehicle or careen into the icy creek below the road. Or she could make it to the rendezvous with Eric Underhill and find herself in more trouble than she'd dreamed of in her worst nightmares.

The highway, when he reached it, was better only in that it was level. In the snowy darkness he could barely see beyond the Hummer's powerful headlights. Had he missed something in the canyon? Should he turn around and look again? Torn, he kept on driving. The police scanner he'd installed in the vehicle was a jumble of static and half-understood voices. He could make out nothing about a wrecked Bentley or a young girl.

If he found her safe things would be different, he

vowed. He would try to be the father she'd missed growing up, and he would be there for Mikey, as well. The qualified people on his staff could manage the resort just fine. He could easily take time off to be with his daughter and grandson—and with Leigh. She'd told him she was leaving but he hadn't given up on her. If she showed so much as a spark of feeling for him he would build on that. He wanted her in his life. He wanted a second chance at a real family.

Lord, what would he do if the worst happened tonight?

The flash of red and blue lights ahead shocked him out of his reverie. A cold, sick feeling crept over him as he glimpsed wreckage through the falling snow.

Swinging onto the shoulder, he braked and vaulted out of the Hummer. A siren blasted his ears as the ambulance pulled in from the road. Sprinting closer, Wyatt could see the rear end of the wrecked car. It lay crumpled on its side in the barrow pit, its license plate visible in the flashing lights. He groaned out loud. There was no mistaking the Bentley.

At first he couldn't see Chloe. Then he spotted her. She was slumped in the backseat of a police cruiser, her shoulders wrapped in a blanket. Someone next to her was holding a bloodstained towel to her head.

"Chloe!" Wyatt nearly ripped the door off getting it open. She glanced up and saw him.

"Oh, Daddy!" She was sobbing. "I wrecked your beautiful car. I'm so sorry!"

"It's all right." Wyatt tasted bitter tears. He tried to hug her but could only reach far enough inside for an awkward pat. "It's all right, honey," he muttered again. "It's only a car. You're okay, sweetheart—that's all that matters."

An officer had come up behind him. "Looks like she slid off and rolled," he said. "The worst part was, nobody saw it happen. She was conscious when we found her, but she must've been in that car, trapped by her seat belt, for a good forty minutes before a patrolman came by and called it in."

Wyatt's gut clenched as he thought of his daughter, helpless, bleeding, cold and alone. What if no one had found her? She could have died by the time he got here.

The paramedics had eased Chloe out of the car, wrapped her in warm blankets and laid her on a stretcher. "We'll know more once we get her to the hospital," one of them told Wyatt. "But I'm guessing she's in shock, maybe some hypothermia, too. The head gash isn't as deep as it looks but she's lost a fair amount of blood."

Wyatt squeezed Chloe's hand as they loaded her into the back of the ambulance. "I'll be right behind you," he said. "Hang in there, honey, you're going to be fine."

He was headed back to the Hummer when another officer stopped him. "We just got a call, Mr. Richardson. They've arrested the man who was waiting for her at the school. He's a forty-year-old construction worker with an assault record. Her emails were on his phone. Your girl was lucky twice tonight."

"Thanks." Wyatt felt his knees begin to buckle as the policeman walked away. He made it to his vehicle, slid onto the seat, rested his head on the steering wheel and shook with emotion.

The ambulance was pulling back onto the road. Starting the engine he followed the taillights through the swirling snow.

Leigh would be waiting for his call. He could always phone her from the hospital when he knew more about Chloe's condition. But Wyatt knew he couldn't delay that long. Right now, more than anything, he needed to hear her voice.

* * *

Leigh had fed Mikey and was sitting on the upstairs sofa with him. She'd turned the TV to the local news, praying not to see a wreck or an arrest, but compelled to watch anyway. Wyatt had been gone less than an hour. It could turn out to be a long night.

Mikey had just dozed off when the ringing phone startled him awake. Her pulse lurched when she saw Wyatt's name on the caller ID. Bracing for the worst she picked up.

"Wyatt, what's happened?"

"I found Chloe." Leigh could sense the relief in his voice. "She rolled the car, but she doesn't seem too badly hurt. I'm following the ambulance now. We'll know more when they get her to the hospital."

"Thank heaven!" She sank into the cushions as the tension drained from her body. Chloe was safe, at least. But was that the whole story? Was Kevin out there in the storm, waiting for her in the school parking lot? Had the police picked him up? Leigh had tried her brother's phone again and again with no answer. Her mother wasn't answering, either.

"What about the person Chloe was meeting?" she asked. "Eric Underhill, or whatever his name was?"

"The police arrested the bastard. He's forty years old, a predator who connects with young girls in teen chat rooms. Lord, Leigh, Chloe could've been raped, kidnapped, even murdered. I've never believed in guardian angels, but that wreck likely saved her."

Leigh succumbed to a rush of scalding tears. Chloe was all right. Kevin hadn't been involved. Her secret was safe. But for how long?

"Leigh, are you there?"

"Yes," she whispered past the lump in her throat.

"I'll call you again when I know more about Chloe. For now I just wanted to give you the news."

"Thank you." She paused. "Be careful, Wyatt. And tell Chloe we love her."

There was no reply. He'd ended the call.

Lifting Mikey against her shoulder, Leigh kissed his silky head. His fingers closed around a button on her shirt, clasping tight. He was so precious—so wise in his own baby way. Leaving him would tear out a piece of her heart.

She loved all three of them, Leigh realized—Mikey. His vulnerable young mother, whose journey to womanhood was so fraught with struggle. And Wyatt, who'd do anything to protect and provide for those closest to him. Tonight, in his voice, she'd sensed the fear, the anger and finally the relief. Beneath that flinty exterior was a tender man who cared deeply for others. A man who needed her.

When she'd taken this job she'd warned herself to guard her emotions. But this troubled family had drawn her into their embrace. They had won her love.

And her lie would betray them all.

Tell Chloe we love her.

Leigh's words, which he'd barely caught, came back to Wyatt as he walked into the hospital room. Chloe lay propped in the bed, her hair a splash of color against the bleached pillowcase. A white gauze patch was taped to her forehead where the doctor had made stitches. A monitor above the bed beeped out her vital signs.

She gave him a wan smile. "Hi, Daddy."

"Hi, sweetheart." He squeezed her foot, fearful of hurting her if he touched her anyplace else. "How are you feeling?"

"Not so great, but better than before. I heard about the

man the police caught. He sent me this cute photo and told me he was eighteen. I did a stupid thing, didn't I?"

"Yes, you did. You're lucky to be alive. But we'll talk about that later."

"How's the Bentley? I know you loved that car."

"I'll look at the car tomorrow. Right now the only thing that matters is that you're safe. The doctor says you don't have a concussion, but they want to keep you here overnight. They'll give you something to help you sleep. And I'll be right here in case you need anything."

"Daddy." She held out her hand. Stepping forward he took it. Her fingers were warm from the heated blankets. His were cold.

"I'm a big girl, and the nurses are taking good care of me. You don't need to be here. Go home to Leigh and Mikey. Get some rest."

"You're certain you won't need me?"

Her fingers tightened. "Please, Daddy, you look so tired. I'll be fine here."

"If you're sure." He moved toward the door, then hesitated as Leigh's last words came back to him.

Tell Chloe we love her.

When was the last time he'd told her that? Could he even remember?

He walked back to the bed, bent and kissed her cheek. "I love you, Chloe. So do Leigh and Mikey."

"I love you, too, Daddy." Were there tears in her eyes? "Now go get some rest. I'll be fine."

When he walked out to the parking lot the snow was still falling. The Hummer was blanketed in white. Wyatt turned on the defrosters and brushed off the mirrors and windows. It was after midnight and he was exhausted. But he felt as if a burden had been lifted. His beloved daughter was safe and had hopefully learned a lesson. Maybe they could turn a corner from here.

Plowing through the drifts, he backed out of the parking lot and onto the road. He'd called Leigh a couple of hours ago and told her he planned to stay at the hospital. Since she didn't expect him home, she'd probably gone to bed.

He imagined her asleep, her eyes closed, her hair like a pool of dark silk against the pillowcase. He imagined lying beside her, inhaling the sweet, warm aroma that cloaked her skin. A hunger stirred and rose in him. He needed her, wanted her with an ache that could only be satisfied in one way.

She'd rejected him before. If she rejected him now, that would be the end of it. He was laying his pride on the line, but that was a chance he had to take.

He didn't want to be alone tonight.

Fourteen

Lying awake in the darkness, Leigh heard the Hummer pull into the garage. She'd gone to bed soon after Wyatt's second call, but sleep had refused to come. Without the presence of its owner the house was like a vast, empty cavern—too large and too quiet.

She missed his voice and the sound of his footsteps. She missed sitting beside him while the evening news played out and watching him cuddle Mikey. She missed his laughter, the clean spicy aroma of his skin, and the sense of homecoming when his arms were around her.

Get used to it, Leigh, she'd admonished herself. *Get used to life without him, because that's the only life you'll ever have.*

She'd known all along that when the time came, she'd have to move on. But it would be harder than she'd ever imagined.

Curled in the downy featherbed, she'd listened for what seemed like hours to the howling wind and the snow pelting the windowpanes. She'd told herself that Wyatt's choice to stay at the hospital with Chloe had been a wise one. Even for a brawny vehicle like his, the blinding storm could be dangerous. On the steep mountain road it would be all too easy to overshoot a curve and go crashing down the slope.

Yet—unless she was hearing things—he'd just driven all the way home. Why? she suddenly wondered. Was something wrong?

Bounding out of bed, she threw her flannel robe over the outsized T-shirt she wore for sleep. Barefoot, she pattered down the stairs. She could hear the faint sound of a snow shovel scraping the walkway from the garage to the house. As she reached the entry, the door opened, letting in a blast of snow and icy air.

Wyatt stepped across the threshold and closed the door behind him. Snow clung to his boots, his hair, his eyebrows and the stubble on his chin. As Leigh stood shivering, he flung off his gloves, unzipped his parka and opened the front. "Come here, Leigh," he said.

For an instant she stared at him as if he'd lost his mind. Then, in the glow of the entry light, she caught the twinkle in his eyes.

She flung herself across the space between them, her arms wrapping his rib cage through the woolen sweater. He closed the front flaps of his coat, enfolding her in his warmth.

"Damn, but you feel good," he muttered.

She tilted her gaze upward. "What are you doing back here?" she scolded. "It's a mess out there. I thought you were staying at the hospital."

He chuckled. "I was. Chloe sent me home. Smart girl."

"Can I make you some coffee? Or maybe some hot cocoa to warm you up?"

"I've had enough coffee to sink a battleship. As for

warming me up…I can think of something better than cocoa."

His tone was light, almost joking. But Leigh sensed an undertone of vulnerability. The man had driven home through a Colorado blizzard because he wanted to make love to her. He had placed his heart and his manly pride in her hands. How could she not love him for that?

She hadn't counted on this. But whatever the consequences, there was no way on earth she would deny him.

Stretching on tiptoe she caught his head and pulled him down to her in a long, intimate kiss. By the time it ended they were both breathing hard. Stepping back, she opened his coat and slid it off his shoulders. He reached down and managed to work off his boots. "Fair warning," he said. "I'm chilled to the bone."

"I think I can deal with that." She took his hand and led him toward the stairs.

In the glow of the night-light, Wyatt shed his clothes next to her bed. Still wearing her long gray T-shirt, she slid between the sheets and made room for him. "Come on in, I left you a warm spot," she whispered. Naked and shivering, he slipped into the bed and into her open arms.

Laughing, she pulled him close. "Brrr…you've got goose bumps," she teased.

"I thought you said you could deal with that." Their legs were deliciously tangled, her T-shirt already bunched above her waist. She wore nothing underneath. How could such an ordinary garment be so sexy? He tried to avoid touching her bare skin with his chilled hands, but she took them, slid them under her shirt and cupped the palms over her breasts. Soon they were very, very warm.

By now he was aroused to the point of bursting. Luckily he always kept protection in his wallet, which was still in his jeans. The time he'd slept with Leigh in the hotel had been like a Hollywood production he'd stage-managed. This time was like…just plain lovemaking—sweet, spontaneous, real, and so damned good he could hardly stand it. He wanted this. He wanted it every night of his life.

He kissed her mouth and her lovely face, sucked her nipples and stroked her nub until she dripped with moisture. Then he mounted her eager hips and thrust home where it felt as if he'd always belonged. She made a little purring sound as his swollen length filled her. "Are you warm enough now?" she teased.

"Warm and getting warmer." He withdrew and glided in again, watching the expressions flicker across her face. Making love to Leigh was a whole new world, as much emotional as it was physical. It was a deep sharing, almost as if he could feel what she was feeling, as if her pleasure was his—and he knew it was because he loved her.

He loved her and he never wanted to let her go.

When his male urge became too strong to hold back, he drove into her hard. She arched her hips to meet his thrusts, hands gripping his buttocks, pulling him deeper as sensations crested. She came with a shudder and a soft cry. He clasped her close as his release burst.

Spent, now, he buried his face in the damp cleft between her breasts. Bathed in her sweet, musky woman smell, he lay still as her fingers wove tender paths through his hair. Earlier they'd been joking, making light of their need for each other. Now, for the moment, neither of them could speak.

Shifting to one side he brushed a kiss onto her ripe, damp mouth. "Warm now," he murmured. She replied with a misty smile and moved over to give him more space. The last thing he remembered that night was drifting off in her arms.

* * *

Mikey woke, as usual, in the early dawn. Attuned to the little sounds he made, Leigh slipped out of the warm bed, hurried into the adjoining room and scooped him up before he could cry and wake Wyatt. He gurgled and butted his head against her shoulder, then settled for chomping on her shirt while his bottle warmed.

She put him down long enough to change his diaper. Then, cradling him against her shoulder, she wandered back into her bedroom. Wyatt lay bathed in soft gray light, one arm flung outward over the spot where she'd slept. His eyes were closed, his hair appealingly tousled, his jaw shadowed with stubble. Asleep, he looked so sexy he took her breath away.

Last night in his arms had been pure heaven. But making love with Wyatt had only sunk her deeper into the morass of lies she'd created. Whether she wanted to or not, it was time to start planning her exit strategy.

Returning to the nursery, she took the bottle out of the warmer, found a blanket to cover her legs and settled in the rocker with Mikey. He drank hungrily, making little squeaks as he swallowed—just one of the baby sounds she'd grown to love. Maybe someday she'd have a baby of her own. But that wouldn't be in the picture anytime soon.

She'd given her two weeks' notice and time was running out. But as far as she knew, Wyatt wasn't taking applications for her replacement. Maybe this time he'd decided to go through an agency. Either way, she couldn't allow that to be her problem. Chloe could take care of her baby if need be, or they could bring in Dora.

She'd planned to stay a few more days; but last night with Wyatt in her bed had complicated everything. The sooner she got out of here the less damage would be left in her wake.

Mikey had finished his bottle. Draping a clean cloth on her shoulder, Leigh boosted him upright and patted his back. For a moment she pressed her cheek against his firm little body. As his sweet baby smell filled her senses, tears welled in her eyes. Everything she'd ever wanted was right here in this house. And she had no choice except to walk away from it all.

Wyatt opened his eyes to find her gone. Half-awake, he felt a surge of panic. Then he came to his senses and saw the light from the nursery. Of course, she'd be in there with Mikey. "Leigh?" he called.

"Right here." She stood in the open doorway, wearing nothing but that gray T-shirt that skimmed the edge of indecency. Too bad she was holding the baby.

"Come on back to bed," he said. "That's an order."

"All right. But I'll have to bring Mikey with me. He slept through the night and he's wide-awake. He won't stand for being put back in his crib."

"Fine." As she crossed the floor Wyatt punched up the pillows and turned down the duvet. He'd slept soundly last night, but not *all* night. Sometime in the wee hours he'd awakened. With Leigh's silky warmth nestled against him, he'd gazed up into the darkness, thinking.

There was no way he could let this beautiful woman walk out of his life. If Leigh was still planning to leave, he had to stop her any way he could.

She'd bridled at the suggestion that she remain as his lover. That, in fact, was when she'd announced she was quitting her job. But would she say no to a wedding ring?

Wyatt had resisted the whole idea of marriage for years. He'd been there, done that, and it hadn't worked out. He had one child, and he hadn't done a great job with her.

Why take a chance again—especially with a younger wife who'd likely want children of her own?

But the woman sleeping beside him had made a hash of his objections. He loved her. He wanted her for keeps. For so long, marriage had sounded like nothing more than a trap—but now it was the prize he wanted desperately to win, as long as he could have it with her.

She walked toward the bed, carrying Mikey in her arms. Mussed and tousled, her face bare of makeup, she was still a goddess with the power to take his breath away.

Easing into bed, she pulled the covers up and laid Mikey on top, in the warm hollow between their bodies. Mikey gurgled happily and kicked his feet, clearly liking where he was.

Wyatt gave the boy's tummy a playful tickle. It felt natural, lying in bed with a baby between them, even if the baby was not technically theirs.

Leigh had settled on her side, her head on the pillow and a sleepy smile on her face. "What time are you picking up Chloe?"

"I'll want to be there early. But if the doctor is slow checking her out I may be a while."

"What are you going to do with her, Wyatt? The girl has a child to raise. And you almost lost her last night. She can't keep acting out like this."

"I know." Wyatt shook his head. It wasn't Chloe he'd planned to talk about this morning. "Maybe some counseling, even rehab if her drinking is out of control. But Chloe has to want help. Otherwise it won't work." He drew a shaky breath. "I wish you'd consider staying, Leigh. Chloe and Mikey need you. I need you. You've become family."

"That's exactly why I should leave." She reached across Mikey and laid a gentle hand on Wyatt's arm. "Don't you see? Things are becoming complicated. The longer I stay, the more painful it will be when I have to go."

"You don't have to go at all." He captured her hand in his, searching for the right words. "I know I've got some issues. My father was an alcoholic who abused my mother and me before he died in prison. We were so poor we barely had enough to eat. I never learned what it meant to be a good husband and father. I thought that if I provided for Tina and Chloe financially and didn't hurt them, that was all I needed to do. But I'm learning how wrong I was—learning it every day from Chloe, Mikey and you. Learning how to do it better this time."

He saw a moist glimmer in her eyes. She blinked and it was gone.

"Marry me, Leigh," he said. "I know I'm supposed to do this on my knees with a diamond ring in my hand, but I'm afraid that if I wait you might be gone—and I can't stand the thought of losing you."

Feeling as if he'd just stuck a knife in his gut, Wyatt waited. He could sense her hesitation. Even before she spoke he knew what her answer would be.

"This isn't a good time," she said. "I'm sorry, Wyatt. If things were different you know what my answer would be. But I can't stay. I just…can't." Her voice had begun to break. She pressed her lips together.

"You could at least tell me why."

"No." She emphasized the word with a shake of her head. "Don't even ask me."

"Well…" He threw up a stone wall to hide his devastation. "You can't blame a man for trying. I guess it's time for me to go downstairs and get ready for the day." He swung out of bed, gathered up his clothes and strode toward the door.

"Wyatt, I'm sorry, I—"

He glanced back at her. She looked as if she were about to cry, but he couldn't let himself care. "Don't," he growled. "You've already said enough."

Leigh stood with Mikey at the nursery window, watching the Hummer pull out of the driveway. Now would be the time to leave, before he returned with Chloe. But the roads weren't plowed yet and she couldn't leave Mikey here alone. She had little choice except to wait for her chance later in the day.

But one thing was certain. Her time here had run out.

She bathed Mikey, reminding herself it was for the last time. He chortled and splashed, loving the feel of the warm water. When she wrapped him in his towel he snuggled close, his head resting against her throat. As she held him, the tears came, hot and bitter, trickling down her cheeks. She'd known this time would come, but she wasn't prepared for its impact. She would never see Mikey's first step or hear his first spoken word. She wouldn't see him off to school or help him with his homework. She would love him forever, but he wasn't hers to keep. And neither was his handsome, sexy grandfather.

By the time she'd dressed him and brushed his hair into a curl at the peak of his adorable head, he was hungry again. Leigh fed him and put him down for a nap. Then, as if to convince herself she was really leaving, she dragged her suitcase out of the closet. Her thoughts churned as she packed.

Wyatt deserved far better than what she'd given him. This morning he'd been honest with her. He'd laid his heart on the line and she'd tossed it away. All the while she'd been in torment, knowing she had no choice except to hurt him.

He and Chloe had taken her into their home and treated

her like family. They'd trusted her completely. It was time she faced up to her lies. No matter how risky, the very least she owed them was the truth.

Packing done, she closed her suitcase and slid it back into the closet. Then with a pad of resort stationery and a pen borrowed from Wyatt's office, she sat at the dressing table in her room and slowly, painfully, began to write.

By the time the doctor showed up to check Chloe out of the hospital it was midmorning. Sunlight blazed in a clear blue sky. The skiing would be glorious today. But Wyatt's mood didn't match the weather.

He'd always thought himself a good judge of people, but he'd misread Leigh by a mile. Last night their love-making had been so good. He'd felt so close to her. But this morning she'd rejected him without a second thought.

He'd asked her to marry him! Did she think he did that with every woman he met? He'd bared his soul to her, hoping she'd do the same. But she'd rejected his proposal without even telling him why. He ought to be furious. Instead he was just plain, damned miserable.

What was driving her away from him? A scandalous past? Legal or health issues? A returning lover? The difference in their ages? Maybe she just didn't love him. Knowing the truth might at least make her refusal easier to accept. But Leigh had locked the door on her secret. It was driving him crazy.

"You're awfully quiet this morning, Daddy." Chloe sat beside him, buckled into the high seat. She was sound enough to go home, but the gash on her forehead would take time to heal.

"You've been pretty quiet yourself," he said.

"I was waiting for you to start lecturing me."

"Aside from being grateful you're alive, all I can say is, I hope you've learned your lesson."

"You mean the one about driving a sports car in a blizzard to meet some psycho creep who found me on the internet? Sure I have. But I still have a lot to learn."

Wyatt focused his attention on the road. He sensed that she had more to say. Was he ready to hear it?

"I did a lot of thinking in the hospital," she said. "When I first decided to keep Mikey, it was because I wanted someone all my own to love. But I didn't understand what it took to be a mother. I wasn't ready, Daddy. I'm still not ready. I proved that last night. All I wanted was somebody to pay attention to me, and it almost got me killed."

Wyatt felt his heart drop. "What are you saying?"

Her hands twisted in her lap. "I love Mikey. But the most loving thing I can do is give him a responsible mom. Leigh's been more of a mother to him than I have."

"Leigh's leaving. You know that. Are you saying you'd give Mikey up?"

"I was kind of hoping you could get married and adopt him. You could even marry Leigh."

Wyatt stared ahead at the freshly plowed canyon road. "I already asked her, honey. She said no."

"Oh." The girl fell silent. Neither of them spoke as the Hummer climbed the last mile to the house. The snow-draped pines and azure sky made the setting look like a Christmas card. But today Wyatt saw everything in shades of gray. Not only was he losing Leigh; there was a chance he could lose Mikey, too.

Leigh wasn't at the door to meet them, but the sound of footsteps and water running upstairs told him she was there. With Chloe settled in her room, he ordered pizza and a salad from the resort and went into his office to catch up on some work. Leigh was probably avoiding him. Fine. For now he would spare her the discomfort.

An hour later, when lunch arrived, there was still no sign of Leigh. Wyatt was debating whether to seek her out when Chloe came downstairs with the baby in her arms.

"Where's Leigh?" Wyatt asked her.

"She went down to the resort on some kind of errand. She left me the baby monitor and said to listen for Mikey."

"She took the Mercedes?"

Chloe shrugged. "I guess. I didn't see her go."

Wyatt couldn't explain the feeling that came over him. But somehow he sensed what had happened. Pushing past Chloe, he dashed upstairs and raced down the hall to Leigh's room. Everything was in perfect order. The bed was neatly made. The closet and dresser drawers were closed. But when he looked inside, they were empty. All of Leigh's things were gone.

Fighting despair, he scanned the room, looking for anything that might tell him more. He found it in the form of a sealed envelope sticking out from under the pillow. His name was printed on the outside.

Tearing it open, he sank onto the bed and began reading the handwritten pages.

Fifteen

Dear Wyatt,
I know you won't like my leaving this way, but I didn't have the courage to face you and say good-bye. I'll be picking up my old car at the resort. Your Mercedes will be waiting for you there, with the keys at the front desk.

Leigh's handwriting was as delicate, precise and feminine as she was. Wyatt fought the urge to crumple the pages in his fist and fling them against the wall. He'd believed in her. He'd offered her everything he had. How could she do this?

You and Chloe took me into your home and gave me your trust. I repaid that trust with a lie. Now that I'm leaving, you're entitled to the truth. I applied for this job under false pretenses. I wanted to be your nanny because Mikey is my nephew. His father is my seventeen-year-old brother.

Wyatt stared at the page, feeling as if he'd been knocked flat on his back. He'd been suspicious of Leigh's motives from the beginning—at least until he'd fallen under her spell. But the connection to Mikey had never crossed his mind. How could he have been so blind? Why hadn't he guessed the obvious?

Leigh could have confessed at any time. After all, she'd broken no law. Why had she kept her secret so long?

The next paragraph held the answer to that question.

I hid the truth to save my job, and to protect my brother, a good boy with a promising future. Now I'm begging you not to take your anger out on him. When Chloe informed him she was pregnant, he offered to take responsibility. But she told him she didn't plan to keep the baby. He has no idea that Chloe changed her mind. He knows nothing about Mikey. Neither does my mother.

Under the terms of the nondisclosure agreement, I don't plan to tell them. I'm hoping you won't, either. But that decision should rightly be left to Chloe.

When I saw your ad at the paper I suspected the baby was my brother's child. I couldn't be sure at first. But when I held him all doubt vanished.

My only motive in taking the nanny job was to know my little nephew and help get him off to a loving start. He has that start. Now it's time for me to step out of his life—and yours. Mikey will have no memory of me. But I hope that some part of him will recall how much he was loved.

Chloe loves him, too, I know. She has a lot to learn, but she has it in her to be a wonderful mother.

With your help and support, she will get there and make something good of her life.

As for you and me, Wyatt, there are no words. If things had been different…but there's no use going there. I can only hope that one day you'll understand and forgive me.

Leigh

Leigh drove the rusty station wagon toward town, her eyes burning with unshed tears. By now Wyatt had probably found her letter and read it. He would be shocked, hurt and angry. She could only hope he'd respect her wishes, and Chloe's, and leave Kevin alone.

Would he ever forgive her? Wyatt was a proud man. She had lied to him, deceived him and rejected his offer of love. If he hated her for the rest of his life, it would be no worse than she deserved.

She was headed home for now. But there was no way she could stay in Dutchman's Creek. Tonight she would call her friend Christine in Denver and arrange to bunk on her couch while she found an apartment and a job. Then she'd pack her car and leave in the morning. At least the nanny gig had paid well enough for a new start. Too bad she couldn't afford to give Wyatt's money back. She'd never felt right about taking the generous salary under false pretenses. Maybe someday she'd be able to repay him.

How would Chloe feel when she learned the truth? Leigh had grown to care for Wyatt's high-spirited daughter. But any future contact between them would be out of the question. And Mikey? She couldn't even think about him now—or about Wyatt. For the past few weeks they'd been her life. Now it was time to put that life behind her.

* * *

Chloe finished reading Leigh's letter. Her calm reaction was the last thing Wyatt had expected. "You don't seem surprised," he said.

"I'm not."

"You *knew?*"

"Not 100 percent. But I was pretty sure. The last name was a clue. She looked like her brother, too—same coloring, same build, same eyes. And no stranger could've loved Mikey the way she did. I could tell that right off. It was like she would've fought man-eating tigers to protect him."

They were on the living room sofa. Wyatt had taken Mikey and was holding the boy on his lap while she read the letter. "Why didn't you say something?" he asked her.

"I liked her, and she was so good with Mikey. I was afraid if I confronted her about it, she'd leave or that you'd fire her and we'd have to find a different nanny." She laid the letter on the coffee table. "I was even more afraid that you might go after Kevin and hurt him."

"Kevin? That's his name?" Wyatt felt his jaw tighten.

"Kevin Foster. He goes to Public. But it wasn't really his fault, Daddy. We were at this big party, everybody was kind of drunk, and I was looking at him because he was cute. We got talking and one thing led to another. We used protection but it…broke."

Wyatt glanced down at Mikey, who was trying to eat a button on his sweater. "Good Lord, Chloe, what were you thinking?"

"That's just it. I wasn't." She gave a little sob. "I just wanted somebody to pay attention to me. The next day I felt so stupid that I decided I never wanted to see him again. Leigh was being honest in her letter—Kevin really did try to be there for me, up until I told him I was getting rid of the baby. I didn't want him to be involved. But look what I ended up with—the sweetest little baby ever!"

And now you don't know what to do with him, Wyatt thought, but he knew better than to say it out loud.

"Would you have gone after Kevin, Daddy? Would you have hurt him?"

Wyatt exhaled, feeling the tension leave his body. "I wanted to at first. But what's done is done, and now we've got Mikey. All we can do now is forgive the past and do whatever's best for him."

"If Leigh had known you felt like that, do you think she would have left?"

He shrugged, his emotions still numb. "Who knows? She's gone."

"So why don't we find her and ask her?"

Wyatt stared at his daughter.

"Think about it, Daddy," she said. "Leigh is the best thing that ever happened to you—and to Mikey. Don't you think it's worth another try to get her back?" Standing, she lifted the baby from his arms. "Have your security goons find out where her family lives. Mikey and I will come with you. She can't say no to all three of us."

"I still don't understand why you have to leave town so soon." Leigh's mother ladled steaming homemade chili into three bowls. "Are you in some kind of trouble?"

Leigh glanced up from slicing bread. She was sick and tired of secrets. But keeping the truth from her family was a necessary kindness. "I told you the reason," she said, hating the lie. "When I talked to Christine she told me about a job opening at an ad agency. The deadline's tomorrow and I have to apply in person."

"But surely there are jobs here in Dutchman's Creek.

What happened with that nanny job, anyway? Did you get caught stealing the family silver?"

"Leigh had a nanny job?" Kevin had just come in from shoveling snow and was taking his boots off in the entry. "So that was the secret agent gig? How come I never heard about it?"

"I suppose I can tell you now." Leigh's mother spoke up before Leigh could hush her. "Your sister had a job baby-sitting for some big-name celebrity. But she couldn't tell me who it was."

"I still can't," Leigh added. "I had to sign a nondisclosure agreement."

"But they had a baby," her mother said. "I could hear the little thing crying over the phone."

"Let me guess." Kevin grinned as he pulled off his gloves. "Movie stars? Rock stars?"

"Guess away." Leigh tossed a pot holder at him. "Guess all night if you want. I still can't tell you."

"You might not have to." Kevin glanced out the front window. "You know that fancy SUV you were driving last time you came home? It just pulled up in front of the house."

The bread knife Leigh was using clattered to the kitchen floor. Her first impulse was to flee to the bathroom and lock herself in. But that would only make her look foolish. Whatever business Wyatt had here, she had no choice except to stay where she was and brazen it out.

From the kitchen, Leigh couldn't see the front window. But she could see her brother. He was staring outside. His face had gone ashen. "Oh, my God," he muttered.

"What on earth...?" Their mother set the pan back on the stove. Wiping her hands on her apron, she bustled to-ward the sound of the doorbell. Leigh strode into the living room and seized Kevin's hand, gripping hard. Whatever they had to face, they would face it together.

The door swung open. Chloe stood on the threshold with Mikey in her arms and her father a step behind her. A ski hat hid the bandage on her head. "Hello, Mrs. Foster," she said. "My name is Chloe Richardson, and this is my son, Michael. My father and I are here to talk to Leigh."

Leigh glanced at Kevin. He looked ready to faint. Her own legs felt unsteady, but she couldn't help admiring Chloe. The girl had stepped right up.

Chloe had said nothing about Mikey being Kevin's child. But Kevin would know. Only their mother remained in the dark. She smiled and greeted the visitors as she ushered them into the living room. Leigh was about to speak up when Kevin stepped forward.

"Why didn't you tell me about him, Chloe?" he demanded. "Didn't you think I'd want to know I had a son, and that you'd kept him?"

Chloe met his scowl with a level gaze. "I'm here, Kevin. Right now that's the best I can do."

Mikey's wise blue eyes took in the stranger who was his father. Kevin's anger crumbled into glimmering tears. "Can I hold him?" he asked.

"Here." She passed him the baby. "Careful, you'll need to support his head."

Kevin held his son as if he were made of spun glass. A tear spilled out of his eye and trickled down his cheek. His mother had sunk onto the sofa. Joining her, Leigh slipped a supporting arm around her shoulders. "I'm sorry," she whispered. "I wanted to tell you, but I couldn't."

Kevin turned toward the sofa. "Here's your grandson, Mom. Do you want to hold him?"

"Oh! Oh, my goodness!" She held out her arms and gathered Mikey close. He responded to her warmth and sure touch by snuggling against her chest. She began to weep softly.

Wyatt had remained in the entry, silent as he watched the drama unfold. Now he crossed the room and stopped in front of them. "Mrs. Foster," he said, "If you'll excuse us, I need to talk to Leigh. Alone."

Leaving the others to sort things out, Leigh led him into the small kitchen, closed the door and braced for a storm. "Say anything you want, Wyatt," she said, facing him from across the table. "Call me ugly names, threaten to sue me. But you're not getting an apology. I regret having to lie to you and Chloe. I regret hurting your pride. But my time with Mikey was worth any price I have to pay now."

"And the two of us?" Something hidden flickered in his gaze. "What about that?"

"Don't." She looked away to hide her welling tears. "I don't regret falling in love with you. But I know what I've done. I know that whatever we had, I've ruined it all."

"You fell in love with me?" A smile tugged at a corner of his mouth.

"Don't tell me you're surprised. How could any woman *not* fall in love with you? But what difference does it make? I lied to you. I lied to Chloe."

"Listen to me, Leigh." He strode around the table and seized her hands. His clasp was gentle but she sensed that if she tried to pull away his grip would turn to steel. "Chloe guessed your secret early on. She didn't say anything because she saw how much you loved Mikey, and she wanted you to stay."

Leigh stared at him. Her lips trembled.

"We *both* want you to stay," he said. "Chloe did some very grown-up thinking overnight. She knows she's not ready to be a mother. What she wants is for you and me to adopt Mikey and raise him as our son. For that, I think we need to be married. But above and beyond that, I want to marry you because I love you, and hope to spend the rest of my life with you. So I'm asking you one more time, will you marry me, Leigh? Will you let me spoil you and love you and need you every day for the rest of our lives?"

The tears broke through, streaming in salty rivulets down her cheeks. "Yes," she whispered. "Yes, with all my heart."

He fished out a clean handkerchief and blotted her face. "Well, then," he murmured. "Should we go in the other room and break the news?"

"Not so fast, mister!" Laughing now, she flung her arms around his neck. Their deep, heartfelt kiss lasted a very long time.

Epilogue

Two years later
May

"Mikey, come back here!" Leigh grabbed for her active two-year-old son, but she wasn't fast enough. He ducked under the row of seats and scampered into the center aisle. From there he made a beeline toward the front of the auditorium, where the organist was just beginning "Pomp and Circumstance."

"Stay put. I'll cut him off at the pass." Wyatt slipped out of his seat and circled around the outside aisle. He reached the little fugitive and snatched him up just short of the steps to the stage. With Mikey in a vise grip, he regained his seat. "I'm getting too old for this," he muttered into his wife's ear.

Glancing at her rounded belly, Leigh gave him a grin. "Just wait till his little sister gets here," she whispered. "Then we'll really have our hands full. For now, let's see how long we can keep him quiet."

Wyatt fished a toy rabbit out of his pocket, then turned to watch as the Bramford Hill graduates paraded down the aisle.

Chloe was third in line, her head high and proud, her fiery curls spilling from under her white cap. In the past two years she'd matured into a responsible, confident young woman. Now she was graduating with honors and had been accepted into the prelaw program at a prestigious eastern college. Wyatt couldn't have been more proud of her.

It was a shame her mother wasn't here. Tina had sent a card and a generous check. But she was living in Paris now, with her wealthy third husband. This time, so far, she seemed happy.

Kevin, who'd graduated two years ago, was majoring in physics at the University of Colorado. He and Chloe kept in touch as friends, but life was taking them on different paths, which was as it should be. They would always have Mikey as an anchor.

As for Mikey, he would grow up with Leigh and Wyatt as his parents, Chloe as his big sister, and Kevin as his uncle. He'd be told the truth when he grew old enough to understand. For now it was enough that the little boy was part of a family, and that they loved him.

As Chloe crossed the stage to get her diploma, Wyatt's thoughts drifted back to the day he'd opened the door to see her standing on the porch, forlorn and pregnant. Little had he realized, in his dismay, that heaven was about to open up and shower untold blessings on his head.

Leigh, Mikey, his unborn baby daughter and a fresh start with Chloe—everything had come from that day. And as he clasped his son close and slipped an arm around his wife, all Wyatt could do was be grateful.

* * * * *

A HOME FOR
THE M.D.

GINA WILKINS

Author of more than one hundred titles, native Arkansan **Gina Wilkins** was introduced early to romance novels by her avid-reader mother. Gina loves sharing her own stories with readers who enjoy books celebrating families and romance. She is inspired daily by her husband of over thirty years, their two daughters, their son, their librarian son-in-law who fits perfectly into this fiction-loving family and an adorable grandson who already loves books.

Chapter One

Dr. Mitchell Baker arrived at his rented duplex just as the firefighters extinguished the last flickers of flame. Glumly, he stood in the rain, surveying what remained of his home for the past six years, now a smoldering, blackened shell. Heavy clouds obscured what little natural light remained at 9:00 p.m., so the firefighters had set up portable lighting to assist them as they wrapped up their work. Normally, street lamps and security pole lights would glow at this hour, but the power was out on this whole street.

One of Arkansas's infamous summer storms had crashed through earlier, bringing high winds, booming thunder and dangerous lightning strikes. Somewhere on this tumultuous Thursday night in July, a tree had fallen over a power line, knocking out the electricity to this part of Little Rock almost two hours ago. Mitch's neighbor in the other half of the duplex—the woman he referred to as "the ditz next door"—had lit candles all through her rooms for light and then left to buy fast food for a late dinner. When she returned, the duplex was fully engulfed in flames.

Water trickled down his face and dripped off his chin. He reached up to swipe at his eyes with the back of one hand, clearing raindrops from his lashes. The rain was little more than a trickle now, but without a hat or raincoat, he was soaked. He made no effort to find shelter. Instead, he watched the firefighters gather their equipment and listened to the ditz next door as she told her tale to a woman who appeared to be a newspaper reporter. She wasn't even smart enough to make up an excuse for the fire, he thought with a shake of his wet head. She freely admitted that maybe the dozen or so candles she'd left burning had caught something on fire.

Maybe? He'd always believed the forty-something bottle-redhead was short a few watts in her mental chandelier, but now he figured most of the bulbs were permanently dimmed, to carry the metaphor further.

He thought regretfully of a few valued possessions he'd lost in that fire. A quilt his late grandmother had made that he'd used as a bedspread. Electronics equipment. Souvenir T-shirts from college and medical school activities and from his few travels. Pictures.

Fortunately, his laptop had been in his office at the hospital, and he kept files backed up online, so he hadn't lost the music and digital photos stored in his desktop computer. Most of his truly precious treasures—things that had belonged to his father and grandfather—were safely stowed in plastic bins in his mother's attic because the duplex had been too small to provide much storage. But still he regretted the things he'd lost. All his clothes, for example. The only clothing he owned now was a couple of shirts and two pairs of jeans stashed in his office and the sneakers he wore with the blue surgical scrubs in which he'd left the hospital.

"Dr. Baker? Are you all right?" The woman who lived in the nearest half of the matching duplex next door approached beneath a big, green-and-white golf umbrella. She and Mitch had met not long after he'd moved in, when he'd helped her retrieve her new kitten from a tree that stood between the two rental properties. That kitten was now a fat, lazy cat who liked to come visit him on Sunday mornings and beg for treats. Both Mitch and Snowball would miss those visits.

"I'm fine, Mrs. Gillis. Thank you."

She looked mournfully at the steaming remains of the house, then distastefully at the ditz, who was dramatically wringing her hands for the benefit of a television camera. "I figured that woman would cause a tragedy in this neighborhood, but I thought it would be because of her reckless driving. The way she zips down this street without any regard for anyone—and you know she hit Miss Pennybaker's mailbox just last week. Now this."

"At least no one was hurt, and none of the other houses were damaged." Mitch smiled reassuringly at her. "All the other stuff can be replaced."

"I'll miss having you as a neighbor. Not many nice young doctors want to live in this neighborhood. They all want to move out to those fancy houses in west Little Rock or some place like that."

When he'd moved into the rental, he'd been a very busy, twenty-five-year-old intern who'd been given a month's notice to find a new place after his former apartment had been sold to a developer. He'd looked for someplace available, convenient to the hospital and reasonably priced, all of which he'd found in the tidy duplex in an aging but respectable midtown neighborhood. He hadn't intended to stay more than a few months, but those months had stretched into years while he'd spent sixty to eighty hours a week at the hospital and what little time was left over helping his widowed mother.

Now, two months into his pediatric orthopedic surgery practice, he could afford to buy or build, but he couldn't think about that now. Not while almost all his worldly possessions were still smoldering in front of him.

Heaving a sigh, he rubbed a weary hand over his face and urged his neighbor—his former neighbor, he corrected himself—to get in out of the rain. There was nothing anyone could do tonight. He assured her he had a place to stay. He would crash at his mother's house until he found someplace better.

A few minutes later, he climbed into his car and drove away without looking back at the ruined duplex.

"Oh my gosh!"

Jacqui Handy was accustomed to fourteen-year-old Alice Llewellyn's dramatic appearances, so she wasn't overly concerned late Friday morning when Alice burst into the kitchen with the exclamation. "What's wrong, Alice?"

"My uncle Mitch's house burned down last night! To the ground!"

Startled by the legitimate reason for her young charge's agitation, Jacqui set down the copper watering pot she'd been filling at the sink and turned quickly. "Is he all right?"

"He's okay. He wasn't home. He was at the hospital."

Jacqui drew a relieved breath. She didn't know Mitch well, but she'd always liked him. She was glad he hadn't been hurt—but then, she'd have felt the same way about anyone, she assured herself.

"He lost everything, though," Alice added, her somber brown eyes a striking contrast to her mop of cheery light-brown curls.

"I'm very sorry to hear that. How did you find out about it?"

"I called Mimi to tell her about Waldo's new trick and she told me. Mitch spent the night with her last night."

Mitch's sister, Dr. Meagan Baker, had married Jacqui's employer, attorney Seth Llewellyn, three months ago. Seth had full custody of his teenage daughter. His ex-wife Colleen, Alice's mother, was a high-powered attorney at an international law firm based in Hong Kong. Seth had a distantly amicable relationship with his ex, who stayed in almost daily telephone contact with their daughter. Jacqui worked as full-time housekeeper and occasional cook and personal assistant for Seth and Meagan. In addition, she kept an eye on Alice and served as her daytime chauffeur when necessary. Alice considered herself too old to need a nanny, so they were all careful not to refer to Jacqui by that title.

"Mimi was pretty upset about the fire," Alice confided, pushing a hand absently through her tousled curls.

"I'm sure she was."

LaDonna Baker, widowed mother to Meagan, Mitch and Madison, was very close to her three offspring, all of whom had chosen to stay in Little Rock to practice medicine. She had embraced her new teenage stepgranddaughter into the family with affection and eagerness, and she and Alice had already grown very close.

Alice was the one who had given LaDonna the whimsical nickname of "Mimi," saying it fit in with the rest of the *M* names in the family. LaDonna had accepted the name with delight. Jacqui suspected having young Alice in her life had eased LaDonna's grief somewhat at the loss of her elderly mother at the end of last year.

"So, anyway," Alice continued, "Mimi's expecting company for the next week, so she doesn't really have a place for Mitch to stay until he finds a new place. And Madison has a one-bedroom apartment, so she doesn't have room for him, either. So I said why doesn't he stay here with us? We've got an extra guest room. I know Dad and Meagan would offer if they were here. So Mimi said that was a really good idea, if you and I don't mind, and she was going to call Meagan and tell her everything that happened and make sure it's okay."

"He's going to stay here?" Jacqui asked, following the rambling account with an effort. That was the part that stood out most to her.

She pictured Dr. Mitchell Baker, a tall, sandy-haired man with kind blue eyes and a warm smile that transformed his pleasantly homely face into full-out attractive. He was thirty-one, two years older than Jacqui. She had met him several times during the past fourteen months, although she could count on one hand the number of times she'd actually had a conversation with him. Those conversations had been brief and slightly awkward, at least on her part. For some reason she always became uncharacteristically tongue-tied around Mitch.

"I knew you wouldn't mind—you don't, do you?" Alice asked, suddenly aware, apparently, that she was making assumptions on Jacqui's behalf.

There seemed to be nothing gracious to say except, "Of course not."

Alice smiled with a flash of braces. "I knew you wouldn't."

Normally, Jacqui wouldn't be staying at the house herself. She had her own apartment across town. But Seth and Meagan had left only two days ago for a two-week trip to Europe on a belated honeymoon. They had asked Jacqui to stay with Alice, a request she had been happy to accept—and not just for the extra pay that would go into her savings for a down payment for her own house someday.

She told herself there was really no reason to be concerned about having a houseguest. She suspected that Mitch, a surgeon like his sister, would be at the hospital quite a bit. When he was here, Alice would keep him entertained. Jacqui would perform her usual role, staying quietly in the background. She was good at being a housekeeper, and she knew exactly how to play that part.

"Mimi's going to call you as soon as she talks to Meagan," Alice said on her way out of the kitchen. "I'm going upstairs to pack for the sleepover at Tiff's tonight."

Alice and her friends loved sleepover parties and were always looking for an excuse to have one. Because Tiffany was on the same swim team as Alice, they had decided to stay at Tiffany's house tonight and have her mother take them to a scheduled meet the next afternoon. Alice had assured Jacqui there was no need for her to attend this particular event, so Jacqui planned to use the time to catch up on some overdue chores including grocery shopping. She figured she might as well stay at her place tonight to dust and vacuum and grab a few extra things she needed here.

The phone rang only a few minutes later. She wasn't surprised that it was Meagan, calling to make sure there was no problem with her brother staying at the house for a few days.

"No problem at all," Jacqui assured her employer. "I'm glad to be able to help. Enjoy your vacation. Your brother will be fine."

"I'm so glad to know you're taking care of things there," Meagan said fervently. "I don't know what we would do without you, Jacqui."

Meagan's mother said much the same words when she called a few minutes later to discuss her son's plans with Jacqui. "He'll probably spend another night here with me and then come over there sometime tomorrow. You're sure you don't mind having an extra person in the house?"

"Not at all. I'll be cooking and doing laundry for Alice and me anyway. One extra houseguest will be no trouble at all. Neither Alice nor I will be here tonight, but I'll be back tomorrow morning, so he can come whenever he's ready."

"You're a jewel, Jacqui," LaDonna said warmly. "We're all so lucky to have found you."

During the past year or so, Jacqui had made a deliberate effort to make herself indispensable to the Llewellyn/ Baker family. She liked this job, and she wanted to keep it. In return, they had all been nothing but kind and generous to her. Maybe they even considered her an honorary member of the family.

She wasn't that presumptuous. Besides which, she had learned long ago that "family" was a word frequently used without real meaning. Family members—honorary or otherwise—were all too often expendable, in her experience.

Mitch's steps dragged as he climbed the steps to the front door of his sister's house Friday night. His mother had given him detailed instructions for letting himself in and disarming the alarm system. As tired as he was, he hoped he remembered her directives correctly. The last thing he needed tonight was to be arrested for breaking and entering.

It was after 11:00 p.m. He'd had a very long day of surgeries, meetings and a pretty-much mandatory appearance at a retirement party for one of the surgical department heads, followed by yet another couple hours of paperwork in his office. His amazing and efficient secretary had volunteered to spend her lunch hour picking up a few things for him so he hadn't had to wear scrubs to the party, which had been a casual affair fortunately. He now owned three pairs of khaki slacks, three white shirts, a comb and toothbrush, a few pairs of socks and a package of boxer shorts in addition to the two pairs of jeans, two polo shirts and electric razor he'd kept stashed at work. He'd had to wear sneakers to the party because Jean hadn't risked buying shoes for him.

It amazed him how kind and generous everyone had been at work. Other doctors, nurses, techs, office staff, everyone who'd heard word of the fire had offered condolences and any assistance he might need. His partners had volunteered to cover for him when he needed time to look for a new place and to replace his lost possessions, even though their schedules were all stretched to allow for summer vacations. A few people had even offered extra clothes and household goods. He'd been genuinely touched by everyone's thoughtfulness.

With a duffel bag holding his entire wardrobe clutched in his left hand, he used his right hand to quickly press buttons on the keypad located just inside the front door, resetting the alarm for the night. At least he had a place to sleep for a few weeks. He would have stayed with his mother, but his late father's two sisters had already planned to come for a weeklong visit. They were arriving tomorrow and even if his mom's house had been big enough to comfortably accommodate them all, he hadn't relished the idea of sharing a house even temporarily with the three women. His younger sister, Madison, was a third-year medical resident who lived in a one-bedroom efficiency apartment, so staying with her wasn't an option, either.

Moving in here seemed the ideal solution, and his sister and brother-in-law had agreed. In fact, they had interrupted their much-needed vacation to call and insist he make use of their spare room for as long as necessary.

He had planned to spend one more night at his mom's, but when he'd realized how late he was going to be, he'd called and told her he'd crash at Meagan's a night early instead. His mother had informed him no one else would be there tonight, so he didn't have to worry about disturbing anyone with his late arrival. Still, he made little noise as he climbed the stairs without bothering to turn on lights. Tiny, energy-efficient bulbs illuminated the steps for safety, providing a soft, cozy glow to guide him to the second story.

After the wedding in April, Seth and Alice had moved from their previous home across the street into

Meagan's house. Both houses in the upscale subdivision were approximately the same size, but this one had a pool in the roomy backyard—of primary importance to Alice. Seth had planned to put in a pool for Alice this summer, but they'd all decided it would be easier to simply settle in here. Seth's house was on the market now, although Mitch hadn't heard if it had sold yet.

Mitch hadn't actually visited this house often, even before his sister married Seth. He and his sisters usually gathered at their mother's place on the rare occasions when they were free to get together. He knew the master bedroom was downstairs and there were three bedrooms upstairs. Vaguely recalling that Alice's room was on the left of the staircase, he turned right, arbitrarily choosing the first door he encountered.

He was going to fall straight into bed, he thought with a yawn. He'd worry about unpacking his few belongings in the morning. Opening the door, he entered the darkened room.

He heard someone gasp loudly at the same time his foot made contact with something large and unyielding. Caught off guard, he fell forward, hands flailing in a futile attempt to steady himself, the duffel bag throwing him off balance. His shoulder made solid contact with the hardwood floor, knocking the breath out of him in a startled "oof!"

Lights blazed, assaulting his eyes. He squinted upward. What he saw made him flinch, just in time to keep from being beaned by a heavy, decorative brass candlestick.

"What the—? Jacqui, stop! It's me, Mitch. Meagan's brother!" he added in a rush, just to make his identity clear.

Her petite body still poised to strike or run, the

woman peered suspiciously down at him. Her short, near-black hair was tousled around her face. With her large, sleep-clouded dark eyes and softly pointed little chin, she looked even more elfin than usual—an adjective that had come to his mind the first time he'd met her a year or so earlier. He'd seen her only a handful of times since, but he'd recognized her instantly when she'd wielded the solid brass candlestick in a very efficient manner. He'd been damned lucky she hadn't bashed in his head.

She blinked her long, dark lashes a couple times as though to clear her vision, then stared down at him with a frown. "Dr. Baker?"

Shifting warily into a sitting position, he stretched his arm to make sure he'd done no damage to his shoulder other than the bruise he would undoubtedly sport tomorrow. "I'm sorry I scared you. I had no idea you were here. Mom said Alice had a sleepover, so you'd be staying at your own place tonight."

Jacqui tugged self-consciously at the mid-thigh-length hem of the New Orleans Saints jersey she wore for a nightshirt, revealing surprisingly long, slender legs for such a petite woman. "I was going to, but when I walked into my place earlier I found a leak that must have happened during the storm the other night. I guess some shingles were blown off or something. Anyway, the carpet was soaked, so I called the landlord, then gathered some things in my suitcase and came back here."

"Uh, yeah. I think I found your suitcase." He climbed to his feet. Now that he was upright, he stood a good nine inches taller than her barefoot five feet four inches. For such a little thing, she seemed more than capable of taking care of herself, he thought with a wry glance at the candlestick she still held.

Following his glance, she replaced the candlestick quickly on the nightstand. "Are you okay?"

"Yeah. Just bruised my pride a little. I'm really sorry I frightened you. I didn't know which bedroom to sleep in."

"I was under the impression you wouldn't be here until tomorrow."

"Last-minute change of plans. I hope you don't mind that I'll be staying for a few days."

"Of course not. It's your sister's house and she invited you. You have every right to be here."

She pulled at her jersey again, and he realized abruptly that she was probably uncomfortable with his presence in her bedroom. He reached for his duffel. "I'll move to the other guest room. It's across the hall, right?"

"Yes, directly across."

Moving toward the door, he spoke lightly. "Okay, then, I'll let you get back to sleep. Good night."

She remained standing in the center of the room. "Good night."

He stepped out in the hallway then couldn't resist glancing over his shoulder to say, "Oh, and Jacqui? You won't be needing that weapon again tonight."

Her mouth twitched in what might have been a reluctant smile as he closed the door firmly between them.

Turkey bacon sizzled in the pan while whole-wheat muffins browned in the oven. Sipping her first cup of coffee Saturday morning, Jacqui kept a close eye on the fluffy scrambled eggs cooking in the skillet in front of her. She'd heard Mitch showering upstairs, so she figured he'd be down soon. If he was like most of the men she knew, he'd be hungry.

On awakening this morning, and wincing when she saw her suitcase still lying on the floor, she had decided to put last night's awkwardness behind her. So Mitch had seen her in her nightshirt, with her hair all a mess and her cheek creased by her pillow. Big deal. Starting now, she was back in professional housekeeper mode. She wouldn't let that facade slip around him again.

"Good morning." Dressed in a new-looking white shirt and khakis, his sandy hair still damp from his shower, Mitch greeted her with a crooked smile that crinkled the corners of his clear blue eyes.

"Good morning, Dr. Baker." She removed the muffins from the oven with a potholder, setting the pan on a trivet. "I hope you like turkey bacon and scrambled eggs for breakfast. I wasn't sure if you'd have to report to the hospital this morning, so I thought I'd have breakfast ready just in case."

He studied the food with almost visible eagerness. "Looks delicious, but you didn't have to cook for me."

Having expected that comment, she shrugged lightly. "I was going to make some for myself anyway. Have a seat at the breakfast table. Do you drink coffee? Would you like orange juice to go with it? I have fresh-squeezed."

"You certainly don't have to wait on me. I'll get my own coffee." Moving to the coffeemaker, he poured a cup and carried it to the table.

Jacqui set a well-filled plate in front of him when he took his seat. "There's homemade jam and apple butter in those little crocks. Help yourself if you want some for your muffin."

Mitch picked up his fork, then raised his eyebrows when she didn't immediately join him at the table. "Aren't you eating?"

"I'm going to wash a load of cleaning cloths and then feed Waldo," she answered lightly. "Go ahead and eat. I'll have something when I've finished those things."

Mitch set down his fork. "I'll wait."

"Don't be silly, Dr. Baker. Your food will get cold."

"So will yours."

"I won't be long."

"Then it won't be a problem for me to wait, will it?" Leaning back in his chair, he picked up his coffee cup and took a sip, looking prepared to sit there all morning.

"Fine." Foiled in her plan to eat alone when he'd finished, she placed a spoonful of eggs and a muffin on a plate for herself and carried it to the table, setting it at the opposite end from Mitch. She retrieved her coffee mug from the counter, then took her seat.

Looking satisfied, he picked up a strip of bacon. "Just so we're straight—you work for my sister, not for me. I don't expect you to serve me or to wait until I've finished eating to have your own meal. Nor to address me as Dr. Baker. I answer to Mitch or Mitchell. I don't think my sister or her husband ask those things of you, either, for that matter. I've heard you call them Meagan and Seth, and I suspect you've shared a few meals with them."

"Well, yes," she admitted, stabbing her fork into her eggs to avoid looking at him. "But you're a guest."

"Hardly a stranger. We've known each other more than a year. And you're pretty much a member of my sister's family. There's no need for formality between us."

She spread a little jam on her muffin, busying herself with the task to avoid having to answer.

The table faced a sliding-glass door, on the other side of which lay a rock patio and beyond that, an inground pool. Mitch nodded toward the grinning yellow dog watching them through the glass, tail sweeping the air behind him. "Waldo didn't prove to be much of a watchdog last night. He never even barked when I parked outside and came into the house."

Following his glance toward Alice's beloved pet, Jacqui smiled. "As sweet as that dog is, I would never depend on him to guard the place. If he did catch someone sneaking in, he'd probably just bring up one of his toys and beg to play. I've always heard Labs are very territorial and protective, but Waldo…not so much."

"Maybe he'd react differently if someone were threatening a member of the family."

"I wouldn't be surprised if he showed some spirit then. Especially if it were Alice being threatened. Waldo does love Alice."

"Can't blame him. She's a great kid." He reached for his coffee. "Anyway, if Waldo were any kind of a guard dog, I wouldn't have taken you completely by surprise last night. Of course, that suitcase of yours did make a fairly effective warning system."

The corner of her mouth twitched at the memory of him sprawled at her feet, staring warily at the brass candlestick in her hand. It hadn't been funny at the time. She could still feel her heart pounding when she'd woken with the awareness that someone was in the room with her. But now she could see the wry humor in the situation. The way his eyes twinkled made her suspect he was struggling not to laugh.

Her humor evaporated when she remembered what had brought him there. "I'm sorry about your house. Alice and your mom told me it burned completely."

"To the ground. It was a rental, a duplex. My neighbor in the other half is a few fries short of a kid's meal. No one who's ever met her was surprised that she caused the fire."

She couldn't help being a little amused by the analogy despite the gravity of the situation. "She really left candles burning when she left the house?"

He shrugged. "That's what she said, and the fire marshal concurred it was the cause of the fire."

"Was it a furnished duplex?" Because she'd spent so much of her life moving from place to place, Jacqui hadn't collected many personal possessions. She always rented a fully furnished apartment. She looked forward to finally owning a home of her own that she could decorate with carefully chosen furnishings and maybe even a few nice pieces of art. Someday.

Mitch shook his head. "No, the furniture was all mine. Nothing too fancy. I'd lived there since my first year of residency and just gathered up what I needed to get by, but there were a few items I'll really miss."

"I'm sorry."

Although she could see the regret on his face, he downplayed his loss. "I had renter's insurance. I'd been considering moving to a somewhat larger place, anyway, now that I've finished my residency, but I didn't have to sign a lease there and I liked that. All I had to do was give a month's notice and I was free to leave at any time. Not many places let you do that."

"Not many rental places, no," she agreed, thinking of the one-year lease she'd recently renewed on her no-frills apartment. It was the first time ever that she'd stayed in one place long enough to actually renew a lease.

Recalling that Mitch had recently completed his surgical residency, she asked, "Will you buy a house now?"

He shrugged. "Haven't had time to think about it. I'm

not sure I want to commit to buying right now. I've considered working another year or so here in Little Rock and then maybe going somewhere else for a while."

"Really?" She recognized the restless look in his eyes all too well, having seen that same wanderlust in her father throughout her first seventeen years. Still, she was a little startled that one of the seemingly tightly knit Baker clan was considering a move away.

"Because of school and family obligations, I've never lived anywhere else," he admitted, scooping the last of his eggs onto his fork. "I'm not saying I will move, but it's nice to have options."

He'd leave. In her experience, once a man got an itch to roam, there wasn't much that would hold him in one place. As for herself, if she made the kind of money surgeons and lawyers made, she would buy a nice house with a tidy yard and settle down contentedly for the rest of her life. She'd had more than enough of drifting from place to place.

"Can I get you anything else?" she asked, nodding toward his nearly empty plate. "Another muffin? More coffee?"

He grinned, and she almost blinked in response to the brightness of that smile. Here was a man who never lacked for female companionship, she'd bet. He wasn't handsome, exactly, but definitely appealing. A single doctor with a killer smile—women probably lined up in hopes of catching his attention. She was surprised he was still single, but maybe he liked keeping his options open in that respect. Not that it was any of her business, of course.

"Didn't I just tell you I don't expect you to wait on me?" he asked teasingly.

She spread her hands and said matter-of-factly, "It's my job."

He studied her face a bit curiously but said merely, "Thanks, but I don't need anything else. I have some things to do at my office this morning. But breakfast was very good, thank you."

"I'll be doing some shopping later today. If you'll make a list before you leave, I can pick up any particular foods you like and whatever else you lack in the way of personal-care items. If you need anything—clothes, toiletries, whatever—I've picked up things like that for Seth when he was too busy to shop for himself."

His brow rose a little higher. "You really do make yourself useful, don't you? No wonder the family seems to think the house would collapse without you running it."

"I take pride in my work," she said a little stiffly, not entirely sure whether he was teasing or mocking her.

"That's the way I was raised, too. If you're going to do something, do it well."

It wasn't exactly the way she'd been raised—more a philosophy she'd adopted for herself—but there was no need to go into that. "There's a magnetic board on the side of the fridge. The Llewellyns usually leave a note there if they'll be home for dinner so I'll know to have something ready for them before I leave each evening. Sometimes they prefer to do their own cooking, but I usually cook two or three nights a week. You can write anything you need there and I'll take care of it."

Was she babbling? She did that sometimes when she felt uncomfortable.

Standing, Mitch carried his dishes to the sink, rinsed them and set them in the dishwasher without waiting for her to clear away after him. She could see this man was accustomed to taking care of himself.

"I'm not a picky eater, but I like to have fresh fruit on hand—any fruit, I like them all. I'll leave some cash for you to add to the tab. Neither you nor Meagan should have to pay for my food while I'm here. As for anything else, I'll have to make a mall run eventually and pick up some things—like shoes," he added with a wry glance at his sneakers. "I don't even know what else I need yet."

Despite her tendency to accumulate relatively few personal belongings, the thought of losing everything she owned was daunting. She was sure Mitch had lost things that were important to him in the fire. Sympathy made her speak a bit more warmly. "All right. But if you think of anything, just jot it on the list. Really, it's no trouble at all."

He gave her another one of those smiles that made her pulse trip a little. "That's very kind of you, Jacqui. Thanks."

Hiding her reaction to him behind a rather brusque tone, she turned away to rinse her own breakfast dishes. "You're welcome."

"I think we'll work out just fine as housemates," he said as he moved toward the doorway toward the stairs. "No reason at all to be concerned."

Housemates. Just the word made her mouth go dry. Which certainly seemed to her like a reason for concern.

Chapter Two

Later that morning, Jacqui finished making her grocery list. She had a generous household account to cover anything they needed, but Mitch had insisted on chipping in toward his food. She had intended to leave for the store more than an hour ago, but she kept getting delayed by things around the house that needed her attention—houseplants to water, furniture to dust, floors to vacuum, beds to change, laundry to do.

She knew every inch of this house like the back of her hand. It might belong to Seth and Meagan and young Alice, but she was the one who kept it running like a well-oiled machine, just as she had the house Seth and Alice had lived in previously. She was the one who'd done most of the packing, unpacking and arranging when the busy family had combined their households. They had decided which furnishings to keep and which to store, sell or give away, but Jacqui had supervised that process while the Llewellyns were tied up with their demanding schedules.

She had been greatly relieved that there'd never been any question of whether she would continue working for them after the wedding. With Meagan's hectic schedule as a general surgeon and attending physician in the teaching hospital, Jacqui's help was needed with the housework and with Alice.

They had established a routine that worked well for all of them. When the family was in town, Jacqui reported to work at around 9:00 a.m., after the senior Llewellyns had left for their jobs. During the school year, Alice had already been dropped off at school by that time; Jacqui picked her up every afternoon. Now that Alice was on summer break, the teen spent the days here at home or being chauffeured by Jacqui to various activities. Every day, Jacqui did the daily cleaning and laundry, ran family errands such as shopping and dry cleaning, then cooked dinner before leaving unless they'd notified her they had other plans for dinner.

Some people might have found her daily schedule boring, but she enjoyed it. She liked the family very much, and they paid her well for her services. Most of her weekends were free and she had time during her workdays to read and knit while doing laundry or waiting for the oven timer to buzz.

She was lucky to have found this family when she'd been looking for a full-time housekeeping job just more than a year ago. Her last employer had moved into a nursing facility and she'd needed a new position quickly. Only twenty-eight years old then, she hadn't been the typical housekeeper applicant. Her résumé listed many jobs in several states, only the latter two of which had been housekeeping positions. But the Llewellyns had taken a chance on her, and she was satisfied their gamble had paid off for all of them.

On the other side of the glass door, Waldo barked for attention, his feathery tail swishing rhythmically. He missed Alice today, she thought, stuffing the grocery list in her bag. He barked again, giving her his best please-notice-me grin. Caving, she set her bag aside. There was no hurry to go shopping; she might as well play with the dog for a little while to make him feel less lonely.

Waldo expressed his gratitude with full-body wiggles and eager swipes of his big, wet tongue. Laughing, Jacqui pushed him down. "You silly dog. You act like you haven't seen anyone in a month. I just gave you a good brushing this morning before I fed you breakfast. And Alice will be home in just a few hours. You're hardly neglected."

Panting, he leaned against her, gazing up with happy dark eyes. She sighed. "Okay, I'll throw your ball for you. But do not get me dirty. I don't want to have to change before I go shopping."

She didn't at all trust the grin he gave her in response to that admonition.

Half an hour later, she was still outside, tossing a tennis ball for the dog, who seemed to never run out of enthusiasm for the mindless game. He would have liked even more for her to throw the ball into the pool; there was nothing Waldo loved more than to throw himself into the water after a toy, especially on a hot July day like this one. But she left the gate to the pool firmly closed despite his blatant hinting. With a wet dog climbing all over her, there was no way she'd stay clean enough to go shopping.

"Okay, Waldo, last throw," she told him firmly,

raising the ball in preparation. Like his owners, she'd
gotten into the habit of speaking to the big yellow Lab
mix as though he could understand every word she said.
And like them, there were times when she suspected
he understood quite a bit. "One more time, and then I
absolutely have to go do the shopping."

"Aw, just one more?"

Her heart gave a thump. She turned to find Mitch
standing in the kitchen doorway, leaning against the
doorjamb as if he'd been there a few minutes. "Don't
encourage him," she said with a faint smile of greeting.
"He'd keep me out here all day if he could."

"Can't blame him for that."

Giving the ball one last heave, Jacqui turned toward
the house. Waldo collected the ball and then, sensing
the game was over, moved resignedly to his water bowl.
Jacqui followed Mitch into the kitchen and closed the
door behind them.

She washed her hands thoroughly in the kitchen sink,
saying over her shoulder, "You're back earlier than I
expected."

"I try not to work full days on weekends, unless I'm
on call. Usually have to go in for an hour or two, but
more than that is just begging for burnout. Of course,
there are plenty of times I get tied up there all day even
then."

"I can imagine." She glanced at the microwave clock,
noting it was just before noon. "Have you had lunch?"

"No. After that nice breakfast you made for us, I
haven't been hungry yet."

"I'm just about to leave for groceries. I could heat a
can of soup for you before I go, maybe make a sandwich,
if you like."

"Have you had lunch?"

"Not yet. I'll probably get something while I'm out."

"Why don't I go with you? We can take my car. We can have a quick lunch and then I'll help you get the groceries."

She blinked. "You're offering to go grocery shopping with me?"

He laughed quizzically. "Why do you look so startled? How do you think I've gotten food for myself during the past decade that I've lived on my own? The grocery fairies don't visit this area, as far as I know."

"I just assumed a busy surgeon would pay someone to do that for him."

Chuckling, he shook his head. "Until a couple of months ago I've been a student or a resident. My extra cash has been going toward paying off student loans. I do my own cleaning, my own cooking—when I bother—and my own shopping."

"I'm sure you'd like to relax after working this morning. Just let me know anything you need, and I'd be happy to get it for you."

"If you'd rather I stay here..."

Something about his expression reminded her very much of Waldo's please-play-with-me face. She found herself just as unable to resist with Mitch. After all, she rationalized, he had lost his home. She supposed he was feeling at loose ends today, maybe in need of distraction, even if it was for fast food and grocery shopping.

"You're welcome to come along," she said lightly, tucking her bag beneath her arm. "That way you'll be sure to get exactly what you like."

He smiled. "Sounds good to me."

Her steps faltered a little toward the doorway, but she lifted her chin and kept moving. It was too late to back out now.

* * *

They had lunch at a bakery-café not far from the supermarket where Jacqui usually shopped. Mitch had a turkey panini with chips and a pickle spear; Jacqui ordered half a veggie sandwich and a cup of vegetarian black-bean soup.

Glancing at her plate, he cocked his head in curiosity. "Are you a vegetarian? I noticed you skipped the bacon at breakfast."

She shrugged lightly. "I'm not a true vegetarian. I like fish and chicken, occasionally, but I simply prefer veggies and fruits."

"I like veggies and fruits myself. If you prefer cooking vegetarian, that's perfectly fine with me."

"I have no problems cooking meat. Your brother-in-law is most definitely a carnivore."

Laughing, Mitch reached for his water glass. "Well, he is a lawyer."

She smiled wryly. "Low blow."

"Just kidding. I like the guy. I'm glad he and Alice are part of our family now."

"The three of them make a lovely family."

Jacqui had been a silent spectator during much of Seth's courtship of Meagan. Meagan had initially interviewed Jacqui for the job as Seth's housekeeper when his previous employee had fallen and broken her leg, but Meagan had been helping out only as Seth's friendly neighbor at the time. From the relative anonymity of her job, Jacqui had observed during the next few months while Seth and Meagan had grown closer, then moved apart. The busy attorney and harried surgeon had been afraid their demanding careers and other obligations would be insurmountable obstacles between them.

Jacqui suspected they had worried as much about hurting Alice as about having their own hearts broken. But love had overcome their fears, and they had become engaged at Christmas.

Jacqui had attended their small, tasteful wedding, and she didn't think she'd ever seen a happier couple. Since that time they'd managed to arrange their hectic schedules to allow as much time as possible for each other and for Alice. Jacqui liked to think her capable behind-the-scenes management of their household had smoothed the way for them, at least to some extent.

"Hey, Mitch."

In response to the greeting, both Mitch and Jacqui looked around. Three men in baggy shorts and T-shirts were passing the table on the way to the exit. All of them looked as though they knew Mitch, judging from the way they nodded to him.

"Hey, Nolan. Scott, Jackson. How's it going?"

"Been shooting some hoops in J-ville," one of the men answered for the group. "You playing football tomorrow?"

"Maybe. I'll have to buy some shorts."

"Heard about your house," another man spoke up. "Sorry, bro. Anything you need?"

Looking as though he appreciated the offer, Mitch shook his head. "I'm good, Jackson. Thanks."

"Let us know if you think of anything," the first guy said again, looking at his companions as if for confirmation. They all nodded earnestly.

"Thanks, Scott. Maybe I'll see you tomorrow."

"Co-ed game," Scott added with a flirtatious smile toward Jacqui. "Be sure to invite your friend."

Mitch nodded. "I'll do that."

"Friends," Mitch explained after the trio had moved on.

"Yeah, I got that."

"Hadn't even thought about losing all my sports gear yet." He toyed with the remains of his sandwich, regret etched on his face.

"I'm sorry. It must be difficult to lose everything."

"It's daunting," he agreed. "But I suppose it's a chance to start fresh, too. Too much stuff just ties you down, you know?"

She wouldn't know about that. She'd never really owned enough that she couldn't throw everything in her car and move on a moment's notice. But it wouldn't always be that way, she promised herself. As soon as she could afford her own place, she couldn't wait to buy furniture and decorations. Things that made a house a home.

"I guess clothes are my most immediate need," Mitch mused. "I'm supposed to go on a trip to Peru in September, so I'll need clothes and luggage for that."

"Peru?" she asked, hearing a hint of excitement in his voice. He seemed to want her to ask him to explain, so she figured she might as well humor him for the sake of conversation.

He nodded. "Some friends are making a five-day Machu Picchu trek. Eight days total for the trip. It's something I've always wanted to do."

"Then you should go."

"The fire came at a bad time—not that there's ever a good time for a fire—but now I've got to make living arrangements and replace some stuff. Still, I think I'll be able to put it all aside and take a week off for the trip. To be honest, it'll be my first time out of the country, other than a four-day senior trip to Cancun, Mexico, the summer after high school graduation. Been too busy studying and working to go anywhere since."

She wondered if that trip would assuage the restlessness she sensed in him—or merely whet his appetite for more traveling. From what she'd seen, when a man got it in his head that he wanted to travel, there wasn't much that could hold him back. "I hope you get to go and that you have a great time."

"Thanks. Have you been out of the country?"

"My dad decided to move us to Canada once. I must have been about nine. We stayed in Vancouver for about six months, then moved to Seattle for a while."

"So you didn't grow up in Arkansas."

"We moved a lot," she said somewhat evasively. "We lived in Arkansas for a year when I was in junior high, and it was always one of my favorite places, so when I had the chance, I came back here."

"Where else have you lived?"

He seemed to be making conversation rather than prying, but it still made her a little uncomfortable to talk about her past with this man whose life had been so very different. "I've lived for at least a brief time in fifteen states."

"Fifteen states? Wow. For someone as young as you are, that's a lot of moving around. Especially since you've been working for my sister's family for a year."

"A little over a year, actually. I worked for another man in Arkansas—in Hot Springs Village—for almost a year before that, so I've been back in this state for a while. As for my age, most people think I'm younger than I really am. I'm twenty-nine."

"Do your parents still move often?"

She nodded. "I can't imagine my father ever staying

in one place for long, and my mother seems content to follow him around the country."

The last she'd heard, they'd been in Arizona. But it had been a couple months since she'd talked with her mother, so they could very well have drifted someplace else since then. For the past dozen years, especially, they'd been unable to settle anywhere for long. During those twelve years, they had traveled on their own while Jacqui followed a different path.

"Do you have any siblings?"

The question still made a hard lump form in her chest, even after all this time. "I had a sister. She died."

Although she wasn't looking at him, she sensed Mitch searching her face. She wondered if he'd heard the guilt that always swamped her when she thought of Olivia.

"I'm sorry," he said quietly.

"Thanks." She reached for her purse. "If you're finished with your lunch, we really should get the groceries. I'm supposed to pick up Alice at four."

"I'm done." He swallowed one last gulp of his tea and then stood.

Jacqui moved toward the exit without looking back to see if he followed.

Mental note to self. Don't ask Jacqui personal questions.

Mitch glanced sideways at the woman in his passenger seat as he drove toward the supermarket she said she preferred. He couldn't help being curious about her, despite her reticence about her past. Or, just as likely, because of it.

Although he wouldn't have called her chatty, their conversation had been going pretty well during lunch until he'd started asking questions about her family.

He had definitely hit some raw nerves there. Her relationship with her parents was obviously strained, and her old pain from losing her sister had been almost palpable.

What had it been like for her, growing up without strong roots to either a place or her family? So strongly connected to his own mother and sisters, and to the memory of the father he had loved deeply, and never having lived anywhere but central Arkansas, Mitch couldn't really identify with her experiences, but he would have liked to hear about them. Not that her past was any of his business, of course. Although circumstances had brought them under the same roof for the next couple of weeks, they were merely acquaintances, nothing more. Maybe by the time he moved on, they could at least claim to be casual friends.

It was her suggestion that they stop at a sporting goods store they passed on the way to the supermarket. "If you're going to play football with your friends tomorrow, you'll need clothes," she said.

Stopped at a red light, he looked at the store, thinking how convenient it would be to save at least one extra shopping trip. "You're sure you don't mind?"

"Of course not." She motioned for him to turn into the shopping center in which the sporting goods store was located.

"I won't be long," he promised. "Just need a few things."

"No reason to rush. We have a couple of hours to shop before Alice gets home."

The casual assurance made him realize that her hurry to leave the lunch table had been more related to their conversation than her schedule for the remainder of the day. No surprise.

"Kind of warm for a football game, isn't it?" she asked, glancing at the blazing sun in the cloudless sky.

He shrugged as he pulled into a parking space and killed the engine. "We dress cool, drink plenty of water. We don't start until six, so even though it's still hot, the sun has gone down some. By the way, Scott was serious about you being welcome to join us, if you like. The games are co-ed, and we have several women who show up regularly to play."

"Since it's co-ed, I take it you play flag football? Not tackle?"

He realized only then that she was under a misconception about the invitation his friend had extended. "Wrong game."

She caught on before he had the chance to explain. "Not American football. Soccer."

"Yeah. Scott was being pretentious, I guess."

She shrugged and reached to open her door. "The rest of the world calls it that."

"But in this country, it's reasonable to assume he was talking about our football. Scott likes to catch people in that assumption and correct them with a worldly indulgence toward their naiveté."

"Sounds kind of jerky."

Amused by her blunt assessment, he nodded. "He can be. But he's okay, on the whole."

Jacqui didn't look mollified. "I don't like it when people try to make other people look stupid. Your sister and brother-in-law would never do that, and they're pretty much the smartest people I know."

He hoped she didn't think he'd been having fun at her expense. "No, they wouldn't. And I—"

But she was already out of the car, the door snapping shut behind her. Mitch sighed.

Forty-five minutes later, he tagged behind Jacqui as she wielded a shopping cart through the Saturday-crowded supermarket aisles. She selected her groceries with even more care than he'd used in grabbing supplies at the sporting goods store while she'd browsed the sneakers collection.

She seemed to have no trouble being friendly with other people. Apparently, she knew quite a few employees of the supermarket. Several of them greeted her with obvious recognition and Jacqui responded with friendly smiles.

"How's the new baby?" she asked a young woman arranging roses in the floral department.

"He's doing great," the woman replied, beaming. "You wouldn't believe how fast he's growing. He loves the little stuffed bear you knitted for him. It's so soft and cuddly, and he always smiles when I give it to him."

"I'm glad he's enjoying it."

The florist eyed Mitch surreptitiously as she asked Jacqui, "Need any flowers today? We got some pretty lilies in this morning."

"No, not today, thanks, Latricia. Maybe next time."

A portly man behind the deli counter grinned broadly when Jacqui approached a few minutes later. "Well, hello there, sunshine. The little missy isn't with you today?"

"She had other plans today, Gus." She glanced at Mitch. "Alice likes to come shopping with me sometimes."

"That little girl does love her cheese," Gus commented with a chuckle. "What can I get for you today?"

Mitch stood back and watched as Jacqui placed her order. He was struck by her attention to detail even with simple luncheon meats. She'd been the same way with the other groceries now stacked in the cart, reading ingredients, comparing prices, making each choice with a frown of concentration. He enjoyed watching her at work—and she was very much on the job.

If only she could relax with him as she did with the store employees. Surely she wasn't intimidated by him? He could think of no reason at all for that to be true.

Maybe she just didn't like him? His ego twinged at the possibility. Was he really so conceited that he assumed everyone should like him? He believed most people liked him well enough, with a few exceptions he didn't much like either. But maybe there was something about him that rubbed Jacqui the wrong way.

He'd just have to seé if he could manage to rub her the right way.

That errant thought made him shift his weight uncomfortably. He studied her from the corner of his eye as she took a smiling leave of the man in the deli.

He would be on his best behavior for the next few days, he promised himself. Whatever he might have done to annoy her, he would do his best to change her mind. He wouldn't mind having Jacqui smile at him the way she smiled at her friends here in the supermarket.

If Alice hadn't gotten enough sleep the night before, it didn't show during dinner that night. She chattered nonstop to her uncle throughout the meal, continued to talk while she helped Jacqui clean up afterward, then babbled even more when they joined Mitch in the family room a few minutes later. Jacqui settled in a chair in the corner beneath a bright reading lamp and pulled out the knitting bag she always kept nearby while Mitch and Alice surfed the TV channels for something they both enjoyed.

Mitch glanced Jacqui's way during a momentary lull in Alice's monologue. "What are you working on?"

Figuring he was trying to be polite and include her in the conversation, she lifted her project to show the ruffle-edged black scarf she was halfway through. "It's a scarf."

"Nice. Is this for your friend's store? Meagan mentioned you sell your knitted stuff at a boutique," he added.

She nodded. "A friend in Santa Fe sells handmade accessories in her shop. I met her when I lived there a few years back and I've been sending her stuff ever since. Mostly scarves, although occasionally she asks for baby blankets or hats or fingerless gloves, which are popular right now."

"How long have you been knitting?"

"Since I was a kid." A friendly neighbor had taught her the basics when her family had settled briefly in a trailer park in Utah. The woman had tried to teach Olivia, too, but Olivia hadn't been interested. Jacqui, however, had loved the hobby, something portable she could take with her wherever they went. She had guarded the needles that sweet lady had given her as if they were made of gold and had hoarded the yarn she'd purchased with odd jobs money or the occasional allowance from her parents.

The hobby had long since paid for itself. She would never get rich selling her handcrafted wares in the boutique and on the internet, but she kept herself in yarn and needles and rarely purchased gifts when she could make them herself. She made her own sweaters, scarves, gloves and hats and even made shopping bags, dishcloths and socks.

She was delighted that Alice had been knitting for almost a year. Alice had begged Jacqui to teach her last summer and she'd gotten quite good at it since. Jacqui enjoyed sharing her knowledge, the way that nice neighbor had done with her all those years ago. Alice liked knitting soft little stuffed animals in pastel yarns, which she then donated to the local children's hospital. The same hospital where her uncle Mitch worked, Jacqui thought, glancing at the pediatric orthopedic surgeon on the couch.

"Everything on TV is boring, Uncle Mitch. You want to play a game?" Alice asked hopefully.

"Sure, that sounds like fun," he said, looking as if he meant it. "What have you got?"

She jumped up eagerly and retrieved a stack of games from a cabinet under a built-in bookcase, setting them on the well-used game table in one corner of the comfortable family room. Generally eschewing the video games most kids her age loved, Alice was instead a fiend for board games, nagging anyone available into playing with her. Jacqui was roped into games fairly often, especially with Alice out of school for the summer.

Alice and Mitch selected a game, sat at the table and then both looked expectantly toward Jacqui.

"Can I get you anything to drink during your game?" she asked, motioning with her knitting toward the doorway.

"Come play with us, Jacqui," Alice urged, patting an empty chair at the table.

"Oh, I—"

Alice gave her a pleading, puppy-dog-eyes look that

would have put Waldo to shame. "Please. Games are more fun with three."

"I wonder if I should resent that," Mitch mused aloud.

Both women ignored him. Conceding to Alice's expression, Jacqui set aside her project. "All right. But just for a little while."

Two hours later, they still sat around the game table. Empty soda cans sat beside Alice and Mitch, and Jacqui had just finished her second cup of hot tea. Crumbs were the only thing remaining on the plate of cookies Jacqui had brought out earlier. Scribbled score pads documented individual victories in the games they'd played that evening.

She was startled to realize how much time had passed when she glanced at the clock on the mantel. Those two hours had flown by in a blur of rolling dice and laughter. Mitch and Alice were cute together. A stranger observing them would never have believed they'd known each other only a little longer than a year, that Mitch had not known his niece-by-marriage all her life. He teased her and chatted with her with an ease that proclaimed family bonds. At least the type of family bonds Jacqui had observed while working in this household. Not so much in her own.

How might her life have been different, she wondered idly, if her own family had spent time around a table, laughing over a board game? Or even just chatting over dinner? How might she have been different?

A memory popped into her head, dimming her smile. She and Olivia sat cross-legged on the floor of a cheap motel room, playing Monopoly with a battered, salvaged set. They'd replaced the missing game tokens with different-colored pebbles and had made their own deeds and play money with scraps of paper. They'd had a few little plastic houses and hotels and enough instruction cards to make it possible for them to play. She'd been maybe twelve at the time, which would have made Olivia ten.

She remembered the wistfulness in Olivia's smile when she'd earned enough scrap-paper money to buy a house.

"Don't you wish it was real?" Olivia had asked, studying the little green plastic house in her hand. "Don't you wish we could really buy a house and live in it forever?"

"Not likely," Jacqui had answered with a brusqueness designed to hide her own old longings. "Dad would be ready to move on before we even mowed the grass the first time."

"I'd like to mow grass." Olivia set the little plastic house carefully into position on the game board. "When I grow up, I'm going to have a house with a big yard and I'll mow the grass and plant flowers. Maybe I'll have a garden and grow peaches. I love peaches."

"You don't grow peaches in a garden. You grow them in an orchard," Jacqui had corrected with the wisdom of her additional two years.

"Then I'll have an orchard," Olivia had replied, unperturbed.

Jacqui snapped back into the present when Alice demanded her attention.

"Let's play Monopoly now!" the teen suggested with an eager look at the stack of games they hadn't already played.

Because there were only a few games left in that stack, Jacqui found no particular significance in Alice's choice, despite the coincidence. Still, her throat clenched enough that she had to clear it silently before replying. "That's all for me tonight, Alice. It's getting late, and I have a few things to do before bedtime."

Alice sighed, but didn't argue, to Jacqui's relief. When Mitch announced that he had early hospital rounds to make the next morning, Alice accepted that game night was over and began to put away the supplies.

Mitch helped Jacqui clear away the remains of their snacks. Carrying empty soda cans to the recycling bin in the kitchen, he smiled down at her when they almost bumped into each other as he reached around her to drop the cans in the bin. "Sorry."

This usually roomy kitchen had never felt as small as it did at that moment, with Mitch standing right in front of her and the kitchen counter at her back. All she'd have to do was take one small step forward and she'd be in his arms, plastered against him. Not that she intended to do anything of the sort, of course. It was strictly an observation.

Mitch studied her face for a moment, making her wonder what he might see in the expression she tried to keep carefully blank. And then he moved back a few steps. She drew in air, realizing she'd held her breath while he stood so close. What was it about this man that flustered her so much?

He moved toward the doorway. "I'm going to do some paperwork in my room, then turn in. I need to be at the hospital by six in the morning for a breakfast meeting with a partner. Told my mom I'd have lunch with her and Madison and our aunts, then I'm heading to the mall to buy a few things. Tomorrow evening I'll be playing soccer with the guys, so I won't be around here much."

She nodded, telling herself she should be relieved he wouldn't be underfoot the next day.

"Good night, Jacqui."

"Good night." He didn't seem to like it when she called him Dr. Baker, but she wasn't quite comfortable using his name yet, so she tended to avoid calling him anything.

He didn't look back when he left the room. She knew that because she watched him until he was out of her sight.

Two more weeks, max, under the same roof. She could do this. She assumed the novelty of him would wear off after a couple days of proximity. At least she hoped it would. She wasn't sure how much she could take of having her pulse race this way every time Mitch stood close to her.

As he climbed into the guest bed that night, Mitch wondered what it was about a suggestion of playing Monopoly that had made Jacqui's dark eyes go so bleak it had made his heart hurt for her. The most obvious explanation was that it had something to do with her late sister. Childhood memories, perhaps?

She hadn't said how long her sister had been gone, but it was apparent that the loss was still raw. He imagined what it would be like to lose one of his own sisters, and the pain was so immediate and so piercing that he put the thought quickly out of his mind. He didn't even want to consider the possibility. Losing his possessions was a minor inconvenience; losing members of his family—well, that was very hard for him to handle. He'd already lost one parent, his beloved dad, and that had been a horrible time for his whole family. It had been difficult enough saying goodbye to his grandmother last year, and they had all been braced for months for her death.

He didn't like seeing pain in anyone's eyes, but for

some reason it had especially bothered him to see Jacqui looking so unhappy, even momentarily. That sadness had been in such stark contrast with her laughter only moments before whatever memory had assaulted her.

She'd seemed to have fun during their game session with Alice. She'd teased along with him and his niece, and he'd been struck by her soft, rich laughter. For those two hours, she had even lost some of the reserve she usually showed around him—and that he still couldn't understand. He'd found himself having to make an effort to concentrate on the games rather than the glint of pleasure in her pretty, dark eyes.

Lying on his back in the darkened room, he stared upward, seeing Jacqui's face rather than the shadowed ceiling. Despite her obvious and bewildering wariness of him, he still found himself drawn to her.

He'd been intrigued by her from the first time he'd met her. He'd been surprised that the housekeeper his sister and her new family had raved so much about had been a rather gamine young woman rather than the stereotypically sturdy matron he'd vaguely envisioned. He'd admired her big, dark eyes, pointed little chin and soft, nicely shaped mouth, and although he usually was attracted to long, wavy hair, he'd liked her tousled pixie cut. It suited her.

As busy as he'd been the past year, and as awkward as it would have been to pursue his sister's employee, he'd done nothing about his initial tug of attraction to Jacqui. But now that they were under the same roof and spending more time together, the fascination was only growing harder to ignore. He was still busy, and it was still awkward—not to mention that she'd given him no encouragement at all—but maybe they could at least be friends by the time he moved into a new place. Maybe in the future she would smile warmly when she saw him, rather than that politely distanced expression she usually wore when he was around.

He'd like that.

Chapter Three

Jacqui had no intention of attending Mitch's soccer game. She knew very little about soccer, and she still winced at the way she'd reacted to Mitch's pretentious friend's affectations. She doubted she'd have much in common with a bunch of highly educated soccer enthusiasts—or football, as Scott had referred to it. To her, football would always involve pads and helmets and "Hail Mary" passes and touchdowns, but whatever.

She hadn't counted on Alice wanting very much to go.

"Mitch said there are usually some other kids my age hanging around to watch," Alice explained. "They don't let anyone younger than sixteen play because they're afraid the kids might get hurt playing with adults, but sometimes there's a kids' game on the next field. And sometimes they need help with carrying water and chasing soccer balls and stuff like that. Besides, I want to watch Mitch play. I bet he's really good."

"It's going to be pretty hot at the park today," Jacqui warned. "In the mid-nineties, according to the weather forecast."

Alice shrugged. "It's always hot in July," she said pragmatically. "Can we go, please?"

"Well, um—"

"You could just drop me off if you don't want to stay. Mitch can bring me home."

Jacqui envisioned Alice wandering around the crowded park alone while her uncle was engrossed in his game. Although Alice was fourteen and fairly level-headed for her age, Jacqui didn't like the thought of her being entirely on her own in such a public place. And what if Mitch wanted to go out for beers or something with his friends after the game?

"I thought maybe you and I could go to a movie this afternoon," she suggested in a weak bait-and-switch attempt.

Alice wasn't falling for it. She shook her head. "There's nothing I really want to see right now. I'd rather watch Mitch's soccer game."

Jacqui sighed heavily. "Fine. I'll take you."

Had she conceded too easily? Was her capitulation entirely a result of not wanting to disappoint Alice? Was it possible she secretly wanted to see Mitch at play, herself?

Frowning, she pushed a hand impatiently through her hair. "We don't have to stay for the whole game if it gets too hot or if you get bored."

"Okay." But Alice was grinning broadly in anticipation, seemingly undaunted by the risks of heat or bore-

dom. Jacqui resigned herself to a long stay at the soccer field.

"Can we take Waldo? I'd keep him on the leash."

"No." Jacqui had no intention of backing down on
that issue, even if Alice begged. Waldo was a sweet dog,
but he was rambunctious when he got excited. Alice
walked him around the neighborhood on his leash nearly
every day and Jacqui drove them occasionally to the
nearest dog park, but any new environment sent him into
a frenzy of hyperactive exploration despite his obedience
training. Because Alice wanted to watch the game, that
meant Jacqui would be stuck at the end of Waldo's leash.
"Not this time."

Alice seemed to consider arguing for a moment, then
she must have decided to quit while she was ahead.
"Okay, maybe next time. I'm going up to decide what
to wear."

Studying Alice's pink-and-white-striped T-shirt and
denim shorts, Jacqui asked, "What's wrong with what
you're wearing?"

Alice rolled her eyes. "I just said there could be kids
my age there."

That was supposed to be an explanation? Jacqui
shook her head in bemusement as Alice dashed toward
the stairs. She glanced down at the ultra-casual oversize
T-shirt and leggings she'd worn for the light housework
she'd done that morning. She supposed it wouldn't hurt
to change. Not because she cared about trying to impress
anyone, but because this rather heavy fabric could be
uncomfortable in the heat. And if she chose an outfit
that was a bit more figure-flattering—well, one should
always try to look one's best when in public, right?

When they left the house half an hour later Jacqui
wore a sleeveless yellow shirt of thin, cool cotton paired

with khaki capris and leather flip-flops. She was still casual, but the soft yellow looked good with her dark hair and eyes, she decided.

After consulting with Jacqui on at least three different outfits, Alice had settled finally on a screen-printed, scoop-neck, purple T-shirt and a different pair of denim shorts. Glittery purple flip-flops revealed her purple-painted toenails. She'd tied her curly hair into a sassy ponytail and wore as much makeup as her father allowed—a touch of mascara and tinted lip gloss. The result was fresh and cute and much too casual to suggest she'd agonized for a good twenty minutes over the choices.

The spreading North Little Rock park was still crowded at six on this Sunday evening. Plenty of people had taken advantage of the slight cooling of the day to make use of the 1,600-acre park's picnic areas, hiking, biking and equestrian trails, golf course, tennis and racquetball courts, fishing lake, and sports fields for baseball and soccer and disc and miniature golf. Playgrounds and a small amusement park drew families with younger children. Jacqui had brought Alice to a birthday party at one of the pavilions there last spring, and she'd spent a couple hours exploring the park while Alice enjoyed the party.

Following the directions Mitch had left for them, they found the soccer field easily enough. But it wasn't until Alice spotted Mitch that they were sure they'd found the right group because so many other games were going on around them.

Grinning, he loped toward them. "Glad you could make it. We're just about to start. You want to play, Jacqui? The teams aren't really that formal. Anyone who wants to join in is welcome."

She had hoped the passing hours had given her time to brace herself for seeing him again. She'd told herself that increased exposure would somewhat soften the jolt of attraction that always hit her at the sight of him. No such luck. His sandy hair was tousled, his lean body nicely displayed in a blue soccer shirt and black shorts, his engaging smile warm and contagious. The too-familiar jolt hit her so hard she almost took a step back in response as she struggled to remember what he'd asked. "Um, no, thank you. I'll just watch with Alice."

"You're sure? We have a lot of fun."

She motioned toward her flip-flops. "Wrong shoes. Besides, I don't know the game that well."

Someone called his name from across the field. Or pitch, as Alice had referred to it. Mitch glanced that way and gave a brief wave, then looked back at Jacqui and Alice. "I'd better get back to the team."

"Good luck with your game," Jacqui encouraged.

"Thanks." He turned and dashed toward his friends. They weren't wearing uniforms, exactly, but Jacqui noted that most of the players on Mitch's side of the field wore blue shirts.

She couldn't resist one admiring look at Mitch's firm backside before she made herself turn to Alice. They'd brought folding canvas chairs stowed in shoulder-strap bags, and Jacqui carried an insulated tote bag in which she'd packed bottles of water and a few healthy snacks in case Alice got hungry. Mitch had told Alice the match would last almost two hours counting breaks. If Alice wanted to stay for the entire game, they would be eating dinner later than usual.

In addition to the chair bag slung over her shoulder and the insulated tote, Jacqui carried a patchwork crafts bag that held her latest knitting project. She couldn't sit that long without keeping her hands busy. Her knitting was so automatic by now that she would have no problem watching the game and finishing the scarf at the same time.

There weren't a lot of spectators for the casual game. Most of the people in attendance were participants, either on the pitch or lined up on the sidelines waiting for someone to get winded and need a rest. Each team seemed to have an unofficial coach who kept their side organized, and a couple of volunteers served as officials, running up and down the field and enthusiastically blowing whistles. A great deal of noise and laughter accompanied the good-natured rivalry.

"It's doctors versus lawyers," Alice confided with a laugh, nodding toward the competitors while she and Jacqui set up their chairs on a patch of grass where they could see the action. "The lawyers usually wear red shirts. Mitch said some people on both teams are students and some are older. He called himself one of the 'old guys.' I told him that was silly. He's not old. Not *really* old anyway," she added.

Jacqui couldn't help but smile as she took her seat. To a fourteen-year-old, thirty-one must seem fairly ancient, but at least Alice had conceded that Mitch wasn't quite ready for a cane and a rocking chair.

The match began with a flurry of kicks and head shots. The few spectators—most of whom seemed to be women with small children to entertain, keeping them from participating in the game themselves—cheered and called out encouragement. Although Jacqui made a determined effort to watch all the players, her gaze kept drifting to one in particular. Alice, too, watched intently for a short while, explaining rules of the game that Jacqui hadn't known, but then her attention wandered to a group of teenagers playing idly with a flying disc nearby.

"I think I know one of those girls from swim matches," she said. "Okay if I go talk to them, Jacqui?"

"Of course." Not particularly surprised that Alice's attention had drifted so quickly from the game she'd begged to attend, Jacqui almost advised the girl not to wander off too far, but she resisted the impulse. She had to keep reminding herself that Alice was growing up and understandably disliked being treated like a child.

As her knitting needles clicked in a soothing rhythm, she thought back to when she'd been fourteen. Much less sheltered and supervised than Alice, she'd been more worldly and mature at that age. Her parents had left their daughters alone for hours, sometimes for a couple of days at a time while they'd pursued their own ever-changing interests or worked odd jobs to keep the family in gasoline, cheap motel rooms and food—in that order. Jacqui had been responsible for getting Olivia and herself ready for school. Neither high school graduates themselves, their parents hadn't helped them with their homework or attended school programs with them. They hadn't set curfews or bedtimes, and they'd shown only occasional interest in their daughters' friends and activities.

Eddie and Cindy Handy hadn't been abusive parents. Just ineffective ones. They'd loved each other and their daughters, in their odd ways, but their own issues had prevented them from providing the sort of guidance and support their children had craved. They had grieved when Olivia died, so deeply that the gaping wound had been the final separation between them and Jacqui. They hadn't argued long when she'd told them at seventeen that she wanted to make her own path from that point. They'd stayed in touch in a desultory fashion—but they hadn't been a real family since. If, indeed, they had ever been.

She drew her thoughts abruptly to the present, wondering what had triggered that melancholy little trip into the past. The fact that she was surrounded by seemingly happy families in the park? That she was watching a group of doctors playing with a group of lawyers, making her wonder if any of them could imagine an upbringing like hers? She wasn't naive enough to assume that all these disparate professionals came from privileged or idealized backgrounds, but they had attained higher education, which made them different enough from her.

She turned her attention back to her knitting, telling herself she was being silly. She belonged in this park as much as anyone. And she was perfectly happy with the life she had chosen—despite her occasional vague longings for something she couldn't even define.

After forty-five minutes of play, the teams called a break for halftime. Alice drew herself away from her friends for a few minutes when she saw Mitch walking toward Jacqui.

"You're playing great, Mitch!" she said cheerily, bounding up to join them.

Jacqui smiled wryly, wondering if Mitch was aware of how little notice Alice had actually given to the game.

After taking a swig of a sports drink, he wiped his brow with a hand towel he'd brought in his sports bag and winked at Jacqui before answering his niece. "I'm glad you've been entertained."

Jacqui told herself the wink had only been conspiratorial, acknowledging Mitch's awareness of Alice's divided attentions. He hadn't actually been flirting or anything, so there had been no reason for her heart to skip a beat in reaction.

Mitch glanced at the knitting in Jacqui's lap. "If y'all are ready to go, don't feel like you have to stay until the end of the game for my sake."

"I'm not ready to leave yet," Alice said quickly. "I've been hanging out with some kids my age over at the picnic tables."

Widening his eyes in mock surprise, Mitch said, "I thought you'd been watching my game."

"I can see it from over there," she assured him. "Some of it anyway."

He laughed and tugged at the end of her curly ponytail. "Just teasing. But what about Jacqui? Maybe she's bored sitting here by herself while you're hanging out with friends and I'm playing."

"Not at all," Jacqui answered candidly. "I'm enjoying it. And I've made good progress on finishing this scarf."

"See?" Alice beamed approvingly at Jacqui. "There's no need for us to leave yet."

A whistle blew from the field, signaling that the game was about to start again. Mitch turned that direction. "Okay, see you both later then."

He jogged off without looking back.

"You really don't mind if I'm over there with the other kids?" Alice asked hesitantly before abandoning Jacqui again.

"I really don't mind," Jacqui assured her with a smile. "Have a good time."

"Thanks." Alice turned and hurried back toward the picnic tables, ponytail bobbing behind her. Jacqui picked up her needles again, her gaze on the field as the players assembled for the second half of the match. She'd lost count of the score, but she thought the doctors were ahead by one goal.

"I don't remember seeing you here before."

Her hands going still, Jacqui rested the almost-finished black scarf in her lap and turned to the woman who had greeted her from a nearby lawn chair. The woman must have set up there during the halftime break because Jacqui hadn't noticed her before.

"That's because this is my first time here," she replied with a faint smile.

"Watching a friend play?"

Jacqui laughed ruefully. "Actually, I brought a young friend to watch her uncle play, but she seems to have lost interest."

She intended to make it clear from the start that there was nothing between her and Mitch, even though she was attending his game. She doubted he would appreciate gossip or speculation about them among his friends and professional acquaintances, especially if it became known that she was his sister's housekeeper.

The other woman who was somewhere around Jacqui's age looked tall and curvy even sitting down. Her undoubtedly expensive white blouse and capris were crisp and spotless even in the heat. Her softly curled black hair framed a square face with perfect, milk-chocolate skin and wide-set black eyes, and her smile was friendly enough, if a little reserved. "I'm Keira. I'm here with my fiancé. Nolan."

Keira motioned vaguely toward a man on the field who looked familiar to Jacqui. Had he been one of the three who'd interrupted her and Mitch at lunch yesterday? She thought one of them might have been named Nolan.

"I'm Jacqui. It's nice to meet you."

Scanning the field, Keira asked, "Is Mitch Baker your young friend's uncle?"

She must have seen them talking a few minutes earlier. "Yes, he is."

"He's one of Nolan's pals. They get together all the time to play basketball or soccer or video games or poker. When Nolan's not at the hospital, he's hanging out with the guys. Rather than fight him about it, I just tag along whenever I'm invited. He's tried to talk me into playing soccer with them, but to be honest, I hate the game. All that running and sweating—not my style."

Jacqui chuckled in response to the frank admission. "Nolan's a doctor, too, I take it?"

"Anesthesiologist. He and Mitch were in the same medical school class."

Feeling a little wilted in the heat of the afternoon, Jacqui drew her half-finished bottled water from her tote. "I have an extra bottle if you'd like one," she offered.

"Thanks, but I have one. Have you known Mitch long?"

Keira appeared more bored than nosey. She didn't seem particularly interested in talking to any of the busy mothers swapping mommy stories nearby while keeping one eye on their kids and the other on the game. Maybe Keira thought she'd have more in common with Jacqui.

Doubting that, Jacqui answered candidly, "I've known Mitch about a year. I work for his sister's family."

The other woman looked toward the cluster of teens in which Alice stood chattering and giggling. "Are you a nanny?"

"Alice is a little old for a nanny, though I do keep an eye on her. I'm the housekeeper."

Keira blinked. "Oh. You don't—um..."

You don't look like a housekeeper. Jacqui finished the statement in her head, wondering how many times she'd heard it said in the past two years or so. Why did everyone think all housekeepers looked like Alice from *The Brady Bunch?*

She shrugged. "I enjoy my work."

After a moment, Keira said, "I'm a respiratory therapist. That's how I met Nolan."

"Sounds interesting."

"Most days," Keira agreed, still looking distracted by Jacqui's occupation.

A flurry of activity on the field captured their attention, and they watched as Mitch passed the ball to Nolan, who gave it a swift kick that sent the ball flying past the other team's goalie and into the net. Cheering broke out among Mitch's team and their few supporters on the sidelines. Jacqui clapped to demonstrate her own approval while Keira called out, "Way to go, baby!"

Preening for his fiancée, Nolan flexed victoriously until his teammates shoved him back into action for the next play.

For the next few minutes, Jacqui divided her attention between the game and her knitting while the other woman focused intently on the field, no longer in the mood for conversation apparently. She was almost surprised when Keira spoke again after a rather lengthy silence between them. "That girl you're with? Alice?"

Jacqui glanced instinctively toward her charge, frowning when she noted that Alice and a couple of other girls of about her age were gathered around a young man who looked to be three or four years their senior. The way Alice posed and giggled, it was obvious some serious flirting was going on. The other girls were performing too, all seemingly competing for the older boy's approval. He lounged against a tree, visibly basking in the attention, though he was doing his best to look "cool."

Jacqui told herself not to be concerned; it was normal for fourteen-year-old girls to practice their flirting skills, though she had never been much of a flirt, herself. She'd had too many other things on her mind at that age—like making sure she and her sister had school supplies and their homework turned in on time.

"What about Alice?"

"That boy she and the others are talking to is Scott Lemon's kid brother, Milo. He's eighteen or very close to it. How old is Alice?"

"Fourteen."

Keira nodded. "That's about what I guessed. Just giving you a heads-up."

"I appreciate it. Is it only the age difference that concerns you, or is there something more about him I should know?"

The other woman's hesitation was somewhat of an answer in itself. "I don't really know him well. I've just seen him hanging around a few times with Nolan and Scott and the other guys. He's Scott's half brother, I think—something like twelve years younger than Scott."

And Keira hadn't been impressed with what she'd seen—or heard—about the kid, Jacqui deduced. "Thank you. I'll keep a close eye on her."

"Good idea."

Alice ran back over to Jacqui's chairs only a few minutes later. Her eyes were alight with excitement, her cheeks unusually pink. "Okay if I go play miniature golf? I can get a ride home when I'm done."

Jacqui frowned. "You know that's not nearly enough information, Alice. Who would you be playing with and who would be driving you home?"

"Just some of the kids," Alice answered vaguely. "And Milo would bring me home. He's almost eighteen, and he has a driver's license and a car."

"Sorry. No."

"It's okay, Jacqui. His brother is one of Uncle Mitch's best friends. So it's not like he's a stranger."

Behind Alice's back, Keira looked studiously at the action on the field, pretending not to pay attention. Yet Jacqui saw the other woman shake her head slightly in response to Alice's argument, as if offering silent advice. Advice Jacqui hadn't actually needed.

"No, Alice. You aren't riding with a boy that neither your parents nor I have met."

"But Jacqui—"

"If you really want to play miniature golf with your friends, I'll come along. I can wait until you finish your game, then drive you home."

Alice wasn't satisfied with what Jacqui considered to be a rather magnanimous offer. "They'll all think I need a babysitter. What if Uncle Mitch says it's okay? I mean, Milo is his friend's brother, so Mitch would probably agree."

Jacqui glanced across the park to where Milo lounged against a tree, watching Alice with a look Jacqui didn't care for at all. "Your father left me in charge of you, not your uncle. And my answer is no. Either I accompany you to the miniature golf course and drive you home afterward, or you can stay here with me until the end of the soccer game. Or we can leave now—your choice."

There must have been a note of steel in her voice that Alice had never heard before. Alice blinked a few times, seemed to realize it would do her no good to argue further, then poked out her lower lip in a near-pout. "Fine. I'll just tell my new friends I can't go with them."

"It's your choice," Jacqui replied evenly. "You can make me the bad guy if you want, or you can tell them we have other plans if you want to save face."

Her expression supremely martyred, Alice turned on one heel and walked away, her posture expressing her dissatisfaction. Jacqui let out a low breath. In the just more than a year that she'd been charged with the responsibility of looking after Alice when her dad wasn't around, this was the first time the girl had even come close to a rebellion against Jacqui's authority. Alice had always been cheery, well-behaved, cooperative, eager— in other words, almost the perfect young teen in Jacqui's opinion. Sure, there had been some minor disagreements in the past year but not quite to this extent. And not with such high stakes, as far as Jacqui was concerned.

She had no intention of allowing Alice to get involved with a boy—much less an eighteen-year-old boy—while her parents were out of town. If it were up to Jacqui, it would be a couple of years yet before Alice was allowed to ride in cars with teenagers behind the wheel. Knowing Seth, she suspected he would agree with her on that point. If he'd had the same grim experiences as Jacqui, he would probably never let his daughter in the car with another teen, she thought darkly.

The soccer game must have ended during the confrontation. When she glanced at the field, the players were milling among each other, shaking hands and chatting amicably. Jacqui had no idea who'd won. She recapped her water bottle and slid it into the insulated tote, then folded her knitting and tucked it into its bag.

A towel draped around his neck, his hair and new clothes damp with sweat, Mitch walked toward her a few minutes later. He nodded toward Keira, who was gathering her things in preparation to join her fiancé, then smiled at Jacqui.

"Did you see me make that last goal? The winning one?"

Because he sounded so much like a kid hoping for a pat of approval, Jacqui hated to have to shake her head. "I'm sorry, I missed it. I guess I was talking to Alice. But congratulations."

Was there just a touch of disappointment in his voice when he responded? "Thanks. Where is Alice anyway?"

Jacqui waved a hand in the girl's direction. Following the gesture, Mitch looked that way, then frowned. "Is that Milo Lemon she's talking to?"

"So I was told."

"Yeah, not going to happen." He placed two fingers in his mouth and blew out a shrill whistle that carried over the noise of the slowly dispersing crowd. When Alice looked his way, he motioned for her to join them.

Even from where she stood, Jacqui saw Alice's reaction, but then the girl said something to Milo and the other girls and headed in their direction.

"Huh. I think I just got a teenage roll of the eyes," Mitch commented dryly.

"I know you did," Jacqui said, her own tone wryly empathetic.

"Think Uncle Mitch's whistle embarrassed her?"

"Oh, I wouldn't worry about it too much. She's just

in a teen mood today apparently. I've been the recipient of some of the attitude myself."

"And here I was hoping that sweet little Alice would just skip that moody, hormonal teen stage and go straight into responsible adulthood."

Jacqui laughed shortly. "Hold on to that dream, pal."

Both of them pasted on quick smiles when Alice joined them.

"We won, kid. By one goal. Scored by your uncle, I might add," Mitch boasted.

"Really? That's cool. Sorry I didn't see it. I was talking to some other kids."

"Good thing I have a healthy ego," Mitch murmured, looking only slightly deflated that neither of them had seen him make the goal.

"I was going to go play miniature golf with some new friends, but Jacqui said no."

Jacqui cocked an eyebrow. "I said I'd be happy to accompany you and drive you home afterward. The only thing I said no to was riding home with a teenage boy."

"You know Milo, Uncle Mitch," Alice said in an ingratiating tone. "His brother is one of your best friends."

"His brother is a friend," Mitch agreed. "I wouldn't say one of my best, but that's just semantics. And by the way, I agree a hundred percent with Jacqui. I wouldn't let you go riding around with Milo, either. Sounds like Jacqui made a nice offer to sit around here for another hour or so while you play mini-golf, by the way. She would probably rather go home."

Something in her uncle's tone made Alice stand a little straighter and carefully erase some of the discontent from her expression. "Thanks for offering, Jacqui, but I guess I'd rather go home, too," she said a bit hastily. "I need to take Waldo for a walk anyway."

Mitch nodded slightly in approval. "So I'll see you ladies in a little while."

"Will you be eating out, or are you joining us for dinner?" Jacqui asked him, using what she thought of as her "housekeeper voice" so he wouldn't think she was being nosey.

Wiping his face on a corner of the towel, Mitch replied, "If you're cooking, I'll join you. But don't go to any special trouble for me."

"Alice and I have to eat. I'll have something ready shortly after I get there."

"Sounds good. See you at home."

It wasn't home, Jacqui thought, walking to her car beside an atypically subdued Alice. Not for Mitch, and not for her. Neither of them needed to get too cozy with this setup. He'd be moving out soon—maybe even moving away, if he gave in to the restlessness she had sensed in him. She would do well to keep that eventuality in mind.

Chapter Four

Though she tried to convince him it wasn't necessary, Mitch helped Jacqui clear away the dinner dishes later that evening. Alice had gone to her room to take her almost-daily phone call from her mother in Hong Kong.

"Think she's telling her mother how unreasonable you and I were today not to let her hang out with a bunch of kids we don't know and ride in a car with an older boy?" Mitch asked.

Because Alice had been quiet during dinner and was still obviously irked that her spontaneous plans had been thwarted, Jacqui wasn't able to work up a smile in response to Mitch's half-teasing tone. "I hope not. But if she is, I hope her mother agrees with us."

"From what I've heard of her, she would. She's a long-distance parent, but Meagan said she's made it a point to back up Seth in whatever decisions he makes on Alice's behalf. At least in front of Alice. Seth and Colleen discuss her in private calls so they can present a united front to her."

Jacqui was already aware of that, of course, being a household insider, but she merely nodded. "I only met Colleen once, when she was in the state for a brief visit with Alice and her parents at Christmas, but it was obvious she loves Alice very much. She was very pleasant to me when she picked up Alice to take her to Heber Springs, where Colleen's parents live."

Colleen was tall, strikingly attractive, expensively fashionable. Although she had grown up in Arkansas, no traces of the South remained in her speech patterns— Jacqui would bet that had been a deliberate effort on Colleen's behalf. Rather than the slight drawl Jacqui had grown accustomed to hearing during the two years she'd lived in Little Rock, Colleen spoke rapidly, enunciating each syllable clearly. Her manner was courteous but somewhat brusque, hinting that her time was too valuable to waste on trivialities.

Jacqui supposed some people would be intimidated by the attorney, although she hadn't been. To her credit, Colleen hadn't been dismissive of her ex-husband's housekeeper, but instead had thanked her nicely for doing such a good job watching out for Alice when the other adults were occupied with their careers.

Seth's second wife was also a successful career woman, but other than that Meagan and Colleen couldn't be more different. Whereas Colleen was obsessed with career, Meagan's priority was family. The family she'd made with Seth and Alice, and the one in which she'd grown up, including her widowed mother and two younger siblings. Often she referred to Jacqui as a part of the family, a generous gesture that Jacqui appreciated even as she continually reminded herself that she was merely the housekeeper. If she were to fall and injure herself so that she was no longer able to fill the position, as had happened to the older woman who worked for Seth previously, they would hire someone to replace her, just as Jacqui had replaced Nina.

"Jacqui? Where have you drifted off to?"

She blinked up at Mitch, who was standing by the dishwasher and looking at her quizzically. Hastily placing the dish in her hand on the rack, she shook her head. "Sorry. I was just thinking about that little tiff with Alice. I've been lucky until this point, I guess. She's been absolutely no trouble at all every time I've watched her."

He shrugged. "If one quarrel and a chilly dinner are the worst you encounter, then you're lucky. I remember some of Madison's teen dramas. My folks were ready to lock her in the cellar a few times, I think. Guess it's a good thing we didn't actually have a cellar."

She smiled perfunctorily. "I guess every teen, no matter how generally well-behaved, hates hearing the word 'no.'"

He chuckled. "Oh, yeah. Didn't you have your share of teen rebellion when you were that age?"

Jacqui had rebelled every time her father had uprooted the family and drifted to another town where she and Olivia would be enrolled in yet another new school. Not that it had done her any good. Every time they'd moved, her parents had promised it would be the last time. They'd advised her to make the best of the life they led, to make new friends and experience new things—and to take care of her little sister while Mom and Dad were out doing odd jobs to support them.

The stabbing pain in her chest was familiar but still

agonizing. It seemed as though she'd thought of Olivia more than usual during the past few days. Partially, she supposed, because the anniversary of her sister's death was approaching—less than a month away now. And partially because the more Alice matured, the more she sometimes reminded Jacqui of Olivia—bright and inquisitive and imaginative, sweet-natured but with a stubborn streak that cropped up unexpectedly. Alice was only a few months younger than Olivia had been when she'd died.

There was no way that Alice would be riding in cars with teenage drivers on Jacqui's watch.

Determinedly, she buried the past deep in the back of her mind, though it had a nasty habit of clawing its way to the front when she was least prepared to handle it. Needing a change of subject, she turned the questioning to Mitch. "Have you given any more thought about a new place to live?"

He gave her a lopsided smile as he closed the dishwasher, his hand brushing hers with the movement. "Trying to get rid of me already?"

Something about his tone—or maybe that smile—made his teasing sound suspiciously like flirting. Probably it was just a habit of his—certainly nothing to take seriously.

When she didn't take him up on his verbal bait, he replied more seriously. "I talked to a few people today about some recommendations for Realtors and rental agents. And Mom gave me the name of a woman she knows who works part-time in real estate sales. I'll probably make a few calls tomorrow."

There was a distinct lack of enthusiasm in his voice. If he was thinking about looking for another rental, she didn't blame him for being less than excited about the search. She never liked doing that, either. It would be different when she started looking for a little place to buy, she promised herself. That lifelong ambition was going to be a joy to fulfill.

"Still looking for a place where you don't have to sign a lease?" she asked casually, her gaze on the counter she was wiping with a sponge.

Because she wasn't looking at him, she didn't see him shrug, but she heard the shift of fabric as his shoulder lifted in the negligent gesture. "Maybe. Or at least a place with a lenient lease-breaking policy."

She wrung out the towel and draped it over the sink to dry.

"My mom thinks I should buy a house," Mitch said with a chuckle. "She even suggested a couple of neighborhoods she thought suitable for me."

"I'm sure she's just trying to be helpful."

"Of course she is. Her first choice would be for me to buy Seth's house, which is still on the market. She pointed out how cozy it would be if I lived right across the street from my sister and brother-in-law."

"A little too cozy, maybe?"

He smiled. "Maybe. But I told her I'd think about it."

Outside in the backyard, Waldo barked. Jacqui glanced at the clock. "Alice usually goes out to play with him and give him a treat after dinner. He's probably wondering where she is."

"Does she usually talk this long with her mom?"

"No, not usually."

"Think she's still pouting?"

"Possibly."

Waldo barked again, the sound ending with a hint of a whine. Jacqui frowned. Alice was usually so attentive to her adored pet. She wouldn't punish Waldo because she was irked with the housekeeper; maybe Alice didn't realize how late it was getting.

She turned away from the sink. "I'll go check on her."

Saying he wanted to watch the news, Mitch headed for the den as Jacqui climbed the stairs toward Alice's room. Alice's door stood slightly ajar, and Jacqui could hear the teen laughing and giggling from the top of the stairs. It was not the voice she used with her mother, but rather the sillier, slangier tone that signified she was talking with one of her friends.

"He's so hot. And I think he likes me," she confided breathlessly to the person on the other side of the call. She giggled in response to whatever her friend said. "Yeah, he said he—"

Jacqui cleared her throat noisily.

"Uh, gotta go, Tiff. I'll call you later, okay?"

By the time Jacqui tapped lightly on the open door and stepped into the room, Alice had already disconnected the call.

"Everything okay?" Jacqui asked casually. "Waldo is looking for his evening treat."

Alice tossed back her curly hair and slid her phone in her pocket. "Okay, I'm on my way down. I was going to play with him for a while anyway before bed."

"He'll like that. Um, Alice?"

"Yes?"

Jacqui laced her fingers in front of her, mentally mapping a path to the conversational destination she hoped to achieve. "Milo *is* cute."

Alice's quick smile was both appreciative and suspicious. "Yeah, he's okay," she agreed a little too nonchalantly.

"But you know, of course, that he's too old to be hanging out with a fourteen-year-old. He should be flirting with girls his age—not girls almost four years younger. Just as your own friends should be fifteen and younger."

Alice exhaled sharply in exasperation. "Geez, Jacqui, we were just talking. But still, four years is hardly anything. Dad's almost four years older than Meagan and nobody has even mentioned it."

"It's different after you're eighteen. Trust me, those four years between fourteen and eighteen are a lot more significant than you think. Eighteen-year-olds have less supervision. They're driving and dating and other things you aren't quite ready for yet. You know your dad doesn't want you hanging out alone with boys just yet, and I agree with him. Don't be in too big a hurry to grow up and get involved with relationship drama. Have fun with your friends while you can still be just kids."

"I wasn't going out on a date with Milo. I just wanted to get a ride home with him. I'd have been perfectly safe. He said he's been driving for two whole years."

"It's still better if you don't ride alone with teen drivers just yet."

Jacqui didn't know how to explain that it was more than just the car ride—though that alone would have been enough for her to turn down Alice's request. She hadn't liked the way Milo had looked at sweet, naive Alice—and that would have been hard to explain to the girl. For one thing, Alice was as likely to be flattered by the attention as alarmed by the boy's intentions.

"You're totally overreacting," Alice muttered. "You don't even know Milo."

"I know a little more than you give me credit for,"

Jacqui replied evenly. "I've been around a while longer than you have, Alice."

Alice looked less than convinced. "I'm going down to play with Waldo."

Smothering a sigh, Jacqui thought about how glad she would be when Seth and Meagan returned from their trip. Between Mitch's unexpected stayover and Alice's out-of-the-blue hormonal rebellion, this week was turning out to be much more complicated than she had ever anticipated. She wanted to go back to being nothing more than the daytime housekeeper and part-time cook, efficient but basically invisible. Life was so much simpler that way, with way fewer obstacles waiting to trip her up.

Speaking of hazardous pitfalls...

She crossed paths with Mitch on the stairs as she headed down a few moments after Alice and he was on his way up. Though the stairway was plenty wide enough for both of them, it felt suddenly smaller when she and Mitch stood face to face.

"I was just going up to log some computer time in my room before bed," he explained with a smile. "Thought I'd do some real estate searches and answer a few emails."

"I'll be turning in early tonight, too." She was suddenly very tired, and she was aware that the exhaustion was more mental than physical. "I'll just finish up a few things in the kitchen and then I'll go to bed when Alice does. Is there anything else you need this evening?"

He chuckled. "There's that housekeeper voice again. No, Jacqui, there's nothing else I need tonight. And if there were, I'd get it for myself."

She nodded a little stiffly and took another step down. Because Mitch moved at the same time, and apparently misjudged her path, their shoulders collided. So much for having plenty of room on the stairway, she thought, pressing her hand to the wall for balance. Mitch caught her other arm as though to steady her.

"Sorry. You okay?"

"Of course. It was just a bump."

"My fault. I got distracted—wasn't looking where I was going."

As she recalled, he'd been looking at her face when he'd moved. Was he saying that she was a distraction to him? Or was she being as silly and flustered as Alice by an intriguing guy's attention?

Annoyed with herself, she started to move again, only to be detained by the light grasp Mitch still had on her forearm. She looked up at him with questioningly raised eyebrows. He stood now on the step below her, which brought their faces close to the same level. And he was looking directly at her mouth.

Self-consciously and without thinking, she moistened her lips. His eyes narrowed as though in response to what might have looked like an invitation, she realized hastily. Awkwardly, she took another step down, thinking she would hurry on her way, but all that did was bring her almost into his arms when he shifted on the step to accommodate her.

Mitch chuckled and caught her other shoulder with his free hand. "Hang on, we're going to knock each other down the stairs if we keep this up."

Pressing back against the wall, she tried to speak in the same light tone he'd used. "We do seem to be colliding a lot this weekend. It'll be a wonder if I don't cause you bodily damage before you find another place to stay."

His grin widened. "Is that a hint? Trying to run me off?"

Studying his devastatingly attractive smile through her lashes, she muttered, "I probably should be."

His smile faltered, but she slipped out of his grasp and moved quickly down the stairs before he could reply with whatever he might have said.

Some role model for Alice she was turning out to be, she thought in annoyance. When it came to a cute, completely unsuitable guy with a sexy smile, it seemed that neither of them had a lick of sense.

Brooks and Dunn wailed that "cowgirls don't cry" as Mitch skillfully wielded a number 69 Beaver blade on the adolescent hand he viewed through a magnifying glass. Mitch liked an eclectic selection of music while he worked; his amplified music player held an extensive collection of country, rock and alternative songs. The selection was varied enough that he didn't get bored with it and his assistants rarely complained, as they did about Dr. Burkett's vast library of polka tunes.

Seated at one side of the hand table, gloved and gowned, Mitch worked swiftly to repair the extensive damage that had been done to the boy's hand when a friend slammed a car door on it. He didn't want to take longer than necessary to make the repairs. More than two hours' use of the inflated tourniquet cutting off the blood supply to the hand increased the risk of long-term muscle damage.

His first assistant, a third-year surgical resident, stood at the other side of the hand table, watching the delicate procedure intently and eagerly and performing as much of the operation as Mitch allowed. A fourth-year medical student stood nearby, craning her head for a better view while doing her best to stay out of the way. At the end of the hand table, next to the vigilantly guarded sterile instrument tray, stood a surgical technician with whom Mitch had worked many long hours in various operations. They'd operated together so often that Brenda often knew what he needed before he even asked, handing over instruments in a smooth, practiced rhythm that made the process easier for both of them.

There wasn't a lot of time for chitchat during this procedure, as there was in some longer operations, but Brenda still asked at one point, "How's the house search coming along?"

"Haven't looked much yet," Mitch answered, taking a moment to stretch his neck muscles, which were tightening up from being held so long in the same position. "It's only been a few days."

"Still staying with your sister?"

"Well, in my sister's house. She's on a European vacation with her husband. Her stepdaughter and housekeeper are sharing the house with me for now."

"How old is the stepdaughter?"

"Fourteen."

"Challenging age."

Mitch thought of the chilly treatment Alice had given Jacqui during dinner last night. "You can say that again."

The boy on the table was only fifteen. And right-handed. Mitch turned his attention to the surgery again, determined that the kid would have full use of that hand again. Mitch loved his job—repairing young bodies damaged by accidents or ailments. The hours were long, the physical demands grueling, the emotional toll occasionally high—but he thrived on it. Sure, there were times when he wondered why he hadn't gone into carpentry; it was a lot less stressful to repair broken cabinets than broken bones, especially because he'd chosen a pediatric specialty with so much at risk. But those fleeting thoughts never lasted long. He was doing what he'd been called to do.

Focused intently on the retractor he held, the resident commented through his mask, "Living with a teenager and a senior citizen is probably making you impatient to get back into a place of your own."

Mitch spared a glance upward. "A senior citizen?"

The resident never looked up from his task. "The housekeeper. Just an assumption."

"An incorrect one."

"Oops. My bad."

The medical student giggled, then subsided quickly into silence, as though embarrassed to have called any attention to herself. Mitch didn't even glance her way but finished the operation without further conversation, an image of Jacqui in the back of his mind. How would she feel if she'd heard herself referred to as a senior citizen?

Leaving the capable resident to close, he stood, taking care not to contaminate the sterile field around the patient. He backed away from the table, his gloved hands held above his waist. The medical student moved up eagerly to take over first assistant position while Brenda watched zealously to make sure the sterile field remained unbroken.

Once out of range, Mitch dropped his arms and arched his back to loosen the muscles there. He had another surgery scheduled that afternoon, but he had an hour free for lunch first. He would eat that meal at his desk while he checked messages and returned calls.

The sandwich sat half eaten on his desk and the list of

phone numbers were held unheeded in his hand a short while later. His thoughts had drifted to Jacqui again. Specifically, he recalled that moment in the stairway when their faces were on a level and her freshly moistened lips had been only a whisper away from his. He could almost feel his hands on her arms as he'd steadied her. Her body had been warm through her thin cotton blouse, and he could only imagine how soft her skin would be over the work-toned muscles beneath.

Definitely not a senior citizen.

He supposed he should find another place to live soon. His growing attraction to Jacqui was likely to get awkward if he stayed there much longer. As if it weren't already awkward enough, at least for him.

Fortunately Alice's sulks didn't last through Monday. By the time she and Jacqui had run errands together and shared lunch at Alice's favorite Chinese buffet, the girl was back in her usual good spirits. Neither of them mentioned the disagreement in the park. Jacqui wondered if she should bring it up again, just as another opportunity to make sure Alice understood what had been at stake, but she decided to let it go.

Mitch had let her know he wouldn't be home from the hospital until late that evening, so she and Alice shared a quiet evening together. After a cooling swim in the backyard pool, they spent a couple of hours knitting in front of the TV. Jacqui finished some projects for her friend's boutique while Alice worked on a pale-green bear she would stuff with batting and add to her children's hospital gifts.

"It's kind of quiet around here without Mitch, isn't it?" Alice remarked as they put away their yarns and needles.

Jacqui smiled faintly. "A little."

"He's fun to be around. I'm glad he's my uncle now. And Madison's great as my new aunt, even if she has been so busy lately in her psychiatry residency that I've hardly seen her."

"You're very fortunate to have found such a nice bonus family." Alice didn't care for the term "stepfamily," so Jacqui was careful to avoid using it.

"I am lucky. I've got lots of family now. My dad. My mom. My grandparents in Heber Springs. My mom's sister and her family in Colorado—I don't see them much, but they're nice. My dad's father in Dallas. And now Meagan and her family. Mimi and Mitch and Madison."

Wondering a bit where this was going, Jacqui said lightly, "You forgot to mention Waldo."

Alice giggled. "Anyway, I'm glad I have a lot of family."

"Then I'm glad you're glad."

The girl smiled again.

"I know your grandparents are looking forward to seeing you this weekend." Beginning Friday, Alice would spend a few days with her maternal grandparents in Heber Springs. She would come home next Tuesday, two days before Seth and Meagan returned from their trip.

Her grandparents had hinted broadly that Alice should spend the entire two weeks with them while her dad and stepmother were away, but Alice had politely thanked them and reminded them about her obligations to her swim team. As it was, she would be missing a couple of practices to spend a few days with them. Jacqui knew Alice was fond of her grandparents, and she spent at least one weekend with them a month, but she had confided to Jacqui that sometimes there she missed her friends and activities at home.

Only then did it occur to Jacqui that she and Mitch would be alone in the house while Alice was with her grandparents. When they'd first made all these plans, Jacqui had assumed she would be returning to her apartment during those days, but that was before the leak had ruined her floors. She'd gone by that morning and the new carpeting still had not been installed. Her apartment was a mess at the moment, with her belongings piled on larger furniture and the floors stripped down to bare particle board, some of which had warped from water damage. The manager had assured her the repairs were being done as quickly as possible, but because several apartments had been damaged—and not all the other tenants had someplace else to stay—it was taking a while to get to them all.

She supposed it wouldn't be a problem sharing the house with Mitch for a few days. It wasn't as though he was here all that much. She would take great care to avoid any more awkward encounters like the one on the staircase. Staying in the background as the cook and housekeeper was the safest course—and one she fully intended to follow.

Or maybe he'd find someplace else to stay by then, she thought without much optimism.

"I guess it will be nice to stay with Grammy and Grampa—even though I was just there last month."

Hearing a distinct lack of enthusiasm in the girl's voice, Jacqui spoke cheerily, "You know how they love spending time with you. And your Grampa's going to take you fishing, isn't he? You always enjoy that."

Alice nodded. "Yeah, I like fishing. But I'd kind of like to stay here with you and Mitch, too. That was fun the other night—playing board games, I mean. And Mitch said maybe he'd take me to the hospital to deliver toys and visit with some of the kids this weekend, but I told him I couldn't because I'm staying with my grandparents."

"I'm sure he'll take you another time."

"Yeah, he said he would. But still—"

"Your grandparents would be very disappointed if you cancel your visit with them, Alice."

"I won't cancel," Alice promised. "I know that would hurt their feelings. But don't do anything too much fun with Uncle Mitch while I'm gone, okay?" she added with a teasing smile.

Jacqui forced a smile. "I wouldn't worry about that. Your uncle will probably hang out with his friends again when he's not working, and I have a few tentative plans. My friend Alexis and I have been trying to get together for lunch and shopping, and we're hoping our schedules will both be clear this weekend."

Alexis Johnson was one of Jacqui's few good friends in Little Rock, outside the family she worked for. They'd met in a four-week vegetarian cooking class they had both taken last year and had gotten together occasionally since. Alexis traveled a lot in her job as a flight attendant and was involved in several organizations that took a great deal of her time, but she and Jacqui tried to get together whenever they could for a few hours of girl talk and relaxation. On the surface, the friends seemed to have little in common. Alexis was very much into fashion and appearance, whereas Jacqui had only passing interest in clothes and shoes, but they'd been drawn together by similar senses of humor and a mutual fondness for Indian food.

Looking vaguely surprised, Alice tilted her head in

Jacqui's direction. Was the girl having a hard time envisioning that Jacqui had a life outside the Llewellyn family? Okay, maybe she didn't do much other than work, Jacqui admitted silently, but she did have a few friends and hobbies of her own.

"I thought maybe you and Mitch would do something while I'm gone. You know, like go out for dinner together or something." Alice's tone was just a little too nonchalant, which made Jacqui frown suspiciously. Surely the girl wasn't matchmaking?

"If your uncle wants me to make dinner for him, I'd be happy to do so," she answered evenly. "That's part of my job."

"I didn't mean for your job," Alice insisted, raising Jacqui's suspicions even further. "I mean—well, uncle Mitch is cute, right? And he's pretty close to your age. Not even as much different as Milo and me... even though I still don't think four years is all that much," she added in a grumble.

Jacqui had no intention of getting into another debate about whether it was appropriate for Alice to hang out with an almost-eighteen-year-old boy—it could only lead to another bout of sulks because Jacqui had no intention of changing her mind. Nor did she want to get into a discussion about why she and Mitch were not a good match despite being single adults of close to the same age.

"Would you carry these empty teacups to the kitchen for me, please?" she requested, folding away her knitting as she spoke. "It's getting late. If you want to play with Waldo a little before bedtime, you'd better go on out."

But Alice wasn't quite finished with their conversation. "It's just...well, like we said, it's nice to have family."

"I have family, Alice," Jacqui countered gently. She supposed it was touching that Alice worried about her being alone, even if it was somewhat awkward. "My parents are still living. I talk with them occasionally, even if we aren't as close as you are with your parents."

"But you really like our family, right? I mean, Uncle Mitch and Meagan and Madison and Mimi and my dad and all. And they all really like you, too."

"That's nice to hear. Now go play with Waldo."

"I just thought…maybe…if you were dating someone yourself, you'd be a little more…you know, relaxed about things."

Jacqui nearly sighed in response to the muttered remark. So it all came back to Alice's new crush on Milo Lemon. So much for the sweet motives Jacqui had just attributed to the wily teen.

She glanced at her watch. "You have half an hour to play with your dog before bedtime. Keep procrastinating and you'll find out just how unrelaxed I can be."

Alice sighed gustily and snatched up the empty teacups. "Fine. Be all grouchy. Just because I wanted you to be happy and stuff."

Torn between exasperation and wry amusement, Jacqui merely motioned her out of the room.

Chapter Five

Jacqui found herself preparing dinner Tuesday evening for Mitch's family. It had all begun with a call from LaDonna early that morning. LaDonna had said that her sisters-in-law wanted to come see Meagan's house sometime that day. They were disappointed, LaDonna said, that Meagan was out of town during their visit, but that was their own fault.

"I told them when they called to arrange this visit that Meagan would be out of town on her belated honeymoon trip during this time, but they said it was the best week for them to come," she said into the phone, her voice low so as not to carry to her guests in another room. "They really have no reason to complain about missing Meagan."

"I'm sure she would have loved to see them, too."

"They would like to come see her house. Don't know why, when she's not even there, but they've got it in their heads they want to come by. And to be honest, I'm running out of things to do to entertain them. Do you mind a visit sometime later today, Jacqui?"

"Of course not. It's your daughter's home—you're certainly welcome here."

"Thank you. All we've done the past few days is drive around and dine out or eat here and I just don't know what else to do with them. They seem to only enjoy eating and chatting and riding in the car," LaDonna added with a wry laugh.

Jacqui spoke impulsively, "Why don't you plan to bring them here for dinner? I'm sure Alice would love playing hostess at a dinner party for her aunts."

LaDonna had jumped on that offer eagerly, despite her token protests that it would be too much trouble for Jacqui to put a dinner party together that quickly. Reminding LaDonna that she would be making dinner for herself and Alice and Mitch anyway, Jacqui assured her it would be no trouble to add a few guests. They might as well invite Madison, too, and make it a family gathering.

Jacqui knew it was a little strange that there would be a dinner party in Meagan's home when Meagan wasn't even there, but she was confident Meagan and Seth would be more amused than annoyed. Both were well accustomed to Meagan's aunt's eccentricities. And both would do anything to assist LaDonna with anything she needed.

Doreen O'Connor and Kathleen Baker were twins in their mid-sixties. Jacqui had met them only once, at Meagan and Seth's wedding, and that had been only a fleeting encounter. Although they looked very much alike, Jacqui didn't think they were identical twins. She saw a few differences in them that helped her tell them apart when LaDonna reintroduced them that evening. LaDonna did not refer to Jacqui as her daughter's housekeeper but as a friend of the family. Jacqui didn't bother to correct her, even though she certainly wasn't embarrassed by her job title. She figured the aunts knew her role in the family.

"And here," LaDonna added with a warm smile, "is my new granddaughter, Alice."

The sisters greeted Alice pleasantly, urging her to call them Aunt Doreen and Aunt Kathleen. With her usual ebullience, Alice was soon chattering away to them as if she'd known them for years rather than having met them only once before. She led them off on a tour of the house before dinner. It didn't take her long to charm them with her excellent company manners.

Mitch's sister Madison arrived shortly after LaDonna and the twins. She made a little face at Jacqui, who had opened the door for her. "Sorry Mom roped you into this," she murmured. "Is there anything I can do to help?"

"It's no trouble," Jacqui assured her honestly. "I always enjoy cooking for a dinner party. Everyone is gathered in the living room. I have everything under control in the kitchen, so why don't you join your family?"

"Is Mitch here yet?"

"Not yet. He just called to say he's running a little late and for us to start dinner without him if we need to."

Smoothing her breeze-ruffled blond hair, Madison chuckled. "The surgeon's life. That's why I chose psychiatry. Shorter hours."

Madison always teased about that, but Jacqui didn't believe it any more than Madison's family did. During the one-year-plus that she'd known Meagan's younger sister, it had become clear to Jacqui that Madison was the most empathetic of the Baker siblings. Meagan and Mitch had both chosen surgery because they enjoyed the challenge of fixing something physical that was broken. Madison was more interested in soothing mental and emotional pain, whether triggered by chemical imbalances or life experiences.

Jacqui was just putting the finishing touches on individual Caprese salads when LaDonna wandered into the kitchen. "Can I help you with anything, dear?"

"No, thank you, LaDonna. Everything is almost ready."

The other woman had insisted from the beginning of their acquaintance that Jacqui should call her by her first name rather than the more formal Mrs. Baker. Fifty-nine and widowed for several years, LaDonna Baker eschewed stuffiness and formality, treating everyone with the same easy warmth. A CPA, she had gone back to work four days a week as a bookkeeper after the death of her mother last year. Like her three offspring, LaDonna didn't seem to be content unless she was gainfully employed. She had taken a week's vacation from her job to entertain her sisters-in-law.

"If you think everyone is ready to eat, I can start serving. Mitch should be here soon, but he didn't want anyone to have to wait for him."

"He works too hard. All my children do." LaDonna shook her head in slight disapproval. Something about her expression reminded Jacqui very much of Meagan. Both Meagan and Madison favored their fair, slender mother. Although Mitch bore some family resemblance, Jacqui assumed he must look more like his late father.

Responding to LaDonna's comment, Jacqui nodded in agreement. "Yes, they do."

"And so do you. You've had your hands full taking care of Alice and Mitch while Meagan and Seth are away, haven't you? And I've added to your work by bringing my sisters-in-law for dinner."

"I didn't mind at all."

"I can't tell you how much I appreciate this. I'm running out of ways to entertain them," LaDonna confided in a murmur. "They get bored easily and want me to keep coming up with new things for us to do. At least a dinner party here is something different."

Jacqui chuckled. "Then we'll make sure they're entertained."

She honestly didn't mind helping out with entertaining the women, even if it was just to serve them dinner. Jacqui had grown very fond of LaDonna during the past year. LaDonna had been nothing but gracious to her, and Jacqui admired the way LaDonna had welcomed Alice into her family. Jacqui doubted any future biological grandchildren would be treated with any more interest and affection from their "Mimi."

Jacqui had worried about LaDonna at the end of last year. Already saddened by the untimely loss of her husband, LaDonna had worn herself almost to the ends of her physical and emotional limits caring for her dying mother. She was still too thin, in Jacqui's private opinion, but she seemed to be recovering now from her grief and stress. Her job had helped distract her from that trying time. As had her joy in her three children and her new granddaughter.

"Don't you even think about staying in here and serving while we're eating," the older woman warned with a shake of her finger. "You are eating with us, right?"

The formal dining table seated eight, so there was room for Jacqui to join them, even though she would have been just as happy to eat at the breakfast-nook table where the casual family usually dined. But because LaDonna had already insisted she join them when they'd first discussed a menu for the evening, Jacqui knew there was no use in demurring. "Yes, I'll join you. I can serve and eat at the same time."

LaDonna nodded in approval. "Good."

Jacqui slipped a pan of seasoned salmon fillets and a separate dish of asparagus spears into the oven to bake while they ate their salads; she had a Dijon-dill sauce chilling in the fridge to spoon over the fish she would serve with herbed rice and the lemon-sprinkled asparagus. She'd long since learned that careful timing was the secret to success with a dinner party, especially if she was eating and serving.

Mitch rushed into the dining room just as Jacqui finished setting the salads in front of their guests. "Sorry I'm late," he said a little breathlessly. "I had a procedure that took longer than I expected this afternoon."

Welcoming him warmly, his adoring mother and aunts presented cheeks for him to kiss. Grinning, he rounded the table, planting noisy kisses on those cheeks, then on his sister's and niece's for good measure.

Alice giggled. "You didn't kiss Jacqui."

Jacqui forced her smile to remain in place even as she shot Alice a look. "That's not necessary," she said lightly. "I'm not family."

Chuckling, Mitch leaned down to press a smacking kiss to her too-warm cheek. "Of course you are," he said heartily. "You came with the package."

She busied herself with her salad as he took his seat. Apparently taking pity on her, Madison spoke quickly, asking Alice about her swim team, which started the conversation in a new direction.

Grateful, Jacqui glanced Madison's way, but because Mitch was seated next to his younger sister, she accidentally caught his eyes instead. He winked at her, making her look quickly back down at the tomatoes, mozzarella and basil on her plate. Although this was her favorite salad, suddenly she found it difficult to swallow.

Jacqui fit in very well with his family, Mitch mused during the scrumptious dessert that followed her excellent meal. But she seemed to be doing everything she could to remain separate from them. She jumped up constantly during the meal to wait on everyone, serving from the left and removing from the right with the efficiency of a banquet server rather than an attentive hostess. She might as well have worn a name tag identifying her as an employee of the household. He wasn't sure how, exactly, his mom had roped her into this, but Jacqui handled a last-minute dinner party with the same efficient aplomb with which she did all the responsibilities of her job.

To give them credit, his aunts didn't treat her any differently than they did any of the others at this somewhat unconventional dinner party. With their usual curiosity—okay, nosiness—they eagerly included Jacqui in the series of personal questions they threw at Mitch, Madison and even Alice. Jacqui, he noted, was good at giving polite nonanswers—so skilled at it that it was only later one realized she hadn't really divulged much information at all.

"Do you want to be a lawyer like your father or a doctor like your stepmother and her brother and sister?" Kathleen asked Alice during the dessert. "Or maybe a CPA like your new grandmother?"

"Both my parents are lawyers," Alice replied, carefully including her mother in the list. "But I want to be an orthodontist."

"An orthodontist?" Doreen smiled. "That's not something you hear very often from a girl your age."

Alice grinned, displaying the braces she'd been wearing for just more than a year. "I've had plenty of chances to watch what my orthodontist does. It looks interesting. And I like the thought of making people feel better about their smiles."

"That's very nice," Kathleen approved. "A good reason to go into a field. That's why all LaDonna's children went into medicine, I'm sure—to help people. Not for the money."

Madison laughed wryly. "You really must have stronger reasons to go into medicine than money. In my opinion, no amount of pay is a good-enough incentive alone to get through medical school. There are a lot less stressful ways to make a decent salary."

Alice giggled. "Dad and Meagan are always play-arguing about which is harder, medical school or law school."

"Medical school," Mitch and Madison said in unison.

"That's hardly fair," Mitch's mother commented. "Seth isn't here to defend his side of the argument."

"Wouldn't matter. He'd be wrong," Mitch stated firmly, making Alice giggle again.

"I wish they were here," Doreen remarked with exaggerated wistfulness. "We haven't seen them since their wedding. I was sure we told them then when we'd be here for a visit."

LaDonna shook her head firmly. "You said then that you were thinking about coming in September. It was only after Meagan and Seth made their travel arrangements for Europe that you switched the date to this week. The change worked fine for my schedule, but Meagan and Seth couldn't just cancel or reschedule their one chance at a belated honeymoon trip."

Mitch knew his mom would get chippy if her sisters-in-law continued to criticize Meagan and Seth, even in subtle jabs. He was relieved when Madison, ever the peacemaker, spoke up quickly.

"Jacqui, this cake is absolutely decadent. Sin on a plate but worth every calorie."

Mitch saw the flash of pride in Jacqui's eyes before she replied in a stage whisper, "Don't tell any of the others, but it's actually a healthy recipe. It's low-fat, low-sugar. Applesauce and crushed pineapple are what make it so moist and sweet."

"You're kidding! Then maybe I should have a second slice," Madison teased. "Really, it's delicious."

The others all added their compliments to the dessert, although Mitch noticed Kathleen, the pickiest eater in the family, now eyed the cake with a little more suspicion. Both the twins were heavy, but Kathleen was the bread-and-sweet fanatic, refusing to even consider gentle suggestions that she should make healthy changes in her diet. He found it amusing that she'd been wolfing down the rich-tasting dessert with enthusiasm until she'd heard it wasn't actually so bad for her.

Jacqui really was an excellent cook. He'd heard Meagan and Seth comment about how much they enjoyed the meals she prepared for them. Seth's former housekeeper had been more of a traditional meat-and-potatoes chef, leaning heavily on Tex-Mex recipes. Although Seth had confided that he'd loved Nina's cooking, he had also admitted that Jacqui's lighter touch with fresh vegetables and fruits and leaner meats was a much healthier diet for him and his daughter.

Jacqui took as much pride in her work as any of them did, Mitch mused. Yet he suspected she was as aware as he was that housekeeping hadn't been listed in the potential careers for Alice. It was a perfectly respectable and worthwhile job, but he had to admit it wasn't one that immediately came to mind. He would like to know more about how Jacqui had ended up in this particular career—and if she had any plans to do anything different in the future—but she was so darned skittish about personal questions.

Was it that evasiveness that made him so increasingly curious about her? Was she simply an intriguing puzzle he was drawn to solve? He'd always liked a challenge. But it felt as though there was more to his attraction to Jacqui. Had been from the start. Even though she hadn't given him even a hint of encouragement.

Well, not specifically, anyway. He thought of that moment when their paths had crossed on the stairs and he'd gotten the feeling she felt some sparks between them, too. Had that been entirely in his own imagination?

"Your mother pointed out Seth's house that's for sale across the street, Mitchell," Doreen remarked, seemingly out of the blue. He felt a muscle tense in the back of his neck. "It's a very nice place," she added. "You should consider buying it for yourself now that you need a new home."

Kathleen nodded energetically. "It's lovely to live close to your sister, Mitchell. Doreen and I have never lived more than ten miles apart in our lives, and we don't regret it for one moment."

"Twelve miles."

Kathleen turned to her twin with a frown. "What?"

"The house I lived in with Gerald— That was my second late husband, Jacqui, God rest his soul. Anyway, that house was twelve miles from the town house you lived in then. You told Mitchell we'd never lived more than ten miles apart."

"Oh, good grief, Doreen, there's no need to get that specific. What does it matter if it was ten or twelve?"

"Well, you said ten."

Though he'd hoped the tiff would distract her, Kathleen turned determinedly back to Mitch. "The point is, it's nice to live close to your family, even if they drive you crazy sometimes," she added pointedly. "I think it's a sign that the other house is still available just when your apartment burned down."

Kathleen had always been led by "signs" and "feelings." Despite her own resistance to any well-intentioned guidance toward herself, she didn't mind giving frequent advice to others, something the rest of the family tolerated indulgently. Most of the time.

Although her twin had been widowed twice, Kathleen had never married. She claimed she'd had a lifelong "feeling" that she was meant to stay single and in a position to offer helpful, objective advice to others on maintaining their marriages and raising their children.

Mitch had always figured that for the sake of the twins' relationship, it was just as well Doreen had never had children with either of her husbands. Kathleen would have certainly been compelled to give her sister guidance on how to raise them, which Doreen would probably have resented eventually. As it was, both Kathleen and Doreen had been active, if long-distance, observers of their brother's family life, asking questions and tendering parenting critiques whenever they visited. Mitch wondered if his dad had chosen to move from his childhood home in St. Louis to take a position at the university in Little Rock specifically to get a little farther away from his lovable but meddling older sisters.

He didn't voice that pondering aloud, of course. "I said I would think about it."

"A man—a doctor, to boot—should have his own house," Doreen commented.

"And a family to fill it with," Kathleen added with a sage nod. "You're over thirty now, Mitchell. Time passes before you realize it."

He kept his smile in place with an effort. "I'll keep that in mind, Aunt Kathleen. Thanks."

He shot a glance at Madison, silently urging her to change the subject. But she merely gave him an exaggeratedly innocent smile in return, probably glad the aunts weren't quizzing her about her life choices instead.

"Even if you don't buy Seth's house—and I can't imagine why you aren't jumping at that chance, he'd probably make you a good deal, being family and all. Where was I? Oh, yes, even if you don't buy that one, you should consider buying or building rather than renting. Much better investment of your money."

"Thanks for the advice, Aunt Doreen." He searched his mind quickly for a change of topic. "How's your sciatica been lately?"

"Don't get her started on that," Kathleen cut in quickly. "I agree with her on the buying versus renting. I've done both, you know, and when I was younger, I preferred owning my own place. Now that I'm older, it's just too much upkeep. The senior living apartments Doreen and I are in now are perfect for us. But because you have no plans to leave Little Rock, you might as well invest in a nice house where you can settle down and raise a family."

Mitch noticed that Jacqui was focusing studiously on her tea mug, as if reading futures in the dregs there. He wondered whimsically if she could see his.

Kathleen's eyes narrowed on his face when he didn't immediately respond to her comments. Another one of her "feelings"? "You aren't planning on leaving Little Rock, are you, Mitchell?"

"I get tempting offers from other places occasionally, but I don't have any specific plans to move," he replied lightly. "I just like keeping my options open, you know?"

His mother made a funny little sound, as if she, too, had heard a hint of restlessness in his voice that was new to her. "Mitch? You're thinking about leaving Arkansas?"

Had she really just paled a shade at the very possibility? He tugged lightly at the collar of his white shirt. He'd left the top two buttons unfastened, but it still felt as if it had just tightened somehow. "I said I have no real plans to do so, Mom. I'm just trying to make the best decisions for my future. It hasn't even been a week since my place burned down and I've been pretty busy at work since. You can't expect me to buy a house in only a couple of days."

Taking pity either on him or their mother, Madison interceded then. "Tell our aunts about the trip you're taking to Peru, Mitch."

He appreciated the effort, but he wasn't sure that was the best change of subject. His mother was already fretting about whether he would be safe on that trek with his buddies, even though he'd assured her it was not a dangerous trip. Certainly not on the level of climbing Mt. Everest or some of the other risky adventure vacations he could have taken. Downplaying even a hint of peril, he gave his aunts a quick description of the trip his friends had mapped out for a five-day trek to Machu Picchu.

"I'm leaving in about six weeks with some friends. I'm really looking forward to it," he added candidly. "I need the break."

He answered several questions about his plans, promising everyone again that he would be perfectly safe. Seeing that his mom was looking a little tense again, he was relieved when Alice launched into a chatty description of her visit to Europe with her mother the previous summer. Mitch figured Alice had been quiet for a while to let the others talk, probably in an attempt to not monopolize the conversation, but now the pent-up words tumbled out of her. He was selfishly pleased when the aunts began to question her instead of grilling him about his plans. Ostensibly, they were prompting Alice for more information about her vacation, but he knew they really wanted to hear more details about the woman who'd previously been married to their niece's new husband.

Even if Alice suspected their motives, which he doubted, she didn't mind. She enjoyed talking about her mother, making it clear she had few resentments toward the attorney who had chosen a career path that had taken her so very far from her only daughter. Seth really had done a good job of keeping the lines of communication open between his daughter and his ex-wife, Mitch mused. And Meagan supported that agenda completely.

Which only proved, he thought, that families didn't have to live right next door to each other to remain close and connected. Not that he was planning to leave any time soon—but if that was what it took to fill that growing emptiness inside him, then he liked to think he could do so without sacrificing what he had here.

Looking around the table at the smiling faces surrounding him—his family—he paused on Jacqui. She was smiling, too, as she paid attention to Alice's stories, which she'd probably heard many times before. But there was an expression in her eyes that looked all too familiar to him. As if she, too, was still looking for something she couldn't quite define.

Or was he letting himself be overly influenced by Aunt Kathleen's "feelings"? To be perfectly honest, he had no idea what Jacqui was thinking. Which only made her all the more intriguing to him.

"That was very nice of you to cook for my aunts this evening," Mitch said to Jacqui much later that night. Alice was already in bed, and Jacqui had been checking to make sure the back kitchen door was locked before turning in herself when Mitch wandered into the room.

She hadn't seen him for the past couple hours since his family had left and he'd excused himself to do some work at the desk in his room. She'd spent those hours cleaning up from the impromptu party, watching Alice swim and play with Waldo for a little while, then completing her latest knitting project for a short while after Alice had gone upstairs. Maybe she'd still been wired from the somewhat hectic day; only now, at just after eleven, did she feel relaxed enough to attempt sleep.

Because she'd already turned off all the lights except the night-light over the stove, the room lay in deep, hushed shadows. Even Waldo had gone to bed, judging from the silence in the backyard. A more fanciful person might imagine that she and Mitch were the only two people on the street still awake at this hour.

"You did an amazing job putting together a dinner party on such short notice. The food was excellent, as always."

She had a weakness for compliments about her cooking. She did try very hard to prepare good food that other people enjoyed eating. "I'm glad you liked it. And it wasn't much trouble. I didn't mind at all helping your mom out."

"I could tell she was grateful. She already liked you, but now you're her new best friend," he said with a chuckle.

She smiled. "I like her, too."

Her smile faded when she tried to think of a tactful way to phrase her next question. "Does your mother look—well, healthy to you, lately? I mean, it's probably a silly question with all three of her children being doctors, but she's just so thin."

Although he looked a little surprised, he shook his head. "It's not a silly question. I appreciate your concern for her. She's been a little stressed with the aunts here visiting, but I think she's fine. She's always been slim, and she tends to forget to eat when she has a lot going on. Remember how thin she got that last month of my grandmother's life? We were all fussing at her then."

Jacqui did remember. She hadn't seen as much of LaDonna then because that had been before Seth and Meagan married, but she had seen enough to be concerned. Not even quite sixty yet, LaDonna looked young for her age normally, but that sad and stressful time had taken a toll on her. Since Seth and Meagan's wedding, she'd looked happier and healthier—but the past couple of times Jacqui had seen LaDonna, she'd thought she noticed a change again. And not for the better.

Maybe she was just overreacting to a couple of pounds' weight loss. As much as Jacqui liked all of this family, she supposed she was a little too concerned about their well-being. Her job was simply to take care of this house and watch out for Alice occasionally. And if none of LaDonna's three physician offspring were concerned about their mother's health, then who was she to question their judgment?

"I'll remind her to take care of herself," Mitch said. "That's her problem, you know. She's always so busy caring for everyone else, she forgets to see to her own needs."

Jacqui smiled wryly. "And she raised three caregivers. What a surprise."

He chuckled. "Maybe she influenced us a bit."

"You think?"

He nodded, his smile fading. "Actually, Meagan is the one who's most like her, and she almost paid dearly for that last year. She discounted some pain she was experiencing as intense but ordinary monthly cramps. She was too busy with work to pay close attention to her own symptoms, and by the time she did, she needed emergency surgery. I can't remember if that was before you met her."

"I met her while she was on medical leave to recover from that operation," she reminded him. "She's the one who originally interviewed me as a favor to Seth. He was going through a busy time at the law office and she had some time off, so it worked out for both of them for her to screen some applicants for the housekeeping position."

"And she highly recommended you, as I understand

it. With a strong endorsement from Alice, who'd also met you that first day and decided you were the perfect candidate."

"I was grateful to both of them," she answered candidly. "Without their support, I'm not sure Seth would have even looked at my application twice. He had in mind someone older and more experienced, like his previous housekeeper. She'd been with him for several years and still would be if she hadn't fallen and broken her leg. I know they stay in touch, although he said she seems happy living in Mississippi near her daughter now."

"We're all glad Meagan urged Seth to hire you," Mitch murmured.

Suddenly the kitchen seemed shadowy and intimate again, their lightly casual conversation morphing into something a little different. She swallowed and backed a half step away from him. He wasn't really standing all that close, but she needed that extra bit of distance.

Maybe he sensed that she was more than ready to end this line of conversation. "I guess I'll turn in. Good night, Jacqui."

"Good night."

He paused in the doorway with a frown. "Mitch."

Her eyebrows rose. "I beg your pardon?"

"Good night, *Mitch.* You seem to go out of your way to avoid calling me by name."

So he'd noticed that, had he? It would have been so much easier to keep a firm distance between them if he would just allow her to call him Dr. Baker. "Good night, Mitch," she said.

His smile made it clear that the invisible barrier she'd so carefully erected had just shrunk considerably, despite her efforts. "Good night, Jacqui," he said again. "Sweet dreams."

She swallowed a groan when he turned and sauntered away. She didn't even want to think about the dreams that might plague her that night.

Chapter Six

Mitch wasn't quite sure how to ask Jacqui a big favor Saturday morning during breakfast. Because he'd been busy at work and had a full schedule for the past few evenings, he'd seen little of her since their conversation in the kitchen late Tuesday evening. He hadn't come in until after ten last night, only to find a note from her saying she'd turned in early and he could help himself to the leftover pie in the fridge if he was hungry for a late-night snack.

Forgoing the pie, he'd gone to bed. Even as tired as he'd been after a hectic week, it had taken him a while to go to sleep. He'd lay there wondering if she'd deliberately avoided seeing him that evening because they didn't have Alice as a buffer between them. Alice had left Friday morning for her extended weekend with her maternal grandparents. Jacqui had assured him there would be no differences in household routines while

Alice was away, but it hadn't escaped his notice that she'd gone up to her room earlier than was her usual habit last night.

She had greeted him this morning the way she always did, with a polite smile and a hot, healthy breakfast. At least she didn't try to avoid eating with him this time. She sat at the opposite side of the table with her bowl of steel-cut oats and fresh fruit.

He glanced past her to the glass patio doors, through which he could see Waldo wolfing down the food in his big stainless steel bowl. "Looks like Waldo's having his breakfast, too."

She chuckled. "He didn't get the kisses Alice gives him before breakfast, but I did rub his ears and throw the ball for him a few times."

Kisses before breakfast sounded pretty good to Mitch. Pushing an all-too-appealing image out of his mind, he cleared his throat. "That dog's got a pretty good life."

"He does, doesn't he? He's lucky Seth insisted Alice choose a dog from the local animal shelter when she decided she wanted a pet for her thirteenth birthday. She's been hinting strongly lately that she wants a cat, but Seth has been holding firm that the family is too busy to pay enough attention to more than one pet at a time."

He could understand that. As much as he liked animals, he hadn't had time to devote to a pet since he'd left high school. "You seem to enjoy Waldo. Ever thought of having a pet of your own?"

She shrugged. "I never had one growing up, but I might like to have a small dog, or maybe a cat, when I buy my own house."

He was always interested in those passing mentions of her past, but he'd learned not to follow up with questions that only made her shut down. Instead, he focused on her future plans. "You're buying a house?"

"Oh, not yet," she answered quickly. "I'm saving for a down payment. I'd like to have my own house someday, but it won't be for a couple of years yet."

That seemed as good a segue as any for the favor he wanted to request of her. "Do you have plans for today?"

She paused momentarily in reaching for her coffee cup, as if trying to figure out why he'd asked. "Not specifically," she answered after that almost imperceptible hesitation. "I had tentative plans to have lunch with a friend, but that fell through when something came up she had to attend to. So, I thought I might tackle some window washing this afternoon."

"It's Saturday. You don't normally work on Saturdays, do you?"

"Not every Saturday. Sometimes I come over for a couple of hours when the family needs help with something."

"You probably wouldn't be staying here this weekend with Alice gone if you didn't feel you have to cook for me."

"Not just that," she corrected him. "The new carpet is being installed in my apartment Monday. I could stay there if I had nowhere else to go, I suppose, but it's easier for all involved for me to stay out of the way."

"You don't really want to wash windows today, do you?"

She eyed him suspiciously. "You have something else in mind for me to do?"

Resisting all the inappropriate responses that popped into his head, he gave her what he hoped was a winning and totally innocuous smile. "Actually, I do. How would you like to help me look for a place to live?"

Her brows rose. Maybe he hadn't phrased that very well. "I need to spend today looking at apartments and houses," he explained. "I have a list of several possibilities and I've made arrangements to see them, but it's really not something I want to do alone."

Jacqui frowned a little. "Why would you want me to go with you?"

"If I go alone, I'm going to get bored and overwhelmed and I'll either just pick one to get it over with—which could be a big mistake—or I'll get distracted by something else and I'll end the day no closer to having a new place than I am now. It's pretty much what I did last time I had to find a place. I just grabbed the first available rental. Fortunately, that worked out pretty well—until the ditz burned it down," he added in a grumble.

"Why would you get bored looking for a place to live?" she asked in apparent bewilderment.

He shrugged. "Lack of interest to start with, I guess. I mean, it's not like I'm home all that much, wherever I stash my stuff. I'm either at the hospital or some professional function or at my mom's or hanging out with friends when I get the chance. I know I need to find someplace quick. Seth and Meagan don't want a permanent houseguest. My aunts are leaving today, so I could stay with Mom for a while, but that doesn't seem right, either. Work's going to be hectic for the next few weeks while I try to clear my calendar for my trip to Peru, so I should take advantage of this free weekend to make living arrangements."

"But why would you want me to go along?"

"As I said, I'd like the company. Objective opinions. Madison was going with me, but she called very early this morning and had to cancel because something came up. You always seem so practical and logical about things. I would value your input. I'm sure looking at apartments and houses is hardly your idea of a good time, but I'd buy you a very nice lunch to make it worth your while," he added hopefully.

If it bothered her that she hadn't been the first person he'd asked to accompany him, she gave no sign. He wondered if that actually made it easier for her to accept—making the whole suggestion less personal. More impulsive. It was hard to guess the thoughts that flashed through her mind before she finally replied. "It does sound more interesting than washing windows."

He chuckled. "Thank you for that, anyway."

"If I go, I should warn you that I tend to say what I think. I tell my friends not to ask my opinion about anything unless they really want the truth about what I'm thinking."

"That's exactly what I want you to do," he assured her, taking encouragement from the warning rather than the opposite. "You wouldn't let me sign anything just to get the whole process over with more quickly, would you?"

She shook her head in what might have been exasperation. "Honestly, you'd think a competent surgeon would take important decisions like this more seriously."

He grinned sheepishly. "I do take work decisions seriously. It's other stuff I have trouble concentrating on. Especially something I don't really want to do. It wasn't my choice, you know? I feel like I'm having to do something because of the ditz's stupidity, not because it was something I decided on my own to do right now."

She studied his face for a few moments in silence and

he wondered what she saw there that seemed to intrigue her. "Do you feel like a lot of your decisions are made for you?" she asked after that pause.

Caught off guard by the question, he answered without stopping to think. "For almost all of my life."

Then, because that sounded whiney and ungrateful—neither of which suited him—he chuckled lightly and said, "But isn't that the way it is for just about everyone?"

She merely shrugged, then asked, "What time do you want to leave?"

He glanced at his watch. "Whenever you're ready."

She stood to carry her empty bowl to the sink. "I assume this is a casual-dress outing, so all I have to do is grab my bag."

Her yellow-and-white knit top and jeans looked fine to him. *Very* fine, he added mentally, surreptitiously admiring the way the jeans hugged her slender bottom. He lifted his gaze quickly before she turned back toward him, not wanting her to catch him checking out her backside.

"I'm ready, too," he said, rising with his own empty breakfast dishes. "I'll get the list and meet you at the door."

"Fine."

If she was looking forward to the outing—or dreading it—there was no way to tell from her placid expression. He couldn't help wondering if there was anyone who knew Jacqui well enough to read her emotions when she made an effort to hide them.

Mitch had predicted Jacqui would take the house hunt seriously—she seemed to take most things seriously—but he was rather amused by how intently she went about the search. During the drive to the first apartment, she helped him make out a quick checklist of the things that were important to him. Location, price, privacy, parking. Because he wasn't committed to either renting or buying, they were looking at a selection of apartments, condos and houses.

"There's always Seth's house," he said as he parked in the lot of the first apartment complex. "I'm sure he'd offer me a good deal. I know there have been a few nibbles on it the past week, one fairly serious offer, so if I take that one, I'll have to grab it soon."

She tilted her head his way to study his face as she reached for her door handle. "I don't think you should buy Seth's house."

Apparently she was following through on her warning that she would tell him exactly what she thought today.

"Yeah? How come?" he asked, genuinely curious about her reasoning.

She lifted one shoulder slightly. "You aren't excited about it. It's something you feel obligated to consider because your mom likes the idea and because you think it would be doing a favor for your brother-in-law to take the place off his hands."

"I'm not really excited about buying any house," he reminded her.

"You should be. Buying a house isn't like buying a pair of shoes. You're talking about a home. A private retreat for you and for the family you might have someday. It's a long-term investment and commitment and it should be important to you. Or you might as well just rent."

Maybe she was afraid she'd revealed a little too much about herself in that lecture—as perhaps she had, he mused. Before he could respond, she had her door open and was standing impatiently in the parking lot.

"The location of this one isn't ideal," she said, her tone emotionless now. "A lot of traffic between here and the hospital at rush hour."

"I don't usually keep a typical rush-hour schedule," he commented lightly, locking the car behind them when he joined her. "But you're right, this wouldn't be my first-choice site."

"We should look at it anyway. Maybe there will be other assets that will outweigh the location."

"Of course." He followed her obediently to the rental office.

Jacqui didn't have to tell him her opinion of that first apartment. He had no trouble at all reading her expression as she wandered through the boxy, sterile, white-painted rooms.

"You might as well live in the O.R.," she said as they climbed back into his car after a very short tour.

"I pretty much do," he replied with a laugh and a shrug.

She snapped her seat belt into place. "But there's no need for you to come home to the same environment. You should feel welcomed and comfortable when you walk into your house, not as though you're still at work."

Fastened into the driver's seat, he started the engine. "Is that the way you feel when you go home to your apartment? Welcomed and comfortable?"

The brief pause that followed his question was heavy, but when she spoke, her tone was even. "No," she admitted. "But that's what I'll look for when I finally buy a place of my own."

He wondered if she'd ever had a home where she had

felt safe and welcome. From what little she'd said of her background, he somehow doubted it. Was that why she'd made a profession of taking care of other peoples' homes?

The next stop was another apartment, this one somewhat nicer and in a beautifully landscaped gated complex. Jacqui gave that one higher marks, both for location and decor. He couldn't say she looked enthusiastic, he thought as they drove away, putting a "maybe" checkmark by that place on the list. But then it was just an apartment. He could be comfortable there, so he'd definitely keep it in mind.

They toured one more apartment and a condo before stopping for lunch. As he had promised, Mitch treated Jacqui to a very nice meal at a popular bistro that specialized in the type of healthy foods she preferred. She seemed to enjoy the meal, but she kept their conversation strictly business, discussing pros and cons of the places they had toured thus far and the advantages and disadvantages of buying versus renting.

Maybe he would have liked to talk about other things during the meal, but he kept reminding himself this wasn't a date. He'd asked her to help him find a place to live, and she was focused intently on doing just that. He wondered what she would say if he told her he was actually enjoying this mission that he'd dreaded all week, mostly because he was having a good time watching her reactions to the places they visited.

He supposed it was only natural that the rental and sales agents they had met assumed they were a couple. Jacqui didn't bother to correct anyone's misconceptions, but he saw her tense a little each time it happened. Maybe it was best if he kept his pleasure in her company to himself. At least for the remainder of this outing.

He'd reserved the three houses on his list for afternoon visits. The first was a big, French-themed house in an exclusive gated neighborhood off Chenal Boulevard in west Little Rock near a golf course and country club. Only two years old, the house had been built to impress, with soaring windows and doorways, impeccable landscaping, top-of-the-line kitchen appliances and decadently luxurious bathrooms. It was all very nice, but he couldn't see himself coming home to this place any more than he could the sterile apartment they'd first toured that morning.

"Honestly?" he said to Jacqui as they drove away, "I prefer Seth's house to that one."

"So do I," she agreed.

Although not as visually impressive as the house they had just seen, Seth's previous home was still a very nice place. It was a safe, clean, quiet neighborhood and Mitch figured he would be comfortable there. He just wasn't sure he wanted to invest in a house when there was always a chance he could decide to take a new position somewhere—maybe as soon as next year, he thought with that familiar ripple of restlessness. Seth's house was a prime example. Seth had bought that house only weeks before meeting Meagan and had lived in it just less than a year before they had married and decided Meagan's house was more suited to the family's needs. Now Seth had to try to find a buyer. Even as nice a place as that one took a while to unload these days.

The second house was a Colonial style, also in west Little Rock but in a more established neighborhood. Mitch liked it well enough, but he couldn't say he liked it more than Seth's house. He could tell Jacqui preferred it to the larger house. She studied all the rooms and poked around in the closets and cupboards. He could almost see her mentally arranging furniture and decorating.

"Nice place," she said about that one afterward.

"It was," he agreed. "But I'm leaning toward the second apartment we saw this morning. Good location. Nice, big rooms. Plenty of parking and storage—not that I have anything to store at the moment. Have to sign a year lease, but that shouldn't be a problem. If I should break the lease for any reason, I'd only have to sacrifice a month's rent."

She murmured something he didn't catch, but there wasn't time to ask her to repeat it. They had arrived at the final house he had scheduled to tour that afternoon.

He thought he heard a muffled sound from Jacqui when he parked in front of the Craftsman-style house in one of Little Rock's oldest, still-well-respected neighborhoods. According to his information, this house had been built in the 1920s. It had been renovated several times since but still retained the flavor of that period, as did most of the houses in the historic area.

Although significantly older and slightly smaller than either of the other houses he'd toured, this one was just as expensive, at the top of his price range. He could see why. All the houses on this block were immaculately maintained, the lawns landscaped and manicured. A curving driveway ended in a discreetly placed garage that matched the house. A roomy front porch was furnished with inviting rockers beneath a lazily turning, antique-style ceiling fan. Flowers bloomed in beds around the porch, and a fountain added the sound of tumbling water to the already idyllic setting.

The inside of the house had been just as skillfully staged. Soft lighting from antique lamps and fixtures cast a welcoming glow over the Mission-styled furnishings arranged for comfort and conversation. Because it was July and still hotter than Hades outside, no fire burned in the old site-built brick fireplace, but it wasn't hard to imagine flames crackling there on a dark winter evening. Built-in shelves held old books and pottery, and antique rugs softened the gleaming wood floors.

The kitchen, though still retaining the flavor of the period, had been renovated into a chef's dream. A sunroom opened off the back, overlooking the small but appealing backyard. They toured a laundry room, a study and a dining room downstairs, then climbed the wooden steps to explore the three bedrooms upstairs. Two smaller bedrooms were separated by a Jack-and-Jill bath, and the master bedroom included a sitting area in a bay window, a bathroom that was as charming as it was luxurious, and not one but two walk-in closets. Because roomy closets hadn't been a feature of this style home at the time it was built, Mitch suspected some walls had been removed to create the space, but the construction had been seamless. It all blended very well.

As many amenities as this house offered, it was more warm and homey to him than the newer places they'd toured earlier. Maybe it was the age, maybe the abundance of honey-toned wood in contrast to the white-painted trim of the other two houses or maybe he just preferred this style. Whatever the reason, he liked it better.

Jacqui, he noted, had very little to say about this one. She'd kept up a running commentary at all the other places and it hadn't been hard to interpret her reactions to them. She studied this house just as closely, if not more so, than the others, but she kept her observations to herself for the most part. She spent an especially long time in the kitchen, gazing at the glass-fronted cabinets, wood-paneled appliances, dark granite countertops and amber-glass light fixtures. If he'd had to guess, he would have said she was transfixed, but it was hard to tell when she made a deliberate effort to mask her thoughts.

She was just stepping out of one of the walk-in closets when he started to enter. Had he not reached up instinctively to grab her shoulders, they would have collided in the doorway. Startled, she laughed. "Oops."

He grinned down at her. "Careful. Even as big as this closet is, there's not room for both of us to get through the doorway at once."

"Then you should move aside so I can come out," she advised him humorously.

He found himself reluctant to release her. It felt good to have his hands on her, to be standing so close he could see the little specks of amber in her dark brown eyes and just a hint of freckles across her lightly tanned nose.

Her smile faded. "Um, Mitch?"

"Yeah." He dropped his hands and moved out of her way. She didn't glance back at him as she wandered off to explore the master bath.

He noted that she looked over her shoulder when he drove away a short while later, her gaze on that house until he'd turned onto busy Kavanaugh Avenue and she could no longer see it. Only then did she turn forward again, adjusting her seat belt and looking through the windshield with a pensive expression.

"That was the last one today," he said, breaking the silence between them when he stopped at a red light. "I don't think my brain can process any more choices."

She smiled faintly, though she didn't turn to look

at him. "I'd say you looked at a nice range of options today."

"Yeah. I can tell my mom I saw apartments, condos and houses, so she can't say I'm not taking the search seriously."

She looked at him then, their eyes meeting for a moment before he directed his attention back to the road ahead. "You're looking at houses to please your mom?"

"I'm looking at houses because I need to move out of my sister's guest room."

"But none of the houses you've seen today have excited you. Not even that last one?"

"It's a house," he answered simply, though he didn't miss her emphasis on the last place they'd seen. She really had liked that one, apparently. "A nice house but still just a place to sleep and stash the stuff I'll eventually reaccumulate."

"You shouldn't rush into anything. Maybe you should wait until some place does excite you."

"Honestly? I don't think that's going to happen. I mean, nothing will really change except my mailing address. I'll still go to work every day at the hospital, still be on call for my mom when she needs me, still hang with my friends when I get the time. A house would add some responsibilities like maintenance and lawn care, but I'd probably have to pay someone to do that stuff most of the time. Mowing and weeding isn't my idea of a good time when I'm off work."

"I wouldn't mind taking care of my own yard, if I had one," she murmured. "Maybe tending some flower beds. But I guess that's not your thing."

He remembered how long she'd gazed at the tidy flower beds around the last house. "No," he replied with a light shrug. "Gardening isn't really something I've had a strong urge to do."

"You want to get away from Little Rock, don't you?"

The seemingly disconnected question caught him off guard, so he hesitated a bit before answering, "I think I've mentioned before that I wouldn't mind seeing what it's like to live somewhere else, because I never have. Every time I thought about moving away for a while, something came up with the family and I felt as though I needed to stay."

"So, what's keeping you now? Your family's in good shape. Your surgical skills are probably in demand just about anywhere you want to move to. Or are you still playing George Bailey?"

Mitch frowned. Was her tone just a little cross? And if so, why? "George who?"

"George Bailey. *It's a Wonderful Life.* The movie."

"Ah." He remembered now. "The guy who kept trying to leave home and couldn't because of the family banking business?"

"Yes."

He chuckled. "I'm no George Bailey. I haven't tried all that hard to leave yet. And, like you said, there's no reason I couldn't move now if I want. I mean, I like my job here, and my family and friends are all here, but still, I can see the appeal of checking out new places. Maybe I'll just find a good home base here and travel when I get the chance—like my upcoming trip to Peru."

"You're really looking forward to that, aren't you?"

"I really am."

"Then I hope the trip will be everything you want it to be."

"Thank you."

As he turned into the driveway of his sister's house,

he glanced across the street toward the for-sale sign in the yard of Seth's former house. He knew it would make his mom happy if he bought that place. Not to mention he'd be doing his brother-in-law a favor. It wasn't as if he didn't get along well enough with the family to live that close. It just didn't— Well, it didn't excite him, he thought, recalling Jacqui's words.

As he followed Jacqui into the house, it occurred to him that the only time that day he'd been anywhere close to excited was when he'd stood in that closet with Jacqui's slender shoulders beneath his hands, her face very close to his.

Something told him that wasn't the type of excitement she had urged him to pursue.

Awakening with a start, Jacqui rolled over to look at the illuminated clock on her bedside. 3:00 a.m. Great.

Knowing she wouldn't sleep again with the echo of her sister's voice in her head, she climbed out of the bed. The house was silent, and she figured Mitch was sound asleep, but she still thought it best not to go traipsing around in nothing but a thigh-length nightshirt—even though he had seen her in that outfit before, she remembered with a slight wince. She pulled on the jeans she'd left draped over the foot of the bed. Figuring that counted as at least mostly dressed, she walked barefoot out of the room, making her way silently down the stairs to the kitchen.

She opened the refrigerator door and reached for a bottle of water. A half bottle of wine caught her eye, but she left it sitting there. That was her mother's sleepless-night crutch, not hers.

Too restless to sit, she leaned against the counter to sip her water. She stared at the table across the shadowy room, but what she saw instead was the kitchen of the Craftsman house she and Mitch had toured that afternoon. She had taken one look at that house and fallen in love. Every step she'd taken inside had only fanned the flames of that passion. The house had been perfect. Exactly the style she and Olivia had always talked about when they'd lay awake at night in a cheap apartment or motel and fantasized about the home they would have someday.

She wanted a house like that. Oh, not that particular one. As much as she had loved it, it had been well out of her price range for any foreseeable future. But she could find a less expensive little house in a less expensive neighborhood and decorate in a similar style. She could paint and hang wallpaper, and she figured she could learn to grout tile and refinish secondhand furniture.

Maybe it was time for her to start haunting estate sales and garage sales on her days off, collecting a few things for the little house she wanted to buy. She'd been in the habit of not accumulating possessions so it would be easier to move when the time came, but she hoped her next move would be into a little house where she could stay for a nice long while. Her goal had been to own a home by the time she turned thirty, just less than a year away. She saw no reason why she couldn't fulfill that dream.

If she had needed any evidence of how different she and Mitch were, she figured their outing today had done the trick. He had looked at apartments and condos and houses with little enthusiasm, seemingly willing to settle for the first reasonably suitable option. From what she could tell, he'd seen the houses as potential anchors, more long-term commitment and responsibility than he was looking for. For someone who had just spent—what had he said, six years?—living in a rented duplex, he certainly saw himself as the footloose type.

Just her luck that the only man who had made her pulse race in the past busy year was a restless surgeon related to her employer—so many strikes against him that it was almost funny. So why wasn't she smiling?

Her somber thoughts were interrupted by a strange sound from the backyard. Frowning, she looked toward the door. Maybe Waldo had heard her moving around and was trying to get her attention. It hadn't sounded like his usual whine, though. Something was…

The sound came again. Catching her breath, she set her water bottle on the counter with a thump and ran toward the door. It took her only moments to disarm the security system and open the locks. "Waldo?"

She could tell at a glance that the dog was in trouble. The trees silhouetted by the backyard security lighting threw long shadows over the pool, patio and lawn, but there was still enough light for her to see that Waldo had somehow become trapped in the fencing designed to hold the adventuresome dog in the yard. His head jammed between a post and a fence slat, he was unable to move anything except his hind quarters. He pumped his back legs wearily, as though he'd been trying for some time to extricate himself, and he whimpered in pain and frustration.

It took only a couple minutes of trying before she conceded she wouldn't be able to free him herself.

"I'll be right back," she assured him, as if he could understand. "Be still so you don't hurt yourself."

Leaving him whining, she dashed inside the house and up the stairs, skidding to a stop in front of Mitch's closed door. She knocked on it sharply. "Mitch? Mitch!"

"Wha?" she heard him say groggily from inside. Moments later the door opened. Tousled and bleary, wearing only a pair of navy pajama bottoms slung low on his hips, he peered down at her. "Jacqui? What's wrong?"

"It's Waldo. Can you help me, please?"

Without taking time to ask any more questions, he followed her quickly downstairs. He assessed the situation with the dog in one quick glance, then knelt on one side of the trapped pet while she crouched on the other side. "Looks like I'm going to have to get some tools. Where does Seth keep his?"

"In the garage storage room." She stroked a hand down the dog's back, feeling the muscles quivering beneath her palm. "I'll stay here with him."

"Okay, be right back."

It took maybe ten minutes for them to free the dog once Mitch returned with a bag of tools. Jacqui assisted him by holding a flashlight and keeping Waldo calm. She wanted to think she could have handled the situation alone if she'd had to, but she was greatly relieved that Mitch seemed to know exactly what to do.

"Is he okay?" she asked, leaning over Mitch's shoulder.

"Let me get him inside in the light where I can see better." Mitch stood, lifting the sixty-pound Lab mix in his arms as easily as if he were picking up a bag of flour. Still weary from the ordeal, Waldo lay limply against Mitch's chest, the tip of his feathery tail wagging in gratitude.

Jacqui and Mitch were both barefoot, so she wasn't surprised when he stumbled a little and cursed beneath his breath on the way toward the house. He righted himself quickly and kept walking to the open back door.

She placed her own feet carefully as she followed behind him.

Mitch set the dog carefully on the kitchen floor. "I'm no veterinarian, but I don't see any problems," he said a moment later.

"There's blood on his neck," Jacqui said, her fingers laced tightly in front of her. Alice loved this dog so much, she thought with a catch in her throat. And Alice wasn't the only one fond of the silly, accident-prone mutt.

"He scraped himself trying to pull free. It's not deep, no need for stitches. If you'll find me a first aid kit, I'll take care of it."

Grateful for something to do, she hurried to get the kit. There was nothing in this house she couldn't locate if necessary.

By the time she returned to the kitchen only minutes later, Waldo was already regaining his usual spirit. He was on his feet, wiggling and expressing his gratitude to Mitch with eager swipes of his tongue.

Chuckling, Mitch fended off the wet kisses, glancing up wryly at Jacqui when she opened the first aid kit. "I think we can safely say he'll be fine."

She watched as he dabbed antibiotic ointment on Waldo's scrapes. "I'm so glad. I swear that dog has more lives than a cat. If you only knew some of the messes he's gotten himself into."

"I've heard a few of them."

"Do you think he'd be stupid enough to stick his head in that hole again tonight?"

"Absolutely," Mitch answered with a laugh.

She sighed. "Then I guess he'll spend the rest of the night—what little there is of it—in the garage until I can get out in the sunlight tomorrow to check the fence."

Mitch scratched the dog's ears, eliciting a blissful tail wag. "He was just exploring. Found an opening and just had to see what was on the other side, right, Waldo?"

Mitch sounded as though he identified all too well with that sentiment.

Comfortable that Waldo had recovered from his ordeal, Jacqui shooed him into the garage, telling him she'd be back in a minute with his food and water dishes and a blanket on which he could rest for his next misadventure. Closing the door into the garage, she turned back to the kitchen.

Mitch stood by the sink, washing his hands. Jacqui frowned when she saw a smudged trail of blood on the tile floor. "I didn't think Waldo bled that much from that little scrape. Maybe there's another—"

And then she realized exactly where the trail led. "Mitch, you're bleeding!"

He glanced down, frowned, then lifted his right foot so he could see the sole. "Well, yeah, I guess I am."

She reached for the first aid kit again. "Sit down, let me look at it."

"That's not— Okay, sure."

She wasn't certain what caused his sudden change of mind, but she didn't ask. She merely knelt in front of him when he plopped into one of the kitchen chairs. She lifted his bleeding right foot into her hands to examine the cut on his heel. "I don't think it's too deep," she said in relief.

"I think I stepped on one of Waldo's toys when I was carrying him in. That's what I get for going outside without shoes, I guess."

"We both did. Silly dog scared me half to death."

She moved to the sink to retrieve a clean washcloth, which she moistened and then carried back to where he sat. She hesitated a moment before kneeling in front of him again. It had suddenly struck her that it was after 3:00 a.m., they were alone in a mostly darkened house, she wore a nightshirt and jeans and Mitch only a pair of pajama bottoms. The intimacy of that situation made her a bit nervous all of a sudden.

Mitch's bland tone helped when he asked, "Want me to do it?"

"No, that would be too awkward for you." Telling herself to snap out of it, she lowered herself to one knee so she could better see the cut. She cleaned the area, dabbed antibiotic ointment on the small cut much as she'd seen Mitch do with Waldo and sealed it with an adhesive bandage. "That should stay on until the bleeding stops."

"Thank you, doctor," he teased.

Flushing a little, she used the still-damp cloth to swipe up the smudges of blood from the floor, then stood to rinse it out and lay it over the sink. She would toss it in with the laundry tomorrow—um, later today, she corrected herself.

"I'm so sorry I had to get you up at this hour," she said, glancing at Mitch, who still sat in the chair watching her fussing with the washcloth. "I hope you don't have to be at the hospital early."

He looked at the clock over the stove. "I planned to be there by seven."

Just a little less than three hours away, Jacqui thought with a wince. "I'm really sorry. I hope you can get a couple more hours of sleep first."

He shrugged. "Actually, I'm wide awake now. I went to bed earlier than usual last night."

"Still, you couldn't have had much more than five hours sleep."

"Five hours was a luxury during my residency. Believe me, I've gotten by on much less." He stood and stretched. The movement dipped his pajama bottoms even lower on his hips and made muscles ripple in his chest and abdomen.

Jacqui's mouth went dry. Making a hasty grab for the open bottle of water she'd left on the counter earlier, she downed several quick swallows—not that it helped much. "Would you—um—like some coffee?"

"I think I'll take a shower. Why don't you go back to bed and try to get some sleep?"

"I'm not sleepy now, either. I'll put on some coffee. It'll be ready by the time you finish showering."

Dropping his arms to his sides, he studied her face intently. "You didn't get up because you heard Waldo, did you? You were already awake?"

She nodded. "I came down for a drink of water. That's when I heard him whimpering."

"You couldn't sleep?"

She shrugged. "I guess I was thirsty."

"You sure there was nothing else?"

When had he moved closer? Setting the water bottle carefully on the counter, she cleared her throat. "I don't know—bad dream, maybe."

"Want to talk about it?"

Because she couldn't look at his eyes just then, she glanced downward. Probably a mistake, she realized immediately, because she was now looking straight at his bare chest. Which was several inches closer than it had been only moments earlier.

"Um, no, I'm fine now, thank you."

"Jacqui—"

Slowly, she lifted her eyes. The way he was looking at her...

She swallowed hard. "Yes?"

"Do I make you nervous?"

Chapter Seven

Apparently, Jacqui didn't like his question. Her chin lifted proudly and her dark eyes narrowed in what might have been a challenge when she replied flatly, "No. You don't make me nervous."

He shook his head slightly in response to the blatant untruth but didn't take her up on the challenge. "Good. I want you to be comfortable with me."

She backed an inch or so away from him, which brought her right up against the kitchen counter behind her. "Of course I am. Didn't we spend all day together?"

"Yes." And she had seemed relaxed enough as long as they were focused on something else, like touring houses or discussing the merits of each. And when they'd worked together to free Waldo from the fence, she'd seemed completely at ease, though worried about the dog. It was only when the focus had shifted to the two of them, alone in a quiet, darkened house, that suddenly her manner had become stilted and self-conscious.

She half turned away from him. "I'll make the coffee."

He reached out to catch her arm, his touch light, making no effort to hold her if she chose to draw back. She didn't immediately pull away, but he sensed that she was poised to do so immediately. "Jacqui."

She looked up at him with that shuttered expression he had no chance to read. "What?"

"The last thing I want to do is make you uncomfortable in any way," he assured her. "But—well, I just think I should tell you I've really enjoyed spending time with you this past week."

He simply couldn't help but believe the attraction he felt for her was not entirely one-sided. There had been too many instances when he'd almost felt the exchange of sparks between them. He had been sure he'd seen an answering awareness in her dark eyes occasionally when she looked at him.

"I'm glad you've enjoyed your stay here," she responded in her best housekeeper voice.

"Don't do that," he said with a slight frown. "You know full well I'm not speaking as an unexpected houseguest."

"Mitch—"

"As least you call me by name now," he mused, his frown tilting into a half smile. "We're making some progress."

"Progress?" she asked suspiciously.

"Progress toward having dinner together without running errands to justify it. Toward talking about things other than our jobs. Toward getting to know each other on a more personal basis than as acquaintances with mutual connections to my family."

She was shaking her head even before he finished speaking. "It wouldn't work, Mitch. There's no need to even think about starting something that has zero chance of going anywhere. Let's just keep things the way they are between us, okay? Friendly. Casual. Semi-professional."

Semi-professional? He might have been wryly amused by the description if he hadn't been so baffled by a fleeting expression he saw in her eyes. Granted, her emotions were hard to read, but he thought he'd nailed that one. Why would Jacqui panic in response to his blatant hints that he wanted to ask her out?

He dropped his hand immediately from her arm, taking a step backward to give her plenty of room. "Like I said, I don't want to make you uncomfortable. I just thought you realized that I'm attracted to you. That I like spending time with you and would like to continue to do so. But if you're not interested, enough said. I won't mention it again and you won't have to give it another thought."

"It isn't that I don't like you," she assured him quickly, as if worried that maybe she'd hurt his pride or his feelings. "It's just that it's all too awkward."

"Because you work for my sister, you mean?"

"That's certainly part of it."

He cocked an eyebrow. "What's the other part?"

"Well, you know—" Frowning, she drew a sharp breath. "I'm not interested in playing Vivian to your Edward, Mitch."

"I have no idea what that means," he said with a puzzled laugh.

"Pretty Woman."

"Ah. Another movie allusion."

She shrugged. "I spent a lot of time watching movies on fuzzy motel TVs when I was growing up."

He would definitely like to hear more about her past, but this wasn't the time to ask the questions that buzzed in his mind. Instead, he shook his head. "I saw that movie a few years back. Hardly a suitable comparison. Vivian was no housekeeper."

"Okay, fine," she said with an impatient wave of her hand. "Then let's just say I'm not interested in playing the role of Cinderella."

"And I wouldn't have a clue how to play Prince Charming," he replied evenly. "I'm just Mitch. And I'd like to get to know Jacqui better."

"There's not that much to know. I moved around a lot, have a distantly polite relationship with my parents, clean and cook for a living and do a little knitting in my spare time."

That was how she summed up her life? "You forgot to add that you are intelligent and competent—not to mention strikingly attractive. Or that you do more than clean and cook for this family—you keep them on schedule and reassured that their precious daughter is well cared for while they're pursuing their careers. They trust you with their home and her welfare. That says a great deal about your character."

A hint of pink darkened her cheeks. "That's all very nice of you to say, but still…you and I couldn't be more different."

"Oh." He smiled crookedly. "So I'm not smart, attractive or competent?"

She gave him a look of censure. "That's not what I meant."

"I haven't moved around at all, I'm close to my

mother and sisters and I basically do bone carpentry for a living. In my spare time, I play some soccer. Sure, that's a different background than yours, but you still haven't convinced me why you think we're so unsuited. Unless, of course, it comes back to you being completely uninterested in me."

"It's not that exactly—"

Taking encouragement from the murmur, he moved a little closer again. "Or that you find me unattractive."

"Obviously you're a good-looking man. But I—"

"So answer this. If I weren't Meagan's brother, would you go out with me if I asked?"

"If you weren't Meagan's brother, we'd have never met," she pointed out somewhat brusquely. "Surgeons and housekeepers hardly move in the same circles."

"If I repaired cars instead of bones and we'd met, say, at the grocery store in the produce aisle, would you go out with me?"

Her mouth twitched with what might have been a reluctant smile. "That's a lot of ifs."

He shrugged but didn't look away from her face.

"Okay, maybe," she said after a moment. "If all those things were true—which they aren't—I might consider going out with you. But even then, I doubt it would go anywhere. There are other things that would get in the way."

He figured they could work on those other things later. At least they had established that she wasn't entirely indifferent to him. He smiled. "Then let's pretend and see what happens. If it doesn't work out, then there's nothing lost, right?"

"I've never been very good at pretending."

He lifted her chin and brushed a light kiss over the lips he had been wanting to taste for much longer than he'd acknowledged even to himself. The kiss was too fleeting for her to really respond, but he thought he felt her lips move just a little before he drew away.

Stepping back, he grinned. "I'm going to take that shower now. I have a couple of broken cars to check on this morning."

"Mitch—"

He thought it best to just keep walking. She didn't try to detain him again.

Mitch's rounds at the hospital didn't take long. He had no surgeries scheduled for that Sunday morning and wasn't on call, so he just checked on a few patients, consulted with some parents and had a quick meeting with a couple of residents before calling it a day before noon.

"I was just going to grab an early lunch, Mitch. Want to join me?" a friend asked when they met in the hallway.

"Thanks, Dan, but I have plans. Next time, okay?"

"Sure. See you."

Nodding, Mitch walked on toward the elevators. He liked to keep moving when he was on his way out. Stopping to talk was just asking to be detained for one reason or another.

Connor Hayes, a second-year resident in pediatrics, was already on the elevator when Mitch stepped in. Connor had rotated through the surgery unit when Mitch was a resident and Connor still a med student. They were close to the same age. Connor hadn't started medical school until he was thirty, unlike Mitch, who'd entered right after college.

"How's it going, Connor?"

The other man nodded a greeting. "I'm good, thanks.

I heard about the fire, Mitch. Is there anything I can do for you?"

"Thanks, but I've got everything under control. Sort of," he added with a chuckle. "Still have some shopping to do, but I've got enough to get by for a while."

"Were you able to salvage anything?"

Mitch shook his head. "Lost it all."

"I'm sorry to hear that."

"Thanks. How's your family?"

The elevator door opened into the parking garage and Connor fell into step beside Mitch to reply. "All doing well, thanks. Alexis is eleven now, thinks she's grown. Anthony is five months, and growing like a weed. And Mia somehow juggles her work and motherhood and my crazy schedule without blinking an eye, just like always."

Mitch chuckled. "Tell her I said hello, will you?"

"I will, thanks."

Mitch was still thinking about that brief conversation with Connor when he buckled himself into his car a few minutes later. An Arkansas native, Connor had married a local woman, attended college and medical school in the state and had listed the local children's hospital as his first choice when applying for his residency program. He seemed to have no interest whatsoever in leaving the state where he had spent his entire life, settling happily into marriage, fatherhood and the medical career he had worked hard to attain. Granted, Mitch didn't know Connor well, but if Connor felt at all constrained by his deeply rooted lifestyle, Mitch had seen no signs of it.

Mitch loved his job. Was close to his mother and sisters. Had really good friends here. So what was missing in his life that made him yearn for something more? A house, wife, kids? He wanted all those things eventually, of course, but he hadn't really given them much thought until this point. His restlessness had seemed to tug him in other directions—adventures and experiences outside what he had always known here. And now that his rented house was gone, his possessions few, his family all in good health and busy with their own lives, he wasn't sure what was holding him back from actively looking for someplace new to try.

His thoughts turned to Jacqui, who had been in his mind so much lately. She was certainly different from the women he'd dated before. Was that part of his fascination with her? From what he had gathered, her background was almost diametrically opposite to his, enough to seem exotic to him. Was she right to worry that he was only amusing himself with her while he was at loose ends—if that was, indeed, why she was so hesitant about spending more time with him.

He couldn't accept that unrealistic excuse she'd given about not wanting to play Cinderella to his Prince Charming. Seriously, who thought that way these days? He had never paid attention to social class distinctions, and even if he did, it wasn't as if he came from a high-brow background. His dad had been a sci-fi-loving physics professor at a state university, his mom was an accountant—people who worked hard at their jobs to pay the bills and support their families. The fact that all three of their offspring had attended medical school was mostly coincidence—or maybe the younger two had been influenced by the older sibling's choice. Meagan had teasingly claimed they were always copying her.

As far as Mitch was concerned, it was just a job—a good job, sure, one that required a lot of training and paid well afterward, but still simply the career he had chosen. Jacqui ran his sister's household, which required skills plenty of people lacked. He couldn't see why their choice of vocations should have anything to do with their being friends. Maybe more than friends.

But if Jacqui was fretting about that foolish quibble, then it looked as though it was up to him to convince her differently. There might be other reasons why a flirtation—or more—between them wouldn't work, but he wasn't going to let anything as superficial as tax brackets keep them from finding out for sure. Not if he could help it anyway.

One thing about Mitch Baker, the guy was certainly persuasive. Jacqui wasn't sure how he'd talked her into an outing Sunday evening, but she found herself sitting beside him in a movie theater, sharing a tub of popcorn and watching an action film play on the giant screen. Maybe she'd accepted because it was less awkward being out in public with him than alone in the house. It was hard to be tense and formal with popcorn grease on their fingers and oversize 3-D glasses perched on their noses.

Watching Mitch laughing at a groan-worthy pun from one of the main characters, tossing popcorn kernels in his mouth and peering through the plastic lenses, it was hard to imagine him in an operating room, gowned and gloved and barking orders while piecing together a child's shattered bones. She pushed that image out of her mind immediately. This Mitch, the one in jeans and silly glasses, was someone with whom she could relax, have fun, flirt a little. The other Mitch—well, she didn't even know him.

It wasn't that she didn't think herself good enough to date a doctor, she assured herself. As battered as it had been, her self-esteem wasn't quite that low. The problem was that she didn't have enough in common with that other Mitch—the one with advanced degrees and enough money to look at houses in some of the nicest neighborhoods. The Mitch who could look at those houses and feel no excitement at the thought of owning one and nesting contentedly into it.

He laughed again at an on-screen antic and grinned at her to share the joke. He looked so cute and silly in the big glasses that she had to smile back. There was no reason she couldn't enjoy spending a few hours with this Mitch. It wasn't as if she'd had all that many dates lately—not that this was a date, exactly, she corrected herself quickly. Still, she figured it was good for her to keep her socializing skills from getting too rusty.

She reached for another handful of popcorn.

Of course, every date had to end. In her experience, they most often ended at the door. It was awkward enough dealing with the good-night kiss decision after an ordinary first date. It felt even more strange having Mitch follow her inside, knowing they would be sharing breakfast—and not because she had invited him to stay.

Not that this evening had been a real date, of course.

"How about some tea?" Mitch asked when they walked inside the house. "You like to drink tea at night, right?"

"Yes, I do," she agreed. "I'll make some."

"I'll do it," he corrected her. "I think it's my turn to make the tea. I've watched you use that fancy boiling-water dispenser at the sink, and I know where you store the teas, so I can manage."

A little flustered by the offer, she stammered, "I, uh—"

"Chamomile, right?"

"Yes, but—"

"It'll be ready in just a few minutes."

She blinked after him as he headed for the kitchen. Her kitchen, she thought with a slight frown. Well, not really, but there was no denying she was a bit proprietary about it. She heard a muted crash from that direction and she winced. She'd fed Waldo before leaving that evening, but she supposed it wouldn't hurt to wander casually through the kitchen to check on him—and a few other things.

She forced herself to remain in the living room instead. To give her hands something to do, she pulled out her knitting. She was working on a new pattern, a pretty lacework shawl with a delicate scalloped edge. She'd chosen a fine, shell-pink yarn, and the project was turning out nicer than she had even expected. She usually made heavier scarves and shawls, fashioned more for warmth and comfort than delicacy.

Mitch returned to the room with a steaming cup of tea in each hand, a frown of concentration on his face as he made an effort not to spill them. "That's a pretty thing you're making. What is it?"

She set the project aside to reach for her tea. "A shawl."

"Something you're going to sell in your friend's shop?"

"I haven't decided yet. It could be a gift for someone."

He sat at the other end of the sofa and they chatted about the movie while they sipped their tea. When they'd run out of things to say about the lightweight plot, they fell silent. Jacqui couldn't think of a thing to say to fill the suddenly noticeable quiet. The comfort she had felt with Mitch at the theater was dissipating now, leaving her inexplicably ill at ease again and much too aware of him sitting next to her.

She drained the tea in a long swallow, almost burning her throat because it was still hot. Fortunately, she managed not to sputter. That would have been embarrassing, she thought with a slight wince. "I'm getting really tired. Not much sleep last night. I think I'll go check on Waldo and then head up to bed."

Studying her face, Mitch nodded. "Sounds like a plan. I'll just watch the news and then I'll probably turn in."

Looking as though he'd settled where he was for a while, he reached for the television remote control as she stood with her empty teacup. He didn't act at all as though they'd just been out on a date. So maybe she wasn't the only one who had chosen not to view it in that light.

And how foolish was it that her feminine ego was just a little piqued that his attention had already wandered away from her to the TV?

"Thanks for taking me to the movie," she said, hovering in the doorway. "I had a very nice time."

He glanced away from the screen to send her a smile. "Thank you for going with me. I've been wanting to see that film."

"Sure. So, um, good night. then."

"Good night. I'll be leaving very early in the morning, so don't bother trying to get up to make breakfast. I'll grab something at the hospital."

She nodded, hesitated another microsecond, then turned to carry her teacup to the kitchen. For some reason, she felt as though there was something more she should have said, but she couldn't for the life of her decide what it might have been. Mitch was already watching TV again anyway.

Maybe he hadn't found her as interesting as he'd thought he would once he'd actually talked her into sort of going out with him. So much for her concerns about whether there would come an awkward attempt at a good-night kiss.

Realizing she was pouting a little, she pulled her bottom lip firmly back into place and told herself she was glad that precarious experiment was behind them now.

Mitch waited until Jacqui was out of his sight before releasing a long, pent-up breath. If she'd had any idea how hard it had been for him not to at least try to kiss her tonight, she'd probably have bolted from the room. Her lips had been so tempting when she'd pursed them slightly to blow on her hot tea, when she'd lowered her cup to leave her mouth moist and glistening. But he had been determined to prove to her that she didn't have to worry about staying alone in this house with him even though he'd told her earlier that he was attracted to her.

He had no intention of taking advantage of their situation. Of putting her in an awkward situation with her employer's brother. The fact that they were both staying here was unrelated to what he hoped was a developing connection between them, other than the fact that the enforced proximity had made him realize just how strong his attraction to her had always been.

Now, if only he didn't do anything to run her off—figuratively, at least—before he even had a chance to see where that attraction could lead.

* * *

Jacqui could tell when Mitch dragged in at 9:00 p.m. Monday that he'd had a rough day. She'd gotten a call four hours earlier from his pleasant and efficient secretary informing her that Dr. Baker was in surgery and would not be home in time for dinner. Though she'd been a bit surprised by the call, Jacqui had thanked the woman for the call, and she'd been touched that Mitch had gone to the effort of getting the message to her.

She wouldn't have minded if he'd simply not shown up for dinner, of course. He certainly had no obligation to eat there every evening, whether he notified her or not. From experience with her employers' somewhat erratic schedules, she cooked nothing that couldn't be safely stowed in the fridge and reheated later. But it had been thoughtful of him to let her know.

Taking one look at his face when he walked into the living room, she set her knitting aside and jumped to her feet. "You look worn out. Have you had anything to eat?"

"I'm not hungry, thanks."

It wasn't exactly an answer about when he'd last eaten, but she didn't bother arguing with him. Even at this hour, it was still hot as blazes outside on this first Monday in August, so she didn't offer hot tea. Instead, she said, "Sit down. I'll get you something cold to drink. There's fresh lemonade or a pitcher of iced tea. Which would you prefer?"

"You don't have to—"

"Mitch," she broke in firmly. "Which do you want?"

"Tea, please," he conceded, sinking onto the couch.

"I'll be right back."

He had his head back when she returned only moments later, carrying a glass of tea and a plate of cheese, crackers, carrot sticks and olives, with a couple of cookies on the side—just in case he decided he was a little hungry after all.

"Thanks." Accepting the glass, he smiled wryly when she set the food in front of him, but after taking only a couple of sips of the tea, he stacked cheese on a cracker and popped it into his mouth.

She sat on the other end of the couch, ready to hop up and run for more food if he still looked hungry after finishing this light snack. "Rough day, huh?"

He shrugged. "Tougher than most. Had an emergency come in just as I was getting ready to leave for the day. Eight-year-old boy, both legs shattered in an ATV accident. He was too young to be riding the four-wheeler at all, of course, but at least he was wearing a helmet, which probably saved his life. We were in the O.R. for three hours. And that was after an already long day of procedures, one of which had complications that made it take longer than it should have."

"So you've been on your feet all day?"

Crunching a carrot stick, he nodded. "I'm usually on my feet," he said after swallowing. "This was just a longer day than most."

"Let me get you some more tea." She jumped up to fetch the pitcher because he seemed to be very thirsty. He'd already almost drained his glass.

Pushing the empty plate aside a few minutes later, he leaned back against the cushions again with a light sigh. "That was good. Thanks."

"Can I get you anything else?"

"No, really. I had plenty, thank you."

She turned on the couch to look at him. "The little boy who was hurt? Will he be okay?"

"He has a long recuperation ahead of him, but he'll get there. Kids are pretty resilient."

Not always, she thought with a ripple of sadness she didn't want him to see.

But Mitch seemed to be getting better at reading her. He must have followed the direction her thoughts had taken. "Jacqui?" he asked after a pause. "Do you mind if I ask how you lost your sister?"

She felt her chest tighten but answered evenly. "In a car accident twelve years ago. The surgeons worked very hard to save her, but she died on the table."

"Younger or older sister?"

"Younger."

"I'm very sorry."

She nodded. "It's difficult for me to talk about it."

"I won't press you, then. Just know that if you ever need to talk, I'm a good listener."

"Thank you."

Sipping the last of his second glass of tea, he reached up with his free hand to squeeze the back of his neck. The gesture seemed to be automatic, as if he were hardly aware that he was even doing it.

Her awareness of the reason for his discomfort—a long operation on an injured eight-year-old boy—overcame her hesitation. "If your neck is stiff, I'd be happy to give you a quick massage. I've been told I'm pretty good at it."

He dropped his hand, looking first surprised then intrigued by her offer. "My neck is a little sore."

Because he was so much taller, she moved to stand behind him as he leaned back against the couch cushions. The back of the couch was low enough that she had full access to his neck and shoulders, especially when he lowered his chin a little. Focusing strictly on finding and alleviating the knots in his muscles, she tried without much success to ignore the warmth and strength of him beneath her palms, even through his thin-knit shirt. When she worked on his nape, his thick hair tickled her fingers, tempting her to bury her hands in it.

A particularly stubborn knot just above his right shoulder blade required both her thumbs to work out. His low groan of pained pleasure signified the massage was working. The deep rumble vibrated through her, stirring something deep inside her. Her fingers tightened for a moment, causing him to flinch just a little. Murmuring an apology, she lightened her touch, carefully working the knotted muscle into relaxation.

After another few moments, she rested her hands on his shoulders. "Better?"

He reached up to lay his hands over hers, holding her in position. "Much better. Thank you."

"You're welcome."

Twisting his neck, he smiled up at her, still holding her hands. "You were told correctly, by the way. You are very good at that."

"Um, thanks." She was held captive as much by his gaze as by his hands on hers. She found herself unable to look away from the expression in his darkening blue eyes.

His smile faded. "Jacqui."

She would never know what impulse took hold of her then. Whatever it was, she leaned over before she could talk herself out of it and gave in to an urge she'd been trying to resist for the past ten minutes—oh, heck, for the past ten days.

She pressed her lips firmly against his.

Chapter Eight

Mitch was certainly quick. One minute she was standing behind the couch, leaning over to kiss him, the next she found herself tumbled into his lap, his arms around her, his lips moving avidly against hers. It was as if he'd just been biding his time until she made the first move and had been poised for an immediate response.

That fleeting brush of lips the night before had been merely a hint of what was to come, whetting her appetite and stirring her imagination. But this…this was so much more than she had even anticipated. There was no first-kiss awkwardness, no bumping of noses or fumbling of hands. He kissed her as though they had known each other—intimately—forever, his mouth fitting itself perfectly to hers, his tongue greeting hers as if he already knew exactly how she would taste and feel, his hands settling exactly in the right places to give her the maximum pleasure from his touch without making her uncomfortable by going too far.

"Do you know how long I've wanted to do that?" he asked when he finally gave them both a chance to breathe.

She rested her hand lightly against his face, feeling the slight roughness of his late-evening beard, the firm line of his jaw. "Since you fell over my suitcase and I tried to attack you with a candlestick?"

He chuckled. "No—though I won't deny I wanted to kiss you then. The first time I met you I had stopped by Seth's house to give something to Meagan, back when she and Seth were dating and Seth and Alice still lived across the street. You walked into the room carrying a big vase of fresh flowers to set on the table in the foyer, and I remember thinking you were even prettier than the roses in your hands."

She blinked in surprise, clearly recalling the moment he referred to. Meagan had introduced them. "Jacqui, this is my brother, Mitch," Meagan had said casually.

Jacqui's first jolt of attraction toward the nice-looking man smiling at her had been firmly shoved aside when she'd remembered that Meagan's brother was also a surgeon. She had nodded pleasantly, then asked him in her housekeeper voice if she could take his coat and get him anything to drink. When he'd politely declined the drink, she'd made an excuse about work to do and disappeared for the remainder of his visit with his sister. The awareness she had felt for him that first time had never completely gone away, try as she might to convince herself otherwise when she had seen him since.

She was startled that he, too, still remembered so clearly the first time they met.

"I've been wanting to get to know you better ever since," he added, studying her face for her reaction.

"That was almost a year ago. You never gave any indication that you were…well, interested in me."

He shrugged, settling her more comfortably against him. "It was awkward."

She bit her lip for a moment before murmuring, "It's still awkward."

"It doesn't have to be. We're both single, unattached adults. There's no reason at all we can't spend time together when we want."

She could already feel some of her earlier misgivings building inside her again. "And when it ends? I'll still work for your sister, and because of that, our paths will continue to cross occasionally. Can we just go on the way we have been, pretending nothing changed?"

He gave a little laugh and brushed a strand of her tousled, short hair from her temple. "We're just starting to talk about this and already you're worrying about a theoretical ending at some possible point in the future?"

She grimaced. "I can't help it. I like to know what to expect from my future. Where I'll be, what I'll be doing. As much as possible, I try to anticipate all the possible outcomes of any major decisions I make."

His left arm propped on the couch behind her, he continued to toy with the ends of her hair with his right hand when he asked lightly, "Does that need to control the future come from your childhood?"

She still wasn't really ready to discuss her past with him, but she answered candidly. "Probably. I never knew from one week to the next where I'd be living or going to school. All I ever wanted was to settle down in one place and make a home for myself there."

His fleeting frown made her wonder if her admission worried him a little. He'd made no secret of his own restlessness—a result of a childhood that was too settled and predictable, in his view.

Maybe opposites attracted, but there had to be more than attraction to form a lasting bond. But then, Mitch wasn't worried about forming lasting bonds, she reminded herself, studying his face through her lashes. Maybe he was concerned that she was looking for more from him than he had been prepared to offer. Her talk about permanence and settling down could have made him nervous.

She smiled slightly and shook her head. "Like you said, all we've done is share a few kisses. Satisfying our curiosity, I suppose. I'm not worrying about the future tonight."

"That's what you think we're doing? Satisfying curiosity?"

"I suppose so. I have to confess I've wondered what it would be like to kiss you," she said with a smile, trying to downplay her action in initiating that first kiss.

His mouth twitched. "Yeah? So how was it?"

Relieved that he seemed to be following her lead in keeping this light, she said after a moment of feigned deliberation, "It was nice."

His eyebrows rose. "Nice? That's the best you can say?"

She couldn't help but laugh at his tone. "Okay, *very* nice."

Wrapping his left arm around her, he nestled her closer. "I'd like to try for a more enthusiastic endorsement."

She barely hesitated before lifting her mouth to his. Okay, so this wasn't going anywhere. There was no need to try to control the future because there was no future for her and Mitch beyond tonight. Alice would be home tomorrow, so this was the last night she and Mitch would be alone in the house. Whatever happened between them tonight, it ended at daylight.

It certainly wouldn't be the first time she'd metaphorically folded her tents and moved on. She knew how to put the past behind her, how to lock memories away to be savored or suffered in private. She might as well enjoy what she had started.

"Well?" His voice was husky when he finally drew back a few inches, a warm flush of color on his cheeks, a glint of heat in his eyes. As close as she was to him, she knew exactly how aroused he was by the long kisses they had shared. Just as he could probably read similar signs from her.

"Much better than nice," she assured him, her own voice breathy.

He rested his forehead against hers, releasing a long, slow sigh. He stroked his right hand slowly up and down her left arm, his touch both soothing and further arousing. "I'd better go on up to bed. Thanks for the neck rub. And...everything else."

She blinked rapidly, trying to process what he'd just said. "You're, um, going to bed?"

Alone? Not that she necessarily would have agreed to go with him if he'd asked, but—wasn't he going to ask?

Drawing away from her, he gave her a crooked smile. "Yes. I told you, Jacqui, I won't take advantage of our situation. Our sharing this house because of outside circumstances, I mean. It would be different if we were at your place, and you'd invited me in and one thing led to another..." He let the words drift off into a rueful shrug.

So that was why he had focused so fiercely on the TV

the night before, sending her off to bed after their movie date with hardly a second look. Why he was drawing back tonight after kissing her until her willpower was decidedly weakened. He was being chivalrous. The jerk.

"I'm quite capable of making decisions for myself without being influenced by 'outside circumstances,'" she said coolly. "If I choose not to be taken advantage of, trust me, there would be no advantage taken."

He looked as though he might have laughed at her wording but was making an effort not to. Wise choice.

Catching his shirt in both hands, she pulled him into another hard kiss. She had started this tonight. She would call an end to it. Eventually.

The buzz of a cell phone broke them apart, winded and dazed and startled by the interruption. Mitch reached automatically for the phone on his belt, then stopped himself when they realized it was Jacqui's rarely used, but always at hand, phone demanding attention.

Glancing at the screen, she frowned. She wouldn't have been overly surprised had she seen Alice's number displayed there, but it made her nervous to realize that it was Alice's grandmother calling. "Hello?"

"Jacqui, it's Paulette Burns," the older woman said, confirming the caller ID. "Have you, um, heard from Alice?"

Jacqui felt herself go cold. "No. Why? What's wrong?"

Mitch stirred beside her, probably picking up on her misgivings.

"She went to the lake with her friends for a picnic and a swim, followed by ice cream in town. They said they'd be back by nine but it's ten now and we haven't heard from her. We've tried calling her cell, but she's not answering. Of course, there are several places up here where it's hard to get service, so she could be in one of those spots."

Jacqui drew a very deep breath and counseled herself to speak calmly despite her rising distress. "What friends is she with, Mrs. Burns? She didn't mention this plan to me."

After a pause, Alice's grandmother said, "She implied that you knew about it. It's a few of her friends from there in Little Rock. Swim team friends, she said, so we didn't worry about them swimming at the dam site. I believe there were four of them going, counting Alice. We told her to be careful and to be home by nine so she wouldn't be out after dark. Harold's thinking maybe he should drive around to see if he can find them."

Jacqui moistened her suddenly dry lips. "Who's driving Alice, Mrs. Burns? One of the mothers?"

"No, it's that young man. Her uncle's friend. He seemed quite nice and responsible. Michael?"

Jacqui looked at Mitch, who was watching her intently. "Do you mean Milo?"

"Yes, that's it. Milo."

"I'll kill him," Mitch muttered with a scowl.

"I'll try to call her, and then I'll call you right back," Jacqui said into her phone. She needed a moment to collect herself, to think about what the next step should be. Call the police? Jump in her car and make the forty-five-minute drive to Heber Springs to look for Alice herself? "Give me five minutes."

"All right. I'm sorry to worry you, but we weren't exactly sure what to do. Alice has never done anything like this with us before."

"What's going on?" Mitch asked when Jacqui lowered

her phone. Both of them were on their feet now, and he didn't take his eyes off her face, which she knew must be drained of color.

Hearing the slight unsteadiness in her own voice, she gave him a quick summary of Alice's escapade. "She led her grandparents to believe I knew about the plan," she added grimly. "When I find her..."

He rested a hand on her shoulder when her words faded into a taut silence. "I'm sure she's fine." He sounded as though he was trying to reassure himself as much as her. "Someone would have called if anything had happened. She's probably having fun and lost track of time."

"I told her I didn't want her riding in a car with teenagers. She knew I wouldn't have approved this plan. How could her grandparents have let her go with them? They're supposed to be watching her!"

"Maybe they've forgotten how to control a teenager. And Alice has never pulled a stunt like this before that I know of, so she must have caught them off guard."

Jacqui nodded tightly. "That's what Mrs. Burns said."

"Okay, first thing we need to do is find Alice. We can call..."

Jacqui jumped when the phone buzzed and vibrated in her hand. A glance at the screen made her close her eyes momentarily in relief before she spoke. "Alice?"

"I'm sorry, Jacqui."

The miserable tone in the girl's voice didn't soften Jacqui's own one bit. "Where are you?"

"I just got back to my grandparents' house. I didn't know it was so late."

"You've forgotten how to tell time?"

Jacqui could almost hear the girl wince in response

to the sharp tone of the question. "I guess I didn't look at the clock," Alice muttered. "I'm sorry."

"First, you should be apologizing to your grandparents for worrying them. And for misleading them that this harebrained idea had been approved ahead of time. You and I will be having a long talk tomorrow. And I have a feeling your father will be discussing this with you when he gets home later this week. I wouldn't be surprised if your mother hears about it when she talks to her parents. She'll probably have a few things to say to you, also."

"You're going to tell Dad?" Alice wailed. That was the warning out of Jacqui's litany that seemed to concern her most—and rightly so. Jacqui had only seen Seth mad once or twice in the time she had known him, and she would hate to be on the wrong end of that cool, lawyer-sharp temper.

Alice wouldn't be pulling a stunt like this again any time in the near future, Jacqui predicted.

"I'll see you tomorrow," she said. "In the meantime, you be extremely polite and considerate to your grandparents so your visit with them doesn't end entirely badly."

"I will. I guess you're pretty mad, huh?"

"You could say that. Are your friends on their way home? Have they called their parents to let them know they're safe?"

"It was just Maggie and Kelly and Milo. Kelly's parents are out of town. She's spending a couple of nights with Maggie. Maggie told her mom they were coming up to visit me at my grandparents' house at the lake and that a friend of my uncle's was driving—and that's true," she added with a just a hint of renewed defiance. "They just called Maggie's mom and said they were on their way home. Maggie doesn't have to be supervised all the time like I do."

Maggie, who Jacqui knew through Alice's swim team, was a year older than Alice and the daughter of a single mother who had never seemed focused enough on parenting in Jacqui's opinion. Alice had been invited to several unchaperoned parties at Maggie's house, which Seth and Meagan had refused to allow her to attend. Jacqui would have done the same, had it been up to her to make the decision. From now on, Jacqui would be keeping a closer eye on Alice's association with Maggie—as she suspected Seth and Meagan would be.

After a few more terse words with Alice, Jacqui disconnected the call with a low groan. "I will be so glad when Seth and Meagan get back in town," she said on a hearty exhale. "They're the ones who should be dealing with Alice's sudden teenage insanity, not me."

"She's okay?"

"Yes."

Mitch visibly relaxed a little when Jacqui repeated what Alice had told her. "I'll have a chat with Milo tomorrow," he promised. "I'll get his number from Scott, who is also going to hear how I feel about his worthless brother hanging around with a group of fourteen- and fifteen-year-old girls. Trust me, after tomorrow, Milo will turn and walk in the other direction whenever he sees Alice."

"She'll be angry with you," Jacqui warned, believing absolutely that Milo would avoid Alice from now on. She'd never seen Mitch look quite this intimidating. And it irked her that she responded quite physically to that look.

Mitch shrugged. "She'll get over it. Or she won't.

Either way, she won't be in a car with Milo Lemon again."

"Good."

Wearily, she pushed a hand through her hair, not caring that the gesture left it in spikes around her face. The mood was broken tonight. She might as well go on up to bed. Alone. Not that she expected to sleep well.

She would be glad when Seth and Meagan returned from their trip and life could get back to normal. Everything had been just fine before they'd left her in charge of their house and their daughter and a stormy summer night had left her sharing this house with Dr. Mitch Baker. Despite what he'd said about being attracted to her from the start, despite his surprisingly clear memory of the first time they had met, despite his insistence that their very different careers had no significance at all to him, she still had no intention of letting herself get carried away by improbable fantasies.

"I'm going up to bed," she said. "Good night, Mitch."

If he was surprised by her abrupt departure, he didn't let it show. "I'll stay down here for a while. Maybe watch the news before I turn in. Good night, Jacqui."

She turned without another word and headed for the stairs. It felt as though more than a long day had just come to an end.

Too restless to sleep, Mitch drank another glass of tea while he watched the ten o'clock local news. When the newscast ended, he carried his glass into the kitchen and placed it in the dishwasher. He supposed he really should turn in; he had another long day scheduled tomorrow. But he was still wired. Both Jacqui and Alice had left him tied up in knots that evening.

Women, he thought with a rueful shake of his head.

There was no way any man could fully understand them—and that gender chasm developed young, judging by his niece's behavior. He chuckled when the thought crossed his mind that Jacqui could be upstairs right now thinking that men were impossible to understand at any age. His amusement faded when it occurred to him that he understood Milo all too well—which was why he'd be having a long talk with that young man very soon.

Glancing toward the back patio door, he saw a nose pressed against the glass, a pair of eyes watching him as he moved around the kitchen. "Hey, Waldo."

He wasn't sure if the dog had heard him, but Waldo knew he had Mitch's attention now. The dog yelped and wagged his tail eagerly.

"Now don't start barking. You'll wake everyone up," Mitch chided, moving quickly to the door.

He stepped outside into the still-stifling August night. It was fully dark now, but sundown had provided little relief from the heat and humidity. The weather forecaster Mitch had just watched had predicted temperatures reaching close to a hundred degrees Fahrenheit by the end of the week. The hospitals would be busy treating heat-related injuries. Having lived here all his life, Mitch was accustomed to hot, dry summers, but he had to admit he preferred the cooler days of spring and fall.

He sat for a while on the patio, patting Waldo, who had recovered nicely from his fence encounter. Surrounding them were the sounds of a Southern summer night as the mostly young professionals in the neighborhood settled in to sleep in preparation for the next workday. The soothing chirps of frogs and crickets in the narrow band of woods at the back of the subdivision blended with the occasional rumble of passing cars on the quiet streets. A siren wailed in the distance, the fading sound coming from the direction of downtown. A dog barked from a neighboring yard, answered by another farther down the block. Waldo cocked his head in response to that brief, canine conversation but didn't join in. He seemed completely happy to sit at Mitch's feet having his head and ears rubbed.

Though the security lighting in the neighborhood dimmed the cloudless night sky, Mitch could just see the glimmer of stars overhead and the blinking lights of a high-passing plane. A nearly full moon floated serenely over the sleepy scene, its reflection glittering on the water of the inground pool that took up about half of the good-size backyard. The pool was surrounded by a decorative, wrought-iron fence. Meagan had laughingly confided that Waldo would play in the pool for hours if they didn't keep it fenced and that the dog enjoyed tossing toys, sticks and anything else he could find into the water they tried to keep clean.

Life in a peaceful Little Rock neighborhood. These were the sounds and sights Mitch had experienced all his life. He had spent a month one summer during high school working on a friend's rural family farm, and although he had enjoyed the experience, he'd learned then that he wasn't really suited to country living. He liked living in the city.

Because it was separated into such distinct neighborhoods, Little Rock was known as a good-size city with a small-town feel. The largest in the state, the capitol city had a population of just less than 700,000. It had its share of urban issues, like any metropolis. Some neighborhoods struggled with poverty, crime and drugs, and he had seen the results of those problems all too often during his training at the teaching hospital. The children's hospital where he worked now had received national acclaim for its excellence, and he was proud to be associated with it. And yet...

He wished he knew for sure whether the restiveness inside him was a result of wanderlust or some other deficiency in his life. Would he be more enthusiastic about settling permanently into a place of his own— like those houses he'd toured the past Saturday—if he had someone special with whom to share that house? A family to fill the empty bedrooms? His own dog in his own backyard?

For some reason, he glanced up toward Jacqui's bedroom window then, seeing no lights shining there. Was she lying awake replaying their kisses in her mind? Did she, too, ache with a hunger to carry those embraces further? Were her nerves still thrumming, her skin still oversensitized, her pulse still erratic—as his were? Or was she sleeping peacefully up there alone, maybe even relieved that they had been interrupted before they'd both gotten carried away by attraction and proximity?

He rose abruptly. "Okay, dog, I'm going to bed. Alice will be home tomorrow, so you'll get plenty of attention then."

Assuming, of course, that Jacqui didn't lock the girl in her room until her father was home again to take over her supervision, he thought, only half-jokingly. He couldn't say he would blame Jacqui for being tempted to do just that.

Locking the kitchen door behind him and resetting the alarm system, he turned out the lights and headed quietly up the stairs. He had to pass Jacqui's door on the way to his room. He paused when he heard a sound from inside. Had she said something to him?

The sound came again, and this time he heard the

distress in her voice. Nightmare? He tapped lightly on the door. "Jacqui? You okay?"

When there was no answer, he cracked the door open just to be sure she was all right, peeking through the opening into the darkened room. "Jacqui?"

She stirred restlessly against her pillows, making another soft but infinitely sad sound. Abandoning discretion, he moved across the room, sitting on the side of the bed to place a hand lightly on her face. "Jacqui. It's okay. You're dreaming."

He could just make out her face in the shadows. Her eyes opened, their depths glittering with unshed tears. She sounded dazed and disoriented when she said, "What?"

"You were dreaming," he repeated gently. "Sounded like a bad one. I just wanted to make sure you're okay."

She reached up to rub a hand over her face, swiping her cheeks as if to make sure they were dry. "I'm okay. I hope I didn't wake you."

"No, I was just passing your door on my way to bed. I wouldn't have even heard you if I'd been in my room."

"What time is it?"

He glanced at the clock. "Eleven-thirty. I've been outside chatting with Waldo."

Apparently, he'd sat outside longer than he had realized.

She drew a deep breath, and he was pleased to note that she sounded steadier now. "Go get some sleep, Mitch. I'm fine, thanks."

"Sure you don't want to talk about it?"

"I'm sure."

Still, he hated to leave her alone when he suspected

her hands were still trembling. "That incident with Alice tonight really rattled you, didn't it?"

"I was concerned," she replied a little stiltedly. "It was bad enough that she was out running around with a bunch of kids I don't really know, but it was really unlike her to be an hour later getting home than she agreed to."

"I know. She gave everyone a scare."

"I hope she won't do anything like that again."

He gave a little shrug. "I hope not, too, but I'm sure she'll misbehave at least a few more times before she's grown. Most teenagers do, even the best ones."

"Unfortunately, you're probably right." Jacqui shifted in the bed, pulling the sheet a little higher.

He supposed she was self-conscious at lying in the bed in her nightshirt with him sitting fully dressed gazing down at her. He really should let her go back to sleep—but he had to admit he was reluctant to leave. What he really wanted to do was crawl beneath that sheet with her, no longer fully dressed.

Instead, he asked a question he suspected she wouldn't really want him to ask. "Was a teen driver behind the wheel when your sister died?"

She went very still and, though it was difficult to be certain in the dim room, he thought he saw her pale in response to the clearly unexpected question. "Yes," she said after a taut pause.

"That's why you worry so much about Alice riding with teenagers."

"I would worry about that regardless."

"So would I. But I wondered if that was what triggered your nightmare. Were you dreaming about your sister?"

He wasn't sure she was going to answer. Finally, she

turned her face away from him and murmured, "Alice and Olivia were both in my dream. It was bad."

Mitch reached out to stroke a damp strand of hair from her face. "I'm sorry. I can't imagine how much it must still hurt you."

She looked up at him then with her chin lifted. He guessed that Jacqui didn't like to be seen looking so vulnerable. "It was just a nightmare, Mitch. I don't have them often. I'll be fine. Go get some sleep."

He nodded, then made himself stand. "All right. If you need anything, you know where to find me."

"Thank you. I appreciate your concern," she said, her too-formal tone making him smile.

He paused in the doorway to glance back toward the bed. "Jacqui? Just so you'll know, I'm not entirely noble. I was very tempted to climb into that bed with you."

"I was very tempted to ask you to," she replied after only a momentary pause.

He groaned. "Thanks for sharing that. Now I won't sleep tonight, either."

He thought he heard her laugh softly when he closed her door behind him. At least he'd left her smiling, he thought as he crossed the hall to his own lonely, borrowed bed. For a moment anyway. He would bet her smile had faded the moment he'd left her alone in the dark.

Pulling his shirt over his head, he tossed it onto a chair and reached for his belt buckle. He found it difficult to smile now. He kept hearing the echo of that soft, sad sound Jacqui had made in her tormented sleep.

It wasn't too much of a stretch to guess that Jacqui had been the teenage driver when her sister had died. And it killed him to think she was still carrying the guilt from that long-ago accident. Maybe it was the physician in him that wanted to do something to alleviate her pain—or maybe he was beginning to care too much about her. The problem was, he could repair a broken bone—but a broken heart was beyond his skills.

Although Jacqui slept only half an hour later than she usually arose, Mitch was gone by the time she woke, showered and dressed the next morning. She had to admit she was relieved. She wondered if he had deliberately slipped out before she got up to avoid any potential awkwardness from the night before.

It had definitely been a eventful evening, she thought, busying herself with housework in a futile attempt to keep herself from replaying every minute of last night. Heated, arousing kisses on the couch. The disturbing call from Alice's grandmother. The nightmare—still much too clear in her mind. Then waking to find Mitch sitting on her bed, his touch so gentle on her face that she'd had to forcibly stop herself from burrowing straight into his arms.

She wasn't accustomed to having anyone there when she woke after a bad dream. As much as she told herself she wasn't a child and didn't need to be comforted after a nightmare, it had still been nice to have someone stroke her and speak to her soothingly until the horrifying images faded. She could get used to that—which was an unsettling thought.

Maybe it was because of that dream in which she had lost both Olivia and Alice in the devastating car accident, but she couldn't be too angry with the girl when she returned home, chastened and wary. Her grandparents dropped her off. Jacqui invited them in for coffee, but they were in a hurry to return home. Jacqui noted that the couple parted affectionately with Alice, who saw them off with a murmured promise that she would never cause them worry again. Apparently, she'd gotten a good talking to from her grandparents—only a hint of what would come from her father, Jacqui thought with a twinge of sympathy.

"I'm not going to fuss at you anymore," she said after Alice had sullenly apologized to her again. "It's up to your dad to take it from here. All I'm going to say is that when you're left in my charge, you're going to have to follow my rules. You knew I wouldn't approve of you riding in a car with Milo, but you implied to your grandparents that Milo is a trusted friend of the family. That was both dishonest and dangerous, Alice."

"I know I should have been back when I said," Alice conceded, looking close to tears. "And I guess I shouldn't have been in the car with Milo. He drove sort of fast. I think he was showing off. I told him to slow down, but he just laughed. You won't tell Dad that part, will you?"

"I'm sure he was showing off in front of you girls." Jacqui swallowed hard at the thought of what could have happened with that boy driving recklessly with three young girls in his car. "I hope you at least wore your seat belt."

"Of course I wore my seat belt. I always do." Alice sounded ironically indignant that Jacqui would even suggest differently.

"As for telling your Dad, I think you should decide what to tell him when you talk with him about last night. But I would advise you to be honest and penitent about breaking his rules."

Alice sighed gustily. "All the other girls my age are allowed to go out."

"You're telling me Tiff's mother would let her go riding around with an almost-eighteen-year-old boy?"

Alice grimaced, as aware as Jacqui that her friend Tiffany's mother was every bit as firm and protective as Seth. "No, I guess not."

"You know not."

Alice merely sighed again.

"Why don't you go out and play with Waldo? He's missed you."

Alice escaped eagerly. Jacqui figured the girl was looking forward to spending time with her dog, who thought everything she did was perfectly delightful.

Later that afternoon, Jacqui debated awhile before knocking on Alice's bedroom door. Alice had been in there for more than an hour, having said she wanted to play on her computer and maybe read a little. Jacqui suspected Alice was still sulking, embarrassed by the fuss she had caused. Alice was also worried about what her father was going to say when he heard about the incident.

After being invited into the room, Jacqui opened the door and stepped inside. The teen lay sprawled on her bed on top of the comforter, an open book in front of her.

Jacqui crossed the room to perch on one corner of the bed. "How's the book?"

"Pretty good. It's the third in a series."

"That series about the rescue dogs?"

"Yeah. Guess I told you about them already."

"You mentioned them."

Closing the book, Alice sat up, her legs crossed in front of her. "What's that you're holding?"

"It's an old picture. I thought you might like to see it."

Alice waited a moment. When Jacqui didn't immediately hand her the photo, she prodded, "You were going to show me the picture?"

Taking a deep breath, Jacqui handed Alice the faded, creased photo. In it, two little girls, ages eight and ten, sat side by side on a concrete step eating ice cream cones. The older had dark hair rumpled in spikes around her solemn face, whereas the younger girl's hair was lighter, wavier, her expression blissful as she enjoyed the melting treat.

Frowning in concentration, Alice pointed to the older girl. "This is you, isn't it?"

"Yes. I guess I haven't changed much."

"You were very cute."

Jacqui smiled a little. "Thanks."

"Who's the other girl?"

The smile faded. "My sister. Olivia."

Alice's eyes went wide. "You never told me you have a sister."

"Had," Jacqui corrected gently. "I had a sister."

Alice bit her lip before asking, "She died?"

"Yes. From injuries she sustained in a car accident when she was only a little older than you are now. It will be twelve years ago next week."

Blinking rapidly, Alice looked down at the photograph again. "I'm sorry. She looks nice."

"She was."

"You must really miss her, huh?"

Jacqui took the photograph again, glancing down at it before replying, "Yes. I do."

"Is that why you freaked out that I was in a car with Milo?"

"Partly. I've seen the results of an inexperienced driver being distracted by passengers. I want you to stay safe, Alice. I want you to grow up to finish high school and go to prom and college and become an orthodontist or whatever you eventually decide to be. All the things Olivia never got to do. I'm not saying you should be covered in bubble wrap and never allowed to leave the house—tempting as that might be for your dad and for me—but I do think you should take reasonable precautions. Look both ways before you cross the street. Don't stand outside in a lightning storm. Wear a helmet when you ride your bike. And don't ride in a car with a reckless teenage boy who's showing off for a group of younger girls."

"Was Olivia riding in a car with a reckless teenage boy?" Alice asked, subdued.

"No." Folding her hand around the treasured photograph, Jacqui stood. "Just a driver who was too young to react quickly enough in a dangerous situation. I want you to understand why your family and I are so concerned about the ground rules they've developed for you, Alice. Your dad will probably chew you out when he gets here, but it's only because he wants you to stay safe. You'll get a little more freedom with each passing year, but I expect you'll have to demonstrate first that you're ready to take each new step."

"By not breaking the rules, you mean?"

Jacqui smiled. "That's definitely a good start."

She reached out to stroke a hand over Alice's soft, curly hair. "Don't dread your dad getting home, Alice. He'll fuss, but he'll be very happy to see you, too. He loves you very much. You know he can never stay mad at you for long."

"Thanks, Jacqui. And I'm sorry about your sister. Will you tell me about her sometime?"

"Sometime," Jacqui promised. "Not today."

"Okay." She set the book aside. "Maybe I'll go swim for a while. Do you want to swim with me?"

"I'll sit outside with you while you swim. I'd like to get some knitting time in before making dinner."

Leaving the girl to change, she walked to her own room to put away her photograph. She wasn't sure why she'd brought it out today. Maybe she was simply ready to talk about Olivia again. And maybe Mitch had something to do with that.

She and Mitch had shared a house for less than two weeks and already she felt as though some things in her world had shifted. She had been so content before—or so she'd convinced herself. She hated to think her life would be in any way less satisfying when this atypical interlude came to an inevitable end.

Chapter Nine

Seth and Meagan returned Thursday afternoon in a flurry of baggage and gifts and hugs. Alice threw herself happily into her father's loving arms, then gave her stepmother an equally fervent welcome-home hug. It had been only a couple of weeks since they'd all seen each other, and Jacqui was sure Seth and Meagan had enjoyed their rare time together, but they were obviously happy to be back home again.

Keeping one arm around his daughter's shoulders, Seth greeted Jacqui. "Well?" he teased. "You aren't holding a resignation letter behind your back, are you?"

She smiled. "No. We've gotten by just fine."

"Uh-huh." Seth had heard a little about his daughter's mini-rebellion over the phone—but not from Jacqui, who had left that task to Alice and her grandparents. He gave his daughter a look that promised a talk later, then hugged her again before releasing her.

Meagan smiled at Jacqui. "To add to your chores while we were gone, I hear you've also been taking care of my homeless brother. You certainly had your hands full, didn't you?"

Jacqui forced a smile. She'd hardly seen Mitch since he'd left her bedroom after her nightmare two nights earlier. He'd been busy at work—or maybe busy avoiding her once Alice was there to observe them. He hadn't talked to Alice about the incident at her grandparents' house, probably figuring there were enough adults on the girl's case about that, but instead had teased his niece just like always during the brief times they were both home. His manner toward Jacqui had been friendly, casual, deliberately proper in front of the girl. But the expression in his eyes when their glances had occasionally collided had let her know he hadn't forgotten one moment of the time they had spent alone together.

"It was no trouble at all," she assured Meagan, hoping no one could tell she was lying through her teeth.

Meagan smiled wryly. "Right. Thank you anyway for everything you've done."

"No problem." She figured she had earned every penny of the generous bonus she had been promised in her next paycheck.

A short while later, she left the family to catch up while she returned to her newly renovated apartment. She had the next three days off, and she planned to enjoy the leisure time. It would be nice to be responsible for no one but herself for the long weekend.

Her apartment smelled like new, cheap carpet and adhesive, but she saw at a glance that the work had been adequately done. What few possessions she'd left there were still intact. The new flooring and a few new furnishings made the inexpensive furnished rental look a little more updated than when she'd first moved in. There was even a new laminate countertop in the tiny galley kitchen, she noted in satisfaction. The old one had been in pretty bad shape.

Her rent would probably go up when the lease came up for renewal, she thought resignedly. She hoped it would still be reasonable. This was a decent place to live until she found a house she could afford, which would be at least one more lease cycle.

She unpacked and put everything away, then settled onto the new plaid couch with her knitting. Her TV was small and she had only very basic cable, so she didn't bother trying to find anything to watch. It was nice to just enjoy the quiet for a while.

It felt good to be back in her own place, she assured herself. Now that Seth and Meagan were home, everything could get back to normal. School would be starting again soon, and her days would settle back into a predictable routine of cleaning and shopping and laundry, picking up Alice after school, then cooking dinner for the family before returning here to her apartment. A comfortable, pleasant, generally stress-free schedule. Exactly the way she liked it.

Her sigh echoed in the silent room, making her frown in response to the plaintive sound.

"Stop being an idiot, Jacqui," she muttered, forcing herself to concentrate on the intricate pattern taking shape between her rapidly moving knitting needles.

Her phone rang a couple of times that afternoon. Her friend Alexis called to reschedule their previous lunch plans for the coming Saturday. "I promise I won't cancel on you this time. No matter what comes up, I'll tell everyone I already have plans."

Jacqui chuckled. "I'll look forward to it. It's been too long since we've managed to get together."

"I know. I want to hear everything you've been up to lately."

That wouldn't take long, Jacqui thought, wincing a little as she disconnected the call. She could tell Alexis a little about the past two weeks, but she wouldn't be comfortable sharing too much of the Llewellyn's personal business. As for anything that had happened between her and Mitch—well, she wasn't prepared to talk about that with her casual friend, either. She wasn't actually close enough to anyone with whom to discuss her complicated feelings for Mitch, she thought wistfully. That was the sort of intimate discussion best held between the very dearest of friends—or sisters, perhaps, she thought with a pang.

Oddly enough, she thought she could talk to LaDonna about her confused feelings, had the circumstances been a bit different. LaDonna always seemed so caring, so levelheaded and accepting. Jacqui wished she could feel as comfortable turning to her own mother as she would be to her employer's mom, if the current dilemma didn't involve LaDonna's own adored son.

Almost as if fate had intercepted that thought, the second call she received that afternoon was from her mother. Jacqui glanced at the caller ID screen with a wince, realizing that it had been almost two months since they'd last talked. "Hi, Mom. How are you and Dad?"

"We're doing well, thanks, sweetie. We're in Denver. We moved here last month and your dad has already found a good job doing maintenance for an apartment complex. I'm going to be helping out part-time in the rental office. In exchange, we get a free apartment and enough pay to provide the necessities. I think we'll be staying here for a while."

Jacqui had heard that before. She wondered exactly how long it would be before her father decided another pasture sounded greener. "That's great, Mom. I've heard Denver is a nice place to live. I hope you'll be happy there."

"You're still in Little Rock?"

"Yes. Still working for the same family. It's going well."

"I'm glad for you, sweetie. I know how you like your routines."

Jacqui frowned a little, wondering if she'd just been subtly patronized, but she decided to let it go. There was no reason for her to take offense by anything her long-distance parent said. "Yes, I'm quite content here," she said simply.

"Maybe you could take a vacation soon? Come to Denver to see your Dad and me? It's been a long time since we've been together, you know."

"I have got some vacation time coming. I'll try to get out there for a few days."

Assuming, of course, her parents were still in Denver when she took her planned two-week vacation time in October, a month she had chosen because it was a fairly slow time in the Llewellyn household. She wasn't enthusiastic about digging into her savings for airfare, but she supposed she should make an effort to see her parents at least once every year or so, and it had been more than a year since the last visit.

"Oh, that would be wonderful. I know your dad will be happy to see you. And so will I."

"I'll do my best."

"Our apartment is only one bedroom, but we have

a nice couch. You won't mind sleeping on that, will you?"

"Of course not." It wouldn't be the first time she'd slept on a couch—or a pallet on the floor, for that matter. Her parents hadn't always been able to provide enough beds for the four of them.

"So, what's been going on with you? Are you seeing anyone special?"

"Not really. But I have friends. And I stay busy. It's a good life."

"Well—I'm glad. You, um, you know next week is—"

Her mother's voice faded, but Jacqui was able to finish the sentence in her head. Next week was the anniversary of her sister's death. She hadn't needed that reminder. "Yes, I know."

"She would want you to be happy, sweetie. We all want that for you."

"And I am, thanks, Mom. I hope you and Dad are, too."

"We're getting by," her mother replied vaguely. "I should probably go. We thought we'd go out for a little while this evening. There's a nice little tavern nearby. Good music, nice people. We stop in occasionally for a drink."

Probably more than occasionally, Jacqui thought, but that was their business, not hers. "Okay, well, have a good time."

"We will, sweetie. Thanks. Um—talk to you soon?"

"Sure. I'll let you know when I finalize my vacation plans."

"I'd like that. I— Goodbye, Jacqui."

"'Bye, Mom."

Tossing the phone aside, she shoved a suddenly weary

hand through her hair. She couldn't help thinking of the lively conversations she'd overheard in the Llewellyn and Baker households—all the teasing and squabbling and I-love-yous. She did love her parents, she mused somberly, but such expressions of emotion had never been easy for them.

She glanced at her watch. Almost 6:00 p.m. She wasn't really hungry, but she was too restless to sit any longer with her knitting. Setting the project aside, she rose, glancing toward the little kitchen across the room. She'd stopped by the grocery store on the way home, so she had a few things to prepare. Maybe she'd see if anything looked appetizing.

She had taken only a couple of steps in that direction when someone knocked on her door. Blinking in surprise, she turned. She was popular today, she thought, wondering who was dropping by unannounced. Probably the landlord, making sure everything was satisfactory. He'd been very grateful for her patience during the renovation; because she'd had another place to stay, she hadn't pressed for immediate action as she was sure some of her neighbors had done.

Glancing through the peephole from force of long habit, she swallowed a groan and rested her head against the door for a moment before opening it. So much for the relaxing, decision-free evening she had envisioned.

"Hello, Mitch."

He stood in the open doorway, searching her face as if to decipher her reaction to his surprise call. "Hi. I got away from work a little earlier than usual today. I hope this isn't a bad time for me to drop by."

Without answering, she moved aside to let him in, closing the door behind him before turning to look at him. He was the one who'd shown up at her home out of the blue; she figured it was up to him to start whatever conversation he'd come here to have.

She was aware that her apartment was hardly luxurious, especially in comparison to the places they had toured last Saturday. She'd never visited his duplex, but it had probably been more upscale than this little furnished rental. Still, she refused to be self-conscious about her modest surroundings. The apartment was clean, the neighborhood lower income but relatively safe, and she could easily afford the rent and still put away savings every month. It worked for her.

His mouth quirked, as though he was amused by her rather challenging silence. "Okay if I sit down?"

So maybe she wasn't being the most gracious hostess. That was his fault for showing up without an invitation, she told herself, even as she relented. "Of course. Have a seat. Can I get you anything? I can make coffee."

He chuckled. "There you go again. You aren't on the job now, Jacqui. No need to use your Mary Poppins voice."

"Mary Poppins wasn't a housekeeper—she was a nanny," she muttered, vaguely embarrassed.

His grin widened. "Sorry. You're the one who's always making movie analogies. Guess I'm not as good at it."

His teasing was making her relax a bit, as he probably intended. She motioned toward the couch. "Sit down, Mitch. Tell me why you're here."

Catching her hand, he tugged her down beside him when he took a seat. "I think you know why I'm here."

She moistened her lips. "Not entirely," she said honestly.

He reached out to toy with the ends of her short hair,

a gesture that appeared to be becoming a habit for him. It seemed little more than an excuse to brush his fingers against her cheek, leaving trails of sensation behind. "Because I can't stay away from you."

All the differences between them flashed through her mind, all the reasons why this was such a bad idea.

He searched her face, probably trying to read her emotions. "We're on your turf now," he reminded her. "All you have to do is ask me to leave and I will. No argument."

Despite all her qualms, all her logical, sensible warnings to herself, she simply couldn't make herself utter the words that would send him away. Not tonight. She sighed lightly and leaned toward him. "Don't go," she murmured.

He had her in his arms, his mouth on hers, before she'd even finished speaking.

Neither of them was in a hurry. Jacqui, for one, had nowhere else to be. Tonight they didn't have to worry about discretion; they had complete privacy here in her apartment. They took full advantage of that freedom.

They left his shirt on the couch when they moved toward the bedroom. His shoes were shed somewhere along the way. By the time they reached her bed, her jeans were on the floor. His mouth seeking hers again, Mitch reached for the hem of her knit top.

She had only a momentary qualm before she raised her arms to allow him to tug the shirt over her head. It wasn't entirely modesty that gave her pause. Mitch's gaze zoomed straight to the reason she had hesitated.

His touch was so very gentle when he traced the scar that crossed her abdomen. "Spleen?"

"Gone."

"The accident?"

"Yes." She had spent six weeks recovering physically from that surgery. She would never fully recover emotionally, although the pain had lessened somewhat with time.

She had to be careful of infections and take a few routine precautions, but otherwise, she could live a full, normal life without a spleen. A doctor had told her after the surgery that she was fortunate to have lost only that relatively unnecessary organ. Still half-crazed with guilt and grief, she had screamed at him that he was an idiot. She had lost so much more than a spleen in that accident.

Catching her face between his hands, Mitch brushed his lips across hers, the kiss so sweet, so tender that it brought a lump to her throat. His mouth moved lightly across her cheek and down her throat, his hands exploring her back with long, smooth strokes that were as arousing as they were soothing. Lowering her to the bed, he kissed her throat and then the rise of her breasts above her white lace bra. He touched his lips to the scar before returning to capture her mouth, unfastening her bra as he did so.

She was not busty, but he seemed to approve of the way her breasts fit into his hands. His thumbs rotated lazily, and she arched with a gasp of reaction. It had been a while since she had allowed anyone this access, since there had been anyone with whom she had wanted to share these intimacies. Her rapidly overheating body was letting her know just how much she needed this release.

Mitch had come prepared for lovemaking. She decided to wonder later if he'd been so confident that she would invite him to stay, or if he had simply hoped she would. Whatever the reason, for now she could only be grateful.

For all the reasons she had listed earlier of why they were so poorly matched, they were certainly an ideal fit physically. Their bodies moved together, meshed together as perfectly as if they'd been built as a set. Once again, she sensed no awkwardness or hesitance between them. Sure, there was a giddy, first-time excitement— and yet an odd familiarity at the same time, a sensation she had felt with him before. If she were the fanciful, romantic type, she would imagine they were meant to be together. Fortunately, she was more sensible than that, she thought, even as she drew him closer.

They climaxed together, their soft cries sounding in perfect harmony.

Propped on one elbow, Mitch gazed down at Jacqui as she lay beside him, both slowly recovering their strength. He loved touching her hair, he mused, brushing a strand from her flushed face. It was so soft and thick, the cute, choppy cut tickling his fingers. Some guys were obsessed with long hair, but he thought Jacqui's style was perfect to best display her graceful neck and the pretty face highlighted by those big, dark eyes that could so easily mesmerize him.

He loved touching her skin, too, he thought as he allowed his fingers to slide down her throat to her shoulder. So warm and smooth and taut over her slender, toned body. The occasional splatter of golden freckles enchanted him. The scar that bisected her firm abdomen saddened him but made her no less attractive to him.

She opened her eyes and gazed up at him. Her expressions were becoming more readable to him, he thought optimistically. He thought he saw the lingering signs of pleasure there, physical satisfaction—and maybe a hint of the misgivings that were probably creeping back into her mind now that they had satisfied their desire for each other. Temporarily satisfied, he corrected himself, knowing he would soon want her again.

"Are you hungry?" she asked, her voice still a bit huskier than usual. "I could make you something."

He almost told her that she was so damned cute, but he suspected that would get him punched—and she had access to a few too many vulnerable places at the moment. Instead, he teased lightly, "Always trying to feed me."

She shrugged against the pillows, her own lips twitching. "That's what I do."

"You're very good at it," he assured her with mock solemnity. "You're very good at everything you do," he added, dropping a kiss on the end of her nose.

He was delighted when she giggled, the sound so rare he couldn't help laughing in response.

"Why, thank you, sir. But you still haven't answered me. Are you hungry?"

"Not really." He was perfectly content to just lie there for a while, savoring the aftermath of the best sex he'd had in…well, ever. "Are you?"

She shook her head. "No."

"Then maybe we could just talk for a while."

He saw the faintest hint of nerves cross her face in response to his suggestion. He wouldn't have been able to detect that a couple weeks ago. He liked to think he was getting to know her better despite her reservations.

"We don't have to talk about anything that makes you uncomfortable," he assured her. "We can chat about the weather, if you want. I just enjoy being with you."

She smiled. "We don't have to chat about the weather.

For one thing, that's too boring in Arkansas in August. Hot and dry with a chance of afternoon thunderstorms. Pretty much sums it up."

Chuckling, he nodded. "Yeah, pretty much. Gets kind of boring, huh?"

She didn't respond, exactly, but asked, instead, "What will the weather be like in Peru?"

He wasn't sure what had made her think of his upcoming trip. "Somewhat cooler. It's winter there, you know."

"Yes."

"I wish you could go with me. I guess it's too late to make the arrangements."

She frowned, obviously startled by his impulsive comment. "Go with you? To Peru?"

"It's going to be a fun trip. Lots of hiking and sightseeing. I'd enjoy sharing it with you."

"Like you said, it's too late to make arrangements for that."

He wondered if he heard a hint of relief in her voice that she wouldn't be forced to make that decision.

"Anyway, I've already made a commitment, sort of, for my upcoming vacation," she said a bit too offhandedly. "My mother called earlier. She wants me to visit her and my dad in Denver for a few days."

"They're living in Denver now?"

"Yes. Managing an apartment complex there. She said they like it."

"Was that one of the places you lived with them?"

"No. They've only been there a month."

"Think they'll stay there?"

She sighed almost imperceptibly. "Who knows? I wouldn't be entirely surprised if I get a call saying they've moved on before I can even make plane reservations."

"Did you have a good talk with your mom?"

"The usual. She told me what they were up to, asked if I'm still in the same place, called me boring, then asked me to come visit."

He lifted an eyebrow in response to one item on that list. "Your mother called you boring?"

"Well...maybe not in so many words," she admitted.

"What words did she use?"

"She said that I've always liked my daily routines."

He thought about that for a moment before asking, "Well? Don't you?"

Her own pause was a bit longer. "Yeah. I guess I do," she muttered. "It was just the way she said it...made it sound so dull."

Mitch laughed. "Trust me, Jacqui. There is nothing dull about you."

She looked pleased by the compliment. "Thanks."

He tapped her chin with one finger. "You're welcome."

Looking at him through her lashes, she said, "My mother reminded me that next week is the anniversary of my sister's death. An unnecessary reminder, of course."

"Do your parents blame you for the accident that killed your sister?" He took a risk asking, but he really wanted to know.

She stiffened a little. "I never said I was driving."

He merely looked at her.

Jacqui sighed. "I guess it was obvious. I was driving. I'd had my license for less than a month, and had little formal training behind the wheel. Dad just handed me the keys and told me to go get Olivia and me something to eat because he and Mom had other things to do. They planned to spend the evening in a bar close to the motel where we were living, just outside Chicago. A teenager in a sports car ran a red light and hit the old car I was driving, right in the passenger door. I've already told you Olivia died on the operating table. I damaged my spleen and had a few broken bones, but she took the brunt of the crash."

"How old were you?"

"I was almost seventeen. Olivia had just turned fifteen."

"And you blame yourself? Even though the other teen driver ran the light?"

"I don't blame myself, exactly. The boy was at fault. But if I'd been more experienced, maybe a little less distracted by something Olivia was saying or by trying to decide where to eat…"

"You do blame yourself. That's a heavy burden to carry, Jacqui."

"I carried it a long time," she admitted. "I've learned to let it go. Most of the time."

"The other driver—was he injured?"

"Yes. He had a head injury that was expected to cause him lifelong challenges. I don't know how he's done since, haven't really wanted to find out. It was a tragedy for him and his family, too. He was just a pampered kid, driving too fast in a car that was too powerful for a boy his age. Some friends were following him in another car, and he was showing off for them. They're the ones who called the paramedics."

"It must have been a horrible time for you and your parents."

"It was. His insurance covered the hospital bills and

the funeral and supported my parents for a couple of years, but it couldn't soothe the pain of their loss."

"Or yours."

"No."

He suspected that Jacqui hadn't received a penny of that money, other than to pay her hospital bills. "What happened after that? With you and your family, I mean?"

"After a few months, Dad needed to move on. Running, that time. Mom started packing, the way she always does, but I told them I'd had enough of wandering aimlessly from place to place. I was ready to find someplace and stay awhile. I found a job at a restaurant, and I stayed behind when they left. It was the best choice for all of us."

"And you were seventeen?"

"Yes."

"Still so young."

"I've always been old for my age."

She'd had reason to be, he thought, guessing from some of the things she'd said about her parents that she must have been placed in charge of her younger sister from the time she was quite young. Which would have made her feel even more responsible for Olivia's death. "I'm very sorry about what you've been through, Jacqui."

She shook her head impatiently. "Other than losing my sister, I haven't had such a bad life. My parents have their faults, but they never treated us badly. I've had jobs I liked, met some great people in my travels—like the sweet neighbor who taught me how to knit when I was a kid and my friend who owns the boutique and sells my work there. I have a couple of good friends here— I'm having lunch with my friend Alexis this Saturday.

I liked my last job for Mr. Avery in Hot Springs, and I love working for your sister's family. I have nothing, really, to complain about, though I do miss Olivia, of course."

She was so determined not to be pitied. He understood her well enough by now to know she valued her competence and independence, and he couldn't blame her for that. She'd been on her own a long time—even before that physical separation from her parents, he thought. She'd made her own way in the world and had done so quite successfully. She deserved to take pride in that.

"You know, I think I am hungry after all." She rolled abruptly and reached for her clothes. "I'll take the bathroom first. You can wash up while I cook."

He lay on his back, his arms akimbo behind his head. "Take your time."

He would just lie here for a while longer, thinking about some of the things she had said and wondering where they would go from here.

Chapter Ten

Jacqui felt as though she were living a double life. She continued to report to work at the usual time and performed her usual duties once there. She cleaned and did laundry, chauffeured Alice for some back-to-school shopping, wrestled Waldo into the car for a visit to the vet for his annual shots, ran errands and cooked dinners for the family before leaving every evening. She doubted that anyone in the family had any suspicion at all that her life had changed dramatically during the past week.

She saw Mitch nearly every day. Saying he thought it was better for all concerned, he'd moved out of his sister's house the day after Meagan and Seth returned from their trip. His mother had urged him to stay with her, but he'd chosen instead to check into a hotel near the hospital until he could make more permanent arrangements. He'd told his mother that he didn't want to disturb her with his erratic work hours, but Jacqui knew he had moved into the hotel so no one knew he was spending most of his free time with her.

She had made him promise not to tell anyone they were spending time together. Much less that they had become lovers. Although he'd argued that he didn't care who knew he was seeing Jacqui, he had conceded to her request. He thought she was putting off telling everyone because she needed time to adjust to the change in their relationship. Time to get used to thinking of them as a couple before letting anyone else see them that way.

What would he think, she wondered, if he knew she was keeping their affair a secret because she fully expected it to be short-lived and hoped to avoid as much awkwardness as possible when it inevitably ended? Would he accuse her of conceding defeat before they even had a chance to make it work, or would he secretly appreciate that she was trying to spare him discomfort with his family?

As much as she was trying to protect her heart, she knew she was going to miss him badly if—when—this all ended. The physical part of their relationship was amazing. Addictive. Like nothing she had ever experienced before. But even more, she savored the interludes afterward when they lay snuggled together in her bed, talking about their days or whatever else popped into their heads.

He made her laugh with stories from his childhood, and she found herself telling him little anecdotes from her own, something she never did with other people. They talked about his adventures—and misadventures—with his sisters, and she told him some of the scrapes she and Olivia had gotten into. It didn't hurt so much to talk about Olivia with Mitch, she discovered. Maybe because he knew how her sister had died and didn't seem to judge her for it. Maybe because finally breaking her silence about Olivia with both Mitch and Alice made each mention of her a little easier.

Or maybe it was just that Mitch was incredibly easy to talk to.

They didn't talk much about the future. She supposed he was doing something about finding a permanent place to live, but he didn't discuss it. Mostly, when they looked ahead, it was not beyond Mitch's rapidly approaching trip to Peru. He was so excited about that trek. She hoped it would be as much fun as he thought it would be. He would be so disappointed if it wasn't.

She was going to miss him while he was away. But then, who knew if they'd still be together by the time he left anyway, she reminded herself. She wasn't making any plans. She was simply going to enjoy it while it lasted. And when it ended—well, she had a lot of experience with moving on. She could still be friendly enough with Mitch on the rare occasions they would see each other through his family. And no one else would ever have to know about their temporary insanity.

The end came even sooner than she had predicted.

They had been lovers for just more than a week when Mitch reluctantly dressed to leave her apartment Monday night. It wasn't all that late, but he had an early surgery the next morning. He thought it best that he go back to the hotel for a few hours of sleep first. He lingered for quite a while at the door as one good-night kiss led to another—and then another.

Finally she drew herself out of his arms and stepped back, warding him off when he laughingly reached for her again. "Go," she ordered. "Get some sleep."

"I'm going." He heaved a sigh. "It gets harder to leave."

"You're just tired of that hotel."

"That, too." He opened the door, then paused in the doorway as if a thought had just occurred to him. "Jacqui—Madison's birthday is next weekend."

Lifting an eyebrow, she nodded. "I know. Meagan and Alice mentioned that they're going shopping tomorrow evening to find her a gift."

"We're having a get-together at Mom's Saturday night. Casual. Just family."

She felt the muscles in her chest tighten as he spoke, making it more difficult to breathe. "Mitch—"

"Go with me, Jacqui. Everyone would love to have you there."

As a matter of fact, LaDonna had already invited her. Jacqui hadn't yet given an answer. She had wanted first to confirm with Mitch that they could both attend the party without giving anyone a hint of their true relationship. Now she wasn't so sure.

"You're, um, asking me to be there—just as a guest of the family?"

"As my guest," he corrected. "I'd like us to go together."

Twisting her hands in the tie of her short terry robe, she shook her head. "I don't think that's a good idea. Everyone would start wondering what's going on. You know Madison, especially, would be asking questions. Right now everyone thinks we're just friends, but if we start attending parties together, they're going to get different ideas."

"The right idea, you mean."

"We're not ready for that to come out yet." If ever.

"You're not ready. Frankly, I don't see the need for

all the secrecy. I mean, sure, it was nice to have this past week all to ourselves without any outside scrutiny, but it's inevitable that people are going to find out. What better time to make the announcement than when everyone's already gathered together?"

It must have been panic that made her blurt tactlessly, "Make what announcement? That you're sleeping with your sister's housekeeper?"

As soon as she said them, she wished she could call the words back. Not because they weren't what she was thinking, but because they led to a line of discussion she wasn't sure she was ready to get into tonight.

Mitch closed the door deliberately. Planting his hands on his hips, he frowned at her. "Considering that you are a very intelligent woman, that was a really dumb thing to say."

She flushed a little but lifted her chin and stood her ground. "Maybe. But still true. Why does everyone need to know our private business?"

"Because I don't want to get in a position of lying to my family. Or sneaking around behind their back with you. Look, I know it's still very early in our relationship..."

"We don't have a relationship, Mitch. We're just having a little fun for now while you're at loose ends with your future plans, and there's nothing at all wrong with that, but there's no need for everyone to know about it. I don't want anything to change between me and the rest of your family, once you and I— You know."

"After we stop sleeping together?" he asked a bit too politely.

She shrugged.

"You never intended to give this a real chance, did you?"

"You're the one who said you're not at a point in your life where you're interested in long-term leases," she reminded him.

"That's hardly fair. I was talking about real estate, not us."

She shook her head sadly. "Don't you see, Mitch? It's all tied up together. I *am* the type who wants a long-term lease once I find exactly what I'm looking for. I don't mind an occasional short-term stay in a decent place while I'm searching for a permanent home, but I always know going in that it's only temporary."

He looked baffled by her tangled analogy, and she supposed she couldn't blame him for that. Still, she thought maybe he'd gotten the message. When it came to giving her heart, it was all or nothing with her. Until she found someone who felt exactly the same way—if that ever happened—she was keeping that vulnerable organ locked safely away. Even if it hadn't been for all the other obstacles between them, Mitch had made it clear enough during the past couple of weeks that he wasn't looking for long-term commitments.

"I love my job, and I don't want to ruin my relationship with your sisters and your mother," she repeated quietly. "I'm very fond of them. When you're off exploring Peru or looking for exciting new jobs in places other than where you've lived all your life, I'll still be here with them. I don't want them feeling as though they have to take sides between us or treat me any differently than they have before. I'm Meagan and Seth's housekeeper, an occasional nanny for Alice—and, for now anyway, a friend of the family. I'm content for things to stay that way."

"So it's a no on the party."

Her heart twisted in response to his expression

because they both knew she was turning down more than a simple invitation.

She agreed somewhat sadly. "It's a no."

He looked as though there was more he wanted to say, but he merely stood there for a moment in silence before he said, "Fine."

"I'll make an excuse to your mother. Other plans."

He nodded. "Whatever you want to tell her. I won't cause you any problems. I'd better go." He reached for the doorknob again. "I'll, uh, call you."

Knotting the robe tie more tightly around her blood-less fingers, she managed a faint smile. "Right."

He took one step outside her apartment, then paused once again. "Jacqui?" he said without looking back. "For the record—your job has never been an issue with me. I think you're damned good at it."

Despite her pain, it was still nice to hear him say that. "Thank you, Mitch."

"Good night." He closed the door behind him.

Moving forward to turn the locks, she sighed heavily. He had said "good night," but she thought she heard an echo of "goodbye" in her now-silent apartment.

She walked slowly over to the couch, where she sank onto one end and automatically picked up her knitting. She wouldn't be sleeping for a while yet, so she might as well be productive while she sat there brooding.

So, it hadn't lasted very long at all. Just over a week. Even with her brief history of ill-fated relationships, that was a record.

It was probably best this way. Short enough so that every moment had been close to perfection, at least until the very end. They hadn't had to deal with fights or makeups or conflicts of time or priorities that inevitably caused friction in long-term relationships. Because it had been so brief, and so private, she wouldn't have to deal with other people's sympathy or advice or disapproval. And because her routines had been disrupted for only a few days, it wouldn't take her long to fall back into them. She had been satisfied with her life before Mitch literally stumbled into it; she would be again, she promised herself.

It hadn't escaped her notice that he hadn't taken issue with her reminder that he wasn't looking for a long-term commitment. She hadn't expected a declaration of undying love or a flowery proposal of marriage—not after only a week of being together, certainly—but he could have argued that he was open to the possibilities. That he, too, was only waiting to be sure he'd found the right one before he made any binding promises.

Only he wasn't looking for commitment. Not now. Not when he was still nagged by curiosity about what lay beyond the borders of his first thirty-one years. He'd known commitment all his life—to his family, his education and career training, his job. She didn't really blame him for not wanting to tie himself to another anchor.

It was a good thing she had protected herself, she thought, glaring fiercely down at her knitting needles. Had she not, she would be in a great deal of pain right now. She would probably be feeling as if her tidy, carefully organized world had just crashed around her ears.

It was a very good thing she wasn't feeling that way now, she thought with a hard, aching swallow.

A worried couple awaited him when Mitch walked into a small, private hospital consultation room late Friday afternoon. They held hands as they watched him enter, followed closely by a surgical resident, who closed the door behind them. Mitch gave the parents a reassuring smile, offering his hand to each before inviting them to have a seat at the small, rectangular table in the cubicle-size room.

Sitting across from them, the resident seated quietly and observantly nearby, Mitch asked, "You were told that Jeffrey did very well during his surgery?"

"Yes, the volunteer and the nurse kept us updated," Laura Dickerson assured him, her voice quivering just a little with nerves. "There were none of the possible complications you warned us about?"

"No, everything went just fine."

No matter how many times he had done it, it always felt good to see the relief in worried parents' eyes when he consulted with them after successful operations. Just as it always grieved him to have to report otherwise. Fortunately, in his specialty he didn't have to relay heartbreaking news often. And in this particular case, the report was all good.

"I was able to cut his tibia and fibula very close to the growth plate, and the bones realigned very well. He'll have to wear the fixator I attached for between eight and twelve weeks, and he'll have physical therapy three times a week. We'll have to make adjustments in the fixator during the process and then evaluate at the end of three months to determine if any further corrections are necessary. It's going to be a challenging time for the whole family, but when it's all over, Jeffrey's legs will be as straight and strong as your own. You'll be racing to keep up with him again."

The three-year-old had been presented to Mitch with Blount's disease affecting his left leg, which had bowed during growth, making it somewhat shorter than his right leg. It hadn't been the worst case Mitch had seen by far, but he knew any procedure was drastic to the child's adoring parents. He expected young Jeffrey to benefit significantly from the operation Mitch had just performed, leading a full, active life afterward. That was just one of the reasons Mitch loved this job.

Fifteen minutes later, after answering a dozen questions and offering a dozen more reassurances, he left the conference room, gave the eager resident a list of instructions, then headed for his office. At least something in his life was going right, he thought as weariness gradually overpowered satisfaction. He hadn't been sleeping well this week. He'd been on call Wednesday night, and it had been a long one, leaving him drained and grumpy. Okay, so maybe there were times he didn't love his job so much. That was normal, too.

He was greeted by quite a few coworkers on the way to his office. He'd made a lot of friends here, he thought. He passed a couple of parents of young surgical patients, returning their greetings with friendly nods. He was accustomed to the respectful manner with which he was often treated—after all, these people had literally placed their children's well-being in his hands. He never wanted to let himself take that trust for granted or to let himself get jaded to the jumbled emotions his patients and their families had to deal with during medical crises.

Accepting a stack of messages from his always-organized secretary, he carried them into his office and tossed them onto his cluttered desk before falling into his chair. He had calls to return, reports to file, dictation to do—but it could all wait for just a minute, he thought, scrubbing his hands over his face.

"Here. Looked like you could use this."

His secretary placed a steaming cup of coffee on his

desk and gave him a sympathetic smile before returning to her own work.

Gratefully, he sipped the freshly brewed beverage, thinking he really should buy her some flowers or something. She'd gone beyond the call of duty during the past month. He hoped she knew how much he appreciated how efficiently she kept his professional life running, his schedule straight, his correspondence completed. Glancing at the door she had closed behind her, he wished fleetingly that he could turn over all his problems to her and have her handle them with the same firm hand.

Maybe then he could go to bed again without lying awake wondering why he had let Jacqui send him away. Wondering if he should have fought harder to hang on to something that had been so special. Wondering what kind of an idiot walked away from a woman like that just because she had very bravely and honestly informed him that she was the long-term-commitment type.

Hadn't he really known that all along? She'd certainly made it clear from the start that she'd had enough of drifting in her rootless childhood. She'd told him she was saving for a home of her own—and he had seen the pure lust on her face when they'd toured that Craftsman-style house in Hillcrest. Unlike him, Jacqui knew exactly what she wanted, and she was pursuing it with single-minded determination. He wished he had her clear-sightedness, her certainty of what it would take to make her happy.

With a wince, he remembered the way she had compared him to a short-term lease while she looked for a place to settle for the duration. Her words had been blunt, a little jumbled, but ultimately effective. He'd gotten the message clearly enough. She wasn't willing to settle. Wasn't willing to risk too much on a guy who wasn't prepared to offer forever.

What she hadn't said was whether she would be interested if he did want to spend the rest of his life with her. Was he no more to her than another furnished apartment—nice enough to spend some time there while she looked for the place she really wanted?

Another real estate metaphor, he thought, muttering an exasperated curse. But apt enough to make his shoulders sag in despairing self-recrimination.

He never wanted to hurt Jacqui. He'd do anything to prevent that—even stay far away from her, if that was what she wanted. But apparently he'd left more behind than he'd realized when he'd walked away. Judging from the emptiness inside him, he'd left a sizable piece of his heart. Did he have the courage to offer her the rest of it? And would she even accept it if he did?

Heaving a long sigh, he turned his focus to his work. As always, he had a stack of responsibilities waiting for his attention.

Jacqui tried to ignore the guilt she felt while sitting across the kitchen table from LaDonna Baker, sharing tea and cookies on Wednesday afternoon, eleven days after Jacqui had broken up with Mitch. Not that there had been much to break up, she told herself as she toyed with a cookie she didn't really want, just to have something to do with her hands during this visit.

LaDonna had dropped by with a pretty top for Alice that she'd found on a sale rack that afternoon. "I couldn't resist it," she'd admitted to Jacqui. "The color will look so pretty on Alice."

Unfortunately, Alice wasn't there to accept the gift. School was already in session during this final week of

August, having started Monday morning. After school, Alice would be competing in her last swim match of the season. Seth had arranged to attend that match, then he and Alice planned to meet Meagan for dinner, so Jacqui would be headed home soon. No one to cook for tonight but herself, she thought. Maybe she'd order a pizza and watch a little TV. That sounded like a perfectly nice evening. She wished she could look forward to it a little more.

Jacqui had invited LaDonna in for a snack and a chat, and the older woman had eagerly agreed. She didn't work on Wednesdays and it was sometimes difficult to entertain herself, she confessed. But maybe she had overdone it a bit that day. She was tired from her shopping excursion, and tea and a chat sounded like a lovely way to recuperate.

"You'd think I'd be over empty nest syndrome by now," she said as they lingered over the tea. "After all, my youngest child turned twenty-eight last week."

LaDonna's house had been empty only since last November, when she'd lost her mother, who had lived with her for several years. Jacqui thought it wasn't so unusual that LaDonna's home still felt empty to her at times after living there so long with her late husband, her now-grown children and then her mother. It must be difficult to make that transition from a full house to a quiet one. And LaDonna was still relatively young. It was no wonder she sometimes felt at loose ends.

"Did you buy anything for yourself during your shopping trip?" Jacqui asked.

"No," LaDonna admitted. "Just the top for Alice and that bag I described to you for Madison. Oh, and I got a lovely set of hand towels for a nice young couple from my church who is getting married next month. Half off, plus I had an extra-fifteen-percent coupon," she boasted.

Jacqui laughed. "Congratulations."

"I saw lots of nice things I thought Mitch could use, but because he can't seem to make up his mind if he's going to buy or rent his next place I wasn't sure exactly what he'd need. It's been five weeks since his duplex burned, and I know that's not a lot of time, but still, he should be making some progress in deciding what he wants. I swear, all that boy can think about is his work and his upcoming trip to Peru."

It took all her fortitude for Jacqui to keep smiling and speak lightly. "He's still very excited about that trip, I suppose."

"Well, yes."

Something in LaDonna's tone made Jacqui's eyebrows rise. "That didn't sound very certain."

"It's just that—well, he was so excited up until a week or so ago. Now he just seems distracted all the time. And he looks so tired. I guess he's been working like crazy to clear his schedule for the time off. I fussed at him over the phone yesterday, told him he's going to have to start getting some rest. Which would be easier, I said, if he were sleeping someplace other than a hotel. I wish he'd just move in with me while he makes his decision."

"I suppose he doesn't want to cause you any trouble," Jacqui replied, feeling guilty again that she was keeping so much from LaDonna.

Did Mitch miss her as much as she missed him? Did he, too, lie awake remembering the nights they had spent together and aching for more? Did he also wish things could have been different for them?

"As if having my son as a guest would be any trouble," LaDonna fretted.

Leaving her cookie untouched, she took a sip of her tea. Her pale face was creased with a frown when she lowered the cup. "Jacqui, do you have an ibuprofen available? I have a little headache."

Jacqui stood and moved to the cabinet where she kept a bottle of over-the-counter pain reliever. "Headache? Is that something you have often?"

"More often during the past few months," LaDonna admitted. "They seem to be getting worse. I suppose I should see someone about it."

Jacqui frowned at the older woman in concern. "With three doctors in your family, I'd have thought you'd have mentioned it to one of them."

"I hate to bother them with medical questions. They get enough of that at work. My annual physical is next month, so I'll mention it to my doctor then."

"I hope I'm not being too personal, but I've been a little worried about your health lately," Jacqui admitted, reaching for the high shelf where she stored the bottle. "You seem to have lost some weight and you look a little pale to me. I've been wanting to mention it, but I wasn't sure you'd—"

Her voice trailed into shocked silence when she saw LaDonna slumped in the chair. Throwing the plastic bottle of ibuprofen on the counter, she rushed forward. "LaDonna? *LaDonna!*"

Chapter Eleven

Mitch didn't know what his family would have done without Jacqui during the next three days. When he and his sisters and Alice reacted with panic to his mother's collapse and subsequent rush to the E.R., Jacqui remained calm, her soothing manner and outward confidence helping them all to remain optimistic.

It was Jacqui who had reacted so quickly to get his mother to the hospital and who had called each of them to give them the news of her illness. The first fear had been that LaDonna had suffered a heart attack. Instead, she was diagnosed as severely anemic, which led to the discovery of previously untreated bleeding stomach ulcers.

When the family reeled in shock from that news, Jacqui pointed out that LaDonna was in an excellent facility with highly skilled physicians and surgeons to care for her. When guilt and stress caused the physician siblings to snap at each other, mostly over who should have seen the signs that their mother had probably been ill for several months, Jacqui stepped in quickly to play peacemaker. She handled the brief conflict so skillfully that they were soon apologizing and working together to make the best medical decisions for their mother.

Jacqui fetched coffee and bottled waters, made phone calls, nagged everyone to eat and rest and served as a buffer when well-intentioned friends flooded them with calls and visits during the first hours after LaDonna's hospitalization. When Mitch's mom insisted that no one should miss work or school to sit in the hospital room with her while she recuperated enough to be discharged, Jacqui made them all feel more comfortable about leaving by offering to stay in their place. She promised to call each one if problems occurred. All of them checked on their mom every chance they got, but Mitch, for one, was able to concentrate better on his work knowing Jacqui was staying with her. He was sure the others felt the same way.

Jacqui had tried to warn him that his mother hadn't seemed well to her during the past few weeks, but he had basically brushed her off. He regretted that deeply now. Under questioning from her doctors and family, LaDonna admitted that she'd had some pain for several months, but had treated herself with over-the-counter medications. She had taken a lot of ibuprofen for stress headaches during her mother's long illness, she confessed on further questioning. Taking too much of the drug was associated with the formation of stomach ulcers.

There had been other symptoms, she said now. Long accustomed to caring for others, she'd gotten into the habit of neglecting her own pains. Besides, she hadn't wanted to worry her children.

"What is with this family?" Seth asked in exasperation on Saturday, the third day of LaDonna's hospitalization. He looked from one Baker sibling to the other as they rested for a few minutes in a visitors' lounge while their mother was undergoing another test. "Meagan ignored the signs of her ovarian torsion for so long she finally had to have emergency surgery. Now LaDonna has suffered in silence until she collapsed. You may be a family of doctors and caretakers, but all of you have to start taking care of yourselves, too."

"Amen," Jacqui said, entering the waiting room with a tote bag full of cold drinks and snacks.

"You're one to talk," Mitch accused her, even as he gratefully accepted a diet soda. Having just spent the past eight hours straight working before breaking away to check on his mother, he needed the caffeine. "Who's been taking care of all of us for the past few days?"

Jacqui's gaze met his for a few moments, but then she looked quickly away, moving to hand a drink to Madison. She had been attentive to Mitch during this crisis but in no different a way than with any of the others. He suspected that he was the only one who could detect the invisible wall she'd placed between them, holding him at a distance even as she had seen to his needs.

There had been more than one time during the past three days when Mitch would have liked to just take her into his arms and hold her, seeking courage and reassurance from her when his own had wavered at the thought of losing his mom. Had it not been for that imaginary wall, and for knowing how important it was to her not to let his family know about their brief affair, he might well have given in to the impulse.

"I've been making sure I've had plenty of rest and food during the past couple of days," Jacqui commented. "You guys are the ones who have to be reminded."

"Whatever you pay her, Seth, it isn't enough," Madison remarked, popping the top on her soda can. "Thank you, Jacqui. I needed this."

Mitch wondered if he was the only one who saw the slight wince narrow Jacqui's eyes for a moment before she moved on to hand Alice a bottle of flavored water. He knew very well that Jacqui hadn't been looking after them because she was paid to do so but because she genuinely cared about this family. She loved Alice and Seth and Meagan. She loved LaDonna.

Being loved by Jacqui Handy was a very special gift. Loving her in return was impossible to resist—at least for him, he realized abruptly.

He sank heavily into a straight-backed visitors' chair, nearly splashing soda on the white coat he wore over his blue surgical scrubs. As if he hadn't had enough shocks in the past few days, now he had a new one to deal with. He was in love with Jacqui. He'd been an idiot not to admit it earlier, especially when he'd been fortunate enough to be with her. Not to mention during the long, lonely nights that had passed after she'd sent him away.

With typical Baker oblivion, he had completely missed the symptoms of his own condition. He'd even misdiagnosed the signs that should have been glaringly obvious. Had he waited too long to do anything about it? Or had he ever really had a chance with Jacqui in the first place?

He watched her chatting with Seth across the room, both of them smiling. Probably lamenting together on how dense the Baker clan could be when it came to their own well-being. Now that it was apparent that LaDonna would make a complete recovery, everyone had relaxed a little, although he suspected his sisters were still struggling with the same guilt he was that they hadn't been more observant.

He wished he knew how to approach Jacqui with his new realization. Should he ask her out again, try to start all over with her? Or simply tell her the truth—that he missed her, that he'd been a fool to take so long to figure out what he'd been looking for all this time?

Would she give him another chance, or would she build yet another invisible wall between them? When would the time be right—if ever—for him to tell her what he felt?

Jacqui jabbed the doorbell button at LaDonna's house Sunday morning before she could change her mind. Mitch had moved out of the hotel and into his mother's house since she'd been hospitalized. Jacqui had driven there straight from an early visit with LaDonna. She had taken fresh flowers to decorate the hospital room in preparation for the after-church visitors who were sure to stop by later that day, and after talking with LaDonna, she had immediately come in search of Mitch.

She had taken a risk that he'd still be here. His car was in the driveway, so it looked as though she'd arrived in time to catch him. She was a little nervous but determined to talk to him.

He looked surprised when he opened the door to him. He smiled automatically to greet her, then stopped smiling in response to her expression. "What's wrong? Has something else happened?"

"Why did you cancel your trip to Peru?" she demanded without preamble.

He frowned. "What?"

"I just left your mom's room. She's very upset with you for canceling your trip."

"How did she find out? I haven't even told her yet."

"One of your friends told Madison, who told your mother, who told me. Why, Mitch?"

"Come inside, okay? No need to have this conversation on the porch." He ushered her in and closed the door behind her before saying, "I would think it's obvious why I canceled. I can't take a trip to South America with my mother just out of the hospital."

"She knew that was the reason, and she feels terrible about it. Your trip isn't for another two weeks. She'll be out of the hospital long before that, and your sisters and I will be here to take care of her. There's no need for you to stay."

"I just want to make sure she's okay. It'll take a couple of weeks for her to get her strength back and for us to make sure the treatments are working well and that she hasn't done any lasting damage. Anemia can wreak havoc on internal organs, even weaken the heart, you know."

"Your mother's heart has been checked very carefully, and it's undamaged," Jacqui shot back. "She'll have a period of recuperation, but I've heard the doctors say they expect a complete recovery. With proper treatment and precautions, she'll be just fine."

"Still, I'll be around to keep an eye on her here. I know you and Meagan and Maddie will all be available to her, but I need to know for myself that she's okay."

Jacqui planted her hands on her hips and studied his face with a frown. She read him very well these days. "You're blaming yourself because she got so sick, aren't you?"

Pushing a hand through his hair, he sighed. "You tried to tell me. I should have listened."

"She kept telling you she was fine, Mitch. You couldn't read her mind."

"No, but I should have seen just how thin and pale she had become. I was too wrapped up in my own issues, with work and the fire and planning for the trip and…"

And with her, she added mentally when his voice trailed off.

"Go on your trip, Mitch," she said more gently. "You've been looking forward to it for so long. Your mother wants you to go. She'll feel awful if you miss it because of her."

"It's too late," he said with a slight shrug. "I've already canceled. I called first thing Thursday morning. I lost my deposit, but that's no big deal. I'd rather stay here and make sure Mom's okay. To be honest, I'd sort of lost enthusiasm about the trip anyway."

Frowning, she took a step closer to him, trying to determine if that was the truth. "But why? You were so excited about it."

"Because you weren't going to be there," he answered simply.

She stared at him in shock. That was one answer she had not expected at all. "I don't—"

"I didn't want to go that far away from you. Not until I had a chance to tell you how much I've missed seeing you. Being with you. I've been trying to find the right time, the right words, to convince you that we're a perfect match, no matter how different our backgrounds might be."

"I, uh— I think I need to sit down." She sank onto

LaDonna's comfortable, overstuffed flowered couch, her head spinning a little.

Mitch sat beside her, looking at her so intently she flushed. "I'm not sure what you're trying to say," she admitted, having been completely unprepared for this conversation.

"I'm trying to say I love you, Jacqui. Something I should have told you the night you sent me away."

Shock jolted through her again, making her glad she was sitting down this time. "You…?"

"You said I wasn't ready for a permanent commitment, that I was afraid to sign a long-term lease—and maybe for a little while I wondered if you were right. Mostly I wondered if you weren't just using that for an excuse because you weren't interested in the long run with me."

"You're the one who said you wanted to keep your options open," she pointed out, her voice not quite steady.

"Yes, I did say that. I was looking for something, and for a time, I figured I needed to go somewhere else to find it. I guess I thought that because I hadn't been able to leave Little Rock, that must mean what I was searching for lay out there somewhere. But the truth is, I've been free to leave for months. My residency was almost finished, my mother and sisters were well and I didn't have a lease. Yet I stopped sending out applications to other hospitals about a year ago. Just about the time I met you. I was just too dense to make the connection until now."

She remembered him telling her how clearly he remembered that first meeting. That he had been attracted to her then and had wanted ever since to get to know her better. She'd been shocked then by that admission—she was even more stunned by what he was telling her now. *He loved her?*

"But you said you didn't even want to sign a lease," she said weakly. She knew she was repeating herself, but she couldn't seem to think clearly.

With an impatient shake of his head, he reached out to rest a hand on her shoulder. "You keep looking for hidden meanings in my lack of interest in real estate. I don't care whether I live in a house or an apartment or a condo or a tent, for that matter. I just hope there's a chance that someday you'll live there with me. I love you, Jacqui."

Her mind whirled with all the arguments she'd given herself. "I don't want to be another anchor around your neck. I don't want to be the reason you look back someday with regrets about the things you never got to do."

"I can still do anything I want. I can travel on vacations—with you, I hope. Maybe you'll enjoy traveling again when you know you have a permanent home to return to when the trip is over."

That was exactly the way she'd felt about traveling lately. Knowing she wouldn't have to keep pulling up roots and trying to settle somewhere new made it somewhat more tempting to see different places just for pleasure.

Before she could respond, Mitch added, "I don't see my family as anchors, Jacqui. I love them very much, and I treasure the time we're able to spend together. I don't blame any of them for the circumstances that kept me here in the past—it was always ultimately my choice to remain close to them when I thought they needed me. Just as it is my choice to stay close to Mom now while she recuperates rather than traipse around Peru with some people I like but who don't mean anything to me in comparison to my family. Or to you."

She drew a deep breath. "I've been trying so hard not to fall for you."

That smile of his was impossible to resist. "How's that been working for you?"

She placed a hand on his cheek. "Not so well."

Catching her hand, he placed a kiss in her palm. "You? The incomparably efficient Jacqui Handy? You never fail at anything."

"Of course I do," she said with a low sigh.

He stopped smiling. "If you're talking about the wreck, that wasn't your failure."

"I know," she said quietly. "Which doesn't mean I won't always feel some measure of guilt about it."

He kissed her hand again, then lowered it to his lap, his fingers laced with hers. "Any time you want to talk about it, I'm here, okay? And any time you need a distraction, I'm here for that, too. Let's just say I'm here for the duration. Whatever you need from me."

Tears threatened, but she blinked them back. "I'm not used to that."

"You'll have plenty of time to get used to it," he promised. "The rest of our lives, if you'll have me that long."

This conversation was scaring the heck out of her, she thought candidly—but he certainly knew the right things to say to tempt her to take risks.

"There are other problems between us," she said—as much to herself as to him.

He sighed with exaggerated patience. "You don't want to be Cinderella. The doctor and the housekeeper thing. I can tell you right now, that's bogus. No one, least of all me, cares to judge what you choose to do with your time. You want to keep running my sister's household and trying to keep my teenage niece in line, I say go for it. You're good at it. But if there are other things you want to pursue, I'll back you in that, too. I know you can do whatever you set your mind to, Jacqui."

She looked down at their interlaced hands. "There are still things you don't know about me."

"I look forward to learning them all."

"I never finished high school," she blurted in a rush. "I dropped out when my parents moved the last time. I got an equivalency degree a few years later, but I don't have the education your family values so much."

"Nobody cares about the framed papers hanging on your wall," he said with a shrug. "If you want to take college classes in something that interests you, do it. I can't imagine you having any difficulty with any subject. If more school doesn't interest you, don't do it. Believe it or not, I don't choose my friends by the degrees they hold. For that matter, I've played soccer every Sunday for years with a few people I consider friends, and I couldn't tell you for certain if they went to college or dropped out of school in junior high."

"You have an answer for everything, don't you?"

He smiled crookedly. "Not really. I'm still waiting for you to tell me how you feel about me."

She swallowed hard. "I... I think I love you, too," she whispered.

His face lit up again with his beautiful smile. "I'll take that—for now."

There were so many things still to be settled between them, she thought. How would his family react to him getting involved with her? How would she fit in with his friends? And she still didn't know what would happen between her and his family if for some reason she and Mitch couldn't make this work. But that no longer seemed to matter quite so much. As much as she cared for the rest of his family, her feelings for Mitch were stronger. If she had to make the hard choice between him and them at this moment—she would have to choose Mitch.

The realization actually surprised her with its sudden clarity.

"But," she warned quickly, fending him off when he would have tugged her toward him, "I'm not committing to anything just yet. We need to take our time. We need to be sure any decisions we make are what we both want, what's best for both of us. We shouldn't…"

"We shouldn't sign any long-term leases just yet?"

His teasing interruption made her flush a little, even though she had to smile. "You're the one who said we should stop with the real-estate metaphors."

"They do seem to keep cropping up, don't they?"

She reached up to grab his collar and tug lightly. "Maybe we should just stop talking for now."

He smiled against her lips. "I've been waiting for you to say that."

She wrapped her arms around his neck and snuggled into his embrace, deciding they could deal with any potential issues later. They had more pressing matters to attend to just now.

They lay snuggled together in the bed in Mitch's old bedroom, though he commented that the decor had changed a bit since he'd lived there last. The sports and rock-band posters had been replaced by earth-toned paint and landscape prints. LaDonna had kept a masculine feel to the room so Mitch would be comfortable whenever he stayed there. Jacqui tried not to think about LaDonna's reaction to what had just taken place in this room.

Such speculation didn't seem to be disturbing Mitch. He looked quite pleased with himself, actually, as he smiled at her from the pillow beside hers. "I'm very glad you stopped by today," he said. "I've been wondering how to get you alone to talk about my feelings for you. I didn't expect you to show up on the doorstep today."

"I was so perturbed when your mother told me about you canceling your trip to Peru that I guess I just stormed over here without giving myself a chance to think about it," she admitted.

"Because you didn't want me to be disappointed about missing the trip. I'm touched by that, Jacqui."

"Maybe I just wanted to get you out of the country for a few days."

He chuckled. "Sorry to disappoint you."

"You're sure you don't want to—"

"I'm sure," he cut in. "So, how would you like to maybe go to Peru with me this time next year?"

Her smile wavered a bit, though she kept her tone light. "That's very long-term planning."

"True. But that's one deposit I wouldn't hesitate to make. I keep telling you, I'm in this for the long-term, Jacqui."

The more he said it, the more believable it sounded. And although she was still afraid to let herself believe too much in what she wanted so badly, she had to trust that he meant what he said.

He let out a long breath. "Guess I should get dressed and head over to the hospital to see Mom. I need to reassure her that missing the trip to Peru isn't the worst thing that's ever happened to me. Want to go with me?"

The question was seemingly casual, but she knew

exactly what it meant. If she and Mitch went together to the hospital now, there would be no more pretending that they were merely friends. "All right."

His smile curved his nice mouth and gleamed in his blue eyes. "Thank you."

Drawing a deep breath, she told herself she would take almost any risk in exchange for Mitch's beautiful smile. "I'm a little nervous," she admitted.

"I know. But I'll be right there beside you. Now and for always. I love you, Jacqui."

She leaned over to kiss his smile. "I love you, too."

How could she not? She'd been searching for Mitch all her life.

Epilogue

Six days later, Jacqui stood beside Mitch on the sidewalk outside the house in Hillcrest, gazing at the front door with a bone-deep longing. The keys to that door dangled in Mitch's hand, and she wanted nothing more than for him to open it and let her walk inside to explore again. He'd borrowed the keys from the Realtor who'd shown them the house before, saying he wanted to look at the place with Jacqui one more time before making an offer—just to make sure this was the right choice.

It was still hot on this first Saturday in September. The sky was a deep, cloudless blue overhead, the afternoon sun beating down on the heat-shriveled trees and grass. A few flowers still bloomed in the beds, but their colors were fading and the beds needed tending. Jacqui's fingers itched to play in those small gardens, weeding and pruning and planting colorful mums for the coming fall. She would rest between chores with a glass of lemonade on that lovely porch, she thought wistfully, her gaze moving to the inviting wood rockers. This was exactly the house she had always dreamed of.

She turned resolutely away. "I don't think you should buy it," she said abruptly to Mitch.

He looked at her in visible surprise. "I thought you loved this house."

"I do," she had to admit, because she was always honest with him. "It's perfect. But you shouldn't buy it for that reason."

He spun to face her fully. "Jacqui, you know I'm hoping you'll share this house with me. I've gotten accustomed to having you under the same roof. Even more accustomed to sharing a bed," he added in a low, affectionately teasing tone that brought warmth to her cheeks.

"And I will live with you," she assured him around a lump in her throat. "But I want you to make very sure it's what *you* want before you commit to a purchase this big."

She drew a deep breath. "If you still want to try living in a few other places before you buy a house and settle in for the long-term, I think you should do it, Mitch. As for me—I'll go where you go. I'll support you completely in whatever you need to do, just as you've promised to do for me."

For the first time in her life, she understood her mother a little better. Troubled as she was in so many ways, Cindy Handy loved her husband and she wanted to be with him wherever he drifted. Jacqui was dissimilar from her mother, and she had different priorities in her life—for one thing, if she ever had children, which she hoped to do someday, she would strive to give them much more of a sense of security and emotional support than she and Olivia had received. But she understood now what her mother had meant when she'd said that "home" wasn't necessarily a place but a feeling.

As much as she loved living in Little Rock, Jacqui understood now that she could make a home with Mitch wherever they went. For one thing, she knew he would always put her needs and desires first—something her own rather selfish father had been unable to do for anyone else. The fact that Mitch was willing to buy this house just because he knew she loved it, that he had always put his loved ones' best interests ahead of his own, was all the proof she needed that she had given her heart and her trust to the right man.

Mitch took both her hands in his, the keys cupped between his right palm and her left. His eyes were dark with emotion when he gazed down at her, his mouth curved in a loving smile. "The fact that you offered to move away with me means more than you could ever possibly realize. I know exactly how hard it must have been for you to make that offer. You love it here."

"I love you more," she said, her voice a bit shaky now.

He leaned down to brush a kiss over her lips, oblivious to the car passing on the street behind them, to anyone in neighboring yards who might see them. Again unlike her parents, Mitch was open with his emotions, unabashed at having anyone see that he was in love with her.

He had made it clear to his family that he had chosen Jacqui for his life partner. It wasn't as if this was a decision they'd made overnight, he had added when they had reacted with delighted surprise. He'd been in love with Jacqui for more than a year. He'd just been a little slow to do anything about it, he'd admitted.

Jacqui had been overwhelmed with gratitude by how enthusiastically Mitch's family had approved his choice. Especially his mother, who was recovering nicely from her health scare under the watchful eyes of her still-guilt-ridden physician children. LaDonna confided that she'd watched Mitch's behavior around Jacqui for several months with a suspicion that he was smitten, and she couldn't have been more delighted to have been proved right.

As for Alice, she smugly claimed credit, saying she really should go into the matchmaking business someday rather than orthodontia. She also claimed responsibility for getting her dad and Meagan together.

"I am exactly where I want to be," Mitch assured Jacqui now. "My family is here, my work is here, but most importantly, you are here. I can't imagine any other place on this planet having more to offer me."

After twenty-nine years of protecting herself from disappointment, it was difficult to put so much faith in anyone else. But she was getting there with Mitch. "Just don't rush into it on my behalf," she said. "There will always be other houses if you want to keep looking for a while."

He nodded, squeezing her hands before dropping his own. She noted that he had passed the keys to her. She wrapped her fingers around them, feeling the tug of temptation to use them.

"I was thinking that porch could be taken down and replaced with a sunroom," Mitch commented, turning to eye the front of the house again. "Maybe brick with lots of glass. And all that stained wood inside? Maybe we could update it a little. You know, paint it white or something."

She gasped. "You will do no such thing! That porch

is perfect. And don't you even think about getting near that beautiful wood trim with a paintbrush. This house is—"

She fell silent when she saw the grin cross his face.

"Yours," he finished for her in somewhat smug satisfaction. "This house is yours. It has been from the first moment you saw it. Might as well admit it."

Her knees went weak as her fingers tightened spasmodically around the keys to her dream house. "Fine," she managed to say after a moment. "But I'm putting my savings toward the down payment."

"That isn't necessary. I—"

She poked his shoulder with one finger as they moved toward the front door. "I haven't worked and saved for the past ten years just to have someone come along and buy a house for me, Mitchell Baker. I told you, I'm no Cinderella. Maybe this is a nicer house than I could have afforded on my own—okay, it's definitely more than I could have managed—but that doesn't mean I won't be fully invested in owning it. It won't be all mine—or all yours. It will be ours."

"Ours," he repeated. "I like the sound of that."

"So do I," she said, her vision misty as she fitted the key into the lock of the house they would make into a home together. "So do I."

* * * * *

The perfect gift for
Mother's Day...

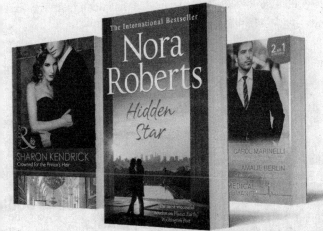

Mills & Boon subscription

Call Customer Services on
0844 844 1358*

or visit
illsandboon.co.uk/subscriptions